# DRAGON VOID

## IMMORTAL DRAGONS BOOK TWO

OPHELIA BELL

Dragon Void

Copyright © 2016 Ophelia Bell

Cover Art Designed by Jacqueline Sweet

Photograph Copyright © DepositPhotos.com and Period Images





ISBN-13: 978-1-955385-07-7

Published by Animus Press

UNITED STATES

❀ Created with Vellum

Whoever fights with monsters should see to it that he does not become a monster in the process. And when you gaze long into an abyss the abyss also gazes into you.

— FRIEDRICH NIETZSCHE

# CHAPTER 1

## MARCUS

*Ultiori Headquarters, Canadian Rockies*
*Present Day*

When the devil's on your tail, the instinct is to run. Marcus wanted to run—time was not on his side and hadn't been for decades—but Elites like him had to set an example for the other Ultiori hunters in the compound.

He desperately needed to be with Evie *now*—before the man Fate had chosen as her mate came to claim her. And before the man Fate had chosen to be his torturer came to kill Marcus.

There was no way his master wouldn't bleed him dry the second he discovered Marcus had betrayed him. Marcus would happily accept his fate by the time Nikhil realized he'd been instrumental in Evie's rescue. He only had a few hours, at best, to see Evie before his world ended. To tell her one last time that he loved her. And to ask her forgiveness for bringing her to this place.

Nikhil was distracted for the first time since Marcus had

served as one of the Ultiori leader's primary soldiers and enforcers. For the first time in five decades, the ancient man's dark mental presence wasn't lurking around in Marcus's head.

His master would come for him. And if the events of the last few hours were any indication of true hope, Evie's *true* mate would come for her.

He exited the elevator the very second the doors opened on the sub-level floor of the Alexandria Institute's Canadian headquarters. Only he, his master, and his fellow Elites had access to this floor, where the most valuable captives were held. But there was one cell Marcus lacked the clearance to open and he hoped he'd find one of the two people who could open that cell. Naaz and Sterlyn were the only ones who could give him access to see Evie.

Before he rounded the corner of the wide hallway, Naaz's deep voice reverberated faintly from the distance, then paused. In his mind, Marcus sensed his fellow Elite's unarticulated question to him. He sped up, heart racing with anticipation and hope that Naaz would be willing to do this one final favor for him.

A sudden, loud crash made him turn his head. One of the two thick polycarbonate cell doors on this corridor vibrated with the violent impact of the huge body on the other side of it. Marcus paused long enough to stare at the big, muscular ursa male who raged beyond the transparent portal of glass.

On the other side of the corridor, another figure moved into view beyond a similar thick door. He didn't have time for this.

The satyr on the other side gestured at Marcus and pointed toward the intercom on the side of the door.

Marcus scowled at the prisoner, prepared to ignore both interruptions, when Naaz pushed in front of him and tapped the button to activate the speaker.

"What is it, Calder? We don't have time for your apocalyptic bullshit today, or for Nicholas trying to tear down the goddamn mountain."

Naaz gave Marcus the weary look of a man who's been relegated to holding down the fort. For the last week, only Marcus and his fellow Elite Sterlyn had been out, carrying out their master's wishes.

"This is the last time I'll ask," Calder said, his deep, serene voice sending a trickle of ice down Marcus's spine. "Today was the day the currents shifted. The dark waters have been disturbed, enough for the river to split. You need to let me into Nicholas's cell one last time so he doesn't drown in the deluge when Fate's flood reaches us."

"Naaz, leave him. I need you to do me a favor quickly," Marcus said, unwilling to entertain the crazy satyr's cryptic rambling.

"I've got you, brother," Naaz said. "Just need your help to handle this crazy fucker first." He glanced over his shoulder at the opposite cell where the white-haired ursa male still pounded at the door, a little less destructively, but no less emphatic. "Not sure which of the pair are crazier, but at least we'll have some peace when we put them together."

Naaz quickly keyed in a code on the pad by Calder's door, then pressed his thumb to the small biometric scanner above it. As the door slid open, Marcus cursed softly and raised his hands, exerting his will to push the magic that had flowed through his veins for the last fifty years out through the centers of his palms. Naaz did the same, the magic coming from his hands manifesting as a red swirl of smoke that their prisoner inhaled along with the dark shadow of Marcus's magic.

Calder's pupils expanded until the deep blue of his irises were completely black, and his face went utterly blank, his knees buckling as the combination of Marcus and Naaz's powers neutralized him. Marcus knew what Naaz's power felt like mixed with his own—a combination of paralysis and overwhelming arousal, which was evidenced by the tent in Calder's loose-fitting drawstring pants as he sagged to the floor. His cock was the only stiff thing about him when Naaz and Marcus stepped in and hooked the satyr beneath the armpits. They hauled him bodily across the hallway to the door of the now more subdued ursa's cell.

Nicholas stood back and obligingly sank to his knees, indicating he had no intention of giving them trouble now that he saw his needs would be met.

"What do you think he meant about the currents?" Marcus asked, keying in the code to unlock Nick's door, followed by the final biometric scan.

"Something big's about to happen. He's only ever ranted like this when there were about to be major changes. He did it fifty years ago before you showed up, and two hundred years before that, just before the whole fiasco with Nick and his mother."

Marcus had only heard brief tales of the Ultiori's experiences after capturing the queen of the matriarchal race of bear shifters. The female had been the first ever to become pregnant in captivity after undergoing several of the Ultiori's experiments. The experience proved to the Ultiori how dangerously volatile a mother ursa could be when she escaped shortly after giving birth. It had taken two elites, Nikhil himself, and an army of Ultiori hunters to subdue the ursa queen long enough to retrieve the child. They had to give up on taking the mother back into custody after she'd killed half their soldiers, but they'd managed to keep the cub.

Marcus had witnessed the ursa male's periodic rages and the resulting damage that had prompted reinforcing all the walls of his cell, including installation of doors that were impervious to his strength. He never wanted to come face-to-face with a female ursa if his fellow Elite's stories were true and she had managed to be too powerful for them to recapture.

When the door slid open, he helped drag Calder into the room. Nicholas held out arms the size of tree trunks and immediately scooped up the unconscious man, cradling him against his large chest as if he were a doll, in spite of Calder being nearly as tall. The satyr had a lithe, swimmer's physique, so was dwarfed in the ursa's huge arms.

Nicholas glowered at the pair of them as they retreated, not even voicing any words of thanks. When the door was securely locked again, Marcus and Naaz watched the large ursa carry his friend to his bed where he tenderly laid him down and curled up next to him with his head on his chest.

Marcus shook his head. "I've never really understood those two. I get the whole ursa fertility cycle and how the males pair up, but that he can substitute another race entirely makes no sense."

"It's like any surrogate, really," Naaz said, crossing his arms and regarding the pair inside the cell. After a moment the scene became more intimate as Calder regained consciousness and Naaz swiped his hand across the control pad to obscure their view. The glass clouded until it was entirely opaque white. "Tiger cubs raised with golden retrievers don't really care they're not the same species. Nicholas wouldn't have survived adolescence if Calder hadn't known what he needed."

Marcus's chest tightened at the reminder. What Evie needed wasn't Marcus. Somewhere out there a certain immortal black dragon was on his way and would soon arrive to claim her and take her away for good. Marcus set his mouth in a grim line. Fate didn't seem to care about mixing two different races, either. She certainly hadn't cared about the creation of abominations such as Marcus and the other Ultiori Elites.

"You want to see her now, I take it," Naaz said, already turning to head in the direction of the last turn in the corridor, at the end of which were three more cells that housed the most valuable prisoners—the three females that kept Marcus and the other Elites from mutiny.

When they rounded the corner, Marcus saw a blond man at the end of the hall, sitting cross-legged outside the last cell. The cell door was clear and back-lit from within. Inside, lounging against the other side of the door, was a striking auburn-haired woman with eyes the color of rubies. Both turned to look at him and stood with smiles on their faces.

His other fellow Elite, Sterlyn, came toward him with a hand extended. They grasped wrists and hugged briefly.

"Come to take advantage of the respite and see your girl?" Sterlyn said.

"I don't just want to see her today. I need you to open the door."

Naaz stopped short and stared at him for a beat, then nodded. "Right. And I suppose you expect Sterlyn and me to scrape your carcass off her floor when Sayid finds out?"

"He's busy, if you haven't noticed," Marcus said, tapping at his temple. "He's been out of my head for the last two hours. I figure as long as he's with the love of his life, we have a reprieve from him filtering through our minds. I plan to take advantage of that."

"You know you can't take her out of here. Her shackles won't let her teleport, and if she leaves this floor the entire facility will be on instant lockdown.

"I don't plan on taking her out. I'm going in. Brother, she belongs to one of them… the Dragon Council … the fucking *Void* claims she's his mate and is on a warpath to find her. If anyone can get her out of this godforsaken place, he can. I just want one last night with her."

Behind Sterlyn, the red-haired female inside the cell said, "If what you say is true, you had best hurry. The Void is not a dragon to trifle with, but I believe you know that, don't you Marcus? It's his blood that powers you, is it not?"

"Zamirah, you are as perceptive as you are beautiful. That's how I know he's the one for Evie. I don't believe she'd still love me now if not for his blood running through my veins."

The red-haired woman shrugged. "Even if Sterlyn hadn't told me, I can see the dark magic in your eyes as clearly as I can see the white magic inside my love's." She gave Sterlyn an adoring look. "But any dragon would know not to test the Void, or any other member of the Dragon Council. I know I may lack company in this opinion, but I prefer the punishment of my incarceration here over any punishment they would mete out on my kind for misbehaving."

"I'm sure Sterlyn wouldn't hesitate to let you go if he could ensure your freedom, despite what our master might do to him after the fact. I want Evie to be free, and if that means I stay behind to appease Sayid with my blood or my loyalty, so be it. As long as she is free."

He turned to look at Evie's door, still opaque for privacy. The feature could be overridden from the panel in the hallway if needed, but until one of his fellow Elites agreed to open it, he didn't want to disturb her sleep. The door opposite hers was clear, however, and a gorgeous, mocha-skinned woman with shining curls smiled at him from the other side.

"Hey, hot stuff," Naaz's twin sister said, her smoky voice sounding tinny through the intercom.

"Neela, looking delicious as always," Marcus said, his suggestive greeting earning him an air kiss that he fake-caught and tucked in his pocket.

"You're not here for me or Zamirah today, are you," Neela said, the immortal dragon blood that infused her allowing more than a casual glimpse into his thoughts. He didn't try to hide from her, though. Naaz's sister was the only Elite who didn't get to leave the compound—she was far too valuable as collateral to keep her brother loyal to their brutal master. She was also one of the five people in the world he'd be willing to die for, if it came to that—all the others were on the same floor with him now.

Marcus shook his head and gave Neela a sad smile. "Sorry, sweetheart. My heart belongs to another. And I know yours does, too."

"It's nothing, honey. I was just telling my brother it felt like time for someone to stir the pot. Nikhil being out of our heads is the perfect time for it. Just don't get yourself killed, okay?" When Marcus remained silent, Neela cursed. "You fucking lovesick idiot," she said, pressing her palm to the door. "She had better be worth it."

"He doesn't have to find out," Naaz said. "I'm not going to tell Nikhil what Marcus is doing, and neither will the rest of you." He gave the others a stern glare that would have been utterly menacing to an outsider. Marcus knew his fellow Elite far too well to be alarmed by his expression.

Marcus shook his head. "It doesn't matter. He'll find out when he discovers she's gone. I'm prepared to take whatever he dishes out when that happens. All that matters is that she's out of here."

"Fuck me," Neela said, in awe. "You found a way to get her out? For real?"

"I'm not going to be the one to do it. But if anyone can override the power of the shackles, the Void can."

"The Void..." She trailed off and shivered while unconsciously rubbing at the dark designs inked around her wrists, the magical shackles that prevented her and every other captive from escape in case their cells failed to hold them. "He's the only creature who ever came close to killing Nikhil. Naaz and I were barely old enough to remember the aftermath of that. I'd rather have him on my good side. Do you think he'd know you carried his blood if he saw you?"

Marcus met Neela's gaze and nodded. Swallowing the jagged lump in his throat, he said, "I only have a fraction of the power he has, thanks to that magic. I'd have gotten her out long ago if I could, but the best I can do is obscure her tattoos for moments. Not long enough for a full escape." He frowned, a thought occurring to him as he glanced around at the others. "I could find out if he'd help you…"

All four of his friends cut him off with objections.

"No," Naaz said. "If you want us to run interference at all, we need to be here. We can't expect Evie's mate to save everyone. If she really is his, he might not want to, anyway. We just can't…"

His and Neela's protests were a little too emphatic and Marcus and Sterlyn both raised both eyebrows, glancing between the pair. Marcus didn't need to ask to be able to sense their desperation.

"You won't leave because of them." The pair seemed to have an unhealthy attachment to two hibernating dragons Nikhil had found ages ago. All Marcus knew was that the so-called treasures were yet another reason the twins had stayed with Nikhil for so long, in spite of the fact that their master kept the two stone effigies securely locked away and never let Naaz and Neela close.

"We would give our lives to get them away from him, if we could," Naaz said. "But you are right, we won't leave as long as he has our mates."

Marcus was debating whether to tell him the details he'd learned over the past day about the true identities of his friends' mates, when light hit the side of his face from the other side of the hallway and he heard a light tapping sound at the glass of the third cell door.

His heart pounding, he turned to see Evie standing backlit by the lights in her cell, the glass of her door clear enough for him to see the petite woman smiling at him. She gave him a small wave and tilted her head, one eyebrow raised as if to ask whether he was there for her.

"Naaz…" Marcus began, too breathless at the sight of her to get more words out.

"I got it, brother," Naaz said, quickly stepping across the hall and keying in the code to unlock the door before pressing his thumb to the pad.

Marcus's heart raced as the door slid open. He'd seen her only infrequently over the past five decades, and only through the glass barrier that blocked the opening of her cell.

Today he could touch her… hold her… and if that look she had meant what he hoped—make love to her.

Unwilling to consider the silent reminders of why she might look at him that way, Marcus stepped into the cell and swept her up in his arms. His mouth found hers and their kiss heated his entire body, his blood surging in his veins like she'd set him on fire. He was only peripherally aware of the cell door sliding shut behind him and the light dimming as it went from clear to opaque again.

God bless Naaz for understanding.

In his arms, Evie moaned and clawed at the buttons of his shirt. Marcus wasn't ready for that yet. He knew he only had a few hours, at most, to be with her, but he wanted to savor every second, commit it all to memory. Because if there was an afterlife, he would take the memory with him as his surest way to Heaven.

He grabbed her hands and put them around his neck while he lifted her up, burying his face in her neck and inhaling the scent of her. She still smelled like that spring day when they'd met in Central Park, of fresh azaleas carried on a crisp March breeze. He moved the few quick strides it took to reach her cot, and set her down, cupping her face in his hands and slowly savoring the taste of her mouth while she let out urgent little whimpers.

"Marcus, I need you," she whispered when he drifted his lips over her jaw and proceeded down the side of her neck. Sweet Jesus how he needed her. His cock had never been so hard, but he warded off her hands again.

"Just let me have this first," he murmured. "Let me experience you without distractions."

She let out a frustrated laugh when he pushed his hand beneath her knit tank top and teased the underside of her breast.

"I don't know if I can keep from reacting. I need an outlet, too. It's been so long … do you have any idea how long?"

"Fifty years, six months, nineteen days, ten hours…" He hazarded a glance at her and smiled at the surprise there. "Fine, sing if you need an outlet, but let me focus on loving you one last time."

Evie stiffened under his touch, her wide eyes flashing with fear for the briefest second before understanding made her relax again. The acceptance was accompanied by a look of sadness that made him pause, and he realized what he'd said.

"I found him…" he began, but she surged at him, her lips slamming against his in a desperate kiss that took his breath away.

"I don't want to know… not yet," she said when she pulled away.

Marcus nodded. Words would only be a waste of time between them now, so he chose actions instead. He pushed insistently at her top, and Evie raised her arms allowing him to strip it off her. He pushed her down onto her cot and she raised her hips so he could strip her of her drawstring pants.

*Slow down,* he told himself, overeager to delve into the fragrant, juicy core of her but needing to make sure he let every moment of this experience sink in. Then she started singing, the bittersweet tune setting the exact tempo he needed.

He rested back on his heels between her ankles, gazing down at her creamy skin. Her eyes sparkled with unshed tears, her emotions making the song rougher as the lyrics flowed from her lips. He didn't understand the words, but had the feeling he knew exactly what the song meant, and it was perfect for the moment.

Evie cupped her breasts and spread her thighs, opening herself for him. Marcus bent and slid one hand beneath her knee, down the back of her thigh and up her hip until his elbow rested on the bed. He kissed the inside of her other knee, brushing his lips along her inner thigh, breathing her in as he went as though her scent sustained him.

He paused with his lips close enough to her core to feel the tickle of feather-soft fringe that covered her folds. The scent of March blooms was ever prevalent, and even more earthy here, and brought back the early memory of his wish to fill her with his child, to marry her and keep her close forever.

She'd told him the child couldn't happen, and she'd been right, but every time he thought of her he still had the same wish. He'd been ready to propose the day they came to this place fifty years ago. He still carried the engagement ring with him wherever he went even now, despite knowing a marriage to her was out of the question.

With a groan to dispel the foolish fantasy, he pressed his mouth to her and kissed, using his lips to part her flesh while his tongue dipped between. He tasted her in one long, slow sweep, from the bottom of her opening all the way to the stiff, throbbing nub of her clit. He pressed the tip of his tongue there and teased, flicking gently up and down until her hips rose up with urgency.

His mouth watered at the tangy flavor of her and he drank her in, plunging his tongue deep into her channel to taste as much as he could before sweeping upward again and sucking that delicious bundle between his lips again.

Evie's song continued, the shifting tempo enough to signal her state and urge him on. He devoured her over and over, hearing the need from her voice as much as sensing it from her body. When her pitch changed and her body tensed, he was right there with her, ready to carry her over and eagerly lapping up every drop of her essence when she collapsed to the bed.

She only paused for a breath before she was on him, pushing him back in a daze and ripping at his shirt and belt.

"My turn," she growled and Marcus was too buzzed from the power of her orgasm to object. All he could do was kick off his boots in time for her to push his cargo pants to his ankles, the gear attached to his belt clattering onto the floor in a heap. Then she was on him, her lips tangled with his as she straddled him, wasting no time before sinking down on his stiff, throbbing shaft.

They let out simultaneous gasps of pleasure at the tight friction and he reveled in her control, letting her ride him for a moment before forcing her to slow down. He dug his fingers into her hips and held her against him, breathing deeply to try to fend off the release that rapidly threatened to overtake him. He planned to come as many times as possible while he was with her, but wanted to make sure the first time didn't catch him off guard.

"Baby, please. Slow down. Let me have this."

Evie pushed her fingers through his hair and bent to kiss him again, more slowly and tenderly this time.

"All right, but you'd better tell me this big secret of yours while we're doing it. I heard a hint of a time limit in your voice. How much time do we have and what's going to happen at the end of it? You can't lie to me and you know it."

He slid his hands up her narrow waist to tease his thumbs over the tips of her breasts. She took advantage of the freedom and rose up his length, hovering with her folds just encompassing the aching tip of his cock.

Her stormy eyes flickered with sparks of lightning, expectant and clearly willing to torture him if he failed to deliver.

"Hours maybe," he said, relenting. "Sayid is usually inside my head so I couldn't get away with seeing you like this before."

"But he's not now? Where is he?"

"Distracted... probably just the way we are right now. But he'll be back and when he comes, he won't be happy with me."

"So, you don't let him find out."

"My love, I am pretty sure your absence will not go unnoticed. And I fully expect he'll take out his anger on me."

She sank down onto his cock suddenly, the sharp, exquisite sensation making his vision blur and his breath leave his lungs in a rush.

"How...?" she asked, not moving again, though the heat of her sank into him in a way that made him regret the distracting conversation.

But he had to tell her the truth.

"Baby, I know why you look at me the way you do. You didn't love me like this when we met, and I remember distinctly the day when that changed. I hated that it didn't happen until there was a goddamn cell door between us, but when I understood why, I admit I was a little grateful for it."

The tears were back in her eyes, and he hated himself for causing them to return. "Why…" she began shakily. "Why do you think it changed?"

"I didn't put it all together until last night. All I knew was that angels like you don't just fall in love. There was someone out there for you already, and it wasn't me. Calder… the satyr down the hall… a while back he told me how your kind works. How seeing your one true love is all it takes to know they're the one. And that something wasn't right if you didn't look at me that way from the start. It didn't happen until after we came here—after that bastard fucked with my blood, filled me with an infusion of some other creature's blood—that was when it changed."

Evie began shaking her head, her tears flowing freely now. "You *are* mine, Marcus. I don't care if you weren't to start with. I wanted you to be. I wished for it every day we were together for the first year after we met. Because if you were, then that meant I *could choose* who I loved. I don't give a fuck how you wound up with his blood inside you. We belong together."

She clung to him, wrapped her arms around his neck. Her elbows dug into his shoulders as she kissed him with wet, tear-coated lips, and began moving her hips again in earnest.

Marcus groaned, his own hips rising to meet her, thrusting deep as she came down on him. His head spun from the emotional weight of it on top of the long needed physical connection with her. He gripped her arms and pulled her away, made her sit back and look at him.

"Evie, you don't understand. I've loved you since the second I laid eyes on you, but you were never mine. Last night I understood for the first time why. I saw the Void—the dragon whose blood is the root of my power…"

Evie began shaking her head, chanting, "no, no, no" under

her breath as though she didn't want to hear what he was saying—couldn't bear to know the truth.

"He is the one, Evie. Your *one*. He knows you are his." Marcus closed his eyes, swallowing his own grief to get the rest of the words out. "He knows, and he is coming for you. And as God is my witness, I want him to have you because I never deserved you."

"You always did," she said, holding his face in her hands. "I don't want to leave you, Marcus. Don't you get it? You may not have belonged to me when we met, but you do now, and that's all that matters. If he comes and takes me away, I'll lose you. Nikhil will kill you for letting me go and I'll lose you."

The emotion he'd struggled to keep at bay broke through. Marcus let out an anguished groan and wrapped her in his arms. He hated that this would be the last time for them, but he needed her like he'd never needed anything in his life. Evie seemed to sense that the conversation was over at least, and they continued making love until Marcus lost himself in her heat, her scent, and the beautiful sound of her voice as she sang him to completion.

# CHAPTER 2

## MARCUS

They lay curled snugly on her narrow cot. Despite the uncomfortable bed, Marcus had never been as comfortable as he was when Evie was in his arms after making love. She was tucked against him, halfway on top of him with one leg slung over his hips and her cheek against his chest. Her cell was warm enough that they didn't need covers.

Marcus stroked his fingertips over her shoulder, reveling in the silken feel of her skin and the weight and press of her breasts against his side. The longer he lay there with her, the more the sense of urgency tightened his gut. He could only savor her for so long. He needed to be well clear of her cell before Nikhil returned, and he certainly didn't want to be here when the Void came to claim her.

"I don't think you need to be frightened of him," he said, flattening his palm against her back and rubbing in a slow circle. "When I saw him last night, he looked…" He paused, trying to find the right words for what he'd seen in the Void's eyes while he secretly observed the huge black dragon and his sister discussing the plights of their respective mates. "He looked how I feel all the time. Desperate to keep you safe."

"I'm not frightened of him," she said. "If I'd met him in the middle of a crowd the way I met you, nothing could have kept me from going to him, being with him. I know nothing can keep that from happening now, but that doesn't mean I'm ready to give you up to have it."

"Evie, I can't go with you when he comes. Nikhil's out of my head for the moment, but I know it's only temporary. Not that the Void would want an old boyfriend of yours tagging along, anyway."

She raised her head and rested her chin on his chest. Her gray eyes were calm, sated, but determined. "If you won't find a way to join me, at least give me one gift."

She trailed off, dropping her eyes so her dark lashes cast shadows on her pink cheeks. Opening her mouth as if to speak again she stopped, licking her lips and stalling as she toyed with the copper hairs around one of his nipples. Marcus's cock twitched, rousing again in response to the teasing touch.

"What is it?" he asked. "If I can give it, I will."

Evie swallowed, seemingly distracted by her fingers tracing soft lines up and down his torso now, straying ever lower. She shifted her knee away from his hips and his cock sprang up, fully erect now. She gripped his length and stroked him slowly, then looked into his eyes again.

"It's a little thing…"

Marcus raised an eyebrow, darting a glance to where she held his cock, fingers not quite able to meet around his girth.

"That's not what I mean!" Evie blushed and laughed, then slid on top of him. "What I want is just a gesture, really. Something my kind does when we share a deep connection with a lover and want to show each other how deep it really is. We share breath. It's intimate and powerful, and—" Her eyes grew glassy with fresh tears and she took a deep, shaky breath. "—and a way for me to carry something of you with me if I have to leave you behind."

He bent his knees and sat up, cradling her against his pelvis and wrapping her in his arms. "Anything that keeps you close to me after tonight is worth it. Just tell me what to do."

Evie settled closer, her warm folds pressed against his cock as she wrapped her legs around him and rested her hands on his shoulders. "Just follow my lead. When I exhale, you inhale, and then we switch. My power will fill your lungs. You might get a little high from it, and feel light-headed, but it'll feel good—like you're flying."

"Mmm, that sounds nice." He slid his hands down her back and cupped her buttocks, but Evie reached back and grabbed both his hands, placing them gently on her shoulders.

"No fooling around until we have a rhythm. You'll know when."

Marcus nodded and relaxed as she placed her hands back on his shoulders. Their gazes held and Evie leaned in, tilting her head slightly. Her breath tickled his lips, faint words audible to his ears—*Boreas lélegzik nekünk, amit belélegzünk egymást.* Words in the old language of the songs she sang that he still never knew the meaning of, but considered beautiful nonetheless.

At the last second, Marcus exhaled and then opened for Evie's mouth as she pressed her lips to his. She was warm and sweet, her kiss light, but sure. When the first wisps of warm air hit his tongue, he closed his eyes and inhaled, breathing her in until he could take no more. His lungs burned and his eyes teared up from the astonishing power that filled him. The sensation was close to what he'd felt the first time he'd regained consciousness after the blood infusion that had given him his Ultiori Elite powers. Evie's breath filled him, the magic seeping into him, making his blood sing for her.

He sensed her slight mental shift as their balance tilted and the breath was pulled back the other way. Marcus caught on immediately and took control, exhaling slowly past his lips, into her body.

Then he was inhaling her again. Somewhere in the middle of the next exhale, as she was breathing him in, her hips moved and he was inside her warm, wet depths, her body taking him in twofold.

When they began to move together, Marcus lost track of where he ended and Evie began. Her breath filled him repeatedly until his consciousness was in the clouds, and it seemed like the most natural thing when her beautiful dove-gray wings unfurled and spread behind her, blocking his view of the rest of the room. But Marcus didn't care about anything but this little bubble they had created for themselves, and when they reached their pinnacle at the same time, it was as if they'd both launched into the heavens as one.

In that moment he knew he would always love her, and would never forget the sacrifice she'd made to be with him. But an angel like her should be free to fly, and he would let her go.

He pressed his forehead to hers when their shared breathing ceased, struggling to catch his breath on his own again. This was the moment when he should say goodbye but he dreaded having to say the words out loud. Her wings were still gloriously outstretched and he reached a hand up to delicately trace the edge of her feathers.

"My God how I love you, Evie North."

Evie shivered and smiled, then stiffened at the sound of her cell door opening.

Marcus frowned. It wasn't like his brother Elites to interrupt—not with the close mental connection they had.

But then the shadow of another teased at the edge of his mind, familiar, and more dreaded than the thought of leaving his lover.

His master had come too soon.

A guttural roar reverberated through the room, loud enough to make Marcus's ears ring. He started to push Evie away, move in front of her to protect her, but he was too slow to react, still buzzed from their lovemaking.

A large hand wrapped around Evie's throat, lifting her off of Marcus like she weighed nothing. She was a light little thing, lithe and warm. She'd always had a buoyant personality before he brought her here.

She dangled in Nikhil's grip like a rag doll, clawing at the fingers gripping her neck before he tossed her across the room. Her shoulder hit the wall and she crumpled to the floor shaking her head and struggling to get up.

Marcus cried out and lunged at Nikhil, nearly reached him before agony split his skull, forcing him to his knees. He could only watch, half paralyzed with the pain of the presence in his mind as Nikhil turned his black gaze back to Evie.

"This is payment for what your brothers took from me," he said, his voice icy. He reached for her beautiful wings.

Evie let out a heartbreaking cry when the first wing came clear of its socket, and the other wing followed. Blood and feathers flew around the room and Marcus struggled to push himself into motion again.

Nikhil's shirtless back streamed red with blood from fresh wounds that had just appeared above his shoulder blades. Evie's blood flowed down her back from identical wounds. It made no sense to Marcus, though he was sure he should understand.

The pain in his head was too much, yet he managed to crawl across the floor toward his lover, calling her name and reaching for her.

When Nikhil turned back to him, the pain lessened, but he'd been weakened too much to put up any defenses. Nikhil saw everything—all Marcus's secrets were bared to his brutal master, including the impending visit from Evie's brother and whatever dragons they could rally to come save her. His master's laugh grated at his eardrums, taunting and wicked and somehow seeming to echo from some other dark place beyond his consciousness.

Nikhil glanced away for a moment, and Marcus moved, no longer caring about anything but reaching Evie, because if Nikhil had blood on his mind, he'd have to go through Marcus before he could get to her, and Marcus would rather die as her shield than watch her get ripped apart by this madman.

A hand wrapped around his ankle and hauled him back.

Evie let out an anguished cry and reached for Marcus. He twisted and sat up, raising his arm to ward off the large blade that Nikhil brandished – Marcus's own hunting knife that had been discarded on the floor with the rest of his gear. Then the strangeness of the scene registered. Nikhil was half naked, barefoot and shirtless, and clad only in a pair of drawstring pants like the prisoners wore.

"I thought you were worthy of serving me, but no more. You will bleed for your treachery," Nikhil said.

Before Marcus could react, the blade arced down, striking into the top of his thigh and slicing inward. His blood flowed hot and thick between his thighs. He struggled to reach down and stanch the flood, but his master's iron control of his mind prevented him from moving more than a little.

In the haze of semi-consciousness he felt Evie's warmth slip in behind him, her hands pulling at his head to cradle it in her lap. She was crying, small, hiccuping sobs in between melodic lyrics.

"Forgive me, my love," he whispered as the world faded to blackness.

# CHAPTER 3

## KED

*Brooklyn, New York*
*The Same Day*

*L*ove at first sight wasn't a dragon thing—the turul had the honor of that particular, crippling feature of their romantic lives. Dragons had the honor of choosing their mates, but Ked knew enough about dragon magic to know that some of the same rules applied to them, too. Fate so often chose for them, and she was pulling his strings at this very moment.

He stared at the photo for way too long. Evie North's brothers had given the faded Polaroid to him just hours ago, moments before disappearing into the bedroom where Ked's sister—they're new mate—was recuperating. They hadn't resurfaced in some time, but that was for the best. Ked's newly pregnant sister needed her mates now more than ever, especially because the second they came up for air, they would be leaving on a rescue mission.

Ked itched to get moving now that he knew the enemy

was likely already on his way to the same destination, if not already there. But he wouldn't leave without Evie's brothers, and they were still indisposed, so he forced himself to wait while he continued studying the photo.

It was hard enough for Ked to even process the static image of the turul woman in the photograph. He'd been away from the human world for so long. He cursed himself for his disorientation. He wished he could have left the Glade over the last few centuries and acclimated to the changes occurring in the world. If he had, he might not have wound up in this situation, where he was staring blankly at a too-realistic painting of a woman and getting a headache over how it worked.

The woman in the photo was his mate. And he couldn't even process her tiny, beautiful countenance on the square piece of paper he'd been handed.

*Evie.*

His heart hurt looking at the photo, which was impossible. He didn't have a heart. Contrary to what his siblings believed, he knew his chest had been occupied by a swirling void of nothing for centuries.

Still… something inside him *ached* to find this woman. The sensation was new and uncomfortable, but it felt right. She was his.

His pulse quickened and he clenched his jaw.

This beautiful woman—the image from his recurring dreams—was *his.* And she'd been taken from him.

The voices around him grew louder and he jerked to attention. Losing track of events probably wasn't a good quality in an immortal. Ked forced himself back to the present and said something he hoped was at least coherent to answer a half-heard inquiry directed at him. He kept looking at the image of Evie, unable to tear his eyes away from her, hoping there might be clues in the picture that would help him know whether she would accept him.

She wasn't alone in the photo. Beside her stood a hulk of a man in a pilot's uniform, his gaze raptly set on Evie while Evie beamed at the camera.

That man was the enemy. Ultiori to the core, though maybe only a new recruit at the time, from the look of him. He looked so full of love and hope in the photo—with not a hint of the devious hunger possessed by the other Ultiori that Ked had encountered.

*Marcus,* he said to himself. Evie's brothers knew him, had told Ked everything about him, including the fact that he was eager to see her rescued and had even given them the location of the Ultiori facility where she was held prisoner.

Yet Marcus had been her seducer. The Ultiori hunter who had stolen her away. The man Ked would gladly kill to get her back.

Evie was his. Fate said so. Or his dreams did, at least, and they were the only connection he had anymore to what Fate intended.

But the image of Marcus intrigued him as much as Evie did. Partly because of how he looked at her, and partly because his presence in her life back then was a conundrum. If he hadn't already become a hunter, he must have become one very soon after the image was captured. Iszak and Lukas would have known him for a hunter, as would Evie, if he'd already joined the Ultiori ranks.

"Are you sure he wasn't turned yet?" Ked asked, looking up from the photo to meet the gazes of the two turul males who grabbed seats across the table. Ked's two brothers leaned against the wall nearby.

Iszak shook his head. "He was harmless. We'd have never let her keep seeing him, otherwise. She would have known better, too."

Lukas nodded in agreement. "She had this crazy idea that she could find love with someone other than her true mate. Every decade or so, she'd get impatient and find some poor schmuck, blow his mind for a few years, then move on when the mystery wore off. She's had more marriage proposals than we can count."

An amused chuckle carried from the other side of the sunlit kitchen they sat in. Ked looked over to the back of the elderly woman who was chopping vegetables and shaking her head. She paused and turned, pointing the knife at Lukas.

"You two used to do the same thing. Ever since you were old enough to notice a pretty girl, you were chasing them, no matter they weren't your Belah. I could set a clock by your escapades."

"Oh, do tell me more, Nanyo," Belah said, smirking at her mates as she entered the room, looking flushed and sated. She joined their grandmother at the counter.

"In time, my dear," the elder North said. "Right now, your brother must focus on my granddaughter. What do you see in the photo, boy?"

Ked raised an eyebrow at the diminutive, but let it go. Sofia North may not have been even half his age, but she still commanded the respect of any matriarch. He'd have loved to have known her in her prime. He glanced back down at the photo of her granddaughter, wondering if the elder had been as beautiful when she was younger. His eyes shifted to Marcus again and he studied the young man.

"There's something about him. Without seeing his aura, I can't put my finger on it." He wished he could have been there—Evie's beauty shone as bright as any aura, but this man had a bearing that drew Ked's attention as much as Evie's did. The man's fixation on Evie seemed familiar somehow, and it was more than just the look of a man devoted enough to give away his captive's location to his enemy.

Ked swallowed, confused at the conflicting emotions that welled up inside him. His mouth watered as he thought of how Evie's magic might taste when they made love. But Marcus… the hunter… his sly eyes made Ked itch to know his secrets, to delve into the darkest depths of the man's soul and understand him completely.

Yet he was her captor, and if Ked were going to carry out the mission ahead of him, he'd have to kill Marcus and any other Ultiori who stood in his way.

"What did you see the day you met him?" he asked, directing the question at Sofia. The woman had a reputation as a powerful seer that was well-known among all the higher races. Ked had no doubt the woman knew much more than she was sharing about her granddaughter's disappearance with this man. He refrained from using his powers on her, however, simply out of respect. If the woman wanted her granddaughter back as much as she seemed to, he had to trust her to share anything she knew that would help.

"I saw a young man in love with an ideal. He believed he was in love with her, but it was only her nature that drew him to her. It is the way of the blessing, of course. The blessing's power drew her to him, too."

Ked's head jerked up and he stared at her. "Blessing? Are you telling me this man was a Blessed human? Did Evie know?"

"To be Blessed during a renunciation is a lonely time," she said, ignoring his question. "Dragons won't take mates so late in a cycle, yet his path was laid out for him from before his birth. He followed the only course open to him, as did my granddaughter." Sofia's voice never wavered, nor did she avert her piercing gaze from his as she spoke.

Ked's vision narrowed as he stood and glowered down at the small woman. The room darkened, his shadow blocking out the light so thoroughly that not even the sunlight outside broke through. He ignored the alarmed exclamations of the others, even the warning admonition of his sister.

"Do you understand how grave an offense it is to divert a Blessed human from their journey to find their dragon mate? He belongs to my kind. And now the enemy has him. And if he is a Blessed, that means he isn't merely a hunter—they have turned him into an Elite." *And whose blood runs through the man's veins now? Is it more mine or one of my brothers'?*

Sofia set her jaw and stared him down. "You would do well not to question Fate. While your kind were busy abandoning your children, my Evie was ensuring your Blessed found his path."

"Straight into the belly of the beast. Even if he could have been redeemed, I'll have no choice but to kill him now." Ked didn't hold back his anger, letting it spill forth, a roiling cloud of black in the already dark room. This meddlesome woman had been instrumental in not only her own granddaughter's abduction, but the turning of a Blessed human into the enemy. The worst kind of Ultiori, too.

Sofia's stubbornness was a beacon in the center of the void his powers had rendered, bright and determined to compete with his anger. She held up her kitchen knife to point it at him. The tip caught some errant scrap of light that seared his eyes.

"You are a fool, Immortal. Your own power has blinded you to the possibilities. The world does not operate at the extremes your magic seems to. Find a way between the darkness and the light, Ked. Your race's Shadows understand this, yet you do not. You are too consumed by the absolutes to see how to balance them."

A dull howling pricked at his ears, growing louder in the moments the two held each other's gazes, both too resolute to be the one to look away first. Sofia's hair suddenly whipped around her head from the gale-force wind that rushed through the room, seemingly from nowhere, buffeting Ked's body so violently he lost focus. This was no normal wind, either. Within the din he heard the voice of one of the few powers greater than his and his siblings'—the words chilled him at first, before the clarity of them forced him to his senses.

*Between light and darkness, between life and death, between power and submission, lies love and truth.*

Ked's skin prickled. It was an admonition, something he rarely had to endure at his rank. Sometimes he forgot that there were powers greater than the Dragon Council. The North Wind was a power he respected, and even feared. As a dragon, he depended on the winds. If he pissed one of them off, he'd be hurting. Few other higher powers could damage him or his race as much as the winds could.

He withdrew his darkness and sat back down with a sigh.

"We are allies, Sofia, and I intend to remain your friend. I will find your granddaughter. If Marcus is willing to atone, I'll decide what to do with him after."

Sofia's shoulders sagged and she came toward him. She was so small. Most turul women were petite and bird-like. Only a few broke the mold. He'd observed her power growing from within the Glade for most of her life and had always admired her tenacity. She'd have made him a perfect mate in her prime. Her granddaughter was the one fated to be with him, though, and the one in the most danger now.

Sofia came around the table and rested her hands on his shoulders. "The path was never meant to be a straight one for them, nor for you. Yet it was the path they were meant to tread. You are their doorway to the next part of their lives." She dug into his shoulders with her steely fingertips and leaned closer to his ear. "*He* is yours as much as she. Never sacrifice your heart for the sake of your soul when you can keep them both."

Sofia went back to her cooking, her shoulders sagging. Belah gave Ked a stern glance before following, sending an admonitory message directly into his mind.

*"She's losing strength, brother. That wasn't fair of you. Your power is too draining on a woman as old as her."*

He frowned and sent her a wordless apology, then turned his attention back to the other problem in the room.

"You're my sister's mates. I cannot, in good conscience, ask you to come, but I have a feeling she'd argue more strongly for me to take you than even you would—because she loves you."

Lukas glowered at him. "Not even your sister could keep us from joining you if she asked us to stay. Perhaps that's what you really mean to say? And you know she's letting us go as much for your sake as for ours."

Ked hated the admission—not that his sister had found love again after so long, but that she was willing to sacrifice it to see *him* find love for the first time in his life. He would do anything to avoid taking that away from her.

"We have a bigger issue, however," he said. "The trip will take us hours and my fear is what state we'll find her in when we get there. You said Marcus assured you she was safe, but Nikhil escaped." He cast a quick glance at Belah, carefully choosing his words. "Since Nikhil may still be *under the influence* of some greater evil, we have to assume he is unstable. We need to fly quickly. My brothers and I can get there within a few hours, but you won't be able to match our speed."

"What if we don't need to fly?" Lukas said. Standing again, he went to his grandmother. "You still have the potion you gave us before… the nymphaea blood that helped us tele-port to where Belah was being held. We can use that."

"No, child." Sofia gave him a defeated look. "There was only enough for you to save your Belah. That was all I had."

Magic as powerful as nymphaea blood would have been welcome just now. Ever since the Ultiori Elites had acquired the ability to teleport, or to *drift*, as they called it, the higher races had been at a distinct disadvantage. Ked and the mortal Shadows had the ability to sublimate their physical forms into smoke, and carry passengers along for the ride, but they were still restricted by distance. Unfortunately the nymphaea had been in hiding even longer than the dragons and finding an ally among them at such short notice was impossible.

"We will have to do without nymphaea blood and just hope we reach the Ultiori compound soon enough, but you two will have to ride instead of fly if you insist on coming…"

The tall, pale-haired Aodh stepped silently forward, his expression intent and a little chagrined. Ked looked up at his quiet brother, eyebrows raised.

In a deep voice that was no more audible than a whisper, Aodh said, "We need not fly, brother. I can take us there now, if you wish. I just need the location."

Ked stopped breathing, his mouth hanging open in surprise. Belah came back into the room and simply stared at Aodh, while Gavra stood up straight and said, "The fuck you can. Dragon's don't teleport or fucking time travel like the nymphaea can. You want to explain yourself, brother?"

Aodh bowed his head. "Forgive me for keeping this a secret for so long. We have all carried heavy weights that we would rather not burden each other with. This is my burden."

Iszak stood, angrily clenching his fist, which he raised, unfurling one finger to point at Aodh. "Burden my ass. If you can transport us around the way the Elites travel, you should have said something. We should fucking *be* there already!"

Ked raised a hand, the invisible force of his magic pushing Iszak back into his chair. In an even tone, he said, "Tell us how this happened, Aodh, but make it quick."

Aodh nodded, spreading his hands and staring down at his fingers. "Early on when I was between human mates, I dallied with a nymph. A pretty little water sprite with a wicked, creative mind. She called herself Meri or Marnie or Marea, depending on her mood. We melded, and the exchange of consciousness while we were physically merged was even more enjoyable than any of the human lovers I'd had. So, we did it again, but the second time she begged me to taste her blood as well as her essence."

Ked grimaced inwardly at the start of the confession, already seeing where it was going. He had no room to criticize Aodh for what had happened. He had his own dark secrets from his early life that few knew of. His brothers and sisters had not criticized him.

Aodh gave them all a humble smile. "I did not know that doing this would give her such power over me. She stole my body, leaving my spirit in the wind. It took the powers of Neph and Nyx and several of the other *thiasoi* chasing after her to bring her back—she did not want to give up the immortality and power she had in my dragon form. She was punished for it—exiled from the nymphaea's Haven, but ever since that day some of her nymphaea powers have been a part of me. I have rarely had cause to use them since, but now I think it's time."

"Brother, that is one hell of a secret you've been keeping," Gavra said. "But I have to know, are the nymphs..."

"No time," Ked said. "The two of you can compare notes later, *after* we've gotten Evie back. Aodh, can you carry all of us?"

"Yes."

"Good," he said, turning back to Iszak and Lukas. "You two will follow my lead, and answer to me at every point."

"I take it you have a plan for after we get there?" Iszak asked.

"You'll do aerial reconnaissance of the compound. From there, I'll access the compound from the air with my brothers' assistance. They can null the security sensors to allow me to go in silently. Aodh and Gavra can distract the hunters inside, sending their breath through the ventilation ducts from the roof." And they would have to just pray that there were no Elites on the premises who would be immune to their tactics.

"And we just sit in the woods with our thumbs up our asses?"

Ked scowled. "You can do whatever the fuck you want, but when she comes out, you remind her who she is. They indoctrinate their captives. She's been in there for five decades, and she doesn't know me."

"What about him?" Lukas asked, pointing at the man in the photo.

"I won't know about him until I see him—talk to him—if that's even possible. If he's still loyal to Nikhil, he's a lost cause. If he remained loyal to her, he may already be dead."

Ked stared down at the photo again, taking in the red-haired man. Another Blessed. They were rare and highly desired. Fated to be a dragon's mate. And desired just as much by their enemy for the magic they carried.

If they had made another Elite hunter out of Marcus, his Blessing would have merged the power of the three Immortal brothers into one man. He would also be able to sense dragons as well as any of the other higher races the second he was near them or heard their voices. Ked had only met a few Elites over the years, and each time they were stronger than before—harder to kill, and learning to harness more of the power carried in their blood. But for so long, there had only been two Elites.

He'd killed one himself before going into hiding in the Glade. The Elite he'd faced had been a female, beautiful and fierce. Full of the kind of fiery light that he almost believed could be his redemption, but a shadow clung to her. Her Blessing had made him want her almost too much to end her life, but she was too far under the Ultiori's spell to be redeemed. The worst part was that he knew without a doubt that the shadowy power and the lust that flickered in her eyes were a result of *his* blood in her veins driving her.

The Blessing was all she'd needed to find him. That was all they ever needed. He'd nearly fallen under her spell at the time, until the truth became clear to him. She hadn't been easy to kill, either. Once he recognized what she truly was, there was only one way to end her life. Only his own black flames could destroy her body, along with that piece of himself that had turned her into what she was.

Chills prickled Ked's skin at the idea. He was responsible for this, more than his sister was. In order to save her life, he and his brothers had been forced to make a trade—their blood for hers. But the amount of blood Nikhil had bargained for was three times the volume of Belah's blood that remained. Enough to sustain Elites for thousands of years. After Ked killed the female Elite, he and his brothers had counted on another Blessed being too hard to find.

It was too late now. The enemy may very well have three Elites who, when working together, could sense any dragon when they were near, including Immortals. He and his siblings were all in danger if Marcus had indeed become an Elite.

If Marcus truly carried Ked's blood, he would be a formidable opponent. If any of the other Elites were in the compound, Ked may find himself as trapped as Belah when her old lover had tied her down and bled her dry.

It was a necessary risk. Aodh and Gavra would have to remain safely outside the walls while Ked went inside to retrieve Evie. Risking his freedom would be a small price to pay if he could make sure Evie North was safe. He would trade his life for hers, if it came down to it.

# CHAPTER 4

## KED

*Canadian Rockies*
*Present Day*

The journey was dizzyingly fast and left Ked holding his head to regain his balance for a moment after they arrived. When he opened his eyes he found they'd reached the edge of the remote research facility that served as the Ultiori's Canadian headquarters. Nestled deep in the northernmost ranges of the Rocky Mountains, built into an evergreen-covered hillside overlooking a raging river, it would be tough to differentiate it from the wilderness around it with an untrained eye. Ked and his brothers shifted and flew in a wide circle around the valley while the North brothers put themselves back together. It seemed turul were more sensitive to that type of instantaneous travel than dragons were.

Ked inspected every detail of the terrain beneath them. Vegetation was lush, which was a good sign. It meant that the Ultiori leader was not in residence. If he had been, there would be a swath of dead foliage surrounding him, a side-effect of his Blessing having ultimately transformed into a curse.

Ked sensed almost no wildlife around the compound, which was no surprise, but at least the forest was healthy.

He spied a moonlit clearing atop the ridge nearest the compound and folded his wings in a dive to reach it. His brothers followed silently. On any other flight they might have bellowed out their elation, but this was not the time. Not even the beauty of the place they landed in captured Ked's attention tonight as his claws dug into the rich earth.

"Does the Wind have anything to tell us?" he asked, looking at the two huge falcons that perched upon a pair of boulders nearby. Both birds tilted their heads, listening, their profiles eerily framed by the moon behind them. If he didn't know their grandmother, he'd consider it an ill omen to see two falcons cast in moonlight so starkly.

"Nothing good," Iszak said. "The place is filled with sadness, pain. But none of it is ever let out."

"Can you get a read on how many are inside? Their level of power?"

Lukas launched into the air and flew up, weaving a figure eight high above the secluded ravine. When he came back, he shifted into his full human form and dropped down to his knees, hugging himself and shaking.

Was he crying? Ked shifted and bent down beside his sister's mate, resting a hand on his shoulder.

Lukas shook his head. "It's not right in there. There are too many captives. Our kind chained. The hunters are there, maybe two dozen, but they're settling in, business as usual, the bastards. The Elites are there, too. All three. Two are asleep, and Marcus... Marcus seems... broken, near death. I think we may be too late."

Ked nodded and as he pulled away, Lukas snapped one hand up and grabbed Ked's wrist. "The Elites. They smell exactly like you and your brothers. The Wind carried all their scents to me, bits and pieces of their magic. Can you explain why the fuck they smell like you?"

Aodh and Gavra tilted their large, horned heads to look at Lukas.

*"You tell him, brother,"* Aodh spoke in his mind. *"He has a right to know the truth now that he's mated to our sister."*

Ked met Lukas's gaze and relaxed his hand, moving it to the back of the other man's head. What he had to tell them couldn't be processed easily. He hated using his power this way, but he had to. They could hate him later, as long as they were with him now.

Slowly, he let his breath out and directed it into Lukas's lungs. Lukas's eyes went wide and he fell back, supported by Ked's hand.

"I will save your sister the same way I saved my own sister, but this time, I have a few… roadblocks. The Elites are made from dragon blood. I'm only telling you this because if I don't come out, you need to know what to expect. They have the same powers as me and my brothers, in varying degrees. They can't fly, at least… physiology can't be faked. Magic can be acquired, though."

"How did they get your blood?" Lukas asked, recovering and settling against a tree trunk. Ked pulled away.

"We gave it to them."

# CHAPTER 5

## KED

*Canadian Rockies*
*Present Day*

"You gave it to them," Lukas repeated. "You gave *what* to them?"

"Our blood. Our power." Ked closed his eyes, envisioning Nikhil destroying his sister and reliving the blood rage he'd experienced in that moment. He'd have given anything to heal her wholly, but he'd had nothing to give then. She'd been on the edge of death for decades, wishing for it, but never able to pass beyond due to her immortality. Even the healing waters of the Glade and her siblings' magic weren't enough to restore her health. Too much of her blood had been lost.

She was safe now, and fully healed, but he could still picture her skin cut to ribbons and her blood collected in a myriad of receptacles scattered around the room as he carried her out. His sister's physician had been the one to warn him something was wrong. After he'd dealt with

Nikhil, all Ked cared about was making sure Belah was safely away from her torturer.

"Why the hell would you do that?" Iszak asked, stepping into Ked's space and glaring at him. "So you're telling us it was never Belah, but you and your brothers who were to blame all along?"

Ked clenched his teeth and stared down at Iszak, forcing himself to resist letting loose a wave of darkness to remind the other man why they were here. Aodh stepped forward and placed a hand on Iszak's shoulder, speaking in his low, soft tone.

"We only cared about saving our sister. She needed her blood. We negotiated to get it back. This was his price."

"Why didn't you destroy him? None of this would be happening if you had!"

"We tried, but our fire was never enough to kill him. We had no choice but to negotiate. The important thing is that we got her blood back, and she is yours now."

Iszak's glare softened at the mention of Belah and he nodded. "I would have done the same, and I would trade my own blood for Evie's life right now, if I thought it would work."

"You won't have to," Ked said. "The one small blessing is that their leader is not here. Only the three Elites are, and by your accounts, one of them is out of commission. The other two... will be a challenge, if I run into them. Thanks to having mine and my brothers' blood in their veins, they have more power than I have on my own."

Lukas stood and came forward, a fierce look in his eyes. "Enough power to fight all five of us if we go in together? Why shouldn't we take the whole compound, release their captives? There's so much suffering inside."

"An army of normal hunters could easily overtake you two," Ked said. "Two Elites may not be enough to overtake me and my brothers all at once, but there would be too much collateral damage if they believed they were under siege. I don't want to risk your sister being harmed before we can get to her. The other captives will have to wait. We'll come up with a plan to help them soon."

The North brothers had equally grim looks, but nodded in spite of their obvious disappointment at not being allowed to go in fighting. It had to be Ked alone for this. He was the only one of the three Immortal brothers who could get in and out of the compound without having to breach their exits. He could have gotten in without any assistance, but didn't know what kind of state Evie would be in once he found her, and sublimation with a passenger was never very easy on the passenger. Having her brothers right outside would ensure she knew she was safe at the end of it.

With a glance, Ked's brothers both nodded and launched themselves into the air. He followed them to the compound and the three of them circled once. Aodh and Gavra both released thick clouds of red and white smoke from their nostrils that swirled and sparked in the night air, descending snake-like to the open vents scattered along the roof. Ked focused his energy until his mass dispersed to become no more solid than a breath, his body dissipating into darkness that sank like black fog. As the embodiment of shadows, he waited, watching the last of his brothers' breath finally disappear down the open vents.

They would send their breaths through the corridors, blending both the calming white smoke and arousing red that would intoxicate the residents, hopefully leaving them lethargic and more concerned with pleasure than alertness. With any luck, no one would be the wiser after Ked got in and out again with Evie. The Elites were still the wildcards. They would recognize the smoke for what it was, but with any luck, Ked would have enough time to get Evie out before it dawned on them.

Aodh and Gavra circled one last time and then flew back toward the clearing, signaling Ked that it was time.

With barely a thought, Ked filtered his shadows through the vents, letting pieces of himself spread through the ventilation system and into every accessible room in the compound, searching. As mere shadows, he could be in almost any space he chose. Each piece of him explored, eliminating possible holding locations before combining and working his way down from ground level to subterranean level. He had no idea how deep the place went, but as he crept around the dimly lit hallways, he sensed his brothers' breath at work. Every so often he'd pass a closed door with the unmistakable sounds of lovemaking echoing from the other side.

He searched, fascinated by the labyrinthine architecture of the building. There were corridors upon corridors, some lined with doors, others that came out onto landings that faced the expanse of plate glass windows lining the side of the compound overlooking the ravine. Beyond, the mountain vistas stretched for miles, the dark ribbon of the river snaking through with patches of white water letting him know how treacherous the landscape really was outside this place.

More treacherous inside, however. On the next level down, Ked could sense the despair. The corridors were sleek and modern, the doors nothing more than shining panels of white glass with no knobs. Each one had a glowing rectangle beside the glass, with a keypad glowing underneath. He paused long enough by one to manifest a finger and touched the numbers lightly. The glass was smooth and cool, the number behind it glowing brighter and making a soft pinging sound.

If Ked didn't know better, he'd have thought it magic. But if it were really magic, the residents inside would have been able to call on their goddesses to release them.

There was no goddess of shadows. Only Ked could get into these rooms with his own powers. He'd considered recruiting the First Shadow, Kol, to accompany him inside, but didn't want to risk the new father's life. Now that he observed how deep the compound went and how advanced the security was, he wasn't sure Kol could have made it this far anyway.

More eerily lit, opaque glass doors lined the hallways at closer intervals, the residents inside a heart-wrenching combination of captives representing the higher races.

What was worse was when he'd passed through dozens of rooms and realized the one thing they all had in common: they were almost all females. Most were turul and ursa females, many were dragons. Only one of the higher races—the nymphs—was poorly represented, though for that, he supposed he should be grateful. On the lowest level, however, he found the sole males among all the captives. A pair of males were locked together in a cell, one a huge white ursa in his natural form, the other a satyr, half-shifted with the hooved lower body betraying his *thiasoi* parentage. The satyr stood beside the roaring ursine beast, and ranted blindly at the floor with one hand tangled in the ursa's fur.

Ked paused, shocked at the sight. The male members of the nymphaea race had been extinct for hundreds of years, or so he'd believed. If this male existed, he was likely the only one still alive. Why had they kept this one alive, and for so long? The satyr raised his head and stared into the shadows where Ked hid. His eyes swirled wildly, his lips mouthing words. After a moment, the sounds became audible, but grated, as though scraped across hard gravel before reaching Ked's ears.

"Fate's flood is upon us, the river splits. Black and white. Don't trust the white ones when you find them, they are filled with secrets and lies."

Ked glanced down at the white-furred creature by the satyr's side. The bear showed his teeth and a low growl rumbled up from within him.

The man shook his head. "Not this white one. The humans with the blood-filled needles and chemical smells, their white coats and bright lights—they are the monsters. They are under the Lamia's spell, just like the master was. The master of this place thinks he is free now, but we are all Fate's captives. Even you, Void. But perhaps you can find happiness in the illusion, perhaps you can find some semblance of freedom from her song. Follow her song, Void. Let the music free you."

Impulsively, Ked reached out with his power, sending darkness into the satyr's mind to drown out all but the keenest of his emotions. Deep regret lay shining among all the dimmer feelings, regret for a love he felt but could not show, because of his knowledge of things no man should be forced to know: his own future.

Ked moved on, leaving the satyr and ursa to their shared misery. He understood the feeling, having carried regrets of his own for centuries. He tried to tell himself that they would have been all the weaker not having Belah at full power. Once the deed was done, and her blood consumed by her lover, there had been no going back for any of them.

When Ked and his brothers found Nikhil to bargain with him for their sister's blood, he had been as far gone as that poor satyr. But what if his sister had been right? When her mates had rescued her from Nikhil a second time, from a second attempt at stealing her blood, Belah had insisted that Nikhil was under the control of some darker force.

*The Lamia's spell.* The female creature who, like his own

sister, had become infamous among all the races over the centuries for her seductive nature and her thirst for blood. No one knew why she did what she did, or what her origins were. But she'd disappeared ages ago, not long before Belah's own infamy took hold. Since then the Lamia had become no more than a myth—something to frighten children into behaving, much like his own sister.

Yet he had no evidence of that creature's existence. Nikhil, on the other hand, was still a very real and present problem. There was no denying their old enemy had captured Ked's sister, held and tortured her for seven days, at the end of which he'd stabbed her and let her bleed. The act was too similar to that night three thousand years ago when Ked had found his sister all but dead and the only way to revive her was to make the most impossible bargain to bring her back to life.

Belah's state hadn't been the only thing driving their decision when Ked and his brothers approached her power-hungry former lover. They'd woken up one morning after having a series of shared dreams. In them, he and his brothers had witnessed Belah's torture. Her veins cut open and her blood running freely. And in the dreams, her blood had spilled onto the floor and immediately taken shape into every magical creature in existence. One after the other, each drop became something more fantastic than the last. Creatures they knew of, and then creatures they'd never seen before.

In the dreams, the new creatures had fought to the death against the old ones. Dragons, turul, ursa, and nymphs all fought on a field of Belah's blood against the other creatures that arose from the red lake that surrounded her.

That was when Ked and his brothers realized that a female's blood held the power of creation. They couldn't let Nikhil keep that power. It might be too late for Belah's old lover, but at least they could retrieve her blood before Nikhil understood the value of it.

Now, he had the blood of countless females. They may not be immortal, but Ked couldn't deny the chill that ran down his incorporeal spine at the thought of what the Ultiori could possibly want with so many females. The understanding that it was Nikhil—the man who had drained his sister's blood—who had orchestrated this ongoing abduction over the centuries, made his teeth manifest and clench hard together, and his fingers tighten into solid fists. Darkness flowed out of him in waves and he had to force himself to pull it back, to return to the shadows.

It didn't matter whether his sister forgave Nikhil. Ked would find a way to kill the man, if it was the last thing he did. To put an end to the abductions and the suffering.

Tonight, he couldn't, though. He'd made a promise, and his heart lay at the end of the corridor he drifted down, his shadow shifting along the edges to avoid the dim light.

He moved toward the music that drifted down the hall, seeping into his soul. Toward Evie.

He would like to greet her as himself the first time, but it would be too dangerous to become fully solid until he got her out.

Rounding the last corner toward her voice, he paused, swirling cautiously as he assessed the unexpected scene before him. There were three cell doors at the end, one the same opaque white glass as most of the others in this place, but two were clear. Slumped to the floor against the two clear doors were two of the Ultiori Elites Ked had worried about running into. "Sleeping," the North brothers had said, but they looked unconscious to him, and their minds were in an almost catatonic state.

Testing them with his own mind, he found remnants of a dark presence that had controlled them briefly, but was gone now. They would wake soon, as would the pair of female captives that were similarly slumped unconscious against the other side of each door, inside the cells.

It was a curious scene that Ked felt warranted more scrutiny, but the strangeness alarmed him enough to move quicker.

He turned to the one opaque cell door where her beautiful voice came from and slid beneath it. Once inside, he let his shadow seep through the cracks and into the corners, surveying the dark room to determine what, if any, threats were inside and what state Evie might be in before he took her out.

All he found was a pair of bodies crumpled together naked on the floor. Their limbs were entwined as though they'd been making love, but the woman was halfway sitting up, with the man's torso draped across her lap. She wept silently, running her fingers through his dark red hair as she sang to him.

A pool of blood surrounded them, originating from a deep gash in the man's upper thigh—a wound no human man could survive for very long. A set of bare footprints crossed through the red fluid. Someone had been in here and done this barefoot, but Ked had seen no bloody footprints in the hall. It had to have been Nikhil.

His impulse was to rage at the sight, but her song prevented it, kept him still and enraptured simply being in the room with her finally.

Ked stayed in the dark corner, mesmerized by the sight of her. She was every bit as beautiful as her picture, but mussed and naked now. Her long hair hung in messy tangles around her shoulders, almost covering her small breasts. The man's arms were wrapped around her hips, his head turned to one side, his cheek resting on her thighs. His skin was as pale and smooth as marble, and he was completely, utterly still.

Tears streamed over her cheeks unchecked. The song changed from what he'd believed was her mating call into what was now a low, haunting melody in an ancient language Ked understood. He sank down to the floor and closed his eyes, entranced by the song that reminded him so much of the day he'd rescued his sister from the same kind of ordeal. He had no tears today, though he might have if he'd been corporeal. All he had was anguish and regret about all the things he'd done wrong in failing to see how dangerous his sister's lover was.

He closed his eyes and let Evie's song sink into him, owning the ache that had so long been a part of him yet had remained unrecognized. His failure as a brother in spite of his power as a leader, and even as a god.

In that old language, Evie sang about love so deep it went through you and wrapped around again, binding you tightly to the other person. Then she sang about how deep the loss was when half of your soul died and that binding disappeared, leaving you too weightless to exist, like gravity had suddenly been turned off and you had no way to maintain purchase on the earth.

That made Ked's heart stop. He'd been weightless his entire life. He wanted solid ground, but he feared it, too. Dragons were meant to be airborne. Yet they had legs, and human forms.

He remained still for another moment, waiting for a lull in her song when he could take action. He needed a moment to catch his breath after his revelations.

The singing stopped.

"I know you're there. Show yourself, please. And tell me it's not Fate's cruel trick that I lose one true love and find another in the same night."

# CHAPTER 6

## KED

*Canadian Rockies*
*Present Day*

"You've been listening for a while. I also know who you are, Ked, and what you are. And I know—" Evie's voice shook. "—I know you are mine. Like he was mine for so long." She dipped her head and kissed the bare temple of the too-still man on her lap, tenderly brushing his hair back over his ear.

Ked pulled himself out of the corner and summoned his shadows back to him. Standing before her, he manifested his human form, disregarding his own mandate that he keep to shadows until he got her out; disregarding his desire to tear down the walls of this place with his bare hands and destroy every hunter in residence.

She needed to see him, now that she'd called him out. That was all she needed. No heroics, no destruction.

"You loved him?" he asked.

"More than anyone else. Until you."

Ked closed his eyes. She was a turul, he reminded himself.

She would know him instantly as her true mate, if they were meant to be. He let out a deep breath and collapsed to his knees beside her.

"What happened?" He placed his hands on the back of the inert man on Evie's lap. The body was warm, but he didn't sense a pulse.

"*Sayid* found us together. Marcus hadn't come to me in so long. I missed him. I didn't care what would happen because he said he was getting me out finally—that you'd received his message and you were coming for me, but then *Sayid* showed up. He wasn't happy."

The name she used made Ked pause. She must mean Nikhil. Was *Sayid* the name he went by now? No, it wasn't his name. It was his title. A fresh wave of guilt and regret washed over him. He and his siblings had hidden themselves for too long. They'd been fools to leave their race to the wolves the way they had. The hibernation cycles meant to protect the dragons had only served to alienate half their race, to the point they broke the laws to avoid the cycles of sleep. As a result, too many of them had been taken and were locked up in the cells Ked had passed before arriving in this room. And he knew this wasn't the only Ultiori facility. There might be hundreds more. He couldn't think about that now, though. The broken-hearted woman in front of him was his reason for coming in here to begin with.

"Marcus was the one who sent the message?" Ked looked down at the body draped across her thighs. It still held a dim aura around it, so similar to the faint aura of his sister the day he'd taken her away from her lover, bloody and broken. The man wasn't dead—at least, not entirely.

"He did it because he loved me, and for once, I let go of my resentment and loved him back the way I craved to do ever since he became like you," she said. Her lips quivered and her eyes filled with tears. "He always loved me, but until tonight, I never loved him enough. He still tried to save me even though he didn't think he could be saved, himself."

"He saved you both," Ked said. "Someone got his message to me that you were here. A female dragon said she was approached by a hunter who gave her your name and this location. She was told to take the information to the Council. Not an easy task for a dragon of her low rank, but she did it. I'm here to get you out, Evie. Your brothers are waiting nearby."

Evie's face was wet with tears, her eyes shining with those still unshed. "I'm not leaving. Not unless you bring him out, too. I know he's dead, but I won't leave him here for them."

Something about her bearing seemed stiff to him. She barely moved her head when she turned to look at him, and she hadn't shifted a muscle of her body. The only movements were her hand on the dead man's hair and the occasional flux of her facial expressions.

That was when he noticed the wall behind her back was coated with blood, the scent strong. She was still bleeding from unseen wounds.

Ked's power surged, blotting out the light in the room. His nostrils flared as he reached a hand out to her.

"You're hurt," he said.

She flinched back from his fingers. "You just ruined the mood."

Ked drew his hand back and stared at her.

Evie shrugged enough to wince at the pain. "It wasn't a good mood, I admit, but you succeeded in making it worse."

"What did he do to you?" he growled.

Ignoring the question, she said, "Can you please turn the lights back on? I spend too much time in the dark as it is."

He blinked at her, surprised at her lack of reaction to his power. He willed the lights to illuminate again.

Evie regarded him for a moment before speaking again, seeming to consider her words. "It was one of the strangest encounters of my life, believe it or not. After he took my wings and stabbed Marcus in the leg, I thought he was going to kill me... I believe I was his target, at any rate, but he didn't expect Marcus to be in here. At the end just when I was sure he'd end me, I started singing. He just fell to his knees and listened, and it was like a veil lifted from him. Then he apologized, swore he didn't mean it and left as though he were on a mission to kill the thing that had hurt us. Like he hadn't just been in the room the entire time, holding that knife."

"He's a mad man. We've known this all along."

Evie shook her head. "No. I know madness when I hear it and I've seen him act strangely before. When he came into the room he was like a juggernaut, his eyes were wild like some unnatural rage powered him. But when I sang, it was as though he became another person. Every word he spoke at the end was the truth. I believe he really was used by some other power and now that he's free he's after that thing's blood."

"You and my sister can compare notes when we get you safe," Ked said, losing patience with her story, though he reluctantly began to wonder whether Belah's insistence that Nikhil had been controlled by something else might be true. "I'm taking you both out of here now. It won't be pleasant, but it won't kill you. Just... hold on, okay?"

"Good luck with that," Evie said, lifting one hand up in front of her face. Around her wrist was a tattoo that glimmered with faint silver light. Through the bloodstains that covered her other wrist and her ankles he saw more. Shackles that were likely designed to keep her in this cell somehow.

Ked had no time for such tricks. With a breath and the

power of a thought, Evie's shackles were gone, but he could do nothing for the bloodstains or the wounds yet.

Ked bent and slipped an arm around her waist, hoping he was avoiding the worst of her injuries. When she leaned into him, he finally caught a glimpse of her bloody back. Two ragged, semi-symmetrical wounds graced each shoulder blade, and it was then that he noticed the floor around them was covered in feathers, and her amputated wings lay atop her small cot.

"Don't look at them, please," Evie whispered shakily. "I just wanted to be his angel for one night. That's all. I guess I was the angel of death."

Ked's rage returned, blotting out the light again and illuminating the profound emptiness and grief that overwhelmed Evie. To lose one's wings would be the most horrific torture imaginable.

He clutched her to his chest and wrapped his other arm around the naked man draped across her lap. The body slumped into him coldly as he gathered his power to get them out.

The swirling void of shadow opened for him, and he flowed through as easily as ever, pulling his passengers along. At the other end they would be safe. Perhaps not whole, but at least Ked would have time to help make them so.

# CHAPTER 7

*Canadian Rockies*
*Present Day*

When he reappeared in a cloud of dark smoke in the clearing, Ked fell into a pile with the other two wrapped around him. Marcus's unconscious face met his, expression as serene as carved stone.

Ked had considered ignoring Evie's plea and leaving the man behind, but he couldn't deny the Blessing Marcus carried now, along with a connection that went even deeper. He was effectively dead, yet his aura still glowed strong. If Evie hadn't noticed, Ked guessed that he was the only one who could sense the black glow emanating from the unconscious man. He recognized it because the aura was identical to his own, so dark it seemed to suck the light away. And for that reason, Ked knew the man wasn't truly dead—that he could be revived.

He was in the same state Belah had been when Ked had found her so long ago, her own blood drained from her to feed her lover's mad need for power—or so he'd believed until very recently. Regardless of what had compelled Nikhil to drink it, Belah's blood had rendered him immortal, the same way Ked knew his blood had done for Marcus.

Marcus could be killed, but Ked hoped that wouldn't be necessary, at least not right away. He hoped he could revive him just enough to glean some information about their enemy, and perhaps learn whether the Norths were correct in trusting him again after his betrayal. After that, he would have to decide the best course of action based on what Marcus shared.

The lingering presence of Ked's own magic provided a connection that should assist with the interrogation. Almost as strong as actually being marked by Ked, though not enough to heal Marcus fully.

Evie's brothers gently carried their sister away, leaving Ked alone with the man he'd thought was a traitor, but who he desperately hoped would be redeemed. The last time he'd killed an Elite, it had left him with a hollow ache inside that had never really gone away in the intervening centuries.

He reached out a hand and touched the man who lay beside him. All it took was a fingertip on his arm and a dark, violet spark shot between them. Marcus's eyes opened.

Ked clenched his teeth hard when he looked into those light green eyes. The allure of his Blessing was strong. Ked was overcome by a powerful urge to mark and mate the man. The fact that Marcus hovered at the edge of death's abyss didn't change his compulsion to possess him. He only knew of two ways to save him, if he proved worth saving, and if the darkness he sensed in the man meant what he believed, it would take work before Marcus accepted either of those options.

"What did you do to her?" Marcus rasped, grasping at Ked's forearm with a grip so fierce it contradicted his weakened state.

"She's safe. You're both safe now."

Marcus closed his eyes and sighed. "Good," he said. "I can die now. Please make it quick."

"That's not going to happen, not until we talk. You're too important for me to kill."

Important was an understatement. What Marcus may know about the enemy only scratched the surface. Blessed humans were so rare, it was nearly impossible for a dragon to control themselves when they found one. Wars had been fought over them in the distant past, and for centuries their enemy had systematically used them against the higher races. Regardless of what Marcus may have become since joining the enemy, Ked rejected the idea of killing a Blessed, particularly one who still carried a piece of Ked's own power in his soul.

Marcus blinked up at him, panting to catch his waning breath. "I'd rather die now. If you want to kill me, go ahead. Evie already thinks I'm dead, doesn't she? The blood drain is deceiving—makes us appear dead and wish for death even more. He does that sometimes to torture us when we misbehave, then transfuses us again. This time he let me bleed onto the floor instead of into a bag. No coming back from that."

"You don't get to die. She doesn't want it. And neither do I."

Ked glanced at Evie, crying in her reunion with her brothers. He would have time with her, but right now he needed to see to Marcus.

"I'm taking you home with me," Ked said. Not that the limp body beneath him could object.

He signaled to Aodh who joined him.

"Can you carry us out the way we came in?"

Aodh frowned and crouched down next to Ked, placing his hand against Marcus's forehead, then his chest, then his lower abdomen.

"We had better not. The *drift* is hard enough on a healthy person. If you intend to gain any intel from this one when we return, we'd better fly. Gavra and I can heal them with our breath while we're airborn."

At Ked's signal, the three dragons and the two turul shifted. Ked grasped Marcus in his talons and sent a silent message to his brothers to fly carefully. Gavra would be able to cocoon Evie in healing breath during the trip, at the very least, so Evie would be in less pain.

They grasped their charges in the cages of their talons and prepared to fly. The way ahead was long, but Aodh could extend their endurance if they needed.

The North brothers had excellent stamina in their turul forms, and could keep pace for hundreds of miles at a time. When they tired, they would rest on Aodh's back, taking in his breath to replenish their energy to travel farther. It would take them most of a day to reach the dragons' safest domain: the monastery in the middle of the Pacific Islands.

# CHAPTER 8

## NIKHIL

*Alexandria, Egypt*
*11th Century BCE*

ikhil gasped and collapsed to the floor, clawing at his throat as he struggled to pull air into his lungs. A steady, skull-splitting tempo pounded inside his head, like an army had a battering ram at the gates to his consciousness. He shook his head, trying to fend it off, to catch his breath, and to simultaneously avoid vomiting.

What was he thinking, trying to *drift* without the aid of one of his Elites? Especially to the location and time he'd intended to reach. He could go anywhere in the world under his own power, but any of his secret temporal chambers could only be reached with the blood of two individuals who carried the nymphaea power within them.

Who knows where he actually ended up. Closing his eyes, he relaxed, focusing on one sense at a time. His lungs started working, and he took a slow, shaky breath, letting himself acclimate to his environment.

He felt cold stone under his back—painfully pressed against fresh wounds.

He remembered giving himself those wounds when he tore the beautiful wings off Marcus's little turul lover. She had been far stronger than he expected, and he deserved every ounce of pain he'd inflicted on both of them.

The next sensation that registered was the sticky warmth of blood coating his right leg and the dull, throbbing pain in the wound that still bled. It was already beginning to itch from the flesh knitting itself together, but a wound that deep would take days to fully heal without Sterlyn's assistance.

If only the turul's song had come a few moments earlier, none of this would have happened. If only he'd been clear of that vile, slippery darkness that had occupied his mind, controlled his thoughts for so long, he would have shown them mercy.

No. He would have released them. That's what he should have done. He should have released *all* of them. He had no reason to hold them now, and thanks to his seven days with Belah and then that divine song the turul had sung... *Evie North. You know her name.*

The notes still danced through his head like one of the incessantly irritating little earworms Marcus used to hum when he was in a rare good mood. How did the one song go? *Before too long, I fell in love with her...*

Evie's song was older. Much, much older. And Nikhil found he preferred the way it ran through his mind repeatedly over the sounds that scratched at the outside of his thoughts. That thing... whatever it was... was still out there and wanted in, but the music had banished it for good, and he had the strongest sense that the music would keep it out as long as he let the song linger in his mind.

But his departure from that bloody cell had been premature, he realized now. He had to go back. To fix what he'd done. He had to tear down the walls of his precious Alexandria Institute and release all the prisoners once and for all. Destroy whatever abominations of half-successful specimens were kept on ice in the vaults. He should burn the research. None of it mattered anymore now that he knew *she* existed.

*Asha. My daughter.*

"Papa?"

Nikhil's head twitched involuntarily at the word. Was he wishing for her so hard that he was imagining…

*"Papa, is that you? Can you hear me today, Papa? Please tell me that you hear me."*

He opened his eyes and sat up. This room… he had made it into the very chamber he'd been hoping to get to, but how?

Standing swiftly, he spun around, sure it must be some illusion, some trick of his addled brain. He wasn't sure he could trust his own mind, after all. He shouldn't have been able to get into this chamber without … *blood* … The sticky wetness of his pants made him look down.

It wasn't all his blood that covered him. When he'd stabbed Marcus, a huge volume of the other man's blood had drenched him, the power of his pulse causing it to gush from the wound onto Nikhil's hand. And then he'd knelt in the pool while their blood mixed from mirrored gashes in their thighs. His blood and Marcus's covered him. He'd had plenty of both to get him here.

*"It doesn't matter now, does it? It only matters that you're here, and that you can hear me finally."*

Nikhil stared down at the lovely, reclining figure on the pedestal beside him. The woman that lay there looked like the most beautiful funereal effigy he'd ever seen. She was seemingly crafted from pale lavender stone, with veins of shimmering blue underneath. The stone was either the strangest opal in the world, or it wasn't stone at all.

"I… I can hear you, yes. Is it really you, Asha?" He tentatively reached out a hand to touch her, then drew it back, disgusted that he'd come to her covered in blood.

*"Who else would it be? Zorion is refusing to speak to you for now. I'm the only other one here. I'm so happy you said something back to me finally. Zorion is terrible company."*

The figure on the other pedestal shimmered in the lamplight. Zorion's huge, male shape dwarfed Asha's. His effigy appeared made from obsidian, but had the same eerie undercurrent of shimmering blue veins beneath the surface.

"I suppose I can't blame him for not speaking to me if he knows anything about what I am. I'm ashamed to say that I'm only just learning it for myself. I am sorry I couldn't hear you before, *habibi.*"

The glow beneath the surface of her skin brightened and pulsed in a comforting rhythm. This time Nikhil did reach out and rest his palm against her shoulder. She was warm to the touch, and his skin tingled pleasantly, the power and life within her clear to him now.

*"Papa, you weren't yourself before. I can't see you with my eyes, but I can see you with my soul. Mama's gifts aren't my only gifts. I have everything you gave me, too. I could tell it was you when you found me and Zorion, but I could also tell that it wasn't you. I am glad it is only you now. Will you stay a while and talk to me before you go?"*

Nikhil suddenly never wanted to leave, but he had to return to make amends. If he were going to be worthy of his daughter's faith, and even have a chance at asking for Belah's forgiveness, he had work to do.

"Can I not free you from the stone so you and your brother can come with me? I will do anything you need me to do."

The light beneath her skin shimmered in a playful fashion, and next to her the male figure's did as well.

*"You cannot awaken us, Papa. That is not for you to do. Our*

*mates must find us again, the right way this time. Only those two Blessed creatures can awaken us, but they must prove their worth."*

Again...? The truth hit Nikhil like a blinding light. Naaz and Neela had been the ones to find these two originally. Nikhil had had nothing to do with it. And yet he'd never trusted the twins' strange draw to what he believed at the time were nothing more than two valuable treasures. So, he'd forbidden either of them from seeing the statues since.

"I will bring them now..."

The blue veins flashed. *"No, Papa, you mustn't lead them to us. They must seek us out on their own. They must follow the path Fate laid for them. It's the only way to end our hibernation. The trial is necessary. They found us prematurely the first time, using magic that is not theirs to use. It is better this way."*

Nikhil's shoulders sagged. If Naaz and Neela weren't to be allowed to find them yet, he would have to find a better hiding place, but that would take time, and he would need Sterlyn's help to relocate them. They should be relocated for safety's sake anyway—he didn't trust that whatever it was that had occupied his mind all along wouldn't be able to find them and exploit them.

No, he couldn't wait for Sterlyn's help. He had to move them *now*. But where? He wasn't sure that any place he'd known of in his entire life would be safe. His mind had been a playground for that other thing for so long, what pieces of it were still sacred?

*"Let me help."* This time the voice was not the clear, high voice of Asha, but a much darker, deeper sound that reverberated inside his head like a bass drum. With the voice came a shadowy presence that lingered at the edges of his mind, much the way that other dark presence had. Except this one seemed to respectfully wait for an invitation rather than clawing and banging at the door.

"Zorion, is it? Will it help you trust me more if I allow you in?" Nikhil asked.

Zorion's blue veins shimmered only slightly in response. *"It will help you help us. I could easily command you to do it and you would carry out my wishes without question, but I am not the wicked, vile creature that held you in thrall for so long. I am my mother's son, and you love my mother, so I will help you. Let me in."*

With a sigh, Nikhil closed his eyes and relinquished his control to the shadow, all the while singing Evie's song under his breath.

Bit by bit, Zorion filtered through his memories, examining and then discarding them one at a time. Nikhil observed skeptically at first, then with growing curiosity as he realized every single memory that was rejected was one from the years since he'd lost Belah.

*"Can you show me when it happened? When I lost control?"* he blurted after he saw the memories from the last thousand years go by.

Zorion paused and asked, *"Do you have a landmark that can guide me? It may go more quickly if we look backward from the beginning."*

Nikhil thought for a moment, recalling the early grief and trying to remember an event that had to be distinctly out of character for him. Any mindless bloodshed that was not directly linked to Belah's disappearance... There were so many needless deaths in his past that recalling each one made him sick. None of them contributed to Belah's glory. All of them were about revenge rather than love.

The ones that stood out the most were the executions of the women. For centuries he had sought out females who resembled Belah and bedded them. And when they failed to bear him a child, he had them killed. He remembered the first one clearly, too, because that was the day a small part of him realized he didn't care about anything beyond his singular goal of producing offspring, and that the deaths were simply a messy but necessary part of achieving that goal.

That very decision was entirely contrary to what he'd believed for his entire life before falling in love with Belah. He may be a sadist, and was extremely good at commanding armies, at killing and torture. Yet he knew the difference between needless death and killing for glory or while defending honor—it was a code he prided himself on from the very beginning and not one he would have easily let go of.

With that early memory in mind, he directed Zorion to continue, hoping he could pinpoint the moment when everything had changed. He needed to know when he'd turned into a monster even Belah couldn't love.

The images turned surreal the closer they got to Nikhil's wedding night. His gut tightened with dread, though the memory was one that rarely left his mind. Closer to the night, the images were broken—they were searching backwards so these must be the days just after, when he was healing from Ked's nearly fatal fire.

The only face he saw during those periods was that of Meri, the palace physician who had also been one of Belah's closest friends. She'd been there from the start of his affair with Belah. He always remembered her as kind and gentle, carefully seeing to his wounds after that fateful battle that had brought his love to him.

In the days after his wedding, when he'd wished for death, she'd been there, too. The memories flashed by in brief images from the rare moments of lucidity he'd had. Meri's soft features, her brown eyes, her patient ministrations.

The smooth slide of her naked body atop his once his

skin had regenerated enough that he could feel again... *yes, Nikhil, take me into you the way you took her... my blood and my essence together... We'll be as one...*

"Stop!" The echo in the chamber rang in his ears jarringly. He'd yelled without meaning to.

Zorion paused at that memory and his power increased, pushing deeper into Nikhil's mind, blotting out the distractions and highlighting the events of that moment in stark detail. Nikhil watched it again and again, horrified.

*"This woman meant something to you, and to Mother. She betrayed you in this moment."*

"Show me all the memories of her."

Zorion's shadowy presence in his mind wavered. *"You fear her return enough to find us a new hiding place. If she was indeed powerful enough to control you all these years, we should not waste time. Better to examine what you know when we can do it without worry of discovery or interruption."*

Nikhil cursed. "You are nothing like your mother."

The flickering veins brightened in amusement. *"I am not my parents, but at the same time I am their very essences combined. Because I am my mother's son, I can sense her pain and love, as well as my father's. They are at odds about you. It isn't Mother who you need to redeem yourself to, Nikhil. It is my father, and also my mother's mates. I will help you do this under one condition."*

"Anything," Nikhil said, standing. "I must prove my worth to Belah, too, though."

*"You must prove your worth to yourself. And once I have my mate I will help you do this, but my sister is right, our ascension must be completed as it was meant to be. You will need Mother's help to see to that. But for now, I know where we can go."*

"You know a place where the darkness ... where *Meri* ... can't track us down?"

*"It is your place, Nikhil. You marked it as yours when you were a boy. See?"*

Nikhil's mind filled with images of a sea coast so vivid it evoked deep and long forgotten emotions. Memories flooded forth that he hadn't revisited since his childhood. As a young child, he'd explored every inch of the coast near his mother's village, before he'd been old enough to begin training as a soldier for his mistress's armies. His favorite destination during those daily explorations was a sea cave, only accessible during low tide.

Nikhil hadn't spared the place a thought since growing up, but now that Zorion showed him the images, all the memories rushed back.

"Are you sure this place is safe?" he asked.

*"This is a memory that has been untainted by the darkness. She will not find this place without an effort. It will serve as a temporary sanctuary for us."*

The question was whether he could take them both there now. He had to hope that Marcus's blood that still clung to him would be enough. His wounds were slowly healing, but wetness still coated his thigh and trickled down his back, so he knew his own blood still flowed.

Nikhil moved in between the pair of effigies and grasped the arm of each one.

"Hold on," he said.

Picturing the childhood hideaway in his mind, he called on the *drift* and held his breath as it rushed in to carry them away.

*Canadian Rockies*
*Present Day*

vie ached at the distance between herself and Ked so soon after finding him, after losing Marcus. But soon after her tearful reunion with her brothers, a huge red dragon urged her into the cradle of one large foreclaw and she went, wincing only slightly when her injured back brushed against his palm. While she'd crossed paths with many dragons in her life, she'd never been so close to one.

Staring across the clearing at the large, naked man who had spirited her and Marcus out of the Ultiori fortress, her entire body tingled just as it had deep in the underground room of that horrible place.

For a moment after she felt his presence, she believed he was merely Marcus's ghost lingering behind, unable to let her go. Marcus's final breath had carried the words, "Forgive me," after all, and had been filled with such soul-deep regret she still ached from the sound.

But a dragon's breath was part Wind magic, and carried a

hint of living essence with it that no turul could miss. This dragon's breath had betrayed his presence to her, whether he knew it or not. And in that second, she had known him—first, for his nature, and second, for who he was to *her*. The immense Shadow wasn't Marcus's ghost, but the magical breath of the biggest, most powerful black dragon she'd ever seen in her life.

For a turul to find a second true mate in a lifetime was unheard of, yet here he was, as frightening for his size and potency as for the feelings he incited in her in the aftermath of losing the man she'd believed she was meant to die with.

She had to remind herself that her situation had been an anomaly from the start. Her rebellion against her race's traditions was what made her impulsively seek out a distraction after years of frustration waiting to stumble across her true mate—her *One*. Marcus hadn't really been hers, that first day they'd met—she knew that much—but over the next year, she'd fallen in love with him in what she believed was a more enduring way. She'd lost that only briefly after her capture by the Ultiori, then during the early part of her captivity, somehow, her feelings shifted.

Marcus had come to her one day, filled with promises of escape and apologies for bringing her there to begin with. On that day, the very sight and nearness of him had struck a bright flame inside her that had refused to die, even after five decades of wishing she could hate him for betraying her. The irony of that moment tortured her.

Now she knew the truth—that Marcus and Ked weren't separate beings. Marcus had only been an extension of her true mate, and she was grateful for being granted the gift of being able to love the man as her true mate before he died, even though he'd ultimately been taken from her.

The flame of that love she had for Marcus had only brightened when this dragon appeared, so dark and intent now as he shifted into his full form over Marcus's inert body. A wave of his power washed over Evie as though drawn in by her mere attention. It made her quiver with need for him in spite of the searing pain that covered every inch of her back. The black dragon's gentle treatment of Marcus's body made no sense to her. He was dead, yet the dragon cupped his large foreclaw and let her brothers lay Marcus carefully across his palm in a reclining position before closing his other claw around him. Marcus might have merely been asleep, as comfortable as he looked.

At her side, another large, red dragon lowered his head to eye level and lifted a massive talon to nudge gently at her chin.

"Who are you?" Evie asked, in awe of all three of the dragons who nearly filled the entire clearing now, dwarfing even her brothers once they shifted into their massive falcon forms and readied for flight.

"I am Gavra," he said softly to her. "Ked, the one who brought you out, is my brother. He bade me to guard you with my life." He let out a gust of red breath that enveloped her. "And I will heal you on the way to our destination."

His breath tingled as it seeped into her wounds, stinging just slightly before easing the pain. The names tickled at her memory, but the pain of her injuries still throbbed too much for her to comprehend the full truth.

"I thought Reds only seduced with their breath," Evie said, attempting a light-hearted tone in spite of her pain. "I'm not in danger of that, am I?"

Gavra let out a low chuckle. "No. You belong to my brother. If he wants to share, I wouldn't object, but you are in no condition for seduction. Sleep, if you can. It will be a long flight."

The lumbering form of a huge white dragon ventured

near and gusted pale smoke over her, then spoke. "He is right; you should sleep. We will keep you safe."

Soon after, Evie found herself lulled by the comforting stream of wind over her skin and the undulations of Gavra's body, from the slow, even pumps of his wings in the currents of air high above the earth.

She dreamed of flying. The caresses of her Goddess, the North Wind, kept her aloft and gave her hope again for the first time since her captivity began. The ordeal was over now, but the pain of grief loomed at the edges of her mind. She would mourn Marcus soon, but not until she could do it wholly, and without the distractions of a damaged body and the pull to the black dragon that reminded her so much of her need for Marcus.

Rather than give in to grief now, Evie reverted to her old habit during her worst days in the Ultiori clutches. She played over and over in her mind the memories of her best days with Marcus.

The day she and Marcus met had been a revelation to her, yet she would always especially treasure their last night together, before his life ebbed away in her arms.

*Central Park*

*Spring, 1965*

T

he steady clink of coins almost drowned out Evie's voice. She smiled as she sang. Every coin dropped into her brother's guitar case meant someone loved what they heard. Lukas strummed while Iszak goofed around with his saxophone, flirting with the women who wandered past their spot near the Bethesda Terrace in Central Park.

They weren't here for money, though. Nanyo Sofia had sent them out to find mates, as if a day in the park was enough to snag the one person each of them were meant to be with for life. Her brothers loved music enough that they went along with it, but they were petering out, too. Finding a mate in a day was ridiculous, but Nanyo would make them head out again until she was satisfied they'd exhausted their efforts.

"The One is there for each of you. You never know where he or she will turn up. It could be in the library, or it could be on the street. Give yourself as many chances as possible to find him or her. It will happen, I promise you."

Evie wasn't even sure if she believed in *the One*. She and her brothers were still young by turul standards, but still over one hundred and fifty years old. She'd have thought at least one of them would have met their true mate by now. Whoever it was, it wasn't another turul. The first thing turul parents did when their children were old enough to fly was introduce them to the other enclaves, to try to find their match among their own kind. She and her brothers knew all the turuls there were to know, yet not even a glimmer of interest occurred for either of them.

Humans were so prolific it could take another century to find a mate, if hers was one of them. That is, if she even believed there was one true mate for her. She could probably have picked one out of the crowd of onlookers, if she wanted to. The second she had that thought, butterflies erupted in her belly and she nearly lost track of the lyrics she sang. Could she throw caution to the wind, choose her own mate, and prove to everyone that the ridiculous waiting and searching was bullshit?

She scanned the crowd in front of her, thrilled with the idea of an experiment. Could she forge a deeper bond with someone by choice? She was no stranger to playful trysts with other turul, but had never had a non-turul playmate before. Unless the other person was definitely *The One*, coupling outside the enclaves was frowned upon. And she'd never been inclined to have anything deeper with one of the turul males she knew.

*I'm probably nuts, but I'm doing this.*

She paused for breath in between songs. The crowd applauded and tossed more coins and crumpled bills into the guitar case. Her brothers continued to play random tunes but would easily pick up whatever song she started in with next. It came to her the second she set eyes on the perfect target. She broke into her favorite Beatles song when a tall, striking man shifted to the front of the crowd and stood, tapping his boot-clad foot in time with the music. Except she switched the lyrics the way she always did, swapping "her" with "him," when she saw him "standing there."

If she had to conjure her own ideal mate, at least in appearance, there he was. A little bit bohemian in dress, with a mop of ruddy waves atop his head that was trimmed more neatly from his ears down. He was unique enough that her Nanyo might believe she'd found her One—but not so much as to raise suspicion. He had a wicked twinkle in his eyes when he looked at her, and Evie stared right back, letting her voice and the power of the Wind do all the work of letting him know she noticed him watching her.

She wished she felt something deeper now. The mated turul she knew all claimed that the second they set eyes on their One, they knew instantly. She wasn't sure she believed it, because it still hadn't happened to her. Maybe with this guy, she could take matters into her own hands.

*I'm going to fall in love with you,* she thought, just as she sang, "And before too long, I fell in love with him."

He bobbed his head and clapped after the finale, beautiful white smile beaming at her. She and her brothers took a bow, and while she did, she tried to formulate an excuse to go talk to him. But when she stood up, he was nowhere to be found.

"Dammit!" Evie scanned the dispersing crowd. He'd been a good head taller than most of the other patrons in the park, and his gorgeous, russet hair had caught the rays of the setting sun making him look aflame. And those shoulders—wow, not even her brothers were quite as built as that, though they were sturdy men. He could've been a dragon, as striking as he'd been, but she hadn't sensed a hint of anything magical about him. No, the man had been pure, perfect, human male, through and through. He shouldn't have been very hard to miss, even among the other humans in the park, yet she didn't see him.

"Evie," Lukas called, forcing her to turn her attention back to them. He was squatting beside his guitar case, sorting through their take, and held up a creased piece of paper. "You've got an admirer." He grinned at her.

Evie's stomach fluttered. She took another cursory glance at the surrounding area, then reached for the piece of paper her brother held out to her.

The messy scrawl was almost illegible, but the note was simple enough. *"Angel Mine, Meet me by your sister's fountain. —Marcus C."*

"Angel Mine, huh? Do you know this guy?" Iszak looked over her shoulder. His tone was unmistakably suspicious and more than a little bit protective. Evie elbowed him in the ribs.

"Just met—sort of. But I'm going to fall in love with him."

"You didn't just find your One, did you?" Lukas said, standing up and dropping the handful of coins he held back into the case at his feet. "Holy shit, Nanyo's going to be impossible to deal with if you did."

Evie rolled her eyes. "I'm going to prove to you guys that we don't need to wait for some perfect mate to magically appear. I'm going after this guy because I want to. Screw tradition, screw…"

She almost said "the North Wind," but knew better than to test their protector, their creator, the Goddess who had blessed their parents with three perfect children, then graced those children with the honor of Her name.

She shrugged. "Guys, a hundred and fifty fucking years. With my luck, he's a dragon and I'll be damned if I'm going to wait for the next brood to wake up before I find *the One*." She made air quotes and rolled her eyes. "I might die of horniness by then."

Lukas laughed and shook his head. "Sister, have you ever *been* with a dragon? They like it if you wait for them. The hornier you are, the better. I guess you have to make up for not having actual horns."

She knelt down beside her brother and made quick work of sorting the coins and bills he'd missed. The money would go to a local homeless shelter—it wasn't like they needed it. The enclaves were wealthy in spite of their preference for simple living. They always tended to send their excess to the other wanderers of the world.

She wondered if he—Marcus—would enjoy the simple life. He'd been dressed simply enough, in a pair of dark brown khakis and a loose white shirt—nothing like the mod crowd or the hippies. She suddenly felt a little self-conscious of her own attire. She'd emulated Cher at first, because she had long, straight, dark hair, though she was more pixyish in stature. Her own outfit was racier than Cher's, though. Her brothers had objected, but held their tongues after her first day singing, when they saw the response from the men in the audience.

She couldn't complain, either. It was comfortable, if a little chilly, to wear in early spring. She smiled at the thought of Marcus seeing her nipples pressed against the sheer fabric of her peasant top.

Even if she didn't fall in love with him, she needed a day of fun. No matter how distasteful it was for her to stray from the enclave for release, she really, *really* wanted something different for a change.

"You want us to stay close?" Iszak asked, drawing her up from the closed guitar case and gazing into her eyes.

His intensity always threw her when it came out. "Iszak, fuck. I can take care of myself." She brushed his hand away from her shoulder where it gripped her tight.

Iszak grumbled. "I don't know this guy."

"He's just a guy. A human. I know that much. Don't you want to know if it can happen? If we can choose who we love? Never have to wait until they find us?"

Iszak grunted and shook his head. "Fine. Just be careful."

"I'm always careful. It's my nature as the eldest." She grinned at him over her shoulder as she ran off down the path. Iszak grimaced, but didn't follow.

Evie giggled at her joke. Both her brothers were protective in the extreme, even though she was technically the eldest of the three. Not that the timing mattered much; they were all conceived and birthed within seconds of each other, though her brothers liked to consider their hatching the moment when they were truly born. If they went by that, she came third, but she was first out of their mother's womb. She wondered if that should make her more cautious or more reckless. At the very least it did mean she was slightly more attuned to the messages carried on the Wind.

Or maybe she was just trying to make up for lost time.

She felt a little silly, running as she was, but the rush of a new experience excited her. She had a good feeling, especially when she slowed to a walk on the path as the fountain with the angel came into view.

Marcus lounged at the edge, relaxed and handsome. When she drew closer, he turned his head and saw her, his face splitting into a wide grin that made pleasant tingles erupt all over her. It was an entirely superficial feeling, though—she felt this way every time she met a potential lover among her own race, but it never lasted.

His gaze roamed over her in an overly familiar way that made her pulse pound. By the time she reached him, she was more breathless from the arousal that simple look inspired than from her jog to get here.

Marcus gazed up at her when she paused in front of him.

"You came," he said.

"You must've really wanted to see me alone, if you couldn't come say hi while my brothers were there. The cloak and dagger was a nice touch." She waved his cryptic note in the air. Instead of sitting beside him, she stepped between his spread knees. He widened his legs to accommodate her and she moved in until they were nearly touching. She knew exactly what she wanted, so there was no sense skirting around it. She had a pretty good idea he wanted it, too.

Yet he didn't touch her.

"True, I wanted to see you alone. Mostly I wanted to see if you really were more beautiful than the angel behind me. I usually just come here and enjoy her presence, then go home. But today another angel was singing, and I couldn't help but follow the sound."

"And you found me."

"I found you."

"So, what's the verdict?" Evie asked, glancing behind him to the winged figure in the center of the pool, then back to him.

"I'm a little too dazzled to look at anything else right now," he said, his pale green eyes locked on hers.

Now *that* made her heart do a somersault. Nobody she'd ever met had been quite so fixated on her. It took her breath away.

"I'm *so* going to fall in love with you," she whispered, more sure now than ever. Even though there was none of that tugging feeling her mother described as the moment when she knew Evie's father was the one, Marcus had succeeded in capturing her attention enough that she really wanted to know more about him. And she really wanted to know if it were at all possible to cultivate love with someone she wasn't fated to be with.

Marcus laughed nervously. "Oh? That's a little quick, isn't it? Or are you some kind of psychic who can see the future?" He slid his hands down his thighs until they were aligned with her legs, yet he still refrained from touching her.

"Marcus, you are a mystery. I like mysteries." She brazenly threaded her fingers through his hair, breaking the invisible barrier between them for the first time. She'd been itching to touch those russet locks since she'd first laid eyes on him.

Marcus shivered and closed his eyes. Evie tangled her fingers in his hair, enjoying the smooth, silky feel of it sliding through. He sighed.

"You're the real mystery. I don't even know your name." He opened his eyes to look at her, his gaze growing darker as she let her fingers stray down and scraped her fingernails through the shorter hair at the nape of his neck.

"Evie North. What does the 'C' stand for?"

"Calais," he replied, sighing and tilting his head down, eyes closed as though her touch were the best feeling in the world. "You must be an angel to make me feel so blessed. I bet you'd look good in wings."

Evie paused, surprised by his comment. It sounded

sincere, but hit so close to home that it made her wonder if he really was as human as she'd first thought.

"Worship me enough, I might grow a pair. Of wings, I mean." She grinned down at him.

"Oh, that won't be a problem," he said, his words trailing off into a rough laugh. "But I'm a bit of a bad boy. I'm worried that if I touch you, my hands might burn with holy fire."

"Marcus, even if I do grow wings, I promise I'm no angel." She let her fingernails dig into the back of his neck just enough to reinforce her statement.

His eyelashes fluttered and his gaze slid down her body again. Finally, he ventured a hesitant touch, raising his hands to her hips and resting them there.

Her skin tingled under the warmth of his palms, and holy shit if she didn't dampen her panties a bit. The man had some alluring quality that drew her to him, even if it wasn't the one thing that signaled they were meant for one another. The idea suddenly frustrated her. How in all the winds could he not be the one for her? He pushed all her buttons. She wanted him. And she'd have him. But there was still that glimmer of truth that never left her. The piece that always knew the right path. The piece she was about to ruthlessly rebel against right now.

"Can I take you home with me?" he asked.

"You'd better. Otherwise, I might just have my way with you right here."

An almost primal sound rumbled up from deep in his chest and his hands ventured higher. They were so large, he could have wrapped both of them entirely around her waist and crushed her, yet he didn't. He was so gentle she almost wanted him to squeeze harder just to be sure he was real. Evie's breath caught when he brushed his thumbs along the sides of her breasts. His lust-filled gaze remained locked on hers, his mouth a mischievous curl. Then her mind short-circuited as he boldly stroked both thumbs over her nipples right through her thin blouse. A sharp jolt of pleasure shot through her, and it was all she could do not to wrap herself around him right there.

"I dare you," he said, and swiped across again, causing another flood of tingling warmth to surge between her legs.

"Ohh-kayy," she breathed, gripping his hands and reluctantly peeling them away from her sides. "I think we have someplace to be right now." She turned and pulled him behind her, trying her best to ignore the confusion of sensations clamoring through her body. Her face burned, her heart raced, and a knot of molten heat had taken up residence between her thighs. It was tricky to even take a breath, but somehow she managed to pull sufficient air into her lungs to clear her head and see straight.

Marcus didn't balk at her urgency. He stood and followed, laughing all the way to the subway until they were seated. He asked, "Where are we going?"

"To your place," she said.

"Good thing you put us on the right train."

Evie hadn't even realized how many of his secrets the wind had told her in those few moments when he'd first touched her. They'd sunk in and become part of her. And in the moment she hadn't thought, just instinctively headed in the direction the breeze blew.

"I... thought we might ride a bit until I caught my breath, is all. You live in Brooklyn?" She looked innocently up at him.

"I do."

The train lurched into motion and he caught her against him. He didn't let go.

His warm, solid body felt good against her, his embrace protective and comfortable. Better than the last fifty years of being thrown in front of so many men, dressed up like the daughter of a wealthy merchant sometimes, or dressed down like an itinerant whore other times. Her people exhausted every avenue, and had more avenues to exhaust. This was the first time she'd given herself to the possibility willingly.

His hand fell to her thigh and she sighed.

"You like that?" he asked.

She gave him a quizzical look. "You're a cocky bastard. That's what I like. And yeah, I like your hand right where it is. For now."

Marcus grinned again, and she barely resisted the urge to push his hand higher, but relaxed and leaned against him for the rest of the trip. After a while, his fingers began tracing little patterns through the fabric of her skirt, making her wish he was in contact with her skin. She was still contemplating a change of plan when the loudspeaker announced their destination and Marcus stood. She had a brief view of a tightly muscled stomach under his shirt when he bent over to sling a satchel over one shoulder, and then he unceremoniously grabbed her hand and tugged her along.

*Okay, I guess I'm along for the ride, whatever that means.*

"Where are we going?"

"My place. It's clean, don't worry."

She nearly tripped over an uneven slab in the sidewalk. When she regained her bearings, she increased her pace. "I wasn't worried about your place. Is there anything else I should worry about?"

Her tone must have alarmed him, because he slowed down to a walk. He squeezed her hand and looked down at her, brow furrowed. "We don't have to do this... whatever this is. I just didn't want to lose the thrill, you know? But if you've changed your mind..."

Evie's heart raced. Maybe she wasn't as fearless as she thought. Maybe she was being supremely dumb. He wasn't the One, and she didn't even know him. Sure, she had decades more experience than he did, but not with love, not with her own heart, and there were other things to worry about. Fuck, how could she be so reckless?

"What scares you, Evie?" he asked softly, reaching up to caress her face. He stroked his thumb over her cheek as though trying to soothe a scared kitten.

The truth would betray her nature. What scared her was *them*. The Ultiori hunters. He might be one and working his seduction on her now. She didn't *think* he was one, at least. The Wind was good at sending peoples' secrets to her ears without them knowing, but the Wind wasn't perfect. The Ultiori had their own tricks of deception—how they did it, she didn't know. She'd only heard stories. Suddenly she grew uncertain about this crazy idea of hers.

She had to give him an answer. "You scare me," she whispered, eyes wide. "I'm afraid… I'm afraid we can't go back after this. That if I do it, our choices will be taken from us. We were strangers until a little while ago, but now we're headed down a path that might never let us turn around again."

He raked his fingers through his thick hair. His shoulders hunched awkwardly, almost like he was trying to shrink, like he was self-conscious of his size on the sidewalk beside her. Finally, he simply squatted down and looked up at her. She had the sense that he might be about to beg, but he only rested his hands on her hips and squeezed gently.

"You terrify me," he said softly, and she knew what he said was true. Even if the Wind hadn't been there to verify his honesty, she'd have known it by the wetness in his eyes. "You are the most beautiful woman I've ever seen, and the first one I've ever wanted so much I'd behave like a rutting stag the first time we meet. I don't do this, Evie. What I want to do with you is entirely out of character for me. I know you have no reason to believe that because we just met, but it's the truth."

She laughed, taken aback by his bare honesty. "Surely, there have been others... Look at you." She waved her hand down his sturdy frame, still crouched before her.

He shook his head. "I've tried off and on, but somehow the women I'm most drawn to are wildly inaccessible. You're the first who's given me the time of day. That in itself makes you infinitely more amazing to me. But there's something deeper."

He reached up and placed his palm against the center of her chest. The simple touch stole her breath. "I can't put my finger on it, but I really want to know everything there is to know about you."

Evie found it hard to fill her lungs enough to speak. Finally, in a near whisper, she said, "What if I never trust you enough to share my secrets?"

"Then I'll have to prove to you that you can."

She sighed, relieved that he told her the truth, but also more anxious than ever that she hadn't heard any hint of a lie. If she had, she'd have had an excuse to avoid following through with her crazy plan.

She urged him to stand and laced her fingers through his again. Taking a deep breath, she found that steely will of hers, along with the wicked streak that had urged her to seek him out to begin with.

"Rutting stag, huh? I think I like the sound of that." She grinned up at him. Abruptly he wrapped her in his arms and laid a hot, hungry kiss against her lips. In spite of the cold brick wall he had her pressed into, all she could feel was his heat flooding through her thin dress. She clung to him, melting against him, both of them oblivious to the traffic on the sidewalk passing by like nothing out of the ordinary was occurring. Like she wasn't on the verge of letting this man fuck her silly against the wall right out in public on a cool spring evening.

The honk of a cab made Marcus jump and draw away from her. She held on, reluctant to lose the warmth of his body and the sweet pull of his mouth. A small, petulant sound came out of her and he groaned in response. He placed his hands against the wall on either side of her head and peered down into her eyes.

"You'll be the death of me, Evie North. But I think you'll be worth it."

After placing a chaste kiss on her forehead, he pulled her to his side, leading her down the sidewalk again. In only a few steps, he pulled keys out of his pocket and opened a door in the front of the brownstone he'd just had her pinned to.

"You mean to tell me we were ten feet from your door?" Evie laughed.

"I was overcome," he said, smirking at her. "Besides, if you were a bad kisser, I'd have made some excuse and sent you on your way before letting you know where I lived. Picking up strange women in Central Park is a good way to get murdered."

She gaped at him. "And only murderers can be bad kissers, I take it? I suppose I'm glad you found my skills acceptable."

Marcus stepped through the door, propping it open with his body and gesturing for her to walk through. As she passed by, she caught him subtly adjusting the bulge that filled the front of his trousers.

"More than acceptable," he said, flushing when her eyes went to his hand at his crotch and her eyebrow shot up.

Evie took his hand and stepped close, leaning against his solid form. She threaded her fingers through his, amazed yet again at how thoroughly he stole her breath. He seemed to have stopped breathing as well, his mouth partway open and his gaze fixed on hers. She raked her fingernails up the side of his neck and pulled his head down. When their lips met again, she let herself savor the velvet softness of him and the stiff pressure of his erection against her belly. She pressed her hips harder against his, enjoying the way he moaned into her mouth.

She suddenly had the urge to tease him, to see how long she could draw out his need for her. It was the kind of thing she'd heard dragons would do to their partners, to increase the draw of the magic and the payoff when their partner finally found release. Her kind subsisted on the same magic, but the music was what drew it to them. That wasn't to say she didn't crave the intimate connection that sex provided. After all, there was a kind of sublime rhythm in making love that was as beautiful as any song she had ever sung.

She wondered whether Marcus had ever played an instrument. He had long, strong fingers that had already set her strings humming with pleasure. She pulled his hand to her breast, unclasped his fingers, and pressed his palm against the small mound of warm flesh. Her nipple ached for his touch, but he didn't respond at first. Then, as though reacting to the steady pulse between her thighs, he brushed his fingertips over her stiff bud again. The pleasure vibrated through her so acutely she could almost hear the music of it. Again he stroked his fingers over her through her sheer top, teasing as gently as he might the strings of a guitar, coaxing from his instrument a soft, reverberating thrum.

The music came out as a soft sigh from her lips.

"I'd like to make you sing again, just for me," Marcus murmured into her ear. His fingers found a slow rhythm over her breast, each pass causing vibrations of ecstasy to flow through her. She could only sigh again and nod.

Abruptly, the world tilted and she found herself cradled in his arms. He stepped the rest of the way through the door and kicked it closed behind him, mounting the stairs blindly as he bent his head to kiss her again. Moments later he crashed through another door on an upper landing, elbowed it shut and carried her across the room.

Evie opened her eyes when he finally pulled back from the kiss and set her down. She stood in a dimly lit and very Spartan studio apartment. The full-sized bed was neatly made and the kitchenette pristine. The only signs that the place was lived in were the books and papers strewn across the surface of a wooden table that appeared to serve as Marcus's desk.

"You're a student?" she asked.

His eyes clouded briefly. "For now." He didn't elaborate, but the dark tone carried with it a sense of helplessness that was at odds with his earlier eager lightheartedness.

Evie raised a hand and brushed it tenderly down his cheek. He had a secret that weighed heavily on his conscience. She was more convinced now that, regardless of their lack of a deeper connection, somehow she had chosen him for a reason.

"What would you like me to sing for you?"

His wicked grin returned and he stepped in close, crowding her backward until the backs of her legs hit the side of his bed.

"You'll see," he said. His hands came up and cupped the sides of her head, his mouth descending again, tongue darting between her lips in the sweetest, most urgent kiss yet. The fervor with which he consumed her set her heart racing and her hands groping, trying to find purchase on his sides. He pressed closer, one arm wrapping around her and urging her down to the bed, while his mouth descended to her throat and the bare tops of her small breasts, on display above the ruffled fabric of her blouse.

He tugged her laces loose and spread the fabric wide,

tracing his lips down her sternum and pulling the blouse lower as he went. Evie laced her fingers through his thick hair, stroking as his tongue darted out to tease one pert nipple. He captured it in his mouth and sucked hard, the sharp sensation making her gasp and arch up off the mattress, pulling harder at his hair.

Marcus chuckled around the stiff, pink flesh. "That's right, sing for me."

"Oh!" she gasped louder when he cupped her other breast and tweaked her nipple.

"Christ, Evie, you're destroying me. Do you have any idea how perfect you are?"

She really had no ideas whatsoever, at the moment. Her body was nothing more than a bundle of senses, experiencing every little teasing touch, the lush scent of his masculine musk mixed with the clean aroma of whatever shampoo he used. The small bit of awareness she managed to cling to outside of him was the whisper of the Wind, confirming again and again the truth of his desire and the incongruous rightness of her choice to be with him right now.

He pulled back and simply gazed down at her half-naked body, her blouse shoved down to expose her breasts. With a determined look, he grasped the top of it and pulled it farther making her yelp as she was briefly bound up in it when he tugged it down to her wrists. He pulled even farther, snagging the waist of her skirt and panties, peeling her clothing off until she was fully naked for him.

With a low curse, Marcus raked his gaze down her body and collapsed to his knees on the floor beside the bed. His eyes brimmed with fevered lust and he dug his fingertips into her thighs, sliding his hands higher to grip her hips and pull her toward him. Evie's backside hit the edge of the bed and she wondered if he intended to pull her all the way into his lap, but he stopped and bent to press the most reverent of kisses against her navel.

The warm caress so close to her core caused her to quiver with anticipation. His mouth turned up at the corners and his eyes twinkled as though he sensed her eagerness. Sliding his hands back down, he slowly caressed, rubbing along the tops of her thighs, his fingertips grazing perilously close to her already wet folds with each pass. At the same time, his mouth drifted lower, tongue sweeping out and tickling wetly at the top of her dark triangle of hair.

Marcus slid his hands in another slow stroke up the insides of her legs, pushing them apart, then cupped the backs of her knees and separated them high and wide, spreading her open for him. Glancing up at her, he raised one eyebrow in silent query. Evie only responded with a languid smile, but that was all the acknowledgment he needed. Abruptly, he wrapped each arm around the tops of her thighs and bent his head, teasing her folds open at the same time as his tongue darted out, the warm, pink tip snaking through the slick furrow with deliberate care. Evie nearly came apart from that one lick.

With his mouth latched onto her, he allowed his hands to drift back up her torso to cup her breasts. His thumbs resumed their earlier rhythm, stroking in maddening circles and sweeps over her nipples in time with the steady strum of his tongue over her clit.

In Evie's mind, a composition began to unfold, sweet notes playing for her alone with each note of pleasure he drew out of her. Soon he began to hum along with the beat of her pulse, the soft sounds vibrating over the slick, sensitive flesh of her core. Sounds erupted unbidden from her own throat, ringing sweet and clear through the small apartment. At first the sound was an incoherent collection of random syllables, but gradually converged into words of a song heard long ago in another era, another country. The first love song Evie had ever learned matched the rhythm of Marcus's attention perfectly, but as he conducted her body's reactions toward a growing crescendo, the true meaning of the song became bittersweet.

She kept singing even as her breath hitched and her body writhed, consumed by her climax. His mouth remained tight against her, tongue sliding more slowly over her quivering flesh and drawing out the orgasm for an endless moment, as if he were testing the strength of her lungs to see how long they could hold that final note together.

The last note came out as a breathy sigh, her body finally relaxing, but still tingling with remnants of pleasure. Marcus pressed a soft kiss on her inner thigh and looked up at her, licking his lips.

"Encore?" he said, grinning.

"Who *are* you?" Evie asked, incredulous. She sat up as he rose from the floor.

"Just a man who knows how to appreciate a creature as exquisite as you. You must have been lying to me when you said you weren't an angel. Only angels have such beautiful voices."

"Oh? And how many angels have you made sing like that?" She reached out and hooked her fingers into the waist of his jeans, tugging him close. His eyes darkened as he looked down at her.

"Now that I've met one in the flesh, I'm sure the rest weren't the real thing. You're too perfect to be human, I'm sure of it."

Evie ignored the comment, though the words tugged at an old memory. She couldn't put her finger on why the comment should worry her—she was still too absorbed by the sense of helpless surrender the lyrics of her song had incited in her. Instead, she tried to distract him by slowly unbuttoning his shirt and sliding her hands up the contours of his taut stomach and broad chest.

Marcus slid out of the garment, letting it fall to the floor. He simply watched with that same stormy gaze as she unfastened his belt and undid the closure of his jeans. A little surge of breath escaped his lips when she tugged his zipper down over the tight press of his erection. She didn't overtly touch him, though—not yet. She wanted to draw out the anticipation as long as possible. Instead, she leaned close and rested her lips lightly over his navel, mimicking his treatment of her earlier and teasing at the small cleft with the tip of her tongue.

Careful not to touch him too much, she pushed his pants down his legs and watched with unabashed appreciation as he bent to pull his shoes off, then step out of his clothes. He was more magnificent than any man she'd ever been with. His skin was lightly tanned, with smatterings of darker freckles over his shoulders and chest. Out of his clothes, he seemed even bigger than before, the definition of thick shoulders and thicker thighs evidence that he was a very active man who cared about his physique.

The best part was the thick curve of his cock jutting out of a reddish thatch of curls where the vee of his abdominal muscles ended. She licked her lips, heat surging between her thighs at the sight.

Unable to resist any longer, she took him in her hand, startled by the velvet heat and solid hardness of him. He hissed through his teeth when she gave his entire length one long, slow stroke. His legs nearly buckled when she reached between his thighs with her other hand and cupped his heavy sack.

With a growl, Marcus gripped her shoulders and pushed her back on the bed. She scrambled backward as he followed, prowling across the mattress toward her, his cock swaying like a dowsing rod seeking the vital wetness hidden in her depths. Hovering over her, he reached to the bedside table and opened a drawer, pulling out a small foil packet.

Evie snatched it from him and shook her head. "Angels can't get pregnant," she said, though the truth was that only with her true mate would she be able to conceive. Marcus may be something incredibly special, but he was far from her One. That, and she really didn't want to dull the sensation of having him inside her for the first time.

Marcus's eyebrows twitched. "Are you sure?"

Evie lay back and hooked her feet around the backs of his thighs, pulling him toward her. "If I am an angel, do you really want a barrier between your cock and heaven?"

He grunted and let her pull him lower. Bracing his hands on either side of her head, he bent to nuzzle at her neck and collarbone. "Fine, nothing can come between us, then. Not now, not ever. But you should know I mean to have my fill of you."

"Good," she said, clutching again at his head as he captured her nipple in his mouth and rolled it around and around against his tongue.

His hips rocked forward, pushing his cock along the smooth skin of her belly. She tilted higher, aching for deeper, closer contact. His hips shifted back again and on the next tilt, the tip of his cock slid up through the center of her sodden folds, the friction of the contact making her cry out for more.

One more forward sway of his hips and he hit home, his thick tip seating itself right at Evie's entrance. She lifted up, her channel so tight and hungry it clenched in a painful spasm. She needed so badly to be filled by him she was only barely aware of the soft pleas spilling from her lips into his shoulder.

When he finally entered her, she sang her pleasure into

the air and an answering breeze blew through the room, an affirmation from the Wind of its approval of her choice.

It still made no sense to her, but the Wind and Fate and the magic that permeated her life surely had a plan. The fact that he seemed to be able to see some of her true nature must mean something, too—though what it meant, she had no clue.

At the moment, she didn't care about why or how, or anything else. All she cared about was urging him to fuck her harder, deeper, and, *oh, yes,* to tilt his hips just so and rub the tip of his cock against the sensitive bundle of nerves inside her.

Her climax built more quickly with the combined sensations of his lips on hers and his skin sliding against the insides of her thighs. His pace quickened and he pulled back, staring down at her in wonder, as though he couldn't quite believe she existed. For a split second she nearly confessed the truth of her nature, but held back, clenching her eyes shut and gripping him tighter around his hips with her legs.

With a stuttering moan Marcus dropped his head, burying his face against her neck. His hips jerked hard, slamming deep into her with such force it ripped her orgasm from her in a crash of sensation. Suddenly, the hot flood of something more potent than his semen flooded through her and her eyes shot open.

*Magic? How is he feeding me his magic?*

She only had a second to wonder; when he thrust again the power surged through her, sending her to another peak that made her cry out with renewed ecstasy.

# CHAPTER 10

## MARCUS

*Somewhere over the Pacific Ocean*
*Present Day*

Marcus had often dreamed of flying under his own power since that terrible day decades ago when he'd undergone his change. But today was the first time the sensation of being carried along on invisible currents outside the confines of a cockpit was actually real. His body may have been near death, but his mind was vitally awake and excited, his strong wings stretched taut with the wind.

No, that wasn't right. They weren't his wings. They belonged to the massive black dragon who carried him. He had a strange affinity with this creature who seemed so adamant not to let him die that he was now carrying him away to who-knew-where. Of all the dragons he'd encountered and captured over the last five decades, he'd never once been so attuned with one that he could believe they were one and the same. Ked's wings were *his* wings, his strength carrying Marcus through the air, his eyes fixed on the horizon.

When he opened his eyes, Marcus didn't see the cage of talons that held him. He saw an endless stretch of clouds and sky, tinged red-gold with the rising sun. He didn't feel the dull ache and dizzying weakness of being bled dry, but the chill stream of wind over his body in contrast to a dark and dangerous swirl of power and rage entrenched deep within his being.

And beside him, he saw another expanse of massive wings, red instead of black, and Evie's small body curled up asleep, safe in the other dragon's claws. If she lived, could he find it in himself to live, too, in spite of the terrible things he'd done, the very worst of which was leading her into that trap so long ago? If he had only known, he would have accepted his human calling instead.

*"You can't fight Fate, Marcus. This was the path you were meant to travel. You are a part of me now. And as a part of me, I can't let you die."* The deep voice he recognized as Ked's resonated inside his head.

*"I know it was your blood he filled me with when he bled me of my own. Was that how you found me?"* he asked.

*"We were searching for Evie, not for you. Yet somehow, a female dragon who had no business knowing of Evie's disappearance had information on her whereabouts. We planned her rescue as soon as we knew."*

Marcus's grasp tightened around the large claws on either side of him. He had given up hope for redemption and resigned himself to unending service to the Ultiori. He deserved what *Sayid* had done to him. He sure as hell didn't deserve a female as precious and perfect as Evie North.

His strength faded, the darkness seeping through him again. Marcus hoped this time it meant he might finally be granted his wish to die. He deserved nothing less than Hell.

Yet it wasn't fire and brimstone that met him when his consciousness faded, but the beautiful, lilting song of an angel, and a sensation washing through him—one he'd once been convinced was Heavenly power.

∽

*BROOKLYN, New York*

*1965*

"W

ow, did you feel that?" Marcus asked, still giddy from the rush of the best orgasm of his entire life.

The beauty beneath him stared back, wide-eyed and speechless.

"Evie?" he asked, her silence after her vocal reactions to his lovemaking a point of concern.

Rather than answer, she clutched him to her and he groaned, sinking back down and pressing his hips tighter against hers. His cock had gone soft inside her, but he wasn't ready to separate, and she didn't seem inclined for him to leave her, either.

With a swift twist he turned them both so that his back was against the bed and she was cradled in his arms. She held onto him, her eyes clenched so tightly shut he wondered whether he'd hurt her.

"Baby, talk to me. At least tell me I wasn't the only one who felt like we just blasted through the stratosphere together. Because that was… amazing."

Her words were barely audible, but her lips brushed against his chest as she spoke. "You weren't the only one," she said. She turned her head and rested her chin on his chest. Big, gray eyes peered up at him, glassy with some deep emotion he couldn't quite fathom. "I was only kind of joking before, but I suppose you should be careful what you wish for. I am falling in love with you."

Marcus tensed at her confession. That kind of stark revelation was so alien to him he didn't quite know how to react, but after a second he relaxed again. To be loved by a woman as amazing as her was better than the most detailed erotic dream he'd ever had.

"I..." he began, then stopped, a hard lump lodging in his throat. Something profound had just happened between them while they fucked, and he wanted more of an acknowledgment of exactly how intense it had been. He didn't understand it himself. He'd had sex with women before, but Evie was the first woman who he'd ever felt *that* with. And he'd only just met her.

"What?" she prompted.

"I've never felt this way making love with anyone before. That blast of—whatever—what was that?" he whispered. "Please tell me you felt it, too."

She sat up, her sweet little ass pressing against his flaccid cock, and looked down at him.

"I felt everything." Her mouth spread into a sly grin. "I still feel everything," she added, pushing her ass back against his growing erection.

Before Marcus could continue the conversation, she'd lifted her hips and taken him inside her again. He lost the capacity for speech and simply moved his hips to match her tempo, holding onto her with both hands and relishing her lithe body's writhing churn on his cock.

"Holy fuck, what are you doing to me?"

Her slender hips rocked atop him and he just tried to hold on, tried to stay focused on the sight of her in spite of how gloriously wonderful her tight, slick channel felt rhythmically clenching and releasing his cock. God, he felt so filthy at the idea of shooting his spunk inside her, but she'd objected to the condom so he'd given in. The lack of a barrier made it even harder for him to hold back. He could have come three times in her since she started fucking him, but wanted so badly to hear her sing again before he did.

The lilting melody came a moment later, and this time he was sure there were actual words to the song. They were unfamiliar to him, but unmistakably sweet, spilling from her lips. He sensed from the intensity of her shudders and her gaze that the song meant something personal to her.

Before he could process the thought and voice his wonder, she clenched so tightly around him he was unable to hold back. His balls tightened and his climax exploded inside her, the hot stream of his semen pulling from somewhere even deeper inside him, as though the energy of the entire universe had chosen him as a conduit to flow through his body and into hers.

Evie's head flew back as she worked herself atop him, her smooth neck a perfect, beautiful line undulating from the sounds still coming from deep inside her. Finally, the song faded to nothing but an echo, and then only the sounds of their heavy breathing were left in the room.

She let out a soft sigh and sank down to his chest again, humming with contentment when he wrapped his arms around her.

"Wow," he said, then chuckled at himself for his lack of any larger vocabulary at the moment.

"Stratosphere?" she asked, smiling up at him again.

"I think we must be in another galaxy entirely, after that. And that song… it was so beautiful. What did it mean?"

She shrugged, the movement causing her breasts to shift pleasantly against his chest. "Just an old song I knew from when I was a kid in Budapest."

"It sounded like a sad song. What was it about?"

She remained quiet for a moment, then her back rose and fell as she let out a long, heavy breath.

"It's a love song, of sorts, but a sad one. About all the things a girl would do for her old lover, if she hadn't let him go to war and lost him."

He only managed a short "hmm" around the sudden tightness in his chest. The war was something he'd managed thus far to avoid thinking about, in spite of the mounting protests throughout the country. The ominous clack-clack of the Draft Board's typewriter updating his classification reverberated in his memory.

"1-A," the new copy proclaimed, which meant, "available for military service."

Marcus was no longer a student, having finished his degree just a few months earlier. He had few living relatives and no dependents. His mother was healthy and well-off enough on her own that it wouldn't be a hardship for her if he were drafted. So with the situation in Vietnam escalating, it was only a matter of time. Marcus didn't believe in the war, but he believed in honor and duty. He had intended to enlist the following week, anyway, to preempt the inevitable. Now, he wasn't so sure.

He wrapped his arms tighter around Evie's body, trying to ignore the dread that had settled in his gut and instead focus on how amazing it felt to have her in his arms. He'd told a little bit of a fib to her earlier—he'd been listening to her sing for weeks, but had only today worked up the courage to approach her. Still, he'd been too big a coward to speak to her directly in front of the two musicians she sang with, and was supremely relieved when she divulged that they were, in fact, her brothers. He still couldn't quite wrap his mind around that. They were both large, well-built men with long, black hair. They certainly resembled each other enough for him to believe they were brothers, but compared to Evie's delicate frame with her small features and shining dark-brown hair, the men could have been from another planet and he'd have believed it.

"Something's bothering you," she whispered, sliding off him and propping her head on one hand by his side. She left her other hand resting on his sternum, toying with the thicket of coppery hair that adorned his chest. "Is it because we only just met?"

"Not at all. I was just worried that your brothers might be missing you. I don't want to piss them off."

Evie let out an indelicate snort. "They're harmless. Besides, you're bigger than them." Her gaze drifted down his naked torso and back up.

"There are two of them, so under the circumstances, I'd prefer to stay on their good side. I should take you home before they decide to come beat down my door."

"What you should do is tell me the truth," she said, hooking her leg over his and nudging her knee perilously close to his genitals. "Something you should know about me is that I can spot a lie a mile away. My brothers might intimidate you, but that's not what's really bothering you." She nudged his balls gently and he twitched his hips to pull away. The contact felt supremely nice, but the look in her eyes was too dangerous. Her leg tightened and she raised her eyebrows.

Marcus rolled his eyes and reached down to grip her knee. "If you want to make use of me again, be careful."

"I'd prefer to fall in love with a man who is honest. If you can't be, then I have no use for you." With her knee locked tightly in his grip, she instead slid her hand down and cupped him between the legs, squeezing gently. The threat wasn't lost on him, but her soft touch made it difficult as hell to think straight. Her eyes brightened when his cock started to stiffen again.

"Christ, fine! The song you sang, at least the meaning of it, hit home." He rolled over and rummaged in the pocket of his satchel, hunting for his wallet. A second later he unfolded a small, cream-colored card and held it out to her. "My draft card. Your brothers are probably in the same boat, if I'm guessing their ages right. I'm not the kind of man to shy away from danger—that's not what bothers me—but now that I've met you…"

Now that he'd met her, it still shouldn't have bothered him. He barely knew her, after all. But he'd never met another woman quite like her and the thought of never having the time to explore what could be would break his heart if he let it. She was even more special than he imagined after those weeks of watching her singing in the park.

"You've known me for what, a few hours? Why do you think I'm so special?"

"Mm, well, what you're doing with your hand right now is pretty special."

Evie lifted her head up and waved the hand she'd been resting on at him. "This? It's just a prop." Her other hand tightened around his rigid cock and gave it a long, deliberate stroke. She grinned at the harsh groan that escaped his lips.

"I don't know what it is about you. Something tells me you're so much more than you seem, even beyond a knack for spectacular hand jobs." His hips rose up to meet her steady stroking. Fuck, he was going to come again if she kept that up, which would probably be breaking some kind of record, at least for him. He'd never been so turned on so soon after an orgasm before. And this afternoon, he'd already had two back-to-back. What the fuck was she doing to him?

"Am I special enough for you to believe me when I say you don't have to worry about my brothers? If anything, it's my grandmother you should be afraid of."

The comment might normally have ruined the mood, but

Evie punctuated it by leaning down and taking him in her mouth. Marcus lost it completely then, hips bucking up hard into her. He reached out and grabbed at her thigh, sliding his hand up between her legs to find her slick and wet. She hummed around his girth when he slipped two fingers deep into her. He wanted more of her. Sweet Jesus, he didn't think he would ever get enough of her. With a squeeze and tug of her thigh, he urged her to move so that her knees were braced against his shoulders and her sweet snatch was poised and dripping over his mouth. He gripped her ass and spread her wide open, lifting his head to delve in.

His worry about her family disappeared, and the looming threat of the war became a hazy shadow at the back of his mind. All he knew in that moment was pure, delicious sensation—her mouth steadily working up and down his shaft, her wet, velvet folds sliding against his lips and tongue. He may only have these few hours with her. For all he knew, tomorrow would be the day the letter came, and by this time next year, he might be in a jungle on the far side of the world. He resolved to make this time worthwhile—to find out all her secrets, not just what made her sing with pleasure, but what made her laugh or cry, what foods she liked, whether she were ticklish or loved the autumn as much as he did.

But at the moment, Marcus just wanted to exhaust himself with the pleasure part of the equation. To have her in as many ways as possible. Suddenly the idea of filling her with his hot seed was more alluring. Maybe angels really couldn't get pregnant, but if he had to leave her, he could leave her with a piece of him and hope that when the war was over and he returned, she would remember him by what he'd given her. It would give him a reason to fight, to live, to come home.

He knew now that he would need that, too, because what else did he have? His family was so sparse as to be nonexistent. His mother was an only child and her parents were dead. She still regularly drank herself into oblivion over some old lover who had appeared after his dad had died in that long-ago war. Whoever that stranger was had taken advantage of a lonely, recently widowed, and very pregnant young woman, and had disappeared just as quickly.

A child… an entire family… had been a distant, elusive fantasy to Marcus, and for the first time in his life, he let himself want it.

Except this particular position, as much as he loved the feel of Evie's mouth wrapped around his cock, was not ideal for that purpose.

He dropped his head back to the pillow with a groan and rolled her off him.

"What is it?" she asked, wiping her mouth delicately and staring at him with those beautiful, big gray eyes. Goddamn, she destroyed him. She was so much more than a pretty face and voice.

"I need to fuck you again. From behind this time. Turn around."

"Oh? In a hurry to try every position? We still have the rest of the night, you know. I'm not planning to fly away anytime soon."

His face grew warm at her teasing, and even more at the secret wish that had come upon him a moment ago. Yet she complied with a pleased smile, crawling to him on hands and knees and leaning in to give him a lingering kiss. When she pulled away she leaned down, wrapping her arms around a pillow with her ass poised in the air, legs spread.

"I'm all yours, all night, Marcus. Any way you want me."

He shifted around behind her and couldn't resist pressing his mouth to her glistening, pink folds again. He squeezed her ass with both hands and slid his tongue all the way to her clit, flicking at it until he heard her gasp and her body quivered. Then he licked the other direction, teasing higher and higher, aiming for the rosy pucker between those two perfect mounds of soft flesh.

Evie's quick pants halted, her entire body growing abruptly still. Marcus was afraid he'd crossed a line, until she pressed back harder against him.

"Hmm, you like that? I'd love to have this pretty ass, too, but right now I just want to fill your hot cunt with my come. I hope you were lying when you said angels couldn't get pregnant. We'd make beautiful babies. Little cherubs with wings and chubby thighs."

"Ohhh," Evie moaned when he entered her again. The sound was both melodic and heart-wrenching. It seeped into his ears, sank into his bones, inundated his soul with a kind of sadness that made him want to make love to her until the song she sang was no longer bittersweet, but filled with joy.

He slid his hands down the smooth curve of her arched back as his hips worked his cock in and out of her at a maddeningly slow pace. He'd been so close to coming into her mouth, he needed to go slowly and work back up to climax again. Bending over her, he placed his lips at her ear.

"Would you like that? If we could, would you like me to put a baby in you?"

"Marcus, please! Oh, don't say that. It can't happen."

He pressed his lips to her shoulder, slipping his hand beneath her chest. She was so small and his hand so large he could easily span both breasts with one hand and tease her nipples.

"Maybe not, but a man can dream," he said, teasing his tongue along the sweat-coated back of her neck. "Just tell me you want it. At least tell me you'd like a future with me, because I can't imagine a life with any other woman besides you."

Evie's muscles clenched tight around him, so tight he had

to stop moving lest he lose control too soon. At the same time, she let out a low, mournful moan followed by a single word that spilled from her lips in the wake of a sob.

"Yes!"

Her ass bucked against him and she reared back, still solidly encompassing his plunging cock. He wrapped his arms around her, reveling in the ecstatic repetition of that same word. *Yes, yes, yes, please fuck me, come in me again. Please!*

The sound of the words were as instrumental in his dive into oblivion as her clenching muscles when her own shuddering orgasm took over. He had one arm wrapped around her chest, his other hand between her thighs, rubbing her hot, throbbing clit in time with his thrusts. The power of his orgasm sent his entire soul through the end of his cock and into her. He wished all it would take was the desire to make it happen, but her reaction told him she hadn't been lying before. He forced the thought away.

Whatever it was that made her so certain she couldn't get pregnant would come soon enough, because he made a silent vow in that moment to never let her go. Being a father didn't matter so much as long as he could have her.

# CHAPTER 11

## EVIE

*Somewhere Over the Pacific Ocean*
*Present Day*

Evie drifted in and out of sleep for the duration of the journey. Sometime in midday she came awake, her breath catching in her throat at the vast expanse of nothing but ocean beneath them. She ached to shift and fly beside them—to feel the Wind flowing around her wings and body, cleansing her of the residue of confinement she felt coated in. She flexed her muscles experimentally. Her back twinged when she moved and she let out a hiss at the pain that shot through her.

*"I could only heal some of your wounds with the first breath. Whatever they did to you isn't responding as it should to my healing power."* Gavra's voice resonated through her ears even over the rush of air. *"At this rate, it will take much more healing for the other wounds. You won't be able to fly again for quite a while, I'm afraid. If you're willing to breathe me in now, I can give you more."*

"I've been earthbound for fifty years. What's a few more weeks? But I will take more," she said.

Once she'd taken in another lungful of his spicy breath, she shifted around in the cage of his large claws and peered beneath them. They flew so high, the clouds looked like huge, white islands floating in a crystal-clear sea. This was the world as she remembered it. Her favorite part of the world, too. The part where she'd always been free from worry and at her very lightest. Nothing mattered up here but the state of being *in between*. In between the fiery sun and the earth and water. Touched by all three, but apart from them.

Except she'd been touched even deeper by fire, she realized, staring across at Ked, who flew slightly in front of the rest of the group, their bodies aligned in a V-formation.

The wind rushing over Evie's body might have chilled her if it hadn't been for that burn inside her. Just as it had been with Marcus, she wished for Ked's touch now. She wished for that flame to be fed and fed to the point that it consumed her entirely the way her love for Marcus had consumed her at the end.

As he'd lain there dying in her arms, her only wish was that they had, indeed, burst into flames, reduced to pile of ashes together. She'd even fallen asleep and dreamed through her pain that it was true, that they'd immolated in their last embrace, and that something wondrous and beautiful had burst forth from their charred remains. Not cherubs, like he'd first suggested the day they'd met. No… A creature part fire, part wind, but all the best parts of them both.

$\backsim$

*BROOKLYN, New York*
   *1965*
   E

vie's body shuddered as much from her crying as from her orgasm. She wanted everything Marcus had suggested. More than anything. She'd dreamed for years of finding her One and having a family with him.

Marcus was so perfect. Why couldn't it really be him? Why did she feel such a strong connection, but not the *right* connection to him? She suppressed a soft sob as he pulled her down to the mattress and enveloped her in his arms, shushing her gently.

"What is it, Evie? You can tell me anything."

She snuffled and shook her head, unable to get any words out at all, which was good because she couldn't tell him the truth anyway. If only he were the *One*, she could tell him, and then they could mate and have that baby he so wished for. The one *she* had always wished for, too.

But he wasn't. The tingling rush of magic through her body told her as much. He was definitely human, but he'd been touched by dragons. *Blessed.* That meant he could never be hers. Ever. That was the nature of a Blessed human. They were rare and gifted. It explained how he seemed to know she was something beyond human. It also explained why he was so attracted to her. Her race and the dragons had very similar auras to untrained senses. It didn't help that dragons embodied all the elements while still commanding fire as their primary. Marcus had likely been blessed by a White dragon, to be drawn so strongly to a creature like Evie—a child of the Wind.

The rush of logic didn't stop the tears from flowing. All that remained once those thoughts faded was the one thought: he belonged to a dragon. And she'd just tried to steal him.

Even worse... they'd shared energy during all the times they'd made love so far. That meant he'd have started forging a bond with her simply by virtue of the act. He probably didn't even have a clue what he'd done, either, or why he felt the way he did. Shit, that had to be why he suddenly wanted a baby with her.

"Evie?" Marcus gripped her shoulder and squeezed, then slid his hand up to her cheek and brushed an errant tear from her eye.

Evie sniffled. "I'm okay. I just… talking about some things is hard for me."

"You want what I want, don't you? But…" He paused and let his hand slide over her hip and rest on her belly. "It can't happen, can it?"

Her throat constricted and hot tears seeped from her eyes again. "No," she said, forcing the word past the sob that threatened to escape.

"It's all right. Shush." He squeezed her tighter for a moment then moved to tug a blanket over them.

She let out a heavy sigh once he snuggled back down behind her. Turning in his arms, she peered up at him through wet lashes. "You want something I can never give you. Why aren't you sending me away?"

His lips twisted wryly. "I just met you. I'm not the kind of guy to give up after one try. Or…" He pulled out a hand and tapped the tips of his fingers. "Four? Five? I lost count. And trying is ninety percent of the fun." He waggled his eyebrows at her.

*It will never happen.* The thought destroyed her, but in the cocoon of his embrace she wanted so much to give him hope. Who knew how long it would take her to find her One? After all, it had been a hundred and fifty years already. It could take centuries longer, for all she knew. Why not find happiness with him for as long as she could?

Evie's conscience pricked at that thought. He didn't belong to her. He was Blessed, which meant he belonged to a dragon, and likely one from the new brood that would soon awaken. But by her math, that was still decades in the future. Would he even live that long?

Evie blinked through her tears, an idea coming to her. Blessed humans tended to live long lives, but still had normal human lifespans if they never found a dragon mate. If she kept sharing her energy with him, he *would* live longer. Much longer. She could keep him until the time came to give him up. Or until she found her One.

"Three for you, four for me," she said, sinking back into him, content in her decision. His dragon blessing meant he needed that transfer of energy to prolong his life. Evie would be more than happy to give him all the magic he needed. "Let's try to top it tomorrow."

EVIE HAD NEVER FOUND it so difficult to leave a man's bed before. It didn't help that Marcus seemed distinctly reluctant to let her go. He clung to her when she rolled over the next morning and sat up, hunting for her clothes. His arms wrapped around her naked hips and his cheek pressed against her thigh.

"You said we'd top yesterday." His bright eyes peered up at her from where his head rested on her leg. He gave her navel a flirty lick and then pouted at her.

"You remember my brothers, right? They're going to miss me." Her brothers were probably oblivious to her absence. The truth was she'd lain awake for half the night worrying over her decision. She could see no flaw in her logic—she likely had a true mate out there somewhere waiting for her, and Marcus's blessing would aim him at a dragon the moment the right one showed herself. But neither of those things were likely to happen anytime soon—or so she hoped.

Her grandmother always seemed to have wisdom to share

when Evie was stuck in such a dilemma. She simply had to go home and talk to Nanyo to make sure she was doing the right thing before she committed to the idea.

Marcus groaned and sat up. "Your brothers are probably going to kill me, aren't they?"

Evie looked over her bare shoulder at him and smiled. "They won't if they know how much I like you."

Her heart lurched in her chest at the little lie she told. She more than liked him. It took all her will not to strip back down and crawl back into the bed beside him.

She focused her energy on dressing instead, pulling her blouse over her head and tugging on her calf boots once her skirt was buttoned. She had to get out of there before he tempted her too much, but if her grandmother gave her a favorable answer, she intended to be back in this very bed as soon as she was able to.

She gave him a long, slow kiss and tried to ignore the dejected look in his eyes when she walked out his door.

When she got back to the Brooklyn row house apartment she shared with her grandmother and brothers, Evie tugged off her boots, sank down onto the worn sofa, and buried her head in a pillow. The feeling of longing hadn't left her for the entire short trip. She was alternately elated and despairing. Marcus made her so happy, made her feel so good, but still... he wasn't the One.

A weight settled on the end of the sofa by her feet, a warm, gentle hand resting on top of her knee.

"Welcome home. Did you have an adventure last night?" Her grandmother's low, smooth voice always reminded her of the hoot of an owl. Both eerie and comforting depending on her mood.

"No more than my brothers did," Evie said, pausing for a moment as she noted the general silence in the house betraying their absence. Her brothers regularly frequented clubs after they did their duties in the park and were rarely home before dawn, either. This was the first time in several years that she'd done the same.

Her grandmother's strong hand squeezed hers. "You had a bigger adventure than they did, I am sure."

Evie sighed and pulled the pillow away from her face. "I met someone, Nanyo. But he isn't... *him*."

"But he means something to you." It was a statement, not a question. Damn, the woman always knew her inside and out.

"Yes. But I can't have him, Nanyo. I tried to believe this whole *one true mate* thing was utter bullshit. What if I don't believe there is only one? It's been so long, why hasn't it happened already? What if I don't believe it's possible?" After the night she'd had, she was confused as hell, but she was fooling herself if she really thought the man she was meant to be with didn't exist. She only hoped her conviction that Marcus wasn't the One was an indication of how strong her feelings would be for her true mate when she finally found him.

Nanyo shifted to face her, leaning one arm on the back of the sofa, her hand sweeping in a short, graceful gesture. "If you don't believe there is one, why not just choose this man you met?"

"I would—or I would try—except he could *never* belong to me. Nanyo. He is Blessed."

Her grandmother squeezed her leg again and Evie watched as the elderly woman squared her shoulders and settled in like she did when she had something particularly wise to share. Evie was struck suddenly by the older woman's delicate features, so at odds with her long-standing perception of the woman.

Nanyo was the steel-hardened matriarch of their family. Evie's parents had left to pursue their dreams, trusting their children to the capable hands of the older woman. But Evie and her brothers were long grown by then. She didn't blame her parents for their love for each other and their desire to share the majority of their lives together alone. They'd raised Evie and her brothers after a long love affair and had centuries left to spend together without the burden of parenting children who should be able to take care of themselves.

A light breeze flowed through the room, and in the blink of an eye, Evie's Nanyo was gone, the wizened, maternal woman sinking into the small frame and someone far more intimidating rising to the surface.

Evie sat up straighter, clutching the pillow. She never knew whether to be excited or terrified when her grandmother used her magic, but when Sofia North spoke, Evie listened.

"Denying your one true mate is tantamount to denying the stars in the sky. You know they're always there, even when you don't see them."

Her grandmother reached out and squeezed Evie's bare foot. Evie nodded.

"Your true mate is out there, but Fate likes a meandering path, so how you find him may not be easy. If you feel a connection with this man, don't deny it. Even though he may not belong to you, he may lead you to where you need to go. You may wind up leading each other."

Evie sat up and stared at her grandmother. "You're saying I should *use* Marcus to find the man I'm supposed to be with? Isn't that cruel?"

Her grandmother leaned toward her and cupped her chin in one dry, cool hand. Evie's breath caught as he stared into her grandmother's swirling violet eyes.

"You have to remember that you are his path, too. Sometimes when you cross paths with a person who affects you deeply, you wind up entwined, until your paths diverge and you go your separate ways. Or not."

The older lady grinned and patted Evie on the cheek.

"Or not what?" Evie asked, irritated by the flippant ending to what she'd thought was a deep vision her grandmother was in the midst of.

"Maybe you'll stay together. Who knows? Do you want some ice cream?" The older woman stood up and walked to the kitchen, leaving Evie gaping at her.

"I thought you were making breakfast," she said, following with a distinct sense that what had just happened had all been a dream.

"I want dessert for breakfast. I'm fifteen hundred years old. I should get to have dessert for breakfast."

Evie laughed. "You should. I'd love some ice cream."

When her grandmother handed her the bowl, she held it back out of Evie's reach for a moment. Evie raised an eyebrow, curious about her grandmother's reluctance.

"Your new friend needs to come here. Not right away, but when you feel the time is right. Bring him home… June. Summer Solstice would be right."

Her grandmother nodded emphatically and let Evie have her ice cream.

THE NEXT WEEK Evie sang even stronger in the park, attracting a bigger crowd than before. Her brothers barely managed to keep up with her enthusiasm. They didn't falter, but she could sense their irritation. She was too eager to see Marcus again.

Near the end of their show, she spied him holding a bouquet of daisies at the edge of the crowd.

"Another fan?" Lukas asked her when she rushed to get their gear together.

"The same fan," she said. "I like him. A lot."

"But he's not the One, is he?" Iszak asked, a hint of warning in his tone.

"So what?" she said. "He's amazing enough to be the One. Maybe he is and I just don't know it yet."

"It's supposed to be instantaneous," Lukas said. "When you lay eyes on your One… you just know."

Evie laughed. "You guys still believe that? What if it's bullshit? This guy is… well, he's holding a bouquet of daisies, for one thing."

"So why isn't he bringing them to you personally?" Iszak asked, eyeing Marcus skeptically.

"Because you guys are jerks." She shot Iszak a dirty look and picked up her satchel containing some small toiletries and a change of clothes.

"We're trying to protect you," Iszak grumbled and sulked. In spite of his large, powerful frame, sometimes he still resembled the same sensitive boy she remembered from their childhood. When they were kids, he'd always worked so hard to appear tough. Now, he was much harder on the outside than he used to be, and rarely let his sweet, inner core show in public, but Evie knew it was still there. It came out in his music enough to be undeniable. She wondered briefly if he envied her connection with Marcus.

"You think I can't handle myself with one human male who loves making me happy? He is harmless!"

Lukas jumped in and soon enough she found herself embroiled in an argument with the two of them. The same frustrating argument she always had. They loved her and wanted to protect her—she knew that—but by the Winds could they just let her live her life for once?

"Evie."

It took her a second to register the deep voice speaking her name over the hubbub between herself and her brothers. Finally she turned to see Marcus standing behind her with furrowed brows.

"Marcus… ah… hi?"

He smiled and raised an eyebrow. "I hope I didn't cause this."

Evie shook her head, but her brothers' scowls betrayed the truth. Marcus squared his shoulders.

"My name is Marcus Calais. I'm afraid I've fallen in love with your sister. I really just wanted to give her these flowers, nothing more." He held the flowers out to Evie. She took them, smiling, her heart beating profusely.

Iszak pushed himself between Evie and Marcus, staring into the man's eyes. "Men don't just *fall in love* with our sister. What's your game?"

Evie bristled and pushed herself in the middle again before Marcus could respond. "What the hell? You have ears, you ass. He said it. It's the truth, and you know it." She glared at Iszak, daring him to challenge her. He knew as well as she did that Marcus wasn't lying or hiding anything. Iszak was just being a supreme asshole for the sake of intimidating someone Evie wanted to be with.

She shivered inside at the realization that Marcus really hadn't been lying when he'd said he'd fallen in love with her. But hadn't she told him the week before that she was going to fall in love with him?

She turned back to Marcus, her skin tingling at the very idea of him being here so close. He made her feel so good on the surface. But underneath… she shoved that idea down. There was something missing, but that didn't matter— there'd been something missing her entire life. It wasn't his job to fill that one void, not when he managed to satisfy every other part of her.

"Thank you for the flowers," she said, and leaned up to kiss him. She'd intended to kiss him chastely on the cheek, but at the last minute, decided to piss off her brothers more.

Gripping the sides of his face, she pressed her lips against Marcus's and latched on. He didn't hesitate to wrap his arms around her and devour her mouth like he'd been starving since they parted. Her daisies dropped to the ground, forgotten in her confusion of desire, the same questions popping up again. How could he make her feel so good if he wasn't the One?

He pulled away first, chuckling and glancing over her shoulder.

"I think I pissed them off," he murmured.

"Fuck them."

She grabbed his hand and called blithely to her brothers, "Don't wait up!"

## CHAPTER 12

### KED

*Somewhere Over the Pacific Ocean*
*Present Day*

Throughout the flight, Ked kept sending periodic breaths to Evie to maintain a mental connection with her. Thanks to his blood in the man he carried, he had a solid connection to Marcus, but Evie was still remote to him.

The pair of lovers came together in his mind as though meant to be there. Evie's memories fell into line with Marcus's so perfectly, Ked had no reason to doubt either of them, or their bond to each other.

Ked had only the smallest twinge of envy that Marcus had reached Evie first, for being there in that first moment she'd seen her true mate, though he knew it was his own blood running through Marcus's veins that had drawn her to him.

Deep inside Marcus's mind, Ked sensed the regret. In spite of his deep love for Evie, Marcus would have given everything up to spare her the ordeal of the last five decades. Marcus was letting go, bit by bit, as they traveled. Ked sensed the man's crumbling constitution with every mile, but not because he was dying. Because he was wishing more and more for death, as though he were ready for it, willing it to come to him, willing himself to let it take him because he didn't *deserve* her love anymore—because he didn't deserve life, either.

That wasn't how their world worked, though. And whether Marcus knew it or not, he'd been a part of their world since before his birth. As a Blessed, he'd been marked in the womb to someday become a dragon's mate. How he found that dragon was up to Fate to decide.

Now that Marcus had been irrevocably altered, thanks to the Ultiori ritual to create an Elite, there was only one dragon he could belong to. And Ked wasn't about to let him give up. Not when he knew how tightly bonded Marcus and Evie were, all thanks to his blood.

He knew from the memories he witnessed that Marcus had, indeed, been no more than Blessed when he'd first met Evie, but somehow that had changed. Yet even before it had changed, Marcus's blessing had drawn the pair of them together so swiftly only magic or Fate could be responsible.

Ked would bet his soul that Fate was the bigger player in the scenario. If Ked was Evie's true mate, Fate would not have simply delivered her to his doorstep. She'd make him work for it. He and his siblings had been in seclusion for too long. It would take dire circumstances to draw them out. Making them dream about their mates was what had done the trick, finally.

Just any mate wouldn't do, however. It had to be someone special. Evie's brothers had been the first to be mated, by Ked's sister, Belah. The North siblings were more than just eligible turul. They were essentially turul royalty, the descendants of Boreas, one of the four Winds. Just as Ked was the son of the Mother of Fire, he was meant to mate a descendant of another elemental goddess. The Goddess of the North Wind.

Marcus was unexpected, though not surprising. Fate enjoyed her tricks, that was certain. Ked was no longer fazed by them. Marcus may have belonged to the enemy before, but he'd belonged to Evie first, and he belonged to Ked now. Both of them did.

Saving the man might be a challenge, however, if his dark dreams were any indication. In spite of the passion and love in those first few dreams Ked witnessed, there was an undercurrent of dread, one that couldn't have only revolved around the human war Marcus had once expected to fight in. Blessed humans had always been somewhat prescient. Marcus may have believed his dread related to that old human war, but likely, it was related to the change he would be forced to endure at the hands of the Ultiori.

The dread grew ever stronger as they flew, with Marcus's ordeal unfolding more every moment, and Evie's along with it.

Ked picked up his pace and let out a trumpeting roar, urging his brothers on faster. He needed to reach the monastery before Marcus sank too far into his despair to bring him back out.

Behind him, Evie's brothers let out similar cries and rose up high in the air, swooping down to land on Aodh's back. With the surge of power he and his brothers had put forth, the turul wouldn't be able to keep up for long. If they wanted to be there when they all landed, they would need to ride rather than fly.

Day faded into night as the sun traversed a path over them, and they flew on, the starlit darkness ahead of Ked bright in comparison to the dark pit he sensed in the soul of the man he carried in his claws.

# CHAPTER 13

## MARCUS

*Dragon Monastery, Sunda Islands*
*Present Day*

Marcus didn't have the strength to move, or even open his eyes, when the rush of wind stopped and his body was gently relinquished from his clawed cage onto a soft surface.

His ears worked, however. As did his nose and his sense of touch.

Evie's lilac fragrance hit his nostrils as her soft fingertips brushed his cheek.

"We made it out," she said. "You did this for me, didn't you? I will always love you, Marcus Calais. I will never forget you."

Her velvet lips pressed gently against his, and he wished for nothing more than to be able to kiss her back—to reach up and embrace her. But his arms didn't work, and she was better off if he were dead, anyway, after what he'd put her through.

He just wished he had the power to ask Ked why the hell he wasn't dead.

A moment later, whatever he was lying on lifted up and he felt himself moving. A stretcher? After traveling for several minutes, he heard a door open and was awash in calming aromas and the sounds of windchimes and trickling water. The air grew slightly warmer and he realized he'd been chilled from the flight, though he hadn't been aware until now.

Strong hands lifted him and laid him down gently on a soft bed.

Then the voices spoke, too familiar and heartbreaking to his ears. Voices he wished he could respond to.

"Watch him. He may be a danger to himself and we can't let him die. If he wakes up, get me or my brother or Ked. We need to speak to him."

Evie's brothers.

If Marcus had the strength now, he would try to reassure them yet again that he'd never meant to harm her. But that would be useless, wouldn't it? Not when he'd promised them she was safe, only to find her so damaged when they reached her.

They would need to hear from their sister that she was the one who had begged Marcus to run away with her at the beginning, and that she was the one who had begged Marcus to send her blood-soaked feather to her brothers to make them believe she was dead.

Right now, all he really wanted to do was beg them to do what he knew they must desire most. To kill him.

If that were even possible.

They'd wanted to, fifty years ago. He didn't blame them now. They probably should have. He was no good for Evie, but he hadn't known at the time how bad he would wind up being for her. If he'd known then, he would have stepped off that proverbial train and thrown himself onto the tracks beneath it.

~

*New York*

*Midsummer 1965*

T

he subtle glares Evie's brothers kept giving Marcus didn't bother him as much as the stories they told about their grandmother.

They were on the subway, heading toward Evie and her brothers' neighborhood from Central Park. By her brothers' accounts, the woman he was about to meet had antler horns, spouted poison smoke, and could change your gender with a single look.

He kept one hand cupped casually over his crotch and his other hand linked with Evie's because she seemed to take comfort in his contact, but stayed alert for her brothers to make a move. He'd never dated a girl with older brothers who were this hostile. Hell, he'd never dated a girl with brothers. Or for that matter, one with a grandmother who was apparently the devil incarnate.

Who was he kidding? He'd barely dated anyone. He had no clue what he was doing. All he knew was that he wasn't letting go of this girl if his life depended on it. Brothers or no brothers. Devil or no devil. It had taken him several weeks after Evie's first invitation to warm up to the idea of actually spending time in the same room with her family. Evie was so amazing, he worried he'd fuck it up somehow.

"You can relax," Evie whispered. "She'll love you. I promise."

Marcus wasn't so sure. He hadn't exactly been an outcast growing up, but he hadn't been popular, either. He gravitated toward athletic pursuits as much as academic, which hadn't endeared him much to either group. He'd rarely had girlfriends, and had no practice interacting with families unless he counted his own distraught mother.

He'd started college on an athletic scholarship, but threw himself into his studies as hard as he trained with his football team. He'd succeeded, so far. Gotten his degree just before meeting Evie. But now he was likely on the verge of being drafted, and not by a pro team, like he'd hoped, but by the United States military.

He couldn't tell Evie that, though. He'd only just found her. The Vietnam War was ever-present, a ticking time bomb that could change his life the second his number came up. He was amazed it hadn't happened already.

He just hoped he had time, though time for what, he wasn't sure. Time to fall even deeper in love with Evie? It had been a couple months since they'd met, and every day, he fell more in love with her. Her brothers still gave him dirty looks, but had reluctantly accepted that he wasn't going anywhere. They still did love to give him hell, from time to time, which Marcus had begun to understand was their way of keeping him on his toes. The first time he ribbed them back, he'd earned himself a smile from the gruffer one—Iszak—and a laugh from Lukas. Evie had rolled her eyes and warned Marcus not to encourage them.

The train came to a stop and Evie stood. She tugged at his hand and smiled at him. Marcus had a hard time not letting his eyes drift over her bare shoulder and the top of her breast. She did love wearing clothes that seemed on the verge of falling off her at any moment. Her dark brown hair fell over her other breast and he resisted the urge to push it aside, just to make sure that glorious, creamy mound was unobscured.

"You're such a perv," she said, laughing at him. "We're here. Come on."

He took a deep breath and stood, letting her lead him out into the noisy heat of the subway platform.

"I'm not a perv," he murmured in her ear. "I just prefer you naked."

He relished the soft shiver of her body against him and the way she clung to him for a moment. He was sure she was trying to catch her breath. Even more sure when she reached up to grip his cheeks and pull him down into a luscious kiss.

"I prefer you naked, too," she said, grinning up at him.

"I didn't just hear that," Iszak said, giving his sister a severe look before stepping out and leading the way up the steps to the street level.

Marcus's pulse raced and he held tighter to Evie's hand. The short walk to the row house Evie and her brothers shared with their grandmother seemed to take an eternity.

"You're going to have a panic attack, if you keep that up. She really is a lovely woman," Evie said.

"So, she raised you guys?" he asked, trying to make conversation. "Where are your parents?"

Lukas shared a quick, furtive glance with his brother, then shot a look over his shoulder at Evie.

"Sort of," she said. "Our parents raised us, but they're musicians. They left when we were old enough to not need them anymore, and Nanyo's been there for us ever since."

"Left... as in deserted you?" He tried not to sound accusatory, because deep down, he thought he understood.

"No. They both got jobs with the Budapest Festival Orchestra. It was their first love—the thing they wanted most together, after each other and having a family."

"Ah, musicians," he said, as though that should explain

everything. The truth was, he envied their lifestyle. She and her brothers seemed so free. He had the weirdest sense that they might just fly away at any moment, and he wanted more than anything to keep Evie on the ground with him.

Climbing the steps to their front door, he believed his heart might be a percussive genius the way it kept time with Evie's steps and every single rhythm of her movements. Maybe he was meant for a life in music, too?

At least, he hoped he was meant for a life within *her* music.

The apartment they led him into was nothing like he expected. In spite of the exterior's humble appearance, the interior was cluttered with wondrous things. Everywhere he turned, he spied new details. Old photographs lined the walls up the stairs, each one with a different, ornate frame. The photos the frames contained seemed to stretch back for centuries. In one particularly ancient one, he could swear he saw Evie's face, but the tug of her hand urged him onward.

At the top of the stairs, he was blinded by the sunset through the high windows. When his sight returned he gazed around, awe-struck at the view they had from this seemingly mundane location. It took him another moment to register the eclectic décor inside. Every inch of wall was filled with something. Photographs, shelves of books, knicknacks, or memorabilia. Yet everything was neatly placed and belonged exactly where it was. It had its own rhythm that meshed perfectly with everything he knew and loved about Evie.

Evie led him through the entryway, into the living room. Though Marcus couldn't really call it one room. Except for one hallway that led toward what he assumed were bedrooms, the entire apartment was one big room.

"Do you like it?" she asked. "We had to take out the walls to fit all our stuff in."

"It's amazing. It feels like a..." He couldn't find the word at first, as he gazed around at the sofas and cushions scattered over the immense array of colorful rugs that covered the floor. More bookshelves rose up around an ornate fireplace and even flanked the huge mirror that hung above the mantel. He saw himself in it, with Evie behind him, curled up in the deep sofa like a little bird roosting. The silhouettes of Iszak and Lukas were visible for a second before disappearing down the hallway.

"What does it feel like?" she asked.

"A nest," he said, walking over to sit beside her. "It feels like a nest. A very comfortable nest, too. How long have you lived here?" The collections he'd seen had to have taken decades to amass. Generations, really.

Evie darted her eyes out the window and plucked at his shirt cuff. "Not that long," she said. "It is pretty cozy, isn't it? I love it here. Especially now that you're here."

She threaded her fingers through his hand and squeezed. The mere sensation of her touch made him crave more of her. He looked at her, enthralled again at her beauty. He'd heard her sing so beautifully so many times. Watched her sweet mouth make the words of those songs. Then considered himself infinitely blessed to have that same mouth encompassing him so thoroughly as to make *him* sing her praises. He loved her mouth, and decided to risk a taste of it.

Just as his lips found hers and she leaned into him, her eyelids fluttering closed, he sensed a presence in the archway behind him. He pulled away and looked over his shoulder at the newcomer.

"Are you going to introduce us, or just sit there smooching?" The brittle, ancient voice sounded amused, and totally incongruous coming from the vital, healthy woman standing backlit in the arch.

She could have been Evie's twin, if it weren't for her

forbidding posture and the butcher knife she held in one hand.

Evie stood up abruptly and turned. Marcus followed, resting his hand on her hip.

"Nanyo! This is Marcus. Please be nice, okay?" Her voice held the faintest hint of panic that had his instincts on edge until Evie leaned into him and squeezed his hip in return.

"Marcus, this is my grandmother. Sofia North."

The other woman raised an eyebrow. "So, this is the man." She ventured forward, the knife still raised parallel to the ground. Marcus eyeballed the blade, a little worried, but when he met the woman's eyes, all he saw was devious mirth. She was fucking with him. That should have made him relax, but he couldn't.

There was no way in hell this woman could be Evie's grandmother, but he was pretty sure there was even less a chance he'd survive if he told her so.

"It's a pleasure to meet you, Mrs. North. You are even more lovely than I imagined from Evie's descriptions."

The woman smiled and gave him a once-over. "You are about what I expected. My granddaughter always had good taste in men."

Oddly, Marcus sensed the comment was a challenge. He wanted to be more than that to Evie. More than expected.

"How can I exceed your expectations, Mrs. North? I love your granddaughter. I don't think anyone who simply 'meets expectations' is worthy of her."

The woman in front of him smiled. "What do you think I am, an oracle? I'm merely an old woman who wants the best for her grandchildren. Now, come set the table. Dinner will be ready soon."

Iszak and Lukas appeared from another room when the scent of food became strong enough. Marcus was more comforted by their appearance than he thought he'd be, and their easy banter with Evie and their grandmother took the burden off him. He tried to sink into the background and simply enjoy what was probably one of the most amazing meals of his life while the family discussion went on around him.

"What do you do anyway, Marcus?" Lukas asked, a playful hint of challenge in his tone. They were all intent on testing him tonight weren't they?

"I just finished a degree in Aeronautics. I've always wanted to fly. I hoped it would be commercially, but..." He let the word trail off, his throat unable to let him articulate the rest of his thought. *But I love Evie too much now to fly away.*

The utter silence at the table only became apparent when he finally took another bite of food and the clink of his silverware echoed through the room. As he chewed, he stared around the table at their faces, trying to decide what each of their looks meant.

Evie's brothers both stared intently at Evie, who only gazed down at her plate.

But Sofia North set her gaze directly on Marcus.

"You seem like an intelligent young man, Marcus. Don't fool yourself. Your call will come, just like the others. But this is not your war to fight."

Marcus bristled. He'd heard the liberal-minded argument against the war over and over. While he agreed with it on the surface, he couldn't in good conscience say no. His own countrymen were overseas dying. He owed it to *them,* if nothing else.

"It may not be my war, but if I have something to offer, it's my duty to my fellow soldiers to do so. I'd do it for them."

Fuck, had he just admitted he was doing it? He hadn't even been drafted yet. Sure, he had originally planned to enlist anyway, but the argument somehow seemed hollow now that he said it.

He continued eating in silence. No one else said a word. The delicious food he'd been eating had lost its flavor. Only the slight squeeze of Evie's fingers on his thigh under the table gave him comfort.

He reached down and gripped her hand, wishing fervently that they could crawl into a cave somewhere and come out only when this Godforsaken war was over. He'd abandon it for her. He'd do anything for her.

When dinner was over, Marcus started to help clean up, but as he was about to turn on the faucet to wash the dishes, Sofia gripped his arm tightly.

"There's something I need to show you," she said. "Let them finish cleaning up."

He nodded and followed her down a dark hallway. She kept walking to the end and flipped a switch that illuminated the entire corridor. It was filled with photographs, small and large. They had ornate and plain frames, and as he followed the path, the photos seemed to progress. The same faces appeared throughout, surrounded by different scenery in each picture.

More of Evie's ancestors, he thought, though it was clear she had at least one ancestor who she took after more. Soon he saw photos of men in uniform. Some of them resembled Evie's brothers so closely the likenesses made him shiver.

"We're not a family who is ignorant of war," Sofia said. "Every single generation of this family has seen it, in one way or another. But *this* human war is not your war, Marcus."

She pulled at his arm and reached a hand up to turn his face to hers. He met her gaze and blinked, disconcerted at the colors that swirled in her irises.

"It's all our war," he said by way of argument, but knew he was just making excuses.

"Not yours, and not ours. Your war will come when the shadows fall over you and you truly believe all is lost. The darkest shadow will be your redemption, and your path to the love you seek."

Marcus shook his head when she stopped talking, trying to clear his disorientation. He was sure she'd been speaking another language for the last bit, but had no idea what it was. All he knew was that he'd understood every single word, and the implications sent his pulse racing.

The woman walked away and he watched her pause at the end of the hallway, facing Evie and speaking to her softly in much the same way she'd just done with Marcus. He could hear her clearly now, but the words themselves were unintelligible. Definitely another language. He stood silent while they spoke, staring at Evie's sepia-toned face in a photo that must have been a hundred years old.

Evie's small form pressed into him a few moments later, molding herself to him as though she were meant to be at his side. He slipped an arm around her and pressed his lips to the top of her head, still staring at the photograph.

"Are you okay?" she asked softly, her voice quavering.

"Your grandmother said…" He looked down at her and shrugged, still confused. "Honestly, I'm not really sure what she said. Just that I shouldn't go to Vietnam. But Evie, I won't have a *choice* if my number comes up."

She moved around to face him, resting her palms on either side of his face. Her fingers slid through his hair, making his scalp tingle, and her stormy gray eyes held his gaze. He longed to hold her tight, to take comfort in her soft curves and the taste of her lips, but his heart nearly stopped when he finally registered the terrified look in her eyes.

"Nanyo is a little bit psychic, so if she told you something, please take it seriously. She's had visions my entire life, and they've always come true."

"What did she say to you?" he asked, lifting a hand to brush a stray tear from her cheek. "Whatever it was, it upset you for some reason."

"She said if I don't keep you from leaving, you'll die over there. Marcus, I don't know if we're meant to be together forever, but I don't want to lose you now."

He held her tighter. "I don't want to lose you, either." But the call would come, he was sure of it. Whether or not he would answer it, he didn't know anymore.

~

*New York*

*Spring 1966*

M

arcus had almost started to believe having Evie in his life had charmed him somehow. Months passed with no contact from the Draft Board. No ominous summons to report for induction. Her brothers, Iszak and Lukas, even seemed to warm to him finally, and the four of them had become closer. He spent more time at their house than at his own small apartment, unless he and Evie craved time to themselves.

Oddly, her family didn't seem to have any hang-ups about the pair of them spending the night together in Evie's bed, which they did frequently. Even her grandmother gave him sly looks in the mornings over breakfast. He still preferred to take her home with him when he really wanted to make her sing.

They spent Christmas together that first year, going caroling around the neighborhood, to the delight of every single household they stopped before. Evie even praised Marcus's singing voice, which he knew was, by far, the least impressive. The Norths were the most talented musical family he'd ever known. The brothers seemed to be able to play just about any instrument they picked up. Evie usually sang, but he learned she was just as clever with a saxophone or guitar as her brothers.

For those glorious months of their relationship, they spent nearly every day together in between Evie's singing gigs and his own work as a charter pilot for a small Westchester airport. Life was so perfect his mind began to shift gears—to risk considering taking a bigger step and making things more permanent between them.

Rather than go to the regular Friday evening dinner he had a standing invitation for at the North residence, he told Evie he wanted to take her out instead. He gathered his meager savings and found a jewelry shop in his neighborhood on the way home that afternoon. With the ring in his pocket, he went home to change clothes. She would come to him in just a few hours, since their favorite restaurant was in his neighborhood, so he had time.

He hustled through his door, grabbing the mail before taking the stairs two at a time, his entire body thrumming with anxious excitement.

It wasn't until he was sitting on the bed, dressed in his nicest suit and tying his shoes, that he happened to glance at the scattered envelopes on his desk and his skin instantly turned to ice. On top of the stack was an unmistakably *official*-looking piece of mail, with an emblem in the corner that could only mean one thing. Marcus reached out a shaky hand and grasped the corner of the envelope, right over the presidential seal. He didn't want to open it. Couldn't open it, because that would make it all too real if he did.

In a daze he stood and shrugged into his jacket, stuffed the envelope blindly into the inside pocket, and left the apartment. He needed to breathe for a few minutes, to try to fend off the sense of his world crashing down around him. He walked aimlessly until he found himself stumbling down the steps into the bar around the corner from his place. Without thinking he ordered three shots of bourbon and stared at his hands.

The bartender raised an eyebrow and poured. "I'm guessing it's not good news from the look on your face," he said.

Without answering, Marcus tugged the envelope from his pocket and laid it on the bar. From his other pocket he withdrew the tiny velvet box and opened it, setting it atop the envelope. The glimmering jewel in the ring seemed to mock him for letting himself be too happy.

The bartender's mouth tightened into a grim line and he lined up three more shot glasses. "On the house today, mate. You need this more than I need the money."

And as if to drive the point home, the radio behind the bar announced yet another protest and slew of men being arrested for burning their draft cards.

"Fucking bullshit, all of it," a slurring patron two seats down from him said. "You should take her away, if you love her. Don't let the goddamn government tell you how to live your life. What's it for, anyway? This ain't our war."

Marcus downed another shot and glanced sidelong at the stranger. The man was older and had the look of a veteran. He was clean cut, wore a nice suit, and smelled like Old Spice, cigarette smoke, and whiskey. Of course, that last could have been the bar itself, but it was distinct enough that Marcus believed it came from him.

The man gestured to the items Marcus had laid on the bar. "You love her, right? The worst thing you can do to love is die for anything *but* love. If you go over there, you'll wind up dying for nothing. Even if you don't die, leaving will kill what you have now. Trust me."

"I don't exactly have any other options."

"There's a whole world of options," the man said. "Run

away or go to jail are the top two. Jail might be better than war, but not if you care about your girl." He paused and fished into his jacket pocket, pulling out a flimsy pamphlet which he set on the bar next to Marcus's drink. "I found this little gem on my windshield the other day. Thought it was pretty clever and wished I'd had that option before Korea. The place sounds nice. The best part is it's in Canada."

Marcus warily picked up the brochure with the photo of a smiling couple on the front, relaxed in an idyllic nature setting. "Tantric Healing," the title read. The small logo at the bottom looked like a sword impaling the head of a dragon, which was totally at odds with the photo. It looked like a vacation brochure on the surface, but once he opened it up, the truth became clear.

He flipped back to stare at the front again. This "Alexandria Institute" had a clever marketing scheme. They weren't offering a vacation, but inclusion in a research program that was specifically looking for committed couples to undergo a series of psychological and physical tests over the course of a year. They would be given room and board in exchange for offering their assistance with basic upkeep of the facilities and allowing themselves to be occasionally poked and prodded for the purpose of scientific advancement—while they had sex. He and Evie had fantastic sex, and the idea of being studied *while* they were doing it was oddly arousing.

The notion of running from his troubles didn't sit quite as well with him. But if he could keep Evie in his life and avoid dying, perhaps it would be worth it.

"This looks like a hippie commune," Marcus commented. "But a nice one. Do you know anyone who's gone?"

The man shook his head. "Keep that. I don't need it. All I know is that *honor* doesn't factor in if you're running from someone else's problem. That war..." The man stabbed a finger at the radio. "Has nothing to do with you, me, or your girl."

Marcus nodded his thanks. "Can I buy you a drink?"

"Only if you tell me about her. What's so special you decided to decorate her with such a shiny rock?"

Marcus smiled at the ring just before stowing it again in his pocket. He left the envelope sitting on the bar.

"If you met her, you'd understand."

"Met who?" a lilting voice said from behind him. Marcus turned, sluggish from the alcohol, to see Evie standing behind him.

"You, baby." He smiled at her and then frowned when her worried look registered. "What's wrong?"

"You weren't home when I got there. I was worried. What's wrong? Why are you here?"

He blinked drunkenly at her and raised another shot. "Celebrating," he said, as if that were the best explanation.

"Celebrating..." she said. "Celebrating what, exactly?"

"This man here—" Marcus gestured with the full shot glass and half the liquid sloshed over his hand. He eyed it then tossed the rest into his mouth and swallowed. He pointed the empty glass at his new friend. "He's opened my eyes."

Evie glanced at Marcus's friend. Marcus struggled for a moment for an introduction before realizing he'd never gotten the man's name. It didn't matter now.

"This is her," he said. "Evie. The woman I'd die for. No... I mean, she's the woman I *live for.*"

The man turned and straightened his tailored jacket, reached out a hand to Evie, and gripped her outstretched palm, shaking it gently.

"You are more lovely than words," he said. "No wonder he's so in love with you.

Evie's brows creased and she glanced once at Marcus before shaking the man's hand and smiling.

"Thank you. I…" Before she could finish her sentence, her gaze drifted to the bar and the envelope that still sat there beside the scattered shot glasses. Her hand fell out of the man's grasp and she turned her gaze back to Marcus.

"Is that what I think it is?" Her delicate finger pointing at the creamy white rectangle that held Marcus's fate sealed inside.

"Yeah… I haven't opened it. I already know what it says, though."

"Oh, Marcus." She wrapped her arms around him and he reveled in the contact. He could die happy in her embrace. He would rather die happy in her embrace than anywhere else.

He held tight to her, dimly aware of his friend shifting off his barstool and moving away.

"I'm sorry I wasn't there when you came. I needed to think."

Evie nodded and plucked at the corner of the envelope. "Do you know what you're going to do?"

Her tone was pensive, hesitant to ask the real question he was sure she wanted to ask. He silently thanked her for not articulating the thing that had to be torturing her already. Would he go?

He loved her for that. Christ, he loved her for everything, but he'd put this off long enough. He knew what was inside, but unless he opened the envelope, he'd be a blind fool who never took real action in his life. He just needed her there with him when it happened.

Marcus let out a deep breath and picked up the envelope, ripped it open, and read the letter. Nothing in it gave him any respite from his decision. It was all exactly what he expected.

He turned it sideways and tore it in half. Then folded the pieces together and ripped them through the center. When he was done, the letter was nothing more than a pile of fragments on the floor around them. It might be the only confetti they ever got.

The ring rested heavily in his pocket, pressing against his heart. He couldn't ask her to marry him when he was about to ask her to leave her life for another reason. He wanted her to come not because she felt obliged to join him, but because she genuinely wanted to be with him. Once they got to that beautiful place in the brochure, he'd ask.

"We're going to leave. Together, I hope."

"Why wouldn't we be together?"

"You have nothing to run from, Evie. I do. But if you're not going to come with me, then I have no reason to run."

"Then I guess I need to go home and pack, huh?" She gave him a shaky half-smile that told him everything. Her eyes filled with tears, and all he could do was kiss her.

She clung to him while they kissed. If they weren't in public, he'd have made love to her as fiercely as he could, just to remind her how much he loved her.

"Marcus, go pack. Pick me up in a couple hours. I'll go wherever you want us to go. As long as I'm with you, it doesn't matter."

She pulled away and he clung to her hand, unwilling to lose contact with her now. She might not come back, but he had no real reason to doubt her. She'd never lied before, but there was always a first time. And this ordeal would be one to run from if she chose to run.

"Marcus," she said softly, "I am never letting you go. I promise I'll go with you."

"Good," he said. "I'll see you soon."

She gave him a long look and then fell into his arms again, kissing him so desperately she left him dazed when she released him, nothing more than a blur of motion when she disappeared through the doors of the bar.

"Sounds like you have your answer," his friend said. "Don't disappoint her. She's worth living for."

Didn't he know it...

Marcus threw his money on the bar and stumbled out the doors. He just hoped he was worth running away for.

# CHAPTER 14

## NIKHIL

*North African Coast, near Alexandria, Egypt*
*Present Day*

The cave was exactly as Nikhil remembered it, though the opening was worn much smoother from the centuries of tides rushing in. He'd targeted the destination of his *drift* to the rear-most chamber where he'd spent most of his time as a child, practicing with toy swords on rudimentary dummies made of sack cloth stuffed with straw and tied to stakes.

Nothing remained of that child in here, but he found a small cache of candles that were still intact after all this time. It only took a flick of his fingertips to light them and line them up along the uneven ledges and rocks that surrounded the area.

The room was so much smaller than he remembered— barely large enough to accommodate the two reclining stone figures he'd transported here. They now lay without their pedestals on the dusty floor.

"I apologize for the lack of amenities here, daughter. I am hoping this place is only temporary."

*"We are patient enough to wait a little longer, Papa. For us, even a year or more feels like mere minutes."*

"If I had known who you were sooner, I would not have made you wait," he said. If he had known sooner, so much pain and death could have been avoided.

His path was set for him now, and much clearer than it had ever been. His efforts over the centuries to produce a child to love now seemed hollow and pointless. Now that he'd found Asha, there was much more at stake. Keeping her safe was the most important thing, followed by finding a more suitable sanctuary for her and her brother to stay until their mates could search them out and awaken them.

But the need that drove him most now was to find out where the creature was who had done this to him to begin with. He knew her identity once—she'd somehow infiltrated Belah's court and posed as a trusted friend for years. Nikhil still remembered the day Meri had died—a feeble old woman in her bed, with no children of her own but with several young physicians she'd trained to carry on her knowledge. Had the darkness somehow been passed to one of her protégés? He had a difficult time remembering any of them now, but one or the other had always been privy to his simplest secret—that he never aged and could not die.

Now he knew that she'd been leading the Ultiori through him somehow. That it had only taken the one moment of weakness when she'd first fed him her blood and her essence for her to get inside his mind. That link had been enough to perpetuate the control, and through his powers, the control of those around him.

The strength of his love for Belah, plus that turul's song had banished her finally, but he had no doubt she was still somewhere out there, trying to get back inside. He could not let that happen again. He had to find her and make her pay.

First, to ensure at least temporary safety for his daughter and her brother he needed to draw on the last vestiges of power inside his weakened body. Tracing a circle around them with his steps, he pushed the power out through his fingertips, building the temporal bubble as he went. It wouldn't be much, but as long as the blood still flowed from his wounds, it would be enough to last until he could hopefully enlist the help of his Elites, if they were willing to hear his story.

THE *DRIFT* back to the Alexandria Institute left Nikhil nearly crippled. He collapsed to the floor in his office on the top level, chest heaving as he tried to catch his breath.

The day outside the floor-to-ceiling windows was dark and dreary, raindrops spattering against the glass. The sound of the storm outside was still no competition for the roaring of the river that rushed beneath.

He'd loved this location for the feeling of true, primal power it gave him, and he drew on that power now, even though he knew how dangerous it could be. The natural web of life that existed around the building would feel the brunt of it. In the past he'd never hesitated when he needed it, but was very careful not to stay in one place for too long because his simple presence was like a wick that pulled the life out of his surroundings. The vegetation around the compound would experience a blight today, to help him heal enough to do what he had to do, but he swore to himself it was the last time.

Finally he rose and found his way to his personal bathroom and showered. His wounds were completely healed now, but the water still ran bright red with all the blood that had covered him.

He would have to find a way to make amends with Marcus and his musical lover. He owed them for his life—his sanity—and for helping him truly reunite with his daughter.

After showering and dressing, he made his way down to the lower level where he hoped his Elites would still be. He'd left Naaz and Sterlyn unconscious outside the cells of the two prisoners they cared about the most. In his absence they always ached to visit their females but studiously avoided any attempt at doing so. Each one of them had made the same mistake at the beginning of their service to Nikhil—they all tried it once—tested his ability to control them by breaking the rules and entering the one cell that was off limits to them each.

For Marcus it had been Evie North's cell. The female had arrived with Marcus fifty years earlier. Their love had been painfully apparent from the start, though Nikhil had gotten the distinct impression the emotions were one-sided during his remote viewing of the intake interview his research director had conducted. Marcus adored the petite, beautiful young woman, and while she certainly had seemed to regard him with no small amount of affection, it was not true love for her. Somewhere along the way that had changed, if Evie's behavior when he'd come seeking vengeance were any indication.

Some aspects of the races he captured over the years were still a mystery, and the turul's mating choices were chief among them. He'd always cared more about dragons from the start, at any rate.

The red dragon Zamirah was Sterlyn's particular weakness. She hadn't been of interest to the young knight at first, but over the years as one of her jailers, their attachment had grown. When Nikhil caught Sterlyn attempting to break the dragon out and escape, he'd had to mete out brutal justice on them both. Ever since, Sterlyn had been the most solicitous and well behaved of the three Elites.

And of course, there had always been Naaz and Neela. His godchildren, and the ones he cared for most—or should have. They were loyal from the start, and became nearly as powerful as Nikhil after he first fed them Belah's blood. But after finding the pair of treasures he now knew were Belah's own children, he had never trusted them to behave without some incentive. And so he had Neela locked up to ensure Naaz remained compliant.

He still had a link to their minds, but with Meri gone from his head he lacked the will to use it. It had been her dark power that terrified them, and when he put enough force of his own behind it, kept them in line. He could not enter their minds again without their permission.

So he walked, taking the central stairs in the large atrium to the ground level. From there he would access the secure wing and the elevators that took him down to the subterranean levels where those most valuable prisoners were kept.

That was when he registered the eerie silence of the place. It was past midday, but still early enough for the compound to be bustling with activity. The second floor of this wing was where the hunters were housed and had their training facilities, yet he heard none of the usual sounds of combat training and general chatter that indicated people lived here. He took a detour down one hall and peeked into one of the dormitories, but there were no hunters to be found, and none in the community areas, either.

Rushing down to the ground floor and the science wing, he directed his powers outward, seeking signs of consciousness of any kind. He found only one semi-conscious dragon, half-shifted and shackled to an examination table, her feet up in stirrups and an IV line attached to her arm. Around him in the rest of this wing, he sensed other prisoners, yet none of the staff.

The staff had apparently evacuated, leaving all the prisoners behind. But where had they gone? And under whose orders had they left?

Nikhil hated the lack of control he felt over his world, particularly the realization that half of his consciousness—the darker half—had been the one that held the most control.

His temples pounded the more he explored, finding work stations seemingly abandoned in the middle of tasks and captives all unconscious in their cells. He vaguely remembered the cloud of rage he'd been in when he'd arrived to take out his anger on Evie North—he very well may have knocked out the entire population of the place. But he had lost his connection to the true power that had driven that rage.

Either his Elites had awakened and evacuated everyone, or someone with equal authority had done so. He'd always been careful who he promoted to have that level of authority over the staff of the Institute, and there would only have been a handful of people on-site with that rank, but there were still hundreds of others within the entire corporate structure who could have done so in his absence.

Forcing himself to refocus on the more immediate goal, he abandoned his earlier intention of avoiding mental contact with his Elites and reached out with his mind to search for them, too. Relief flooded through him when he sensed their inert presences right where he'd left them, near the unconscious bodies of the other prisoners on the secure lowest level. Only Marcus was missing, and Nikhil felt that absence like a spike through his gut.

"Fucking dragon blood," he muttered, heading toward the elevator that would take him down to them. Now that the darkness was gone from him, the familial connection to his

Elites through the blood they each carried was too strong to deny. He wondered how it must feel to the dragons themselves when they encountered one of the Elites.

How had it felt for Belah to be near him, with her own blood running through his veins? The reminder of that connection made his chest tighten with longing for her. Discovering Asha's existence hadn't diminished his feelings in the slightest. If anything, they were stronger now that his mind was clear of all the other dark urges that had driven him for so long.

The prisoners on this level were still unconscious, except for one. As Nikhil passed by Nicholas and Calder's cells, he paused, realizing that the pair were both inside the same cell. Calder knocked on the thick glass of the door and Nikhil tapped the button to activate the speaker.

"Welcome to the flood," the old satyr said. "How does it feel to finally be above water again, just in time to drown?"

"Did you know all along I was … submerged?" Nikhil asked, making an effort to speak the satyr's odd language in which everything seemed to pertain to water.

"Aye. You would not have taken so well to the drift had you not had a drop of a powerful nymph's essence mixed with your blood. Did you ever wonder why your brothers were never able to accomplish such a journey on their own?"

His brothers? Calder must be referring to the other Elites, who were in fact his brothers by blood—even if it was stolen blood. "I never permitted them to attempt it. They were only allowed to accompany me on those journeys."

"You still have her essence within you, and I don't mean your heart's true love. The slippery nymph who controlled you left her mark on you. That will never leave until she is dealt with. Have you discovered her identity yet?"

Nikhil caught a hint of a challenge in Calder's tone. He crossed his arms and narrowed his eyes, scrutinizing the other man through the glass. "I may have an idea, but it sounds like you might have information worth sharing. I'd prefer to avoid torture going forward, but I've never been the type to shy from more brutal methods of extracting information when the situation called for it."

Calder threw his head back and laughed maniacally. "Oh, you would no doubt enjoy torturing me, pain whore that you are. The *Thiasoi* and I knew all there was to know about you before I let myself be captured. You'd be surprised to know what I've learned since, even locked up in these cells for so long. I won't keep it from you, nor will I keep any of the truth any longer."

"Do tell," Nikhil said, scowling at him.

Calder stepped closer to the door and raised his hands, placing his palms flat against the glass. Beneath his touch, the glass shimmered, small ripples cascading out across the surface from his fingertips until the barrier disappeared entirely and Nikhil could hear Calder's voice directly, rather than the tinny version that came through the small speaker.

"Your hunters have a hard time capturing us for a reason, but she is even more slippery than most. We called her Marnie when she was young, but she went by Meri when she was banished from the Haven. Neph, one of our twin leaders, once believed she was his perfect mate, but her betrayal of our strictest laws proved how wrong he was. She had to have kept violating those old laws to stay in control of you for so long, but I don't have any more of a clue what her current identity is now than you do. I came here hoping to figure that out, but she's far too careful."

Not quite believing the door could be entirely gone, Nikhil reached out and swiped a hand through the invisible plane where it had been. "If you could do this all along, why did you stay and endure all the torture I inflicted on you? And don't tell me it was her doing it... she may have been in control but I remember enjoying much of what we did."

Calder grinned at him. "Oh, I know who was in control. She fed the dark cravings in you, encouraging you to act on the impulses that would serve her the best. The nymphaea have always been impulsive, but Meri took those urges to disturbing lengths. When she melded with the dragon and stole his body we knew we couldn't allow her to remain in the Haven. It wasn't until the Diviner saw her path that we discovered the mistake we'd made. She should have been executed, not set free into the world, even if we had cut off her connection to the water's power."

The heat of anger burned inside Nikhil's stomach. If the woman had been executed, he may have never committed the atrocities he did in Belah's absence. His lover might have taken him back. "If she had no power, how in Hell did she succeed in surviving so long? She impersonated my physician from the beginning. I trusted her and she got into my head."

Calder's stance shifted, his shoulders dropping. He turned his hands palm-up in supplication. "A nymphaea's spirit still holds magic. There was no way we could entirely strip her of it. But her ability to shift into other forms was lost to her. As you have discovered, the blood of our races is incredibly powerful on its own. So powerful, shedding it for any but the most sacred reason is a violation of every law of *all* the races. She used her blood in ways that it should never be used. Now we need to turn that knowledge against her. When she reveals herself to me, I will return home and gather what assistance and power I can to hunt her down."

"And sitting in this cell with your pet ursa is going to make her show herself to you?"

"After you release the others on this floor, one of your brothers will personally carry messages to the other facilities, and tell the entire staff that I have assumed control of your mind. Your brother will say that as a precaution you and I have been locked into a cell together until the scientists can discover how to release my hold on you."

Nikhil nodded, understanding the deviousness of the plan, yet it was no guarantee. "There is one problem. I have no intention of sitting in a cell with you while we wait for her to come to us. There are too many other things at stake and having lived with her in my head I doubt she would even fall for such a trick. Unless she sees me in there, it would never work."

"It will work because she is nearly impotent without your power to wield, and because of this..."

Calder raised his arms above his head, stretching toward the ceiling with his head tilted back, his black hair swirling around his shoulders as though moved by some invisible, liquid flow. Before Nikhil's eyes, the other man's body began to shift, his torso elongating and then widening in places. His clothing disappeared, his skin darkened to the color of caramel, his thighs thickened, and dark, familiar tattoos began to wind themselves around his upper arms. Then his skin was slowly covered by clothing that materialized like liquid paint flowing over a fresh surface until the figure was clothed in an outfit identical to Nikhil's dark suit pants and dark-red dress shirt.

Nikhil remained transfixed during the transformation, until a moment later the figure inside the cell lowered his arms, and dipped his head again to face him.

Nikhil stared at himself, dumbstruck. The other figure's eyes widened, his mouth falling open as though he, too, were too surprised for speech. When Nikhil lifted a shaking hand to reach for his doppelganger, the other man did the same in reverse... a perfect mirror image of his movements. Their index fingers met in the center before they both dropped their hands and let out simultaneous, booming laughs.

Nikhil's doppelganger continued to grin at him after Nikhil's laughter stopped and he took a breath, holding his stomach.

"You have me fooled, that's for sure," he said, shaking his head. "I still don't see why you didn't escape and fucking *take over*, if you were capable of all this."

"There are a few reasons for that. Our kind have somewhat transient physical forms—I can't maintain this form for long without an available connection to flowing water. The nearby river provides enough for me to use it here, but if I were to travel, my appearance would return to normal within a day. Fresh blood would do the trick, too, but to take it from unwilling subjects would be perpetuating the same atrocities that allowed Meri to slip away from us."

Nikhil frowned and glanced at the sleeping bear on the cot behind Calder. A wave of tenderness tangled with an urge to protect the young ursa male who he'd come to regard as a sort of surrogate son during his few moments of emotional clarity. He hated that he'd think it, but the ursa had the strongest constitutions—second only to dragons—and if blood needed to be spilled, they would survive. "What about a willing subject?"

Calder gave Nicholas an affectionate glance, shaking his head. "I would never ask that of him. Besides, you and I both know that, while his value may lie in his blood, it is not the taking of it that will help. He will stay with me for now, but when he leaves, he must return to his kind. His family will be our allies in the coming conflict."

Nikhil raised his eyebrows. "You know this because the Diviner told you?"

"Because the water gave me the knowledge. The nymphaea's greatest power is in the manipulation of the flow of time. We can manifest other shapes at will, but gain no particular advantage from any of them the way the dragons, the turul, or the ursa do from their true shapes. Meri is the most powerless of us since she's been banished and stripped of her link to the water. She's relegated to hopping between human bodies, but she's been increasing her power bit by bit over the centuries. Somehow she has managed to steal away every male of my kind, save for me, and the only reason I am still here is thanks to my link to the water. When she sees me through your eyes, I am as transparent as glass—practically invisible to her."

Nikhil remembered a time when they hunted nymphaea more avidly. The satyrs of the race were easily seduced and so the Ultiori captured them frequently, but none of them would divulge the secret to capturing their females. They must have known all along that the true enemy was one of their own.

"How do you know she has stolen the males? Your kind got wise to us after a time. We never left a single one alive."

"On the contrary, they do live. Their connection to the flood tells us so. They are like small tributaries whose flow is frequently interrupted, but we can still sense them—they have not dried up yet. We just don't know where they are or what she's done to them. All we know is that the only way for her to gain more power than she has now is to take over a more powerful body. Keeping them must be a means to that end for her. The only reason she didn't take your body completely was the dragon blood you carry. But you should know until today that blood has been tainted by Meri's essence. I would not trust your old supply, if I were you."

"Noted," Nikhil said. His private study would be one of the next places he visited when he woke Sterlyn up. He would send Naaz on the mission to warn the other facilities of Nikhil's supposed control by this satyr. He regarded

Calder silently for a moment, sensing some reticence to divulge one important bit of information, but the man's mind was too fluid for him to pin down the detail without asking. "You are leaving out something, friend. What is it?"

The other man's features rippled slightly, then reformed with their original shape. Calder's eyes were filled with sadness and he glanced back at the slumbering bear behind him. "Our kind have complicated lives when it comes to finding our mates. I have been caught in Fate's net and am bound by three contradicting vows at the moment. The oldest one must take precedence, and that is my vow to find Meri and deal with her once and for all. But the other two may haunt me as a result. At the start of my journey I vowed that I would not take a mate until my search is done."

"And the other two?" Nikhil asked.

"To be with Nicholas until he is released from this place, which is going to be the easiest to achieve, but the hardest one to let go of. When he returns to his kind, he will no longer need me, but letting go won't be so easy for either of us. And the worst part is that Fate seems to have a true mate in mind for me but I cannot be with her when my original promise is left undone."

Nikhil let out a long sigh of commiseration. "I understand. It seems the curse you bear is knowing all this, though. Is seeing the future something your kind always does?"

"Aye, it is a curse, but one I endure in order to do my job. This perpetual connection I have is not permanent, at least. When I accepted this mission almost a thousand years ago, the Diviner gave me an unbreakable link to the flow of time. Thanks to the Diviner's touch, I won't be rid of it until Meri is dealt with. I just hope that the mate Fate has chosen for me is patient enough to wait."

Nikhil frowned, considering his next question and knowing it should be his last one before he said farewell to the satyr and set about putting their plan into motion. Calder preempted his thoughts before he could speak.

"Yes, I do know your future, but no I will not tell it to you. Just know that you are on the right path at this moment. Trust the river's direction, but don't forget that you have to paddle sometimes, too. Now is time for you to do so. Farewell, friend."

Before his eyes, the glass reappeared between them and Calder pressed his palm against it.

Nikhil nodded in farewell and moved on.

Desiring to waste no more time, he used his power to mentally rouse the others. When he rounded the corner to the last three cells on the floor, his Elites were slowly standing and rubbing their temples. The females inside the cells were also standing, looking dazed but otherwise no worse for wear. He tried not to think about the bloody mess inside the third cell, but was relieved that the prior occupants were now safely away from here.

When he reached the end of the hall, he quickly unlocked and opened both cell doors, then stood back while his Elites and the two females they cared about more than life gaped at him.

"I am releasing all of you today," he said looking at each of them in turn. "You are free to leave, but I would like your help before you go. There is much to explain, so if you are willing, I would prefer to simply *give* you all the knowledge of the events that have transpired over the last day. Once I do, hopefully you will understand what is at stake, and why I wish you to stay and help me if you are willing to."

"Sayid…" Sterlyn began, but Nikhil held up his hand to stop his Elite from going further.

"I am no longer your master, Sterlyn. It's my hope that you will see me as a brother, because our blood binds us as brothers. Allow me to earn my place as a proper commander to you, which is what I believe will be required if we are to overcome our common enemy. The evil that controlled me until today is gone. The proof is in my memories, which I will show you if you open your minds for just a moment. This will be the last time I affect your minds in this fashion, I promise."

The two Elites shared a look, then both of them glanced at the third cell door that was still closed.

"Marcus and Evie should be a part of this," Naaz said.

When Naaz moved to open the door to Evie's cell, Nikhil braced himself for the reaction to come. The other man simply stood there and stared at the carnage in stoic silence. Beside him, Sterlyn cursed and clenched his teeth, his jaw working to hold back more as he turned to glare at Nikhil. The two women gasped and covered their mouths with their hands.

Nikhil closed his eyes, willing them all to say what they were thinking.

In a dark, chilly voice as rough as jagged ice, Naaz said, "Are they dead?"

"No," Nikhil said, his throat tightening around the word enough to nearly strangle him. "You both know Marcus can't die any more than we can. I did not kill Evie, though when I came here earlier that was my intention. I believe you may know more about how they left, don't you? I sensed as much in your minds just before I knocked you out and found the pair of them together."

"Are you telling me the *Void* bled them and cut off Evie's wings before he took them?" Naaz asked, his question punctuated by a sharp protest from Zamirah.

Nikhil exhaled, letting the defensive tension seep away. "No. I did this when Evie's brothers came and took Belah away from me. I wanted revenge on them somehow and she was the nearest target, but self control has eluded me of late."

He closed his eyes and all he saw was blood. Evie's and Marcus's blood and before that his beloved Belah's spilling from her chest as he observed. He'd been nothing more than a passenger inside his own body for all of it, his impulses and the dark, foreign presence compelling him to act. But couldn't speak that aloud to his Elites without the words sounding like hollow excuses.

"I know," Sterlyn said, stepping forward. Behind him the red-haired female moved to his side. Nikhil forced himself to recall the dragon's name. She was no longer a prisoner, but would hopefully become an ally. *Zamirah.* She slipped close to Sterlyn, pressing herself into his side with a sigh of complete contentment that bordered on sexual.

"How can you know? You were under my control all this time."

"The power of the dragon blood you gave me shows me lies sometimes," Sterlyn said. "Evie's turul power does the same, with more consistency, but we both agreed that there were times when you seemed to move under some artificial power. She said you seemed like someone was pulling your strings, like a marionette. This is the first time I've seen you act entirely under your own power—trust me, the difference is striking."

Neela, his goddaughter, swiftly embraced her brother and kissed him on the cheek. Turning her dark brown eyes to Nikhil, she gave him a smile.

"Sterlyn's right. You were not yourself before, but you are now. I remember what you were like before. It's nice to have you back, *Bennu*," she said, stepping close and giving him a kiss as well before resuming her spot by her brother's side. "I am glad to see you have been reborn as the man Belah loved. We will accept whatever knowledge you wish to give us."

Naaz squeezed his sister, holding her protectively close, and gave Nikhil a grim nod of agreement.

Nikhil's throat constricted and his eyes watered in response to the fresh term of endearment Neela gave him. He had indeed been reborn, as the fabled Bennu bird from his ancient home.

Unable to speak, he closed his eyes and recalled the events of the last day, from Belah's moment of realization that his mind was not his own to the clarity revealed when Evie's song had banished the darkness for good. Carefully editing out the details related to Naaz and Neela's connection to Belah's children, he sent the images to the others and then waited while they processed them.

They all stood there with eyes closed, their brows equally creased in concentration. One by one, they opened their eyes and Nikhil braced himself for their responses. They said nothing at first, simply glancing at each other for validation and confirmation. Naaz and Sterlyn nodded solemnly at each other.

"We are at your service, brother," they said in unison.

# CHAPTER 15

*Dragon Monastery, Sunda Islands*
*Present Day*

Marcus opened his eyes when a soft hand brushed across his forehead. The image that greeted him was of a beautiful, dark-haired woman with the bluest eyes he'd ever seen. She gazed down at him solemnly, her irises flickering with inner light.

Something in her aura was familiar, reminding him of the dragons who had carried him and Evie away from Hell.

"Welcome back," she said in a low, soft voice that resonated in his mind the way the black dragon's voice had. "I'm Belah. My brother, Ked, wanted to make sure you were taken care of. Are you in any pain?"

*Belah.* He remembered now, but the last time he'd seen her she'd been naked and bound in ropes, with Nikhil's hand around her throat. A moment later his master had drifted away with her.

It seemed like eons ago that he'd been in that room, secretly keeping tabs on this woman for his master—*former* master. Watching while Evie's two brothers let themselves be marked by her, to be bound as her mates. He'd been instrumental in letting her be taken from them, but also in helping them get her back.

"My pain was earned." he said, his voice rasping through a dry throat, the words trailing off to a cough that made his entire body burn with agony. He hadn't protected either of them in the end. Not this woman, nor Evie. *Evie.*

Before he could voice her name, Belah pressed a hand lightly against his shoulder.

"Evie will recover, and I am well. I can feel the worry in you, Marcus. Contrary to what you believe, you helped us, and no one can fault you for that." She paused, glancing over her shoulder. "My mates will come around in time."

"I promised them Evie would be safe. I was wrong."

Marcus looked away, feeling unworthy of the kindness she gave him. As his gaze drifted over the room, he saw Evie's brothers standing nearby and grimaced. They both glowered at him with their arms crossed. He deserved it.

Belah looked over her shoulder again. "Let him have some space for a little while. Go see how Evie is."

"He lied to us," Lukas said. "After what he let happen, why should we let him live?"

"Because nothing you do can kill him. It would be a waste of effort. He's an Elite Ultiori hunter. They can't be killed, except by dragon fire. If you want specifics, go talk to my brother—he's the only one of us who has ever killed an Elite." Her gaze held theirs, unwavering until the brothers let their arms fall to their sides and they both stalked out of the room.

As he left, Iszak turned back. "Call us if anything happens."

The woman only nodded slightly and turned back to Marcus when the door closed.

She smiled down at him, her gaze filled with sympathy.

"Forgive my mates. They're extraordinarily overprotective of me lately." Her hand rested lightly on her abdomen, the slight gesture more than enough to indicate the reasons.

Marcus chuckled. "I never imagined it was possible for the North brothers to settle down. And both of them with you? My condolences."

Belah laughed, and the entire room brightened. Christ, she was a beautiful woman. He inhaled sharply at the effect she had on him, his brows twitching in confusion. Somehow all his emotions seemed to rise to the surface at once and he felt compelled to confess every one of his sins to her.

"They are my heart, but they're confused and hurting now," she said. "They don't know quite how to deal with everything that has happened, but they'll come around, if you help them."

Marcus closed his eyes. "There's no reason they should come around. I deserve their hatred. If I hadn't been so terrified of losing Evie, I'd never have taken her away. When I promised them she'd be safe until she was rescued, I should have known Nikhil could come at any time."

Belah clutched his chin and he opened his eyes. "You were following a path Fate laid out for you. Never blame yourself for that. Lukas and Iszak will forgive you because I know what's in your heart. I saw every moment of your dreams while you were unconscious. You are linked to my brother in a very special way that I am trying to understand for my own reasons. That blood bond is going to be your redemption. And your love for Evie is as bright as any star. Don't give up on her, Marcus. She will need you."

"She doesn't need me. All I did for her was bring her misery. Is she all right now? That bastard made her bleed. He was so brutal with her."

Belah wrapped her hand around his and squeezed. "She is

fine. We are healing her physical wounds, but she will need to see you for her soul to fully heal. She believes you're dead."

That was some consolation, at least. "Let her believe I'm dead. And please, if you have any sympathy for me, make it the truth. You said it could only be dragon fire that kills me, right? So… you're a dragon. Kill me now." He stretched his arms wide, baring his naked chest to her. The despair inside him pressed like a heavy stone against his breast and he wished for nothing less than oblivion.

She only smiled at him tolerantly and he sensed some deeper understanding in her gaze.

"I won't kill you, Marcus. First, you are more valuable to us alive. I hope you understand this. Second, if I killed you, it would destroy Evie. And my mates would never forgive me if I did that, no matter how much they may wish you dead at the moment."

"She already believes I'm dead. It won't matter."

"Not anymore. Ked is telling her the truth now."

Marcus closed his eyes. In his mind he could even hear the dragon talking. He could feel the dragon's arousal, too, it was no different than he'd felt every time he was close to Evie and somehow it didn't surprise him a bit that his counterpart would feel exactly the same. Yet he longed for her.

"Kill me or free me. I need to be with her if you won't let me die. And trust me, I have enough strength left to get to her if I want to."

Belah stood and gestured toward the door. "You are not a prisoner, Marcus. She is in the bath house with Ked now. Find the widest path and follow it up the hill. You should have no trouble finding my brother."

Marcus sat up and stared out the door. He could see all the way through the living area to the open front door. Outside was a long porch with a flagstone path beyond, surrounded by lush vegetation and lined with stone lanterns that cast a warm glow in the darkness. He craved Evie's contact more than anything, yet he settled back onto the pillow.

"No. She's finally free—I won't burden her with my love any longer. Even if you won't kill me, she is better off believing I am dead."

Belah crossed her arms and scowled down at him. Her blue eyes flashed imperiously. "Just like her brothers were better off believing she was dead for fifty years? Perhaps they were, but it broke their hearts to learn the truth. They would have died to save her, and they deserved the chance to try— to have that choice. Evie deserves a chance, and so do you."

"She *has* a chance. With him."

*Dragon Monastery, Sunda Islands*
*Present Day*

Evie lay limp in Ked's arms. Soft didn't begin to describe how she felt against his skin. But she wasn't moving now, and his mind reeled as to why she might have checked out. She'd been alert for the entire trip. He hoped it was only exhaustion.

Her wounds were healed now, thanks to Gavra's breath during their long trip, but her dark hair was matted and stringy, her skin still streaked with blood.

Sweet Mother, in spite of how utterly wrecked she looked, she was so beautiful. She would be even more beautiful once rested and awake.

When they'd arrived, instead of carrying her down to the secluded mountainside bungalow set aside for him, he had turned and walked along a different path, heading for one of several private bath houses situated over the hot springs bubbling up from beneath the mountain.

He sensed Marcus's consciousness in his mind now,

heard his sister's soft voice, as much through Marcus's link to him as through Ked's link to Belah. It betrayed the closeness of his connection to the man. Marcus likely didn't understand what it meant yet, in spite of what Ked had told him when they started their trip. The unmistakable despair still flooded Marcus's mind—his singular wish to leave this world, buried deep in decades of regret, but still filled with the ache of love for Evie that he never believed he deserved.

Looking down at Evie, he knew she would be the key to bringing Marcus back, even though she was the reason for the depth of his darkness.

Ked let his conjured clothing fade away as he entered the lantern-lit bath house and stepped into the fragrant, steaming pool of water. Once Evie's body was submerged, floating on the support of one of his arms, Ked moved to one of the benches around the edge and sat, cradling her on his lap.

Scented soaps and soft cloths were scattered around the edge of the pool, and he used them to wash her. Over and over, he brushed the cloth down her arms, over her chest, over her back, careful of the newly healed marks where her regrown wings would manifest when she shifted. He slowly washed away all evidence of her torture. She was so strong. She had to be, to have withstood so much agony and still maintained consciousness for when he found her.

His own sister hadn't managed as much so long ago, and carrying Evie away from that place had left Ked with the same dark anger he'd experienced that day he'd rescued Belah. Just after he and Gavra had landed and he silently requested that Belah see to Marcus, he shared a long look with her. Belah was his closest sibling, even without having shared that ordeal, and her expression had been filled with purest sympathy when he'd carried Evie away, as if to let him know she understood his pain.

He ventured a surge of dark breath now to check on Evie's state, and was relieved to note that she was merely sleeping. The combination of Aodh and Gavra's breaths could be potent, and healing could be an exhausting process when her body was urged to do it so quickly. Once her body was clean, he simply held her close.

"Now that I've found you, I will keep you safe. For the rest of our lives, you'll want for nothing, and the enemy will never touch you again. That, I can promise." He inhaled slowly, reveling in her closeness, but not allowing himself to become aroused by her soft, naked body against his. All that mattered was that she was here in his arms now. He could wait an eternity for everything that would come after.

"Are you sure you can promise that?" Evie groggily replied.

Ked tightened his embrace and looked down at her. "I don't make idle promises. I also promise to destroy him the first chance I get."

Evie only stared at him, her eyes wide and assessing. Ked held his breath, as though waiting for her judgment, for the first time worried about what another being thought of him. What must she think? He was probably terrifying her with his power, which he realized was nearly blocking out the sparse light in the dim room.

With a slow inhalation, he pulled the darkness back into his lungs and the lights brightened.

Evie's expression grew only grimmer.

"Don't hide yourself from me," she said. She shifted around on his lap, pulling herself up into a sitting position and twisting to face him. "I know you are the one. My One. I want to know every part of you, even the darkest part."

"I am nothing but the darkest part," he said, though at least one part of him felt distinctly like it might start to glow a little bit of its own accord.

Evie's aura brightened and her mouth twitched. "I beg to differ," she said and reached between them to rest a hand against his stiffening cock.

"We don't… you don't have to…" Fuck, why was he stuttering over simply being touched by her? Ked gave up speech and let out a low groan when she stroked him, her hand slowly exploring his entire length beneath the warm water.

His eyes never left hers, and what he saw in her gaze brought back another surge of his power. Just as dark this time, but not with the need for vengeance against his enemy. This time, it slid over him like midnight velvet, arousing all his senses and rendering the lantern light a sultry, intimate glow around them. *Privacy* was the thought that had gone through his mind, even though the residents of the monastery had a tendency to give him a wide berth. He simply wanted to create a more intimate cocoon for himself and Evie if she had the urge to become so familiar with him so quickly.

"I like that darkness," Evie whispered. The dimmed quality of the light cast Evie in coppery gold highlights, the water glistening on her skin making her look gilded.

Ked's eyebrow twitched. "Does it feel good to you?" In his entire existence, he'd never once heard a positive comment about this particular use of his power.

She leaned into him and let her lips brush his ear as she continued to stroke him. "I think anything that comes from you would feel good. That's how it's supposed to work when you find your true mate. Everything you are is beautiful, and the darkness suits my mood."

"You said Marcus was your true mate before. I thought turul only ever had one," he said.

Testing her this way wasn't fair. He knew that her connection to the other man was only due to the change Marcus had undergone after being transfused with Ked's blood. Evie's prior connection could have been with anyone, as long as they'd had a measure of Ked's blood inside them. Of course, it hadn't been anyone. It had been Marcus—a Blessed. Ked distinctly sensed the hand of Fate involved in the situation.

"Marcus was, but I know you are, too. I can't explain it other than to say I think it was meant to be this way. He died in my arms, and then there you were. And I have never wanted to be with anyone as much as I want to be with you now. You're going to mark me, aren't you?"

Ked closed his eyes and released a soft hiss. He would love nothing more than to mark her now. To spin her around in the dark and lay her down on the thick velvet of night he'd conjured around them. To cover her body with his and fill her up with every single bit of him. But now was not the time, not so soon after her ordeal.

They may be entwined in the dark now, but he couldn't keep her shrouded any longer. He wrapped his hand around hers and stilled her stroking. It was all he could do not to squeeze her around him and urge her onward.

"You need to know the truth before you commit to me, Evie. Marcus isn't dead. Not truly. Before I can mark you, I need you to talk to him. Make him want to live."

She struggled to pull away from his grip and he reluctantly released her. "Take me to him," Evie said tightly, standing and hauling herself out of the pool. She glanced around and headed toward the towels stacked on shelves in one corner, robes hanging on hooks beside them. "I have to see him before I'll believe you. His heart fucking *stopped* when he was lying in my arms. He shouldn't have even been in my cell with me, but we hadn't touched each other in so long... I craved it too much not to have you one last time."

Ked closed his eyes and silently cursed at the word she

just used. He didn't even think she was aware she'd done it. *I craved it too much not to have* you *one last time.*

Ked left the pool, absently clothing himself within the two long steps it took to reach her. She cast a sidelong glance at his conjured attire and muttered what he thought was *"fucking dragons"* while shrugging into a soft, woven robe. She winced as the fabric draped over her shoulders, as though her skin was still tender from the torture she'd endured.

As she closed the robe around her, she seemed to wobble, her face growing pale. She reached out a shaky hand to steady herself, but hit only air. Just as she started to topple, Ked caught her, picked her up, and cradled her in his arms.

"You shouldn't be so weak now. Not after Gavra's healing."

Evie let out a bitter laugh. "It's never happened this quick before. Usually it takes a few more days."

"What has happened, Evie? If I'm going to help you, I need to know."

"I'm pregnant. Again."

"Sweet Mother, Evie," he said. "I'm not taking you to see him until you tell me everything." *He'll live,* Ked thought bitterly. In spite of the memories from both Marcus and Evie that he'd already experienced during the trip, he found it difficult to find sympathy for a man who would have turned against a woman as precious as Evie, especially if she was carrying his child.

She clung to him, twining her hands at the back of his neck and burying her face in his chest. Her hot tears seeped through his shirt, warming his skin as he carried her down the path to his private bungalow.

Lanterns lit the high-ceilinged bedroom in a comforting glow. The windows up here had no glass in them, thanks to a temperate climate and an utter absence of insects and other wildlife living within close proximity to the monastery. Evie gasped when she saw the view. Nothing but endless, starlit sky stretched for miles, only broken here and there by lush mountain peaks illuminated by a huge moon hanging low and full over the horizon.

"The last time I saw a view like that was fifty years ago," Evie said. "It was the last time I saw the sky before you pulled me out of there."

~

*Canadian Rockies*

*Spring 1966*

T

he place Marcus took them to turned out to be a huge research compound hidden deep in the Canadian wilderness. Evie's alarm bells went off when they rounded a bend in the curving, narrow road that led through the mountains to get to it. Marcus slowed on the rain-slick pavement and pulled up to a painted concrete guard station and a huge security gate. Beyond the gate, Evie saw more wet road winding up higher through the trees and foggy mist.

In spite of the trepidation that overtook her, she held her tongue. She'd never been so bombarded with conflicting signals in her life. The Wind's messages one moment would carry a warning of danger ahead, but at another moment, would tell her that she was still headed in the right direction.

Finally, she just clenched her teeth tighter and twined her fingers through Marcus's after he put the car in gear again and moved slowly through the now-open gate. She had to believe they were doing the right thing, and even if they were stepping into dangerous territory, at least they would be together.

Around a few more curves in the road, the landscape flattened and they headed downhill into a narrow valley. Along one bank of a raging, glacial river, the compound glimmered like a line of diamonds laid out in a row.

It took Evie a moment to register that what she saw were windows reflecting the sparse vestiges of sunlight that broke through the clouds above them. The facility seemed to be made entirely of glass, which was at odds with the image she'd had in her head of what they might be headed toward. Of course, in her irrational worry, she'd imagined being captured by the enemy and held in a dark dungeon built of impenetrable stone, with iron bars and no windows to see the sky.

The place couldn't be that bad if it had such endless views from every room.

Once inside, she managed to relax. The facilities were comfortable, the people friendly. The entire procedure seemed more like checking into a luxury hotel than anything else. So much so that she could easily pretend that was precisely what they were doing. Not running away, but enjoying a romantic holiday together.

They were escorted to a luxurious suite of rooms on an upper floor with an entire wall of windows overlooking a steep, pine-covered slope and ravine where the white-waters of the river sliced through.

"The director will join you shortly after dinner," the young, pretty woman who had escorted them up told them before retreating back through the door and leaving them alone together.

While they were settling in, the sun set at the end of the ravine in spectacular fashion, enough to steal Evie's breath and make her want to sing at the same time. In the wake of the descending golden orb, an eerie mist built at the other end, stealing down from the mountains behind them and blanketing the lower reaches over the river. It was idyllic, to say the least, yet Evie's skin prickled with a sense of dread as she stood staring out the window.

Marcus stole up behind her and wrapped his strong arms around her shoulders, pressing his lips to her cheek.

"We made it," he said. "It's even better than I'd hoped, but you don't seem sold yet. What is it?"

She closed her eyes and sighed. He'd always been particularly perceptive to her moods, thanks to the faint bond of magical energy they shared through his Blessing. It was an artificial bond, however—not the bond he should have with the dragon mate he was meant for. And not the bond she would hopefully someday have with her one true mate. Yet she couldn't deny she loved him deeply and believed in her grandmother's gifts enough to be here with Marcus in a place where she didn't feel entirely comfortable. She simply had to have faith that she was, indeed, on the right path.

"It's…" She was about to simply say *nothing* when a knock sounded at their door.

They opened it and a starkly beautiful, distinguished-looking woman stood on the other side, wearing a lab coat and carrying a clipboard along with a doctor's medical case.

Before entering, she reached out her hand and greeted them both warmly. "Marcus Calais and Evie North? It is a pleasure. I am Dr. Meryl St. George, director of the Alexandria Institute's research division. We are so glad you chose our humble organization for your needs. Have you been briefed on how your stay here will work?"

"Yes," Marcus said. "You're a scientific research facility and you want to use us as test subjects in exchange for giving us sanctuary."

Dr. St. George grimaced. "I wouldn't use such harsh language. You are a far cry from lab rats. The entire reason we opened this facility was to *save lives*. Lives that may otherwise be needlessly lost in the conflict. Right now war is an inevitability, but through the Alexandria Institute's research, I hope we can find a way to help peace prevail. I choose to employ science to wage war *against* war."

Evie listened closely and watched the woman. There was something unusual about her, but she couldn't put her finger on what it was. Everything she said was true. Nothing about her mannerisms was at odds with her words. Yet she sensed something hidden beneath the surface of her seemingly honest exterior. Either she really was telling the truth, or she was so good at lying the Winds couldn't even tell.

Marcus seemed perfectly comfortable with the woman's speech, however. He invited her to sit and they talked for several more minutes, sharing their opinions about the war. Evie only listened, seeking out any hint of deception from the doctor.

"What do you need from us?" Marcus asked during a pause in conversation.

"That's the easy part. Nothing more than a few blood samples to start with. Once we've analyzed them, we'll have a better grasp on which of our testing programs you're best suited for. I can take the samples now, and the two of you will be free to enjoy yourselves for the next few days until we get the results. In between testing programs, all our residents are expected to contribute to the upkeep and management of the facilities. Our facilities manager will set up an appointment with you both to determine your skillsets. I understand from the forms you filled out that you have Aeronautics training, is that correct, Marcus? That's a valuable skill you kept away from the military. I'm impressed."

"Flying was always my first love," Marcus said and blindly reached for Evie's hand.

She gripped it back, only then realizing her palms were coated in a sheen of clammy moisture. This doctor wanted her *blood*. That was absolutely not something she was prepared to do.

"I can't," she whispered, yanking her hand from Marcus's and staring at the syringe and collection of glass tubes the doctor had fished out of her bag. "Please, don't ask me to do this. *Please.*"

In all the cautionary tales she'd heard growing up, the strongest theme was to never let your own blood be shed by another, and never give it willingly. That was what the enemy wanted. Their reasons were never entirely clear to her. In some tales, they instinctively fed on her kind like leeches or mosquitoes. In others they were monsters, willfully hunting down and draining any member of the higher races for sustenance.

"Evie? Are you all right?" Marcus immediately stood and went to her, pulling her into his arms and stroking a large, comforting palm over her hair. "You don't have to. It's okay." Turning to the doctor he asked, "She doesn't have to, does she? She's terrified of needles, and we didn't know this was part of the process."

The doctor frowned and reached into her bag. "Blood samples are ideal, but no, we have other methods."

Marcus sighed. "Good. I am happy to give you as much blood as you need to make up for it. Just please, don't take hers."

"Not to worry," the doctor said, giving them both a warm smile. "A hair sample will do, provided we get a bit of the root."

Evie closed her eyes, feeling like a fool for being so terrified. "No. It's all right. It will be for a good cause right?" she asked, hopeful and trying to do her best to talk herself into enduring an unpleasant experience. She'd shared bodily fluids with Marcus for an entire year. If he could shed his blood for this, so could she.

# CHAPTER 17

## EVIE

*Dragon Monastery, Sunda Islands*
*Present Day*

"You have strong instincts," Ked said softly, stroking his hand in slow circles over her back while Evie told her story.

"If only I didn't routinely ignore them," she replied, sinking against him while they watched the moon rise.

She ached so much for more of him, but didn't have the strength to ask. The memories of her ordeal bombarded her, yet something about being near him made it impossible for her to hold them in. It had something to do with his power, she knew, though she'd never encountered a Shadow so strong before, and certainly never one that could affect her mind so acutely. In his presence, a veil seemed to drift over every other emotion, every other memory, leaving only the most prominent, terrifying, heartbreaking memories and feelings of loss, fear, and despair looming monstrously in the darkness. The only way to dispel those shadows was to purge them from her mind by letting him take ownership.

"You're doing this to me, aren't you?" she asked. "Making me relive it all? And I have, since you found me. The entire way up here, I dreamed of the first year with Marcus. If you witnessed any of that, you should know what kind of man he is."

"He isn't the same man you ran away with," Ked said. "But I believe a part of that man still lives. What he is now is closer to what I am."

Evie glanced up at him, incredulous at the sound of resignation in his tone. Did he believe his nature was so terrible that he didn't wish it on another?

She reached up and brushed her hand down the side of his face. Ked closed his eyes and held her even tighter.

"If what he became is closer to what you are now, then it's no wonder I loved him more after he changed than I did before."

"Tell me what happened, Evie."

"Under two conditions," she said.

"Anything." And somehow, with that one word, Evie knew he meant everything he'd said to her in the bath earlier. She would want for nothing, and he would kill the man who did this to her, even though she wasn't entirely sure that man deserved to die.

"If Marcus really is alive, make sure he stays that way, but don't tell him I'm pregnant."

Ked's brows drew together and he started to shake his head in disagreement. Evie caught his square jaw between her hands, astonished at how solid and warm he felt.

"Promise me. Yes, the child is his, but this is the third baby I've conceived since undergoing their horrible experiments. None of them survived to term."

"Children conceived with Marcus?" Ked asked softly, as though hesitant to delve into the subject.

"No… this is the first with him. They kept him away from

me for most of the time we were there. We rarely saw each other." She closed her eyes, remembering the ordeal. "The two other babies were conceived when the other Elites were forced to couple with me. I'll tell you about it all, if you promise you'll keep him alive and keep this a secret."

She hoped beyond measure that this child would live, and that its father would, too. That she'd conceived so quickly must mean that her desperate attempt at completing the turul mating ritual and sharing breath with him had worked, but if Marcus died…

"I had no intention of killing him—he is too much a part of me to even consider it. What's your other condition?"

Evie's heart pounded as she stared into his dark, fathomless eyes, suddenly finding it impossible to get those last two words out. Here she was, in *his* arms, after two hundred years of believing he didn't even exist.

After his change, Marcus had incited something like this sensation in her, but even then it had never felt this strong—this all-encompassing. Like the entire universe was a cacophony of clanging bells signaling that *yes*, she'd finally found her true mate.

Before she could even spur her voice into action, his mouth came down on hers, answering her second condition without a single word. Those words she'd been unable to say —*"Kiss me"*—wound up translated into another language as their lips collided and their tongues entwined. Only this language was unconditional, and she realized she never even needed to ask. She could have had his lips at any moment. She could have *all of him* at any moment with the smallest signal of her desire. The very idea of putting conditions on how they shared each other seemed entirely alien to her now, and she wished she could take back the request—the suggestion that she had to qualify her sharing before she would do it.

No. He gave everything to her without even having to be asked. She would do the same. At least, she would as soon as she reclaimed control of her mouth and her voice.

An infinite, wonderful moment later, he pulled back and she took a breath. She stared up at him, lost in the dark gaze, then smiled at the tinge of pink on his cheeks.

Ked raised an eyebrow, but his flushed, swollen lips stayed grimly pressed together, unsmiling.

"You were going to tell me more," he said.

Evie closed her eyes, wishing she could just stay lost in his embrace. She'd never realized how comforting darkness could feel until he'd wrapped her inside his version of it. Usually being trapped in the dark made her feel more alone, but with him, it was different. When he held her, his power blotted out everything but their two souls, bright and shining, like a pair of diamonds on black velvet.

But there was something missing. The something that had brought them together.

Marcus.

"He was dying," she said softly. "He died in front of me."

~

*CANADIAN ROCKIES*

*Spring 1966*

S

omething didn't taste right about their breakfast the morning after their arrival.

Marcus, the most voracious eater Evie had ever seen, didn't seem fazed by it. And she had to admit, it was a spectacular spread. She didn't blame him, either, after spending a week on the road living on peanut butter sandwiches. Her own stomach growled and she took a few bites of fried potatoes and eggs. Then tried the oatmeal.

There was a weird, metallic tang to the meal that seemed *off*. Even the coffee and orange juice had it. She shrugged and ate, because she was as hungry as Marcus looked. She was glad she did, a little later. Being fed and bathed and having the liberty to enjoy the day with him worry-free was one of the reasons they'd done this.

They would have to contribute their efforts soon, but today, she just wanted to lounge inside with him. She was grateful for the rainy weather outside, too. If it were a sunny day, she'd be itching to find the nearest secluded ledge among the nearby mountains and fly, after giving Marcus an excuse that she wanted some time to herself for a little while.

But today, the rain made her happy they had this safe little sanctuary to hide away in. After breakfast they simply fell back into bed, giddy with their freedom, and made love for hours before falling asleep together in each other's arms.

THE SENSATION of something gripping her ankles was what drew Evie out of sleep first. It was unexpected, yet not unpleasant. Her head swam as though she were drunk, and she tried to remember if they'd had anything to drink with breakfast.

Through the haze, she heard Marcus's loud and frantic yells. "Let her the fuck go! You can have me for your fucked up experiments, but let her go!"

The deep, calm, and eerily monotonous tone of the other voice was foreign to her. "Marcus, Marcus, Marcus, you have no concept of how valuable you both are to our research. Dr. St. George and I have been looking for specimens like you both for *centuries*. Longer, really, but my researchers only had the technology to begin the right experiments recently."

Evie shook her head to dispel the last of the haze from it.

She raised a hand to her face and saw that her wrist, too, was cuffed to an anchor somewhere beneath the cold table she lay on.

"What happened?" she asked. "Marcus?"

"Ah, she's conscious." The chilly feminine lilt of Dr. St. George's voice drifted over to her, and a moment later, her distinguished face came into view. "Tell me, Ms. *North*. Would you like to share your secrets with your lover, or shall I?"

How had she not sensed it when this woman walked into the room? How had she not sensed it in the others she'd met the day before? Ultiori Hunters were crafty, but they couldn't hide their natures for very long when encountered up close. They gained the advantage by being able to sense the other races before they were sensed themselves. Only an Elite could have duped her so well, but even now this woman seemed decidedly *human*.

The large, imposing man behind her was definitely *not* entirely human, though. Power exuded from his very pores and his gaze flickered between her and Marcus with hungry interest.

A motor began to whine beneath her, and slowly the cold, steel table she lay on tilted upward, raising her to her feet. She caught sight of Marcus several feet away, chained naked to a bar above his head and looking back at her in utter anguish.

Soon, Evie's feet rested on a ledge at the end of the table. Chains jangled behind her and her wrist restraints shifted. She glanced over her shoulder to see the table being moved away, and the doctor raised Evie's arms up to attach her chains to a similar bar that hung above her head.

"Are you an Elite? Is that how I didn't know you when we met?"

Dr. St. George shook her head. "Not even close. Thank

you, by the way, for volunteering to give your blood yesterday. So very brave of you, considering it had to be at odds with your true instincts. Turul are so very *good* at wheedling the truth out of a situation without even having to ask the right questions. Why don't you explain to Marcus what you *really* are?"

"You don't have to say anything, Evie. I'll get us out of here." Marcus wrenched against his bindings, his entire body going taut and his muscles straining so hard that concrete dust drifted down from the ceiling.

Dr. St. George glanced up and hummed slightly. "Need to get stronger anchors in the future. But you won't be up there long, not once my *Sayid* has his way with you."

The disturbingly silent man stepped over to a tray covered with surgical instruments and picked up a scalpel. Something was odd about him, though. He moved almost mechanically, like a puppet on strings. And yet the doctor had called him "my *Sayid*", which Evie knew meant "Master" in another language.

"No!" Evie yelled, when she saw him head toward Marcus with with the shining blade.

With a sure flick of his wrist, the man sliced a vein in the inner elbow of Marcus's bound and upstretched arm. Then another in the opposite arm. Blood streamed from the cuts down over his thick biceps.

Tears streamed from Evie's eyes and she imagined it was his blood, warm and salty, coating her face. She had done this to him for being ignorant of the trap they walked into, for ignoring her instincts.

The man aimed the scalpel at a lower spot, closer to Marcus's shoulder on his inner arm.

"The first was just a small vein," Dr. St. George explained, her voice close enough to Evie's ear for her to feel warm breath that made her recoil with its stench of low-tide. "The next cut will be bigger, unless you show Marcus the truth."

"Marcus, I'm so sorry," Evie said, regretting every moment of the selfish secrecy that led them to this. She should have broken turul laws to protect him. It was too late now.

She let out a cry that echoed through the lab. In her own ears it never changed in timbre or force, but from the widening of Marcus's eyes, she knew he had to recognize it. He was an aviator, after all, and loved all flying creatures—birds of prey, in particular—for their aerodynamic properties as much as their beauty. It was one of the many reasons she loved him.

She had no doubt that he recognized the cry of a falcon coming from her throat. Just as he must recognize the shape of her body when she shifted into a much larger version of that bird a moment later.

The cuffs around her ankles tightened when she flapped her wings and pulled against them, her first instinct to swoop down onto the doctor's head and claw out her eyes. But no... there would be no swooping. Her wrist bindings had fallen away when her fingertips had shrunk down to wing tips, the narrow bones of her wings too small to be cuffed, but she could do nothing with her talons still bound tightly. Nothing but let out more cries of anguished desperation.

Finally she gave up and shifted back, falling to her knees on the small platform that her ankles were still tethered to.

"I'm sorry Marcus. It's my fault we're even here. My fault they're keeping us." To the doctor, she said, "Please, let him go—he is just a human man. You have no use for him."

Dr. St. George stepped around to face her and crouched to meet her eyes. She touched Evie's chin and the acrid scent of industrial hand cleanser hit her nostrils. It wasn't the scent that caused Evie to pull away in disgust, though—an even stronger aroma of rotting fish emanated from the woman.

"Quite the contrary, young lady. You were instrumental in bringing him to us. He is Blessed. But he is still missing the secret ingredient to make him an Elite."

With that, the man with the scalpel dropped his hand in a graceful arc. At the end of the arc, his wrist moved in a little sweep, slicing the scalpel deep into Marcus's thigh. A torrent of blood gushed out from Marcus's femoral artery and his life's blood flooded over his leg and onto the floor beneath him.

Evie screamed and lunged for Marcus, but her ankle restraints kept her too far beyond reach of him. Still, she scrabbled at the blood-covered floor, struggling to reach him to stanch the flow of blood.

She yanked at her feet and shifted again, beating her wings frantically and hoping that the restraints would slip off her talons somehow. They only grew tighter around her ankles with each tug, like Chinese finger traps shrinking around her the more she sought to escape. Feathers floated around the room, stirred by her struggle until she finally fell to the floor again, exhausted and panting in her human form.

"No. Marcus, please don't die." She buried her head in her blood-covered hands.

A pair of feet came into view, clad in blue surgical booties, tracking through the blood.

Evie looked up to see the doctor again, moving a wheeled IV stand to Marcus's side and prepping his upraised arm with a swab. Another figure passed before her eyes, clad similarly in blue scrubs, but the huge, brutal man who had done the cutting was nowhere to be seen.

A different large man knelt down in front of Marcus and let out a soft curse before wrapping a tourniquet swiftly around Marcus's upper thigh and pulling it taut. The most astounding thing happened then.

Evie couldn't quite believe her eyes, and even ceased struggling against her bonds when the man took a deep breath and exhaled slowly, blowing out against the wound that still seeped blood from Marcus's thigh. Before her eyes, the wound sealed shut.

"It's done," the man said in a deep voice devoid of any emotion. "Shall I do the other wounds? What about hers?"

The doctor answered with a curt nod. "Get it done. Take her down and put her in a fresh cell on the lower level, then come back and monitor him. I need to make sure *Sayid* is satisfied and escort him back to Cairo. He has already been here too long."

"When will you return to oversee the first round of tests?" A new voice asked the question from somewhere behind Evie.

The doctor let out a sigh, and Evie closed her eyes, hoping to catch some nuance of the truth about her from the breath she'd expelled, but all she got was more aquatic rot.

"I'll be back in three days, but *Sayid* won't be able to return for six months. We will have to proceed as far as we can without him."

"We should transfer them to the Mexico facility, if he's worried," the man behind her said.

"No. They're too valuable to move. Any time they leave the facility, we offer an invitation for a breach. *Sayid* will simply have to adjust his schedule if he wants to be here. We can only attempt the most crucial tests once a year, anyway." She checked Marcus's bindings, double-checked the tube that attached to Marcus's arm. Evie could only watch ineffectually from the floor, tugging at her bindings. The doctor stared down at her in disgust. "Sterlyn, control her, please, and clean up this mess when you're done. I will see you in a few days."

"Yes, doctor," the man said as the doctor left the room.

The man in front of her followed, and in their absence, Evie pulled as hard as she could against her bindings. She didn't need her feet. If she shifted they'd heal, anyway. The pain nearly made her pass out, but she clawed at the bloody floor, trying to reach Marcus's limp form anyway.

"Stop, please," a soft voice said. "Even if you get out of your bindings, there's no way out of the facility. Trust me, I have tried."

Evie stilled her struggling and turned to look at the unseen man who had stayed behind.

She stared up into the bluest eyes she'd ever seen, and a spark of recognition seemed to flare for a moment. It ignited a tiny flame inside her that she didn't realize even existed.

But then he blinked. His blue eyes were hidden for a split second, and the connection she thought they had disappeared entirely, replaced by a cold gaze.

Evie studied the man's beautiful face, wishing like hell that feeling would return, but it didn't.

"I need to take you to your room," he said.

Evie was too flummoxed to object.

That was the spark her mother had told her about. She knew it instinctively. But it had fizzled with this man. She kept looking up at him now, willing it to return, but it didn't happen again.

He carried her down a dark hallway, then fumbled to unlock another door.

Just before he carried her inside, he lifted a hand to her chin and made her look at him. His brows furrowed and his lips pressed together. He had the most anguished look in his eyes for a split second before the look cleared. Then he met her gaze.

"*Sayid* and Dr. St. George have us all at a disadvantage. They eventually kill most of the females who come here, but you're too precious. Please don't piss them off. We can't protect you. I need you as much as the others do. The happier they are with their test subjects, the easier it is on the rest of us. I'm so sorry, Evie."

With that, he laid her down on the bed and left silently through the door.

Her tears began to flow at the sound of the heavy bolt locking behind him.

# CHAPTER 18

*Dragon Monastery, Sunda Islands*
*Present Day*

"Six months—he was gone for that long? And the man who helped you…" Ked trailed off.

Evie closed her eyes, remembering the kindness granted to her by Sterlyn that first night. Yet how cold he was to her after that. Dr. St. George would oversee initial tests but Evie rarely saw the woman in person again after that, and the man they all seemed to fear and revere in equal measure was only there for a day or two at a stretch. Evie saw no one else but Sterlyn and his counterpart, Naaz. The two men were the antithesis of each other, yet somehow seemed to have the same trapped look in their eyes when they talked to her.

"I know you're thinking how in the world I didn't manage to escape if the king was away from the castle, and the soldiers left in charge were so deferential to me. I did try, but they just looked so sad every time I asked. It was Sterlyn who finally told me why."

~

*Ultiori Compound*
*1967*

"HE'S GONE FOR *MONTHS*, yet you two still just do his bidding. Why? I know you both have enough magic in you to easily overpower the doctor."

Evie had made the argument so many times and received no answer. If they were all prisoners here and the true master was absent, why the hell couldn't they just leave? Especially if the men who commanded the place in their master's absence had the keys and wanted to escape just as badly.

Sterlyn was the one who broke first. After hearing her needling him and calling him a fucking coward for a week straight, he finally threw her empty dinner tray against the wall so hard it bent.

"Don't you think I *want* to be free of those two? I can't. They're too smart for all of us, and too careful. The second you get free, the woman I love dies. *Sayid* employs magic not even I can unravel to track our activity. As far as I know, he's learned to do it all himself, too. He has a thousand years of experience on all of us. He gets into our *heads* when he's here. He *stays* in the heads of the other hunters—the ones who aren't like me and Naaz. He doesn't need to coerce them into following him the way he does to us. They just *do*."

Evie sank down on her cot. She normally enjoyed the moments when Sterlyn would come and sit with her while she ate. Tonight she regretted haranguing him about helping her escape. But she'd grown weary of asking about Marcus every time and receiving vague replies. She'd been there nearly a year already, but Sterlyn still refused to answer those questions aside from telling her that Marcus was alive.

"I'm sorry," Evie said. "You have no idea how he does it? How he controls you?"

"It must be the blood he transfused us with at the beginning. It made me crazy for the first few weeks after it happened. I'd have sucked the man's cock if he'd asked then. All I wanted was more. The power was *incredible*. I felt like I was whole for the first time in my life. Like I'd been missing a piece of myself that he'd managed to give me. Life had new meaning, until I met Zamirah."

Evie stared down at his dejected form where he slumped against the wall beside the door to her cell. Sterlyn had already told her the story of meeting and falling for the female dragon he and Naaz had hunted and captured more than a decade ago. He'd been a loyal Elite until that moment, and from his words, Evie could tell it was his Blessing bleeding through that had attracted him to Zamirah.

He had rejected his orders to bring her in, but Naaz had made him do it anyway. "We fail and he'll know. He always knows," Naaz had told him.

Ever since, he'd tried and failed to find a way for them both to escape.

Evie would have hoped Marcus might feel the same about her, but since that horrible day when she'd been forced to watch him bleed almost to death, she hadn't seen him. She would do anything to see him, but neither Naaz nor Sterlyn were susceptible to bribery. They both had loved ones locked away in the bowels of this place and could do nothing but continue to follow orders to keep them safe.

"Please help me," she said. "I just need to know he's all right."

Sterlyn turned his tortured blue gaze to meet hers. "He isn't okay," he said bitterly. "Because you're locked up down here, he will *never* be okay. Not until we find a way to get away from that bastard and burn this place to the ground."

He let out a harsh sigh and shook his head. "Sayid doesn't permit us to see them—to see our lovers. But even if Marcus were allowed to visit you, or willing to break the rules to, he doesn't want you to see what he's become, which is understandable."

Evie's eyes widened. "What do you mean? What has he become?"

Sterlyn closed his eyes and whispered the words. "He's an Elite Hunter, like me. A monster. And more ruthless than either I or Naaz ever was. At least, he's afraid that's how you'll see him."

Evie closed her eyes, holding back tears. She only wanted to see him to make sure he was safe. But this… this was more than she'd anticipated.

"You made him like you. Why?"

"He's special. I think you knew that already, being a turul. Why do you think you tolerate talking to me so much? I'm like him, so is Naaz. It took Naaz and me awhile to learn why *Sayid* wanted us, in particular. Why we were the ones who were cursed with the right physiology to accept the blood he gave us. The dragon blood in our veins would kill a normal human. But us, it simply makes stronger."

To illustrate, he held up his hands, palms facing up. Glimmering white smoke rose from them, like the fog she remembered rising from the river outside. Before her eyes, he gestured, crafting the cloud of smoke into the form of a dragon that expelled a tiny, white flame before taking wing and flying straight to her.

The little dragon flitted around her head silently, spouting flames at her intermittently. Evie giggled and swatted at it, but it evaded her, finally hovering before her face, its tiny legs curled up under its belly and its wings flapping slowly. The details of it were uncannily realistic. When she reached out a finger to tap the center of its belly, it disappeared in a puff of smoke. She was oddly sad to see it go.

"That's my essence," Sterlyn said. "I could use that power to control your mind, if I wanted to. I could use it for so many things. That's what we do, though. We hunt your kind, and the other races. Dragons especially. We use our nature to seduce you—because your kind are always attracted to a Blessed—then use our dragon power to keep you docile while we lock you up for his experiments. This combination is deadly to the rest of you. It makes us crave your blood enough to hunt you, and makes us powerful enough to subdue you. Luring you and Marcus here was the highest profile catch we've ever had—a Blessed *and* a turul princess. The only thing that could have topped it is if both of you had been dragons."

"What experiments?" Evie asked. For the past year, she'd only been held captive. Trapped, with her blood drawn daily, but nothing more.

Sterlyn closed his eyes. "If I could protect you from them, I would, but I can't even protect Zamirah from them. Stay strong, Evie."

She let out a harsh breath. "Fine, I can deal with whatever those fuckers throw at me. Just please try to convince Marcus to come see me? If I'm going to be trapped here, I want to know he's safe."

He stood and knocked at the door, signaling Naaz to let him out.

"I'll try," he said. "Forgive me if he's not what you expect when he comes to you."

TWO DAYS LATER, the sound of the bolt sliding open in her door roused Evie from half-sleep. She sat up abruptly as the door swung open. Before the interior fluorescent lights flickered on, all she saw was a large, decidedly male, and very familiar silhouette in the doorway, which disappeared when Marcus turned wordlessly and shut the door behind him.

"I'm sorry I didn't come sooner," he said. "I didn't know how to face you, after what they did to me."

Evie barely even heard the words. Her eyes welled with tears. It was *him*. She knew it without even seeing his face. It was crystal clear when the lights in her room finally flickered on and she could see all of him.

Her entire body ached as though she'd been beaten. Her soul thrummed with need to connect with him.

She shook her head. It couldn't be him. Sure, it was Marcus, without a doubt, but something about him had changed. She'd always been attracted to him—he was one of the most beautiful men she'd ever met, after all. Yet, she'd never had such an all-encompassing craving to be with him before. Like she might just die if he didn't hold her in his arms.

He was the *One*. The singular person who could fill the void in her soul that she didn't even recognize needed filling until this moment. She closed her eyes, trying to gather herself. As she pulled in a breath, she marveled at the fact that her race's laws weren't based on a myth. This draw to him was too real to deny.

"Are you all right, Evie?" he asked.

When she opened her tear-moistened eyes, she saw him take a hesitant step forward, then pause as though he wasn't sure he should go to her. But she needed to feel him so much.

"Marcus… By the Winds, you're all right." She stood and rushed to him, desperate for his embrace. Just as she got to him, his hands shot up and gripped her shoulders, holding her back.

"No, Evie. I'm only here because Sterlyn was worried

about you. I can't…" His face twisted into an anguished knot. "I can't keep you safe unless I do what Sayid asks. The second we cross that line, we're both dead."

"No! I need you, Marcus. You don't know what it's like being locked up in here."

Marcus closed his eyes. A teardrop seeped out of one corner. "I know, Evie. I've seen every corner of this place. I've been locked up for months, too. But I'm going out now."

He reached up and cupped her cheek. "I promise you, if I can find a way to get us out, I will. Even if I die trying."

Then he left, and Evie fell back onto her bed feeling even more lost than before. She shouldn't have been drawn to him that way. A man didn't just start being her true mate halfway through knowing him, did he?

# CHAPTER 19

EVIE

*Ultiori Compound*
*1967*

The experiments started a few weeks later.

At first, she went willingly. Two anonymous hunters in lab coats escorted her to an exam room in another wing and urged her to lie down on a medical table. They undressed her and put her feet into stirrups. One of them injected her in the arm with something before she could object, and a few moments later, the world went fuzzy.

Then *she* was there. Dr. St. George's imperious gaze met Evie's from between her legs as latex-covered hands gripped her thighs. The doctor held an instrument in her hands which she inserted into Evie, her alien fingers unwanted on Evie's tenderest parts. At least she wasn't overly familiar with those parts. She treated Evie like a scientific specimen—analytical and disengaged, even as she shoved something deep into Evie to the point of causing her pain.

Evie gasped at the invasion, at the sudden tight cramp that overtook her abdomen. But then it was gone and the doctor retreated, whispering orders to the orderly who stood at her side.

She was taken back to her room and told nothing more.

A month later, she had the worst period of her life, spending nearly a week doubled over in pain from the cramps and bleeding heavily.

Six months later, they repeated the process and this time Sayid was in attendance, watching dispassionately from a corner while the procedure was completed.

A month after that, Evie broke down in tears when she understood what was happening.

That afternoon, Sterlyn found her bleeding and crying beside her toilet after she'd spent half the day alternately puking and bleeding from a pregnancy that should never have happened.

"I want to fucking kill them," she said.

"Get in line."

Evie stared up at him through hazy eyes. "They're getting me pregnant with those tests. There's no way these babies will ever live. I can't be forced to conceive. Fertility is sacred to all the higher races. It takes more than simple science—cells bumping against each other at the right time—to make a baby. We have to love each other to make it work. Our very essences have to want it."

"He's doing it to Zamirah, too," Sterlyn said. "He wants something with these tests, but I don't know what."

Sterlyn trailed off, and Evie heard what he was unwilling to say. The man who held them captive wanted a child, but only a child that would require this kind of morbid sacrifice to create.

Evie gave the attendants hell the next time she left her room. She didn't give a shit what they were going to do with her; she just wanted out.

She learned quickly that she had no means of escape.

They'd moved her to a cell right across from the lab, so there was little time to rebel, and they were prepared for any eventuality. In the end she simply sang out, hoping the winds would hear her and take notice.

A week later her cell door mysteriously unlocked and she took advantage, but didn't get far enough to escape.

"Gag her," Dr. St. George said when they caught her, and she spent the next few weeks of her captivity with a rag in her mouth except when she needed to eat. Either Sterlyn or Naaz guarded her with their own judgmental looks. *"Damn yourself and damn us in the process,"* their eyes seemed to say.

When she finished the meal Sterlyn had brought her not long after that, she told him, "I'm not going to cry again. I'm sick of the damn gag. I promise, I'll keep quiet."

After that, she didn't say a word. She submitted to the experiments that went on for years and tried to forget each brief glimmer of new life that struggled to take hold inside her womb before fading just as quickly. She stopped considering herself pregnant with the ones that didn't take, except for the ones that came from Sterlyn and Naaz. They were the closest things she had to Marcus. After so long living in a cell, simple contact from those two kind men made her crave their presence even more.

# CHAPTER 20

## KED

*Dragon Monastery, Sunda Islands*
*Present Day*

"*Please, stop.*"

Ked's attention shifted from Evie's story to the voice of Marcus inside his mind. The man's emotions had transformed from dark apathy to an even darker resistance to hearing Evie's story.

Ked had never expected to wind up an emotional conduit between two lovers, but had deliberately left his mind open to Marcus while Evie told him of her ordeal.

"*This is your story, too. One side of it, at least,*" he replied to the man's plea.

Anguish flared in his mind from the other man, but Marcus didn't retreat. A glimmer of curious need arose.

"What is he telling you?" Evie asked softly. She reached up and pressed a palm against Ked's cheek, urging his attention back to her.

"Not much. He's hearing everything you tell me, you know. It's difficult for him to absorb."

"Tell him that I don't blame him. I knew what I was in for almost from the beginning. We were meant to follow that path to get to you. I wish it could have been easier, but we both survived." She smiled and leaned up to him, pressing her lips against his softly, then pulled back and whispered, "Tell him I love him and that this is for him." She slid into his lap and pressed her body fully against his. Ked opened up to her completely, accepting her sweet, velvet tongue and caressing it with his own, melding his mouth with hers until his arousal was reflected back to him by the other man's presence in his mind.

He craved an even deeper connection with them both and impulsively exhaled a breath into Evie's mouth. She shuddered in his arms and deepened their kiss. A moment later, her thoughts flared brightly in his mind, strong enough to make him moan in surprise at the intensity. He'd been aware of the fluctuation of her emotions through her aura, but being inside her mind at that moment nearly overwhelmed him.

In his mind, Marcus said, *"Is that her? Evie?"*

Evie pulled back from the kiss with a sigh and closed her eyes. Ked rested his forehead against hers, cradling her on his lap as the pair of battered lovers tentatively reached their thoughts out through the shadows of his consciousness.

*"I am here, Marcus. Please, don't give up. Not yet. I still need you."*

*"They could have killed you. And all those years of torture—what you had to endure. It's all on me, Evie."*

*"But they didn't. We survived, and here we are. But we have barely even spoken in five decades, Marcus. Let me rest my voice for a while. Tell me what it was like for you."*

After that, Ked simply stayed in the shadows of his own mind, a silent observer to their separate, yet shared ordeals.

# CHAPTER 21

## MARCUS

*Ultiori Compound*
*Mid-1980s*

"The angel in cell 25," they called her, even before Marcus had confessed to the other two Elites that he considered Evie his angel. He often thought back to their first meeting and her sardonic smile at being called an angel. The memory was one of many he'd had with her that made him smile. Knowing what she was didn't bother him—in fact, it had been a relief once he'd found out she wasn't human. There was no way a woman as amazing as Evie could possibly be human.

His two fellow Elites had approached him warily at first, but as time passed, he grew to trust them. He'd eventually developed a rapport with them after working together so closely. During a hunt, their emotions shone brightly in his mind—excitement was what they presented on the surface, but underneath he sensed the same familiar self-hatred and dread he carried, along with something primal, like the pathos of a caged animal.

Because those emotions mirrored his own so well, he sensed without asking that the other two Elites were in similar straits. He confirmed his suspicions when Sterlyn refused to switch a shift guarding one of the female dragon captives while she was being transferred the short trip to the lab for tests.

"He isn't allowed to have contact with that one," Naaz had explained later, but refused to elaborate.

Marcus wasn't allowed contact with Evie, either—not after the one concession had been made shortly after his change. When they started referring to her as *his* angel, he knew they were brothers in arms, even if they were still trapped under Sayid's thumb.

He soon learned not to even *think* about escape, or at least not without shielding his mind with the dark power he soon learned to wield. He learned to do other things, too, such as conjure a cloaking smoke that would render him virtually invisible, and to easily sense the strongest emotions a target was experiencing without them even knowing he was in their mind.

His fellow Elites had to know he used it on them, considering he'd caught them both using their powers on him—testing his defenses every so often as they had during his training. If they caught him, they never gave any indication, but when he tried it with Sayid, the man immediately threw back a blinding bolt of pain that seared through Marcus's mind and left him with dizzy spells for days.

Simply knowing he had allies was a comfort, even if they were impotent at helping each other overcome their master. The first time Marcus tried sending a hopeful nudge out to them both to open up deeper conversation, all he got was a blank wall of denial from Sterlyn and a pornographic image of Sayid fucking him in the ass from Naaz. Both responses were not-so-subtle hints that even the most benign sort of telepathic contact was a bad idea.

Their actions spoke louder than any words, however, and while the three had to be careful in both shared thought and speech, the ease with which they worked together grew into deeper trust. Marcus often imagined if he had joined the military, he might have wound up on a similar team. Their deeper mental connection reinforced that sense of fraternity.

He also reminded himself that if he had joined the military, there was a very good chance he would be dead already. But at least Evie would have been free.

The only time they ventured a deeper conversation was nearly two decades into Evie's captivity, when Sayid divulged the secret of his research. The man wanted the Elites to couple with three of the female captives. Marcus was elated at first, because it meant he could make love to Evie again. That wasn't to be the case, however. His separation from her would still be enforced.

After the announcement and Sayid's abrupt-as-always departure, the three of them had sat around the table in the shared dining room of their private quarters.

"To hell with it," Sterlyn had said. "I love Zamirah, and the thought of sharing her twists me in knots, but she needs sex to survive and until now they've barely kept her from turning feral with the infrequent visits from human hunters to service her. I would rather one of you were the one to fulfill that need for her than any of those crazy bastards. She accepts them because she has no other choice."

Marcus envied the man his telepathic link to his lover. Something about the dragon blood running through their veins allowed the intimacy of that mental contact, which he wished he had with Evie. She had her own subtle power to contact him, though not as directly. Every so often he heard her voice like a whisper in his ear, reminding him that she still loved him, and he would whisper back when he heard it, hoping that his own sentiments made their way to her on the wind. Some days, it was the only thing that kept him moving.

"You are like brothers to me, too," Marcus said. "If it has to be anyone, I'd rather it were one of you. Just as long as it isn't *him*."

Both men nodded, understanding his meaning. Their master had a reputation for brutality in the bedroom, but only had a taste for blue dragons, who sadly never survived a night with him. Marcus dreaded the day their master would send them out to hunt for another.

Naaz frowned, his lips twisting in distaste. "I would rip the man's head off if he went near my sister. Better she's locked up and prodded by his scientists than touched by him."

Marcus and Sterlyn shared a glance that acknowledged neither of them could stop Sayid if he decided he wanted one of their lovers, or Naaz's sister, Neela. The Elite's twin was the collateral that kept Naaz in line. The pair had been in the Ultiori's clutches the longest, the Blessed human female transfused with the same blood as her brother, but kept locked up. If she were to die, Naaz would have no reason to continue serving as an Elite, and the immortal dragon blood was the surest way to keep her alive.

The prospect of making love to either female left a bad taste in Marcus's mouth. He had been their guard for years and knew them both well. They were as much like family as the two men were. And they were helplessly trapped as much as Evie was. As alluring as the prospect should have been, he couldn't in good conscience go through with this without their explicit agreement.

"They have to tell us it's okay," he said. "I'm not going to *rape* your women just because he commands us to. That's what he's asking us to do. We can't let it go down like that."

Sterlyn stared into his cup and nodded, his jaw clenching. He looked up and met Marcus's gaze. "Evie means almost as much to me as Zamirah. Whatever has to happen, it won't be forced, I promise you. If she says no… she says no and we suffer the consequences."

Naaz grunted and nodded, looking at his friend. That was enough of a consensus for Marcus.

"You two have a good relationship with Evie already, but I need her to say she's on board."

"We can do that. When the time comes, we'll make sure it's her decision."

Marcus nodded, strangely self-conscious about the conversation. Clearing his throat, he said, "Whichever of you does the deed, you'd better not leave her hanging when you're with her. Promise me you'll make sure she enjoys it."

Naaz chuckled. In his deeply accented voice, he said, "I was born in a harem. It is against my religion to leave a lover hanging. The bigger danger is that I please her so well she forgets every other lover she's ever had. But if you share your secrets, I will be sure everything I do reminds her of you."

Marcus gave him an agonized look. "I'm not worried about her. She knows what she wants. But Neela and Zamirah… I'm definitely not happy about what has to happen with them."

Naaz sighed. "My sister is a strong girl and not shy. Let her take the lead. Our parents were the honored pets of a dragon goddess. When we first served Nikhil, it was willingly and openly because our parents said that, as the dragon's mate, that made him our godfather. We learned everything we know growing up in that harem. If you know anything about dragons, you know their pets are never deprived of pleasure for long. Neela and Zamirah will both guide you, friend. Just promise me you won't share any details afterward. Sterlyn and I don't want to know."

They stood together and Marcus steeled himself for the night ahead. "Tell her I love her, please? Just don't tell her what I'm doing."

Both men nodded and they made their way to the door. Sterlyn patted his back as he left the room. "You can't rape a dragon," he said. "As long as you're enjoying it, Zamirah is enjoying it. I trust you."

Marcus trusted both of them, too, but he hoped Evie didn't wind up hating him after this.

*Ultiori Compound*
*Mid-1980s*

"The doctor wants to try something new," Sterlyn said when he came to her one day, almost twenty years into her captivity. Evie was feeling particularly vulnerable, wishing for word about Marcus, so was comforted by Sterlyn's presence. He and Naaz saved her sanity and always brought loving messages from Marcus when they came. Today's message had nothing to do with Marcus.

"I don't think I know what 'new' means. What is it she wants to try?" The doctor's cruel experiments had subsided for a few months and Evie welcomed the reprieve but she'd known it couldn't last. The severe-looking woman with the foul smell hadn't aged well over the years and during the last procedure, it was painfully apparent to Evie that the woman's days were numbered. She even went so far as to hope that the woman had finally died, but feared the kind of person who might replace her.

Sterlyn's face flushed and he turned away from her,

pressing his hands against the door to her cell as if he wanted to escape. She knew Naaz was on the other side with the key. All he had to do was say the word and his brother in arms would open the door to release him.

"She thinks artificial insemination won't work. She thinks it needs to be natural."

It took mere seconds for Evie to grasp the suggestion. "She wants you to fuck me."

Sterlyn kept his back to her, his hands pressed against her door, but she could see his muscles bunch under his shirt.

"Should I be insulted that you look so disgusted at the prospect?" Evie asked. She wasn't surprised by this shift of events. Wishing he were Marcus didn't change a thing, though. Sterlyn and Naaz were her best friends in here.

He turned around again and let his eyes drift over her body, roving slowly as though letting himself recognize her femininity for the first time. She almost laughed. At the moment, she was dressed only in a threadbare white tank top and black sweat pants, her lank hair pulled back into a pony-tail. She hadn't been allowed to cut her hair or shave her legs —nothing aside from simple bathing—since she'd arrived. Her smile faded under his gaze, however. How long had it been since either of them had lost themselves in intimate contact?

"You're as beautiful as Zamirah, you know," he said. "She used to give me this look when she wanted me. Her eyes would kind of flash with light, and she would glow a little. It's a dragon thing, I guess."

Evie's breath left her lungs, but she managed to nod.

"Yeah," she finally said. "Totally a dragon thing."

"Except Sayid won't let me near enough to her to touch her anymore. Not since he discovered we'd become lovers. I can still contact her telepathically, at least, but even that is risky."

"Does Marcus know you've been sent to do this?"

"Yes. He…" Sterlyn paused and met her gaze directly, his blue eyes studying her with an unexpected heat lingering deep within. She suddenly felt drawn to him on two fronts—attracted as though he had some latent seductive power, and set alight deep in that secret place only Marcus had touched her, and only once on the day when she'd last seen him.

Sterlyn's voice pitched lower when he resumed speaking. "He told me how you liked to be touched. How to make love to you. What I do with you would be what he asked me to do. To remind you that he hasn't forgotten. It's an abomination of what we are, I know this. I don't want to be the man our master has turned me into. I was built for honor and right-eousness. I'm a fucking *knight*. I don't rape women. But if we don't go through with this, he *will* punish us all for disobeying him. Still, you can tell me now that you don't want it and I will leave. The three of us promised each other that it would be your decision, not ours."

He took a few slow steps toward her and Evie's pulse quickened.

"What about Zamirah? Does this mean that Naaz or Marcus is with her? It would be Naaz, wouldn't it? So Marcus must be with Neela. Is that what this is, one big swap to get us all pregnant to progress his twisted experiments? How in the world can you let this happen?" She stared at him, struggling to comprehend how he could even consider suggesting the idea to her, and how he could condone letting anyone else be with the woman he loved.

Sterlyn's strong features twisted with anguish and he stared at the ceiling. "I've been Sayid's dog for more than a thousand years, Naaz for far longer. Don't you think if we could have left him, we would have? His power is *immeasur-able*. Even if I were to *think* about betraying him now, he would sense it. You may be trapped in here behind that locked door, but I am trapped behind the lock he has on my mind. He only grants us enough slack that we can function, but the second we test our boundaries, the leash snaps tight."

Behind the tension in his words, Evie heard desperation. She had the strongest sense that he might fall to his knees and beg at any moment. She pressed her lips tighter, but her anger dissipated.

"If any of us say no, then would we all be punished?"

Sterlyn shook his head and grimaced. "There's no telling what he would do, but if he wants this badly enough he'll go to every length to make sure we perform to his satisfaction. We may not have the option of *asking* the next time. And you may not have the option of having any control over the situation. If you want me tied to the bed and have your way with me, we can do that."

Evie smirked. "I have a suspicion you might enjoy that too much."

He gave her a sheepish smile and a little shrug. With a more serious expression he came toward her. "I care about you, Evie. I know how much you mean to Marcus, too. I would rather you had the opportunity to enjoy it than otherwise."

Evie frowned. It had been so long since she'd enjoyed anything, the prospect of the kind of intimacy Sterlyn promised was incredibly tempting. And if Marcus or Naaz was with Sterlyn's lover now, and they had talked about this beforehand, why shouldn't she agree? By the Winds, she wanted Marcus here more than anything. To have him hold her, to talk to her in that sweet way he knew she liked. To drive her mad with desire until she begged.

But she didn't have Marcus. One of the other women had Marcus, and she had Zamirah's lover, instead. The prospect of another failed pregnancy made her chest tighten. If she said no to Sterlyn, would she keep being subjected to the horrible experiments? Maybe this would be an opportunity to escape the humiliation and subsequent pain of those horrible experiences. Except the idea of actually producing a child who would likely become a prisoner itself turned her stomach. What choice did they have? The idea of being able by some miracle to give Marcus a child had been a fantasy of hers for so long. If this worked, she might have a child. That old craving hit her full-force for the first time in years. Maybe she would be allowed to keep it in the end. Could she risk it just for the sake of having that chance—a chance she may never get again?

She studied Sterlyn who was watching her expectantly. Her stomach did a little somersault. Oh, but she did care deeply for him, even if he wasn't Marcus.

"I'll do it," she said.

Sterlyn let out a sigh, his shoulders relaxing. With a slight smile, he moved and stood barely inches from her, his closeness causing goosebumps to rise on her skin in spite of his warmth. "How does Marcus make you feel?" Sterlyn whispered, his lips brushing against her ear.

Evie blinked, then caught on to his game. He'd heard Marcus's version of their love life, now he needed to hear hers. She didn't want it any more than he did, but if he could take the ruse as far as this, she could give back. His lover was as trapped as she was so neither of them had a choice. Being the jailer who was himself a captive had to be torture. This had to happen, so they might as well make it good.

Evie focused her thoughts on Marcus, smiling. "He doesn't think he's a musician, but he is. I'm his instrument. He makes me sing when he touches me."

Sterlyn closed his eyes as he shifted even closer to her and brushed his hand up her arm to cup her jaw.

"Can I make you sing tonight, Evie?"

His blue eyes closed, and his mouth pressed against hers while she processed his question.

No. No, this wasn't right. He was being *too* sweet. Too much like Marcus. She didn't want an imitation of Marcus. If she couldn't have him, she wanted something that didn't even come close to reminding her of him. If this had to happen, she didn't think she could stomach a fake.

With Sterlyn's mouth on hers, she could certainly tell the difference. He was already a little harsher in his touch than Marcus, and that harshness spurred her on. She kissed back hard and nipped at his lip, tasting hot copper when her teeth broke skin.

Sterlyn's head flew back, his eyes wide. He raised a hand to his mouth and pulled his fingers back, blood glistening on the tips.

"What the fuck? I thought you wanted this."

"Oh, I want it," Evie said. "But don't you *dare* try to make love to me tonight. If I need to be fucked, that's all it's going to be. I don't care what Marcus asked you to do. If you care about me even a little bit, leave him out of it."

Sterlyn grimaced, his blond eyebrows squeezing together in irritation. "You said you couldn't get pregnant with someone you didn't love. I hoped simulating that love would help."

Evie raised her hands to the sides of his face and pulled him down so that his nose was almost brushing against hers and their foreheads rested against each other.

"How could I not love you after tolerating you all these years? You and Naaz both have kept me sane. But neither of you are *him*, and I'd rather keep it that way. If we need to participate in some debauched experiment to satisfy the asshole you call a boss, I'd rather keep my love for Marcus a million miles away from it."

She raised her lips to capture his and he wrapped his

arms around her, pulling her tight against him. He plunged his tongue between her lips, passionately consumed as much as she was in their kiss.

The little spark inside her brightened like a candle flame showing her the way through the dark, and the path led her deeper into his arms. It wasn't her final destination, just the place she needed to be in this isolated emotional wasteland she'd found herself in. He was her waystation, and she would take solace with him for as long as necessary.

Sterlyn pushed her hard against the little ledge of a table she ate her dinner on—nothing more than a steel shelf attached to the wall of her cell. He lifted her up effortlessly and seated her on it, stripping her shirt off, followed by her pants. She wore nothing else—any other garments were superlative in this place.

He fell to his knees and spread her legs wide, sliding his hands up her thighs with the hungriest gaze, laser-focused on her core. Sterlyn certainly had the smoldering look down to a science. Her core throbbed hard under that gaze and she let out a little squeak when he pressed his lips against her heated flesh.

Goddamn, Sterlyn was talented with his mouth. His tongue flicked adroitly at her clit, swirled around it before he pulled it between his lips and sucked. He pressed two fingers into her tight channel and twisted, hooking his fingers just enough to rub in the exact right spot to make her vision go dark. She wanted to lose herself in the pleasure. To be plunged so deep in it she forgot who she was, where she was, and that the man kneeling before her wasn't really the man she wanted. If she were going to do this, she wanted it to be a binge, because she may not have another chance. Sterlyn alone was not enough.

"I wish there were two of you," she stuttered. "I need more."

"What did you say?" he asked, raising his head and resting his hands on her thighs. His blond hair was mussed and sticking out at all angles from where her fingers had tangled in it. His blue eyes were bright with lust.

"I wish there were two of you?" she repeated, blinking down at him, a little irritated that he'd stopped the glorious things he'd been doing with his mouth.

He grinned. "There are," he said and stood up, wiping off his mouth as he strode swiftly to the door. Halfway there, he hesitated and turned back. "You mean that, right? You want two of us? Naaz is outside the door. If you'd said no to me, he was going to try to convince you himself."

The admission made Evie's eyes widen. The suggestion made her body tingle all over with desire. If Naaz had been the one to initially try to talk her into it, she probably wouldn't have held out as long. "Do you think he'll do it?"

Sterlyn's mouth quirked into a sideways smile. "We're men, Evie. You're the most beautiful woman we get to have contact with on a daily basis. And like you said, it's hard not to love someone who you're that close with for so long. He's right outside."

Evie spent a second trying to imagine what Marcus might think of her if she did this, but she knew already. He'd once told her how he often dreamed of watching her with another man. Besides, he'd given them both his blessing already.

"How close is Marcus?" she asked.

Bewildered, Sterlyn said, "In the guard office up top."

"Can you contact him? I need to hear him say it's okay before we do this."

Sterlyn nodded and banged at the door. It opened a crack, and he whispered something to Naaz. The door closed again for a few minutes, then opened and Naaz stepped inside, a handheld radio gripped in his palm.

"Bruce is watching the door," he said. "Marcus wants to

talk to you." He shoved the radio into Evie's hand. "Tap the lever here to talk to him," he said, indicating a little trigger on the side of the radio.

"Baby?" Evie said into the radio, following the instructions and trying like hell to ignore Naaz's gaze studying her naked body for a second before he turned away and pulled Sterlyn into a corner to talk covertly.

Marcus's voice crackled through the speaker of the radio. "Oh, God, Evie, I miss you so much. I miss hearing your voice. Are they being good to you?"

"Y-yes. Very good." She neglected sharing precisely *how* good Sterlyn had just been to her and grimaced at the wetness on her upper thighs. How in the world could she be talking to him so casually while she stood there, *naked* after another man just had his tongue buried in her snatch?

Marcus was silent for a second. "You agreed, I take it?"

"I did. It might take two of them to make up for the fact that I can't have you, though. But if you aren't okay with that, then I won't."

A low chuckle came through the speaker. "I'm not thrilled, no, but we don't exactly have the luxury of saying no, here. I just want to make sure you didn't think we were jumping at the chance to fuck each other's women. If there were any other way... God, Evie, if it could be me, you have to know I would be the one down there with you. But whatever *you* want is what I want. If the pair of them together is what you need, then you have my blessing. But fuck, I'm going to go mad imagining that situation."

"Are you sure, Marcus? I want you, too."

"I'm sure. I love you."

After that, she only heard dead air. Evie set the radio on the table with her hand still resting on it, unwilling to give up that brief connection she'd had to Marcus. She closed her eyes, trying to hold in her mind the sound of his voice before it faded.

A gentle grip pulled her hand away from the radio. She opened her eyes to see Naaz's huge, dark, and entirely seductive form in front of her. The man was so beautiful it hurt to look at him. He'd been the first of them to try to talk to her, but all she could do was stare at him, marveling at how a man could be made so perfectly and still be human.

Finally, they'd sent Sterlyn instead and she'd relaxed and opened up. Sterlyn was perfectly imperfect. He was gorgeous, but had obvious scars. His teeth weren't quite straight, he didn't wear his exhaustion well, and seemed prone to broodiness. Entirely *human,* right down to his blue eyes and perpetual five-o'clock shadow. On the rare occasions she did see him happy, he virtually glowed.

Naaz was a statue of a god. Bigger than life, more beautiful, and completely devoid of a soul. At least, that was what she'd thought at first, until the day he'd shown his wound to her. It had taken months after first talking to him before his shell had finally cracked, and it had only been for a moment that Evie had seen the truth of the pain he hid inside. His demeanor hadn't changed with her, but her reactions to him had changed. He was simply a deep well. All stone on the surface, but filled with dark waters that would drown you if you weren't careful. The tiny flame inside her sparked again when she looked at him, just as it always did. She considered the pair of men her best friends as surely as she considered Marcus her soul mate.

"You don't want to be loved tonight, so Sterlyn says," Naaz said, his voice as rough and deep as a thunderstorm. One of his large hands gripped her naked hip and squeezed. "You want rough, or gentle fucking?"

His touch made her entire body tingle and she leaned into his hand.

"As rough as you can make it until I tell you otherwise," she said.

Naaz chuckled. "Marcus is a gentle lover, I take it?"

"Not always, but he's attentive. Make me beg."

Sterlyn's warm body slid behind her, trapping her between the two of them. His mouth found her throat, trailing hotly over her sensitive skin. She went rigid from the surprising pleasure at first, then sank back into him, watching Naaz from beneath her lashes.

Sterlyn pulled her back the few steps it took to get to her tiny bed and sat, urging her onto his lap.

"We've got you," he whispered. "Nothing you don't want tonight, all right?"

Evie shifted back as though trying to escape the looming form of Naaz, who finally knelt down and settled between her thighs, gripping them to keep her from moving more.

"I plan on fucking you until you scream, but right now, I want to know if you taste the way Marcus says you do."

Evie couldn't move, trapped as she was with Sterlyn's arms wrapped around her torso, his lips brushing up and down her neck and his hands cupping her breasts, thumbs steadily moving in circles over her nipples.

Naaz gripped her thighs and held them tight enough to bruise. His dark head bent and his lips pressed lightly against her folds in a soft kiss that grew deeper and deeper. His tongue flitted over her swollen flesh once before sinking in and tasting her with a soft moan of pleasure.

"Jesus, he wasn't lying," he said after pulling back for breath.

Evie felt flushed and greedy from his mouth. She wanted more.

"Are you ready to beg, yet?" Naaz asked, smiling a sweet smile at her with lips that still glistened from her juices. Sometimes he was so cocky she wanted to smack the pretty off him, but right now she reveled in being worshiped by a man so inhumanly beautiful.

While he stared down at her and Sterlyn kept kneading her breasts from behind, Naaz sank two fingers deep into her.

"So wet," he murmured, holding her gaze.

Evie whimpered as his two fingers twisted and curled inside her, rubbing precisely the way Marcus's did. Her eyelids fluttered shut and she smiled as the understanding that he had coached these two to touch her this way. Her clit throbbed and she tried to ignore the soft squelch of Naaz's thrusting into her wet depths.

But then he was gone, and her entire body rejected the absence of his touch.

"You bastard!" She opened her eyes to see him sitting back on his heels and smiling wickedly as he slowly stripped off his shirt, then stood and removed his boots and pants.

"You said you wanted us to make you beg," he replied.

Before she could retort, she found herself thrown down onto her cot with Sterlyn hovering over her. His mouth found one breast and claimed it, sucking and toying at her nipple while his fingers teased lightly between her thighs, then ventured deeper. He was gentler yet more persistent than Naaz. Her already aroused senses couldn't handle the increased prodding at her most sensitive area, that perfect little bundle of nerves inside her behind her pubic bone.

She wished he wouldn't stop. Desperation ruled her in that moment while he teased her with his mouth sucking her nipples, back and forth, urging her to heights that would make her scream if he'd only take her to the end. Sterlyn seemed to know the exact right moment to stop.

"We're supposed to fuck you, remember?" he said by way of excuse when he pulled back and stood to undress.

They both stood there by her bed, stroking themselves so

casually she'd have thought they were trying to torture her until she saw the needy looks in their eyes. They were barely restraining themselves.

*Marcus*, she thought. He'd laid down the law. But she wanted them, and they wanted her to beg.

"Please, fuck me. Both of you. Fuck me until I beg you to stop."

She sat up and reached for Naaz. His cock looked so delicious, so long and smooth. He stepped closer and gazed down with a look of pure lust. As she took him into her mouth, Sterlyn slid in behind her, straddling her hips. He gripped her hips with both hands and she rose up, her soaking core aching to feel him inside her. One hand remained on her hip, keeping her poised over his lap while the fingers of the other slipped between her folds, teasing enough for her to lose track of what she was doing with Naaz's cock.

Soon the thick, hot head of his cock replaced his fingers, sliding up and down along her slit until he finally urged her to sink down. The thick weight of him stretched her in the most glorious way, filling her bit by bit, and she savored the slick friction as much as she savored the taste of Naaz's salty skin.

She let Sterlyn set the pace with his hands on her hips, but that wasn't good enough. She let out a whimper of dissatisfaction around Naaz's cock and found his hand against her chin, pulling her off him.

"You need to lose control, baby. Just let go, let us take over."

Evie nodded. Yes, that was exactly what she needed. She found herself lifted off Sterlyn and bodily turned, positioned face down in her pillows with her ass high in the air. Her pussy ached to be filled and soon enough it was. She had no idea whose cock it was, but she didn't want to know. She knew it was one of them, and that was enough.

A hand steadily stroked her back and kneaded her ass and thighs while she was pounded from behind. A bold finger even pressed between her ass cheeks, slid down to gather moisture, and back up again, swirling around the small opening, and she let out a little cry of encouragement.

The finger delved deeper and another joined it. Another hand slid between her thighs in front, finding her throbbing clit and rubbing in slow circles. Still more hands found her breasts and a warm mouth pressed against her ear.

"That'll be my cock in that tight little cunt of yours in a few minutes," Naaz said. "I'm going to fuck you so well you'll forget your own name. Maybe I'll even take that pretty ass of yours while Sterlyn fucks your pussy again. We'll fill you up with our hot spunk until you're overflowing, then fuck you again."

His voice was as smooth and seductive as the man himself, his warm fingers tugging and pinching her nipples until she was nothing but a swirling bundle of sensations, inside and out. Sterlyn's thrusts sped up, his hips smacking hard against her ass, his balls brushing against her thighs with each rough shove into her.

Every sensitive inch of her inner flesh rejoiced at the pleasure. It swelled inside her, growing more potent with each caress, each kiss, each plunge of Sterlyn's invading cock and fingers. He let out a desperate groan and slammed hard, the head of his cock reaching so deep she imagined she could taste him. With that last thrust, hot fluid flooded into her along with a familiar tingling current of the sweetest magic. Evie flew to pieces then, coming hard and slamming back against the cock that filled her.

Evie clenched her eyes shut tightly, bewildered at the sensation of the magic that was so similar to Marcus's, yet so different. The fact that Sterlyn had shared it with her at all meant he was even more like Marcus than she'd realized.

Then it clicked—all three of them were Blessed. All three altered in the same way. It had to be dragon blood that had changed them, and from Naaz's story of how he came to be here, how old he really was, it had to be immortal dragon blood.

Still dazed at the realization, she found herself being pulled off the small bed into a pair of strong, comforting arms. Naaz cradled her against him, stroking her gently while she came down from her orgasm and her revelation. He bent his head to kiss her, and she responded with ardor, wrapping her arms around his neck and moving against him, eager for more. She wanted to feel his power filling her now, to confirm her belief as much as for the pleasure of it. The magic made her feel alive for the first time in years. It reminded her of who she was and what her purpose was. This was only a piece of her journey and as inevitable as the sunrise, which she knew still occurred daily, even though she hadn't seen it in what seemed like eons.

She let Naaz shift her and moved to straddle his hips with his huge cock sandwiched between them. She lifted up and gazed into Naaz's perfect face as she slid down onto him, her pussy slick and dripping with the combined juices of both Sterlyn and herself.

"You're a genius," she whispered.

Naaz looked too enthralled to even answer, his expression lost. "You're the genius," he whispered as he thrust into her. "This is the first time I've come close to forgetting that I can't save her."

Evie pressed her tender lips against his and stroked his cheeks as she fucked him. "We will," she whispered. "If it's the last thing I do, I'll make sure we save them all."

# CHAPTER 23

*Ultiori Headquarters, Canadian Rockies*
*Present Day*

"Maybe she knew something we didn't know, even back then," Naaz said, shaking his head as he bent to pick up a bloody feather from the floor of Evie's cell. He and Sterlyn stared at it almost reverently, making Nikhil wonder if there was something he was missing.

"Why does the turul's knowledge matter to either of you?" he asked. "She wasn't your mate. Marcus was always the one who loved her. Otherwise I'd have caught one of you in her cell with her last night, instead of obediently sitting outside in the hallway."

The two men looked at him in confusion bordering on offense. Their postures both tensed and Nikhil realized he should have chosen his words more carefully.

"You were the one who ordered us to get close to her, then eventually try to breed with her," Naaz said. "Same as you ordered Marcus and Sterlyn to bed my sister, and myself and Marcus to do the same with Zamirah. You couldn't bear to let either of them close to their own mates. Or me to my sister." Naaz's jaw clamped tight, the muscles flexing to keep from spewing the anger Nikhil could easily sense bubbled just beneath the surface. He knew what Naaz left unsaid was Nikhil's refusal to allow him or Neela close to those two treasures that he now knew were their intended mates.

Nikhil shook his head. "I would never do such a thing," he said, though some faint shadow of a memory niggled at him. The image was like a dream, the sound of his voice experienced like an echo reaching his ears again seconds after already leaving his mouth. He had done what Naaz said, but it hadn't been *his* desire driving that order.

Neela stepped between Nikhil and the pair of men who looked ready to rip him apart. She pressed a hand against his chest and looked up at him with a gaze filled with understanding and compassion he didn't deserve. Even deeper lay a small hint of tenderness that caused an ache within that baffled him.

"You did many things, Bennu. Things the old Nikhil never would have done, but not even the darkness that was in you could control every outcome. Those orders you gave my brothers only made the six of us closer. Our bond is strengthened because of it."

Her eyes remained locked to his a moment longer, as if she were searching for something within his gaze. Another memory flitted past and was lost, leaving behind a sense of intimacy with Neela that he'd never had before. He frowned. "Did we..." he began, hoping to draw out what she'd left unsaid, but he was interrupted again by her brother.

"Did you think we wouldn't talk while we fucked?" Naaz asked. "We may have been careful about hiding our thoughts from you, but as long as you weren't in earshot, we had no qualms about saying the things out loud. Evie knew how we felt. That first night Sterlyn and I had her, the number one thought in all our minds wasn't getting off, it was getting *out*, and getting our lovers out, too. That includes…" He snapped his mouth shut, baring his teeth at Nikhil, the unsaid words as loud as a yell.

"That includes her," Nikhil finished for him, tearing his eyes away from Neela. "The treasure you found that day we *drifted* off course. The one I kept from you ever since."

Neela's face pinched with pain when she turned away, and the brief connection he'd felt with her was shattered.

"Keeping us away from them hurt worse than separating us from each other. At least Naaz and I could sense each other's presence. We found some comfort with the others, but there is still an empty space inside me that aches for my mate. If I could just *sense* him in the world it wouldn't hurt so much, but I can't. It's like you made him stop existing, even though I know that can't be true. If he stopped existing, this hole he was meant to fill would have no reason to exist, either."

Her eyes welled with tears and Nikhil watched her struggle to swallow down her emotions while his own anguish rose into his chest.

"It's… oh, fuck." He swiped a hand over his face and stared at the ceiling, trying to gather his thoughts to offer some consolation that wouldn't sound entirely hollow. Anything now was too little, too late, but he had to try. Taking a deep, steadying breath, he said, "For three thousand years Belah was gone… hidden away, because of *me*. And I felt empty. I wonder if maybe that empty place is what made me weak enough for the… the *thing* that took over to bind me with its power so thoroughly. The moment Belah returned to the world again, I knew, and it was like the sun came back out when I'd finally given up and decided night would never end. Belah is the only thing that lights that dark place inside me. Simply knowing she is in the world right now helps me feel whole, even though I don't believe I deserve that feeling."

Neela regarded him with far more understanding than he was due. In his mind, he felt a subtle link with her that reminded him she still carried Belah's blood. It was what had kept her alive all this time and must have been the source of that flash of memory he'd been unable to hold onto. Ever since he'd locked her up he'd seen no point in giving her the same infusions he gave her brother, but she still received just enough of Belah's blood to keep her alive.

Through that link he sensed her hopefulness along with her hesitance to ask for what she really wanted. Nikhil said nothing because he couldn't give her what she wanted. Not yet.

Finally, Neela sighed and nodded as though his thoughts had silently reached her.

"We will follow your lead, Bennu," she said. "We were all wronged by the thing that held you, and we will work by your side to get revenge. Just tell us what you need us to do."

Glancing between Neela and the others, he saw them each nod in turn.

Nikhil accepted the role of commander even though he didn't yet feel like he deserved that level of respect from them. He set Neela and Zamirah the task of releasing the remaining prisoners. The dragons and turul that were being kept would be able to fly away under their own power. The ursa captives would be given the option of being released into the wilderness that surrounded the compound, or flown home by one of the dragons.

Aside from Calder, they held no nymphs or satyrs captive, and he had a sinking feeling that somehow the satyrs they'd captured over the years had seen some worse fate than simply being executed when their usefulness expired.

With Neela and Zamirah off to the other wings where the

less valuable prisoners were held, he returned to Calder's cell with Sterlyn and Naaz and had the satyr repeat his plan to them. Once the plan was set in motion, he turned to his two remaining Elites, meeting their wary looks head on.

"Speak your minds, please. If I am going to earn your respect again… if I ever even had it… please let us have an open line of communication. You both know I can get into your heads to find the answers, but I need to trust you to tell me what bothers you, and I need you to trust me to be faithful to your loyalty now that you know the truth."

"Where is she," Naaz said without even hesitating. "I know you still hold my mate somewhere. I want to know where."

Nikhil winced wishing Naaz still had that link with him through Belah's blood, but that power had long since been replaced by a cocktail mixture of her brothers' blood. "That is the one thing I cannot share with you, Naaz. She is safe with her brother for now. When your task is done, I won't stop you and Neela from seeking them out, but it is not my place to lead you to them."

Naaz's hand shot out and grabbed Nikhil by the throat, slamming him back against the wall with the preternatural strength of the dragon blood he carried. "Where is she!" he yelled. "She is *mine!* You cannot keep her from me!"

Nikhil stared the other man down, controlling his own anger at the affront and channeling it into his carefully chosen words. "*She* happens to be my daughter. She is safe, and you will find her in good time. If it makes you feel better, *godson*, Sterlyn will be coming with me to ensure she and her brother are secure, and that their mother is reunited with them. It will be Belah's choice where they are kept. If you don't trust me to see them safe, trust their mother."

Naaz blinked at him in confusion, his fingers relaxing. He dropped his hand to his side.

"Belah… our godmother is her … her mother? You're sure of this?"

Nikhil tamped down the surge of emotion that rose every time it hit him that he and Belah had succeeded in creating a child together, but he couldn't keep it entirely out of his voice. Shakily, he said, "Yes. When we were together, Belah told me the truth. Asha is her name… I can at least tell you that. Zorion is her half-brother, who I presume Neela is meant to be with."

"Asha…" Naaz breathed, his tension receding. "When can I see her?"

"That I don't know. It's up to her mother." He shrugged, giving Naaz a somewhat sheepish look but secretly enjoyed the warm glow he felt at the very thought of fending off his daughter's suitor and the secret glee at making Naaz jump through hoops to prove himself. The one thing he regretted was not being there for Asha from the beginning.

Naaz opened and closed his fists in apparent frustration, then looked at Sterlyn. "You'll tell me whether she is safe, won't you? And Neela's mate, too… she'll want to know."

Sterlyn nodded solemnly. "You have my word, brother."

With that, Naaz's eyes closed and his head tilted back. His body shimmered slightly, the image rippling as though seen through the surface of a lake. A moment later he was gone, the *drift* carrying him off to the first of several dozen Alexandria Institute facilities throughout the world to carry out their plan and to glean what knowledge he could about who had given the order to evacuate the staff of this facility.

Nikhil turned to Sterlyn. "I would not blame you if you decided to tell Naaz the secret of where his mate is being kept, but he must not know for her sake. It isn't my choice to keep the information from him. It's hers."

Sterlyn gave him an understanding smile. "I know. They've both talked to me during the few visits we had.

Mostly Asha—she's the talkative one. I offered to bring their mates to them even though I knew it would likely get me killed, but they explained why I couldn't. They didn't belong in the place you kept them. For their true ascensions to occur they need a dragon temple."

"They were in no such temple when we found them," Nikhil said.

Sterlyn shrugged. "I wasn't there, so I can't offer any insight. All I know is that Zorion believes the twins stumbled on them prematurely thanks to the power of the nymphaea blood you gave them. They weren't meant to be found so soon. Keeping them hidden away was probably the best thing you could do."

"I hope their mother thinks so when I take her to them. But first I need your help securing the temporal bubble they're in now. I don't want to take any chances of them being discovered by our enemy."

After that, Nikhil would have to take the next step—one he dreaded as much as he longed for it.

He would finally keep his promise to the woman he loved, and bring Belah to her children.

# CHAPTER 24

## KED

*Dragon Monastery, Sunda Islands*
*Present Day*

Ked gritted his teeth in outrage over what Evie had endured. The memories of her pleasure did nothing to overpower the despicable nature of what they had all been compelled to do. Nikhil had outdone himself and Ked's darkness surged forth again with the desire to rip the man to pieces.

"It wasn't him," Evie said.

"Wasn't who?" Ked bit out, his gut churning with rage.

"Nikhil. Most of the experiments weren't done by him. Sometimes he would watch, but it was almost like he wasn't really there… like he was an empty shell, a puppet, whenever the doctor was in the same room with him. The doctor was the one who did all the procedures up until shortly after the last round. I think she must have died, because after my second miscarriage I never saw her again. She was quite old by then."

"You said you'd been pregnant twice before." Ked

squeezed her arm more to comfort himself than her. "How many times were there?"

Evie let out a shuddering sigh and shook her head. "If I don't count all the times before that barely even lasted a day, there were only two. After that first night with Sterlyn and Naaz, I became pregnant, and it almost seemed like it would be viable. I can't say any of us were particularly happy about it once we found out, but they'd done their job as far as Dr. St. George was concerned, and I started to have hope, if you can believe it."

"But it didn't last." In the shadows of his mind, he felt Marcus withdraw again in shame and anger, erecting a new wall between them.

Evie looked up at him with wide eyes glistening with unshed tears. Her eyelids slid closed and she shook her head. "No. Nearly two months later, I miscarried. And the second time was the same, but the pregnancy failed sooner."

"Did they come to you any other times without their leader's instructions? Together or apart?"

"After the first time, yes, but only once. They didn't want to risk Sayid starting to think they had a soft spot for me, or I'd wind up collateral just like Neela and Zamirah."

Evie grew quiet and sank limply in his arms, as though she were exhausted. She'd been wound so tightly Ked found it difficult not to lay a comforting hand on her, but if he had, he'd distract her from the telling and from Marcus's reciprocation of his own part of the story.

Now that she was done, Ked's body was on high alert. His cock raged to take her, yet he simply held her, happy that she was in his arms. She wasn't fully his, though, if her distant look was any indication. As comfortable as she was resting against him, her gaze out over the high balcony told him she was imagining something else.

He brushed his palm over her cheek and urged her to look at him.

When her gray eyes met his, her instant recognition struck hard inside him, triggering his power before he could control it. The room went black except for the two of them. Evie glowed brightly, her aura a stark contrast to the shroud of his power, and her shock was apparent.

"What did you do?" she asked.

Ked let out a low grumble. He needed to keep better control if he was going to be able to wait until Marcus came around before he marked her.

"You do this to me, Evie. But it isn't just you and me in this little bubble right now. Marcus is too important to deny. If it were just you and me, I would make love to you now, mark you and make you mine. You still need him, though, because he's the biological father. Your child carries my blood mixed with his. It is part dragon through the part of me that infuses his body, and unborn dragons need their parents' energy to survive until birth."

Evie smiled absently. "I know that's why I'm so drawn to Marcus." Her eyes widened and she looked at him. "The other two Elites, what about them? I always felt a spark with them, but it was never as strong as it was with Marcus. Do they have your blood, too?"

"Yes, just not as much of it. Judging from what I've learned through Marcus's memories, each of them has a different ratio of blood from myself and my brothers. Doubtless if you had been fated for Gavra or Aodh, you would have bonded with one of the other Elites instead. But it was Marcus, and it is his natural, human energy the child needs as much as mine."

Her eyes clenched shut and he regretted the pain he saw on her face. "I need him, too," she whispered. "I would rather die than lose him. I don't care how close my bond is with you."

When she opened her eyes, Ked knew she wasn't lying.

"He isn't making it easy on us, but we can change his mind together, especially if he knows the baby is his."

"Are you sure that's all the baby needs?" Evie asked, squeezing his arm. "I don't think I can bear it if I lose another child."

Ked hadn't wanted to broach that issue with her so soon, but it wouldn't be able to wait long. If there was even a drop of his brothers' blood running through Marcus's veins, it would be enough to pass on to the child. The baby may not need a lot from Aodh and Gavra, but it would need some. Still, he should wait until Marcus was awake and they could discuss the issue together.

"The baby will live, I promise you."

If Ked had his way, this baby would live to be the bane of the Ultiori leader's existence, no matter what his sister claimed.

He slid his hand inside her robe and pressed his palm against her naked belly. The softness of her skin enticed him to trace his fingertips across her hips, trailing up and down her sides, over the tops of her thighs. She was so warm in his arms, so relaxed and pliant, so accepting that the darkness slipped away from him and the light of the descending sun illuminated them both again.

Evie responded to his touch with a sigh.

"Please," she said, even as her legs parted and his hand cupped the top of her thigh. His fingers brushed the delicate skin of her inner thigh, slick and wet with her arousal.

"Please what?" Ked murmured against her ear. "Please stop? Please go on? You need to tell me what to do. I want you more than I can say."

"Please don't leave me hanging," she said. She shifted in

his arms and her robe fell open, her perfect, pale skin gleaming in the light.

Ked let his hand venture farther up her thigh and beyond the triangle of dark curls that lay between. Evie tilted her hips up and his fingers found her soft, wet center and slipped between, sinking deep inside her. She clenched around him so tightly he nearly groaned. He'd give her this small release now because he sensed her need, but he needed to take her to Marcus, not give in to his burning ache to spend the next week making love to her. If everything worked out, both he *and* Marcus would spend the next week making love to her.

# CHAPTER 25

## MARCUS

Marcus simply couldn't hear another word. Her tale of her encounters with his fellow Elites had been a bright spot, and so arousing he wished again that he had been there to witness—or to join in.

The deeper connection to Evie was what destroyed the illusion. The deep grief over the loss of those babies, and understanding for the first time what she had meant that first day so long ago. She wasn't able to carry his child—or any child—that wasn't sired by her true mate.

That man wasn't him, and had never been. Now that she had Ked, she could heal from those earlier losses that Marcus's actions had resulted in.

His saving grace was that he had ultimately succeeded in his plan to find a way to get word to her brothers that she was alive. Only it hadn't been her brothers who mattered. The *Void* was supposed to be the go-between, yet he'd ultimately been the man who would save them both.

*Shanghai, China*
*Six Years Ago*

FINDING the dragon hadn't been easy, but Marcus had eventually tracked the elusive Blue to a smoky night club in Shanghai. He should have signaled to Naaz and Sterlyn to meet him so the three of them could pool their power to capture her. Yet this time, he hesitated. The other two Elites were not nearby, so this would be the perfect opportunity to test his plan to get word to someone about Evie's whereabouts. Besides, the last thing he wanted to do was let his master destroy another Blue.

The Blue dragon's aura was like a lure to him, and he spiraled closer to her like a moth to a flame. She was a beautiful woman with straight, dark hair that reminded him of Evie's. She was as petite and bird-like as his lover, too, except with sweet Asian features and glimmering blue eyes.

He sensed her awareness of him, and yet she didn't even send him a glance when he sat down at the bar next to her. To her, he was merely an unmarked Blessed human. He had learned over the years that to a dragon, that was the most enticing bait, even more so than a sexually aroused human. It helped that the reminders of Evie had put him in that state. He pushed it a step farther, imagining Evie in the same slinky dress and him peeling it off her before he dropped to his knees for a taste.

The bartender took his order and while he waited, he felt the cool tickle of a breeze blow across his face. The female dragon had taken the bait, her breath a curious test to learn more about him. He inhaled, and increased the detail of his fantasy, making sure the woman believed the images in his mind resembled her more than the woman he wished she was.

As he reached for the tumbler of whiskey on the bar, her hand slipped across the slick wooden surface and halted over his.

"Bring your drink and come with me," she said in perfect English.

Marcus affected surprise, turning his head to look at her with raised eyebrows. He let a slow smile curl his lips and gave her an appreciative once-over that seemed to please her.

"It would be my pleasure," he said.

Satisfied, she slid off the bar stool, still clutching his hand. With his free hand, he grabbed his drink and let her lead him through the crowded room, past the dance floor, and through a curtained doorway in the back. Beyond that lay a hallway with a pair of human bouncers guarding another door. They nodded silently to the woman and opened the door for her, revealing a dimly lit staircase beyond.

On the second floor, she led him through another door which she closed and locked behind them. The room was decorated luxuriously in pale lavenders and blues, with an entire wall of windows that overlooked the dance floor and bar on the lower floor. Comfortable chairs and sofas were arranged around the room, and there was a bar along one wall.

"We're alone," she said.

"I see that." Marcus tossed back his drink and finally let his gaze meet hers. She stood with her back pressed against the door, her breasts rising and falling rapidly and her eyes twinkling with inner light no normal human would be able to see. He set his empty glass down and strode back to her. She was ripe and ready for him, no doubt eager to learn what it was like to make love with a Blessed human.

She wouldn't get the opportunity, however. He wasn't here for sex, after all.

He threaded his fingers through her sleek hair, gripping the side of her head and tilting her face up to press his lips against hers. She let out a soft moan as he claimed her mouth, thrusting his tongue deep. Christ, she even felt like Evie in his arms, and his erection was enough to lend credence to the ruse. He pulled her tighter against him, just to emphasize how much he wanted her, and enjoyed the way her slender arms wrapped around him, her fingernails digging into his back.

Gripping her backside, he lifted her and carried her to one of the sofas and laid her down. Just as he'd imagined earlier, he hooked the straps of her gown with his fingers and tugged them down her shoulders, peeling the slinky fabric off her perfect, translucent skin. Her bare breasts were small and round, with perfect pink nipples. Marcus bent and took one tip into his mouth, sucking expertly. He'd spent a few nights with Sterlyn's Zamirah and learned that dragon females were every bit as pliant as other women, if he took his time.

Her fingers combed through his hair, yet another reminder of how Evie behaved when they made love. He decided he would enjoy making this female fall apart under his touch. It was the least he could do, considering he would wind up terrifying her afterward.

He tugged her dress all the way off, pleased to discover she was entirely nude beneath. He slid to the floor, kneeling before her, and urged her legs apart, pushing one up to drape over the arm of the sofa. Without further preamble he bent his head and kissed deeply between her thighs.

His tongue teased along the length of her slit and he reveled in the tangy flavor of the slick, velvety folds. The more he licked, the more her sweet fluids coated his lips. Her swollen clit burned with heat beneath his tongue and his cock raged with need to fill that slick channel.

Ignoring his need, he worked her deftly until her voice rose harshly and her hips bucked against his face. The sounds of her cries were the most brutal reminder that she wasn't Evie. She wasn't singing her love for him in the wake of her orgasm. The cry still resonated inhumanly in the room, and the power of her climax surged into him like a flood of cool water.

He chose that moment to act, sliding his hands up her torso to cup each side of her head and letting the dark power inside him surge forth from his palms and sink into her.

The dragon's blue eyes went wide and she cried out, "No! Please!"

It was too late for her. He had her mind in the vise-like grip of that darkness, isolating her power and rendering it null, then preventing her from telepathically communicating with any other dragons who might be nearby.

"I'm not going to hurt you," he said in a low voice. "I admit, I was sent to capture you—my master does love Blue dragons in particular, for some reason. My partners aren't far. I could easily take you with me now, but I need a favor instead. If you promise to do this for me, I will let you go. If you do not, then I *will* call my fellow Elites and we'll lock you away with the others we capture." He had no intention of carrying out the threats, of course. This was his best chance to get Evie out of her prison, and if it meant holding his power over this woman to ensure the message was delivered, then he would use it.

"Y-you shouldn't exist," she croaked. "There hasn't been an Elite with your power in centuries. Only one dragon on earth has that power. The Void. Legends say he killed the Elite who mirrored his power."

Marcus had heard the story countless times. Sayid loved to tell it, always with a particularly hungry, vengeful look in his eyes. The Elite in question had been the very first of them, a female who was once Sayid's favorite.

The blue dragon's admission gave him an idea, however. If this dragon was so powerful, he had to have some pull among the higher races. He was only going to ask her to speak to the Dragon Council at first, but why stop there?

"I need you to get a message to this so-called *Void*. Tell him to find Iszak and Lukas North. Their sister is alive."

"Where is she?" the woman asked, growing still, her eyes narrowing with a calculating look Marcus saw right through. He needed Evie's brothers to know she lived, but he wasn't prepared to risk giving away the precise location of the Ultiori facility. If the messenger were caught with that information he would be risking Evie's life.

"She's in North America. Tell him to let fucking *Fate* guide him. Do you understand?" He shook her when her eyes widened at his instructions.

"Yes, but it's nearly impossible for a dragon ranked as low as I am to reach the Council. They aren't even accessible until the Ascension."

"When will that be?" Marcus asked, frustrated.

The woman closed her eyes and pursed her lips, her naked body still tense beneath him. Finally, she said, "Six years, give or take. I will do this for you if I can, but it will take time. Please, forgive me."

Marcus released her and sat back with a sigh. It would have to be enough. They'd been trapped for so long already, a few more years wouldn't kill them, at least he hoped. And the delay may help avoid suspicion.

"All right. I'll come back here on this same date in six years. I expect to hear that you delivered the message."

She nodded and reached to the floor for her dress, tugging it swiftly over her head. When Marcus stood, she eyed his bulging crotch and gave him a small smile. "You can let me take care of you, too, if you would like. As a thank you for not capturing me?"

Marcus merely shook his head. "Six years," he said again and walked out the door.

*Dragon Monastery, Sunda Islands*
*Present Day*

Evie's moans of climax reverberated in Marcus's mind loud enough to make him aware of the renewed connection between himself and his savior. His fingers clenched, skin tingling at the phantom sensation of her tight channel and hot, wet fluids coating Ked's fingers as they penetrated her.

It was as though Marcus was with her himself, doing these things to her, and he groaned out loud at the unmistakable ache that plagued his groin. He only ever got that hard around Evie, but there was a new aspect to his craving. Something inside him reached out, not for the connection with Evie, but for the man who Marcus was somehow inexorably linked to. Marcus wanted to thank him, and to tell him to take care of Evie, the way Marcus was unable to. He wanted something else, too, but the craving was new and alien to him. So alien he couldn't quite process it, so he focused on the need to express his gratitude.

*"I can hear you,"* Ked's already familiar, deep voice resonated in his mind. *"Like I told you before, you are part of me now, so we can communicate at will. You can't block me out if I don't wish you to."*

*"Then you have to know I'm through with this world. Please, let me die. My strength is gone, and she has you now. I'm at peace now that she's safe."*

*"You'll regain your strength, if you are willing to live and let me help you,"* Ked said.

Marcus didn't want to hear more. With the force of the last vestiges of dark power he had possessed for fifty years, he cloaked his mind to block out the voice again. He could still sense Ked's presence lingering in the shadows of his thoughts, but the black dragon thankfully stayed silent.

With Evie's warmth lingering on his skin and her scent in his nostrils, Marcus closed his eyes and let himself revisit the night he'd wished had been their last night together.

HE'D RETURNED to the Shanghai night club six years to the day after his first visit, as promised. The blue dragon he'd convinced to carry his message was nowhere to be found.

Sitting at the bar, he ordered the same drink he'd ordered before and scowled around, seeking out the blue of her aura among the myriad flickering energies of the humans that filled the large room. He even scanned the opaque glass of the windows along the second floor, wondering if she lay hidden in one of the VIP suites above. His senses picked up other dragons, but none of their auras were familiar to him.

Fucking hell. Had she screwed him over after all?

Just when he was about to give up, an attractive, dark-haired man seated himself on the barstool to Marcus's left.

"All the dragons in here are aware of your presence, Elite," the man said in a low voice. "We've been expecting you."

Marcus stiffened and set his gaze on the man's face. "I hope they know better than to act. You don't want the human patrons to find out what this meat market really is to you guys. Your choices would be exposure of your kind, or insanity for the humans in here." His brows drew together as he studied the man's somewhat familiar features. He wasn't the person Marcus had hoped to meet, but he had to be related to the woman he'd given his message to. He had the same sleek, black hair, refined features, and vivid blue eyes, though his cheekbones were heavier, his jaw wider, and his eyes rounder.

"We're not foolish enough to try to take you," he said, his tone calm, but his tension betrayed by the rigid set of his shoulders. "Besides, I admit I'm curious why you entrusted my mother with such a valuable message. She gave up her last reserves of energy to ensure the message was delivered. Power that would have been my inheritance. In the end, I was the one who had to endure the scrutiny of the First Shadow in order to fulfill my mother's dying wish. You spared her, so she felt obligated to follow through, even after her death."

"You're her son. Of course." Marcus had forgotten how significant the timing was. The woman would not have been able to wait for the Ascension. Each subsequent generation of dragons gave up their lives every five hundred years, leaving the last of their power as a legacy to their offspring. "How long has it been since she died?"

"A little over a year. We Ascended shortly after her death, and I came home to find her message." The man let out a sigh and took a slow swallow of his drink. He cast his glimmering blue eyes to Marcus. "You're one of *them*, but you're not loyal.

That makes me very curious. Care to explain why you entrusted my mother with your message?"

"I just need to know that it was delivered."

The man's jaw clenched and he stared down at his drink. "It was. I hope like hell the sacrifice we made to do so was worth it. The First Shadow seemed particularly interested in the details when I delivered it. He told me..." The man's eyes went foggy and he shivered. "He thanked me and said he would reward me once he retrieved the woman mentioned in the message."

"What do you mean, the *First Shadow*. I asked for the message to be taken to the *Void*." His hand tightened around his glass, his scalp tingling with rising anger at his missive being disregarded.

"Do you have any idea what you were asking? Carry a message to the fucking *Void*. If he wanted to, he could carve your mind out and leave you with nothing but an empty core, with your worst nightmare the only thing left behind for you to live with for eternity. There's a reason access to him is limited.

"The First Shadow is the highest ranking black dragon those of my family's rank can speak to. My mother took the message to the former First Shadow shortly after you gave it to her. She begged for an audience with the Void, but was denied. There was nothing more she could do. I followed up last week with the new First Shadow. He assures me there are dragons tasked with finding this woman, but it would have helped if you gave us a more precise location."

"If I were to tell you, my master would find out and either move her or kill her. I can't risk it."

"Then you'll just have to fucking be patient," the man sneered at him. "No one wants to risk pissing off that dark bastard just for the life of one female who isn't even a dragon. If you want to find the Void, go after him yourself."

Marcus gathered his power and raised his hand, prepared to introduce the man to his own brand of darkness, but stopped himself. He lived with that void inside him already. He was weary of using it on others. Weary of carrying the burden himself and being forced to do precisely that to the myriad of victims his master had sent him and his brothers out to capture over the years. No. If Evie could be sent away to safety, he would stop, regardless of the torture he had to endure in the aftermath of her escape. And, God willing, he could actually die.

Marcus would love to meet this *Void* before he died, though. To curse him for his contribution to the last fifty years of purgatory he'd endured. To every dragon he'd met in the intervening years, his own power was considered a cosmic balance of a sort. No one questioned exactly *why* Marcus and his brothers had virtually the same powers as the dragons, even though they manifested theirs a little differently—through their palms as well as through the power of their lungs. But he knew the truth. The trio of males the lower-ranked dragons revered as demigods were the reason for Marcus and his brothers' very existence.

Marcus shut his eyes and laughed softly. He finished his drink and ordered another.

"I'm in the mood for a void of a different sort tonight, my friend," he said to the man beside him. "I have a few hours before my brothers find me. I'm not at liberty to share my reasons for doing what I did, but if you get me drunk enough, details may slip. In the meantime, I'd love to hear more about your mother. She was a lovely woman."

The man's brow furrowed and a perplexed half-smile tugged at the corner of his lips. "You're nothing like I expected for an Elite. In stature, certainly, but demeanor... you look hopeless."

"Not for lack of trying," Marcus said.

The man's gaze drifted over his face slowly, cautiously, and Marcus caught a glint of something more curious and bold in those blue eyes. With a jolt, he remembered this was a dragon he was becoming far too relaxed beside. The fire of attraction in the man's eyes made him realize he'd taken a bigger risk than he intended. He was still a Blessed, and this blue dragon before him wanted a taste as strongly as his mother had. The idea of giving in to someone else's craving for his sex energized him, but not in the direction his companion might have hoped.

"I apologize," he said, flinging cash onto the bar and standing. "I'd love to stay, but I just realized I have somewhere to be."

WITH THE POWER of the *drift*, he returned to the "dungeon," as he liked to call it. He ignored Sterlyn and Naaz's objections when he immediately headed down the hallway that held Evie's cell at the end. Their master was due back within days, but Marcus wasn't about to waste time now that he knew they were coming for her. He wanted just one night before she left him.

He paused outside her cell and closed his eyes, making an effort to gather his wits. He'd been too long apart from her, and his need overwhelmed his senses to the point that he couldn't remember the key code that would let him into her room. When the keypad beeped and flashed angry red lights, he stared blindly at the message on the digital readout. "Biometric Scan Rejected," was all it said. He mashed his thumb onto the tiny surface of the scanner and received the same message.

Marcus was on the verge of smashing his fist into the screen embedded flush into the wall in front of him, the little lights and messages taunting him. He needed to get to her.

"Marcus," Sterlyn said, gripping his shoulder tightly. "You're not authorized to enter her room."

"I have to get to her tonight! You don't understand..." He looked at Sterlyn and snapped his mouth shut immediately when he saw the look of warning in the other man's eyes.

With a soft curse he lowered his hand from the panel. "He's here early."

"Something's happened," Sterlyn said. "He wants all three of us with him tonight. Special assignment, he says. Naaz is on his way up. He sent me to find you and bring you, too. I think he's found her, finally."

The "her" in question didn't need clarifying, but Marcus's sense of dread heightened. He'd heard stories about the dragon that had made their master who he was, and the idea of the pair of them getting back together could only mean more suffering for them all. But he had no choice.

Before him, the opaque white of Evie's door faded to transparent and her petite form came into view on the other side. She gazed up at him wide-eyed with a hesitant smile pulling at the corners of her mouth.

Her lips moved, mouthing the word "hello," though Marcus couldn't hear her. He pressed his hand to the glass and said, "I'm sorry. I love you."

Again, her lips moved, forming the words he still didn't feel worthy of. *I love you, too.*

He had no idea how much everything would change in a matter of days.

# CHAPTER 27

## MARCUS

*Dragon Monastery, Sunda Islands*
*Present Day*

"*Y*ou should have left me behind," Marcus said to the shadowy entity still lurking in a dark corner of his mind.

He sensed Ked rousing to his communication and the male's voice replied, "*The two of you are a package deal, at least where she is concerned. And you intrigue me. I killed the last Ultiori Elite created with my blood, and it has haunted me ever since. Killing you would destroy another piece of my soul.*"

Perhaps if Ked felt that strongly there was hope for him. Especially if the dragon was entertaining the idea of saving Marcus for Evie's sake. The prospect of living sparked a glimmer of energy deep inside him and Marcus forced his eyes open, blinking into the dim room. Once his eyes adjusted, he was greeted with the scowling looks of Evie's brothers yet again.

Despite recent moments when he hoped they might have

forgiven him, the fact that she'd arrived here damaged had clearly not helped their opinion of his worth. The pair of them would definitely prefer it if Marcus disappeared, but he cringed at the idea of being sent away.

*"If I agree to stay, I want your word that I'll have sanctuary. I can offer my knowledge in exchange. Your kind fears me and my brothers, but believe it or not, the most terrifying person on earth isn't you and your siblings—it's our master."*

Ked's essence shifted in Marcus's mind, as though he'd become more alert. *"I am aware of Nikhil's methods. I am also aware of what you did to help my sister's mates locate her when she was held by him. But I need more from you than your knowledge. You are far too valuable to simply give safe harbor to."*

Marcus closed his eyes again to block out the scrutiny of the two men he regretted displeasing the most. Perhaps if he acquiesced to Ked's demands, he could find some way to regain Lukas and Iszak's trust. He would do anything.

*"What is it you need me to do?"*

*"The same thing I must do: be a father to your unborn child. Without its parents' energy, the baby will die."*

Marcus sat up and opened his eyes wide. He struggled to rise from the bed and Lukas and Iszak both snapped to attention, stepping in front of the doorway that led out of the bedroom.

"I need to get to her!" he said, swaying on his feet as he scanned the room for clothes. He spied garments hanging on hooks along the wall beside a large, wooden bureau and stumbled toward them, the room swimming as he walked. His vision blurred and he stumbled, flailing forward. Two pairs of large hands grabbed his arms and held him upright with vicious grips.

"Where the hell do you think you're going?" Iszak growled. He turned Marcus back toward the bed while Lukas snagged the garments from the wall and followed.

"Evie, I need to see her. Just… talk to Ked." How in the world it had happened, he couldn't begin to fathom. He and Evie had only had the one night together. That a child could have been conceived in the midst of the horrors Marcus and Evie had endured was beyond his ability to comprehend. Besides, he really didn't want to be the one to tell her overprotective brothers that their sister was knocked up.

His savior arrived in the form of the brothers' mate. Belah opened the door and came through, followed by a man Marcus had never met, but who definitely carried himself with the same regal stature that most dragons possessed. The man was shirtless, clad only in a wrap-around sarong, his torso covered in the most elaborate tattoo Marcus had ever seen. A huge dragon wrapped all the way from the tops of his shoulders down to disappear beneath the top of the sarong.

While Belah had a quiet word with her mates, the man scrutinized Marcus so closely, Marcus shivered and reached for the clothes, his hands trembling as he struggled to dress himself. The man's eyes were unlike any dragon's eyes he'd ever seen, but it took him a moment to grasp exactly why.

When he did, his head shot up and he stared, open-mouthed at the man.

"You're a Prismatic," he said, dumbfounded. He'd only heard of the existence of Prismatics once or twice—whispers from their prisoners or dragons he and his brothers eavesdropped on when they were hunting. In all his years as a hunter, not once had he encountered a prismatic.

Marcus managed to get the lightweight drawstring pants pulled up to cover himself before Belah turned to face him, though his modesty was far from preserved after the unraveling power of the man's gaze.

"Marcus, this is Kris. He's going to help you regain enough energy for me to take you to Ked and Evie. Ked wants you conscious. He says you can be trusted, which my mates may not yet believe, but I have faith in you as I have faith in your former master."

"Did he tell you?" Marcus croaked, glancing between Belah and Kris, still marveling at the swirling spectrum of Kris's eyes.

Belah smiled and Kris raised an eyebrow.

"Yes, but my mates don't know yet. I will acclimate them into the idea when the time comes."

Marcus heaved out a sigh that eased one worry but left behind the true anguish he'd been seeking to let go of with his death. Fuck him for wanting the easy way out. He knew better.

Kris knelt before him. "I have to touch you for this to work. You might feel a little aroused when it happens, but that's natural. Save it for her."

Marcus nodded. He wanted this as much as the shadow did. The shadow tickled at his mind, impatient for his presence.

Kris's hands gripped his thighs and squeezed. Kris didn't move his hands, but a surge of energy pulsed into Marcus that made his dick instantly spring to attention.

"Fuck!" Marcus blurted, but gripped the bedsheets behind him while the man closed his eyes and let more power flow between them. Within moments, Marcus felt entirely energized. He stared down at Kris, confused by the desire he had to kiss the man—and not in platonic gratitude, but to take his mouth and plunge himself inside with his tongue, devouring him to the point he begged to be fucked.

He closed his eyes to suppress that urge. Fucking dragon magic. When he opened them again, the urge hadn't gone away and he clutched his fingers hard to still that need. He felt the mattress underneath his hands rip until his fingertips punched through the woven barrier.

"You'll want to take care of that," Kris said, smiling and pointing at Marcus's raging erection when he stood to leave. "I would, but I have my orders. You should have enough power to make it through a bonding."

Marcus had never felt more alive in all his life. He lifted a shaky hand and cupped his aching cock. After the threat of death, he didn't believe he'd ever perform again. He had been thankful that his last lovemaking with Evie had probably been his best performance ever.

But he had a bigger mission now.

"Take me to her," he said to Belah after Kris departed.

Belah's blue eyes twinkled with inner light and she gave him a sweet smile. "Good. Just follow me…" She trailed off when he stood, her eyebrows rising when she saw his discomfort and the tent in his pants. She tutted softly and stepped toward him. "Kris has a wicked sense of humor. That wasn't very fair of him. Here, take a bit of my breath and you'll feel better."

Belah cupped both sides of his jaw, holding him steady with cool, soft hands as she parted her lips. Between them, a faint wisp of blue smoke escaped her mouth. Marcus obediently inhaled and the tension in his groin eased to a dull but pleasant ache, his hard-on disappearing.

"Now, are you ready to see her?" Belah asked, taking his hand.

"More than ever." He let her lead him to the door. Beyond the opening, Lukas and Iszak waited warily, falling into step on either side of them as Belah led him through the lush foliage up the flagstone path.

Marcus took a deep breath, trying to quell the anxiety inside him. The power of Belah's smoke had left a tingling sensation deep in his lungs, reminding him of sharing breath with Evie.

"Do turul have power in their breaths, too?" he asked, hoping to engage the North brothers in conversation and perhaps regain some balance with them, if he couldn't get them to actually trust him again.

Neither man answered, their only response was to glance at him with open hostility.

With an exasperated glance at her mates, Belah sighed and said, "Our breaths are sacred, for both dragons and turul. For the dragons, the magic we wield comes from our lungs. You would know this as an Elite—since my brother's blood runs through your veins, you are a part of him and carry his power inside you. You use your breath to manifest it, yes?"

"I do, but something happened when I was with Evie the other night." Or was it last night? He had no frame of reference now for how long it had been. He shook his head to dispel the sense of discontinuity he felt having spent his dreams reliving the last fifty years.

"What happened with Evie?" Iszak said, his words clipped and harsh.

Marcus cursed himself for mentioning it now. The experience had been the most intimate moment of his life, and of his entire relationship with Evie. He had no business sharing it with her brothers, except that he was curious about how much her magic might have affected him, if at all.

"We shared breath," he finally said, opting for bare honesty in hopes that it might earn him points with the pair.

"Oh!" Belah said, stopping short on the path and facing him with a delighted smile.

Evie's brothers had the opposite reaction, both of them ejaculating colorful curses to the heavens.

"Shit," Marcus said. "I did something wrong by doing that, didn't I? I mean, besides all the other things I fucked up, like nearly getting her killed."

Belah let out a small laugh, still smiling, and laid a hand on his upper arm. "No, Marcus. All you did was accept a turul mating bond with Evie. This explains quite a bit, actually." She widened her eyes emphatically without elaborating.

Marcus opened his mouth, grasping her meaning. "Ah…" he said before stopping himself. Christ, that woman was devious. He couldn't help smiling secretly. No wonder she'd gotten pregnant so quickly.

"Dragons do it, too," Belah swiftly said, filling in Marcus's pause and starting to walk again, gesturing gracefully during her explanation. "Not as part of mating, but as a way to share a closer bond with one we love, if we're unable to mate with them for whatever reason. We've always had so many laws that kept some lovers apart. Until recently, two dragons were never permitted to mate each other. And now with you and your bond with Ked, we're discovering that there are so many situations our laws could not have predicted."

She paused and took a deep breath. Marcus couldn't help but sense a kind of desperation in her tone when she spoke again. "It has forced the Council to consider what kind of precedent it sets when a human has been infused with a dragon's blood. The bond goes deeper than the magical bond that's made when Nirvana is shared. It is as if you are a part of him—a part of his soul—separate, yet still intertwined too closely for the bond to ever be broken."

Marcus pulled her to a stop again forcing Belah to cease her increasingly frantic rambling. "I know about the bond," he said gently. "You don't need to explain it to me. I'm honestly grateful for it because it made Evie look at me with true love in her eyes for the first time ever. Now that I know…" He paused, glancing at Iszak and Lukas who both narrowed their eyes at him. "Now that I know she'll still have me, I need to be with her, whatever the consequences."

Belah's smile looked forced now and when he met her eyes, they were brimming with tears. She swallowed and nodded at him. "Good. That's good," she forced out. "Because Ked can't help but love you because of that bond, and Evie's baby needs you even more."

Her eyes suddenly widened and she clamped her mouth shut, covering it with one hand. The other hand rested protectively over her midsection.

"What the fuck?" Iszak said.

"Christ," Lukas muttered. "Evie's pregnant, isn't she? Is it yours, Marcus? It had better fucking be yours."

Marcus braced himself for the confrontation, but refused to dismiss Belah's odd behavior. He turned to the brothers who now stood blocking the path ahead of them, holding his hands out in surrender.

"Evie's been locked in a cell for fifty years. I knew she was about to be rescued and so I went to be with her. We were making love when she asked me to share breath with her. I think that extra bond plus my link to Ked are what enabled her to conceive." He kept a solid wall of dark power in his mind between his words and the knowledge of the other experiments Evie'd been forced to endure while inside. All that mattered was that she was out now.

He stared at both men who he had once considered as close as brothers. "Now, if I understand correctly, her unborn child needs me because of my bond to her true mate as much as the fact that I am the father. Which means you had better not fucking stand in my way of seeing her."

The wind kicked up around the North brothers, rustling the trees around them. Now that Marcus knew what kinds of creatures the pair were, he recognized the signs of turul power being gathered. Belah swiped at her tears and stepped between them, facing her mates. "This isn't the time…" she began, but was cut off by a loud yell from some distance away, and the sounds of running footsteps and flapping wings around them.

Then a dark turbulence pummeled at Marcus's mind, an incoherent rage rising in him that made his blood boil for no apparent reason. Above them the clouds drew together, the the full moon snuffed out behind whatever power had overtaken the night.

A thunderous roar shook the entire mountain. Belah cursed and started running up the path, with Marcus and her mates close on her heels.

"What is it?" Marcus called after her.

"I don't know!" Belah yelled back. "You have a link to my brother, ask him what the fuck he thinks he's doing!"

As they ran closer to the source of the disturbance, the anger built inside him. It took all of Marcus's will to remain in control, but the need drove him to get to Ked, to make sure that Evie was all right. What else could possibly cause the dragon to react this way?

Marcus reached the top of the hill just behind the others. Before him was a huge, circular clearing that reminded him of a heliport. Dozens of dragons of various colors sat around the edges in states of agitation. In the center of the circle, three huge, white dragons paced in circles around a pair of figures Marcus could barely see between the gaps in the dragons. On the opposite side of them, Ked landed in all his black dragon glory, a full head higher than the largest dragon in the clearing. He roared again, the power of the sound causing Marcus and the North brothers to stumble back a step.

Out of the corner of his eye, a figure jogged toward him and he didn't even stop to think before turning in her direction.

"Marcus! By the Winds you're alive!" Evie yelled as she leaped into his arms.

The clearing erupted into chaos then, and Marcus bent over Evie to shield her from the cacophony of roars and gale force winds. For a second he thought Iszak and Lukas were reacting to his contact with their sister, but when he turned to look, he saw a blue dragon facing off against the black one, and a pair of huge falcons circling overhead. Clouds seemed to form like contrails behind the birds and with each circuit the winds grew stronger.

The warmth of Evie's slight body against him made all the rest fade away and he looked down into her storm-gray eyes. She looked haggard, but beautiful.

"Is it true?" he asked, and even though there was no way his voice could be heard over the noise, she nodded. He held her tighter and kissed her.

"What's happening?" she said when they parted.

Marcus shook his head and looked toward the chaos. The three white dragons had disappeared, but had been replaced by an even larger white dragon, and the three now seemed to be in a standoff over the pair of figures in the center. Marcus knew Ked as he knew his own skin, could feel the barely restrained rage that simmered beneath the surface. Rage toward the newcomers, he realized, and tugged Evie closer so they could get a better look.

The blue dragon must be Belah, though he'd missed the moment when she or her mates had shifted.

"Who is that?" he asked, pointing to the white dragon and tilting his head so his mouth was close to Evie's ear. He felt a small tingle of affinity to the white one, but it was nothing like his connection to Ked.

Evie shook her head, uncertain. "Must be their brother. But who is th—"

They moved clockwise a few steps around the group and Evie suddenly grabbed Marcus's shirt. He shot a look at her and then back toward the group and saw what had startled her.

In the center of the clearing on their knees, looking like they were about to become dragon snacks, were the unmistakable figures of Sterlyn and Nikhil.

# CHAPTER 28

NIKHIL

*Dragon Monastery, Sunda Islands*
*Present Day*

The fact that chaos surrounded him now was no surprise to Nikhil. He was more surprised that he'd succeeded in making it this far. It must have been the fresh drop of Belah's blood she gave him before they parted that allowed him to find her so quickly. Not just a drop, he realized, though that second memory was not entirely his own. He had hurt her—had spilled her blood deliberately and greedily and in the process had consumed more than just that one drop. He hadn't earned it because she hadn't given it willingly, and for that he knew he deserved whatever punishment these dragons wanted to give him now, but the blood had served a purpose in the end. It made it easy for him to mentally lock onto her location and *drift* himself and Sterlyn straight to the dragons' secret stronghold after they had completed their task to secure Belah's children.

Now here they were, with three of the most magnificent beasts he'd ever seen looking like they were about to rip him and Sterlyn apart—or rip each other apart, Nikhil couldn't quite decide which.

He dropped to his knees and urged Sterlyn down as well, but that didn't make a difference in the demeanor of the dragons. He turned to look up at Belah, his breath escaping at the sheer size and beauty of her.

"*Tilahatan!*" he yelled. "I have come to keep my promise to you!"

The huge blue dragon craned her head around and peered down at him. "You have angered my brother and my mates, my love. They do not understand what happened to you. They do not believe what I have told them. And even if they did, you should not be here."

"He must die for what he's done, Belah!" the black dragon roared. "Use your fire and kill him and his Elite now!"

Beside him, Nikhil heard Sterlyn utter a foul curse. A huge, white tail smacked down right in front of them, causing dust to billow up and leaving a long indent in the earth.

"No one is setting fire to anyone here!" the white dragon bellowed. He moved closer, his tail snaking around the pair of them protectively. "The Elite is mine to dispose of. He carries my blood!"

Nikhil hadn't recognized him in his dragon form, but that brief statement confirmed that this was Belah's brother, Aodh.

He stood again, holding out his hands and turning slowly to look at all of them. An audience had formed around them, and close behind Belah he saw Marcus standing stock still and glaring at him, an astonished Evie held close to his side.

"I will not make excuses," he said, directing his words to the couple he had nearly killed and raising his voice so he could be heard above the wind. "The things I have done are unconscionable—actions deserving the worst kind of punishment and death. I will accept any punishment you wish me to take, but please allow me to speak first."

He turned his eyes skyward, recognizing the pair of turul above by the power of the winds that howled around them. These were the brothers of the female he had harmed, and his true love's new mates. "Please allow the Winds to prove the veracity of my words. I will not lie to you now. If this is the last moment I have to speak the truth, let it be the truth that lies in my soul, then you may do with me what you will."

Belah bobbed her large head and let out a trumpeting call. "Please hear him, for my children's sake. All of you, please!"

Nikhil stared at her, dumbfounded by her defense of him after the way he'd harmed her. She was magnificent in her true form, and when her huge body shimmered and shrank, her human beauty took his breath away. She walked toward him clad in a flowing blue gown, her shining midnight hair cascading in waves down her back. The two falcons descended and shifted at her sides, naked for a moment until an almost invisible breath flowed from Belah's lips and simple blue trousers materialized to cover them.

The two men fixated on him in the strangest way, their steps as sure and deliberate as Belah's, but when they stopped in front of him he could sense the confusion of hostility and hunger warring in them both.

Belah's shadowy brother's feelings were not so ambiguous, however. A wash of dark energy hit Nikhil's back, making his skin prickle with the absolute lust for vengeance that flooded from the other man. The feeling was beautiful in its stark simplicity. He remembered that feeling well, because it was the one emotion Meri had latched onto in the beginning. The spark that she had found and fueled with her own agenda until it became an all-consuming wildfire he no longer controlled.

The feeling burned in him once more, but this time he

controlled it, and knew precisely where to direct that rage. He turned to face Ked now, stared into the Void of the black dragon's eyes and silently dared the man to look into his soul to see the truth.

Around him, the others took a few steps back, Sterlyn moving toward Aodh's side as though he were a moth drawn to a flame.

Darkness hit Nikhil like a tidal wave and he fell to his knees, gasping. The sensation of utter *nothingness* flooded through his mind, ten times more powerful than the *drift*, leaving behind a stark landscape of regret in its wake. As the darkness filled him, bits and pieces of his unconscious slowly began to rise up to the surface, like flotsam from a shipwreck, the only lucky pieces that made it to shore.

The sensation was not unlike his strange conversation with Zorion, though that one had not been so brutally efficient at picking out crucial details from his memories. Now, he was powerless to control what Ked did inside his mind, and astonished at what the dragon's power revealed to him.

His true desires were the brightest—his love of Belah and his craving to have a child with her. Beyond that, his regard for his Elites stood out, his pride in each of them and his love for them as surrogates for the child he longed for but could not have. Finally, he saw his grief over the loss of Benedetta, one long-dead Elite who was the only other Elite he'd ever created besides the ones who still lived. An Elite who he'd seen as a daughter as much as Neela had always been, but more than that, she'd been a close friend. Her death at the hands of this creature who invaded his mind now had been one of the few moments of pure rage he'd felt in all the hundreds of years since Belah's death, and one of the few memories he was certain was wholly his own.

That bright flame of emotion seemed to burn through the darkness and Ked's power retreated suddenly. Nikhil found himself face-to-face with a man in utter anguish, crippled by his own eternal regret.

"I loved her," Ked said, and Nikhil knew he spoke of Benedetta. "I thought I might never love another after her, until I learned that Evie was out there."

"Benedetta loved you, too, and you killed her," Nikhil said, then immediately backpedaled, holding his hand up to stall Ked's reply. "No. I am not such a fool now that I cannot accept half the burden for her death. *We* killed her."

"You were her master. You could have released her from her bond to you." Ked's voice strained with emotion, with the need for absolution, but Nikhil had none to give.

"I would have, had I been in full control of my mind then. There was a time when my Elites were truly loyal to me, when I considered them close friends. Benedetta was my closest friend during a time when I had very few. Being loyal to me and loving you at the same time tore her apart. I remember it because she told me she would rather die than choose between us. The Nikhil that once possessed a soldier's honor would have released her from her bond and allowed her to be with you. Please believe that I am that man again."

He turned to look at Marcus, whose face appeared more ashen than before and he leaned on Evie as though he'd fall over if not for her support. "Marcus, this may be long overdue, but I release you. I have already released Naaz and Sterlyn, and all the prisoners that were held in the facility where Evie was kept. I know you have no such conflict of loyalty toward me, but my only wish now is for you to find a way to be whole again. I will not stand in your way."

Turning back to Ked, he said, "Your mates appear to need more healing. If Sterlyn is willing to stay, I'd like to recommend his services, but only if his mate may join him later."

Ked tore his gaze away from Nikhil, his anguished look

receding to be replaced with tenderness, and then his brows drew together with worry. He stepped around Nikhil to get to Evie and Marcus, then slung Marcus's arm over his shoulders and wrapped both arms around the waists of his mates.

The display of decisive action gave Nikhil hope. If the three of them could find a balance with each other in spite of Marcus's history, perhaps his sister and her mates could find a balance with him. But when he shot a hopeful look at the three of them, his heart sank.

"How can we believe you aren't somehow hiding your true monster inside you?" one brother asked, his anger evident in his clenching fists and lowered brows.

"Because Belah's brother just stripped my conscience naked and seems more concerned with other things..." Nikhil gave the man a small smile and shrugged. "And because your sister sang it away," he said, and launched into a poor rendition of the tune that had been constantly running through his head for the past two days.

The North brothers both looked startled, their heads jerking back and their mouths hanging open.

Nikhil stopped singing. "She's much better at carrying a tune. Belah is, too..." he said softly, recalling the nights she'd sang him to sleep with a very similar tune.

Slowly, the two men relaxed a tiny bit. The less serious of the two took a tentative step toward him, a look of hungry curiosity burning in his eyes.

"Lukas, what are you doing?" the other brother snapped.

"I need to know if what I felt when we saved Belah was real or not."

"Don't fucking go near him!"

Lukas glared over his shoulder at his brother. "Don't fucking deny you feel it, too, brother. It's the same goddamn thing that Evie has with Marcus. Evie, tell your brother he's a fool not to try to at least understand."

Nikhil observed the exchange, perplexed by what was transpiring. What was it that Evie had with Marcus? To him it seemed like any bond between two lovers, no different from his bond with Belah. That Belah's brother wished to collar two submissive lovers seemed like a perfectly reasonable arrangement to him.

He watched Evie roll her eyes at the more obstinate of her two brothers. "You can't help it, you big dummy," she said to him. "He did horrible things, but that doesn't change the fact that Belah's blood runs in his veins and you used to hate her, too. Her blood makes him your *One* as much as Belah. You can't *not* love him! Just let it happen. You'll be much happier if you do."

Evie turned, clearly finished wasting time on her brothers, and walked with Ked and Marcus away from the clearing.

Sterlyn cleared his throat. "Sayid... er... Nikhil... I'm going to stay and do what I can for the others. I expect there will be more dragons arriving from the Institute soon who will also need assistance. Aodh says that Zamirah will find her way here with the others when they're released. Somehow she knows the way even though I never knew she did. He says all dragons know the way here, even the ones who have never been. Find me when you are ready to go back."

Nikhil nodded at the knight, who simply waved as he trotted off after the large, white-haired dragon. The white brother, Aodh, reminded Nikhil of a certain young ursa who was likely still locked in a cell in the compound and would stay as long as his satyr lover stayed.

Nikhil turned back to the three remaining figures. He sat back on his heels, regarding them. Belah seemed hesitant to approach, as though she were waiting for her mates to make the first move.

"I meant it when I said I'd accept any punishment," he said. "But I must request that it be postponed until after we've located the bitch who had me controlled all this time. I have allies who are helping with this task as we speak."

Lukas moved to stand in front of him and bent down, eyes narrowed as he scrutinized Nikhil's face. The young turul was strikingly handsome, cleaner of feature than his brother, with a sardonic half-smile on his lips and a dark lock of hair covering one eye.

"Allies, huh?" he asked. "More Ultiori thugs?"

"Not Ultiori," Nikhil said. "Former prisoners, in fact. We think the creature that is responsible is a nymph. One of her own kind wants to find her and punish her. The status of the Ultiori organization is … uncertain, but the allies I still have inside are helping determine the truth. My Elites are with me, and I have one of them investigating to find out where the other Ultiori hunters and scientists' loyalties truly lie. If there are any loyal to me still, I can build an army from them."

"Hmm, an army you say? To command the way you commanded Belah?" Lukas said, standing up and walking around Nikhil.

"Lukas…" the other brother said, in an admonishing tone.

"Iszak…" Lukas retorted sarcastically. "I'm curious about him. Want to know what lengths he'll go to for her. If he's telling the truth, this could be fun…"

Nikhil heard Lukas stop just behind him. He wished he'd stood up before engaging them in conversation, but thought that remaining on his knees might make them more receptive. He'd been right, but now sensed he was at an unpleasant disadvantage and had no idea what Lukas was going to do. What, exactly, constituted "fun" for the man?

Lukas moved closer and warmth radiated through Nikhil's clothes into his back. A pair of hands rested lightly on his shoulders, long fingers splaying down across his collarbone. The contact was oddly comforting—not invasive or threatening as he'd expected.

He swallowed, glancing up at Belah and Iszak who stood just a few feet away, watching. Belah's eyes were wide with wonder at the scene. Iszak looked like a tightly coiled spring, his gaze boring into Nikhil. He wanted something… Nikhil guessed it involved introducing both fists to his face.

Lukas, on the other hand, seemed to want something different. His hands traveled down Nikhil's arms and grasped his wrists, then twisted his hands behind his back. The rough sensation of rope snaked across his skin, tightening as Lukas bound him with a quick knot. Then a hand grabbed his hair and yanked his head back hard.

Until that moment, he'd imagined he was simply being prepared for torture. It's what he would have done had he been in control. He'd eventually have told Lukas that he couldn't feel any of the pain inflicted on him, but the inflicting of it might have allowed Lukas to trust him at least a little bit.

But when Lukas's mouth descended on his in a brutal, demanding kiss, his entire body went rigid with the realization of what he was truly in for. And when his groin tightened with arousal as Lukas bit down hard on Nikhil's lower lip, it became crystal clear.

Nikhil hadn't had a hard-on in ages, but the last time had only been when he'd managed to arouse his partner by inflicting pain on her. Just like his own pain, he felt none of it, but any pain or injury he gave another would cut him as surely as if the knife had pierced his own flesh. So it was with pleasure—he only felt it when he gave it to another and it was all the sweeter when that pleasure came from pain.

Lukas was desperately turned on by tying him up and torturing his mouth with the most destructively passionate kiss Nikhil had ever had. The other man's arousal flooded Nikhil with unexpected heat that wasn't entirely unwelcome —not when he could tell Belah enjoyed the show.

By the gods, his Belah would not have mated a pair of men who would simply bow before her, would she?

When Lukas finally released him, Nikhil saw the others through a haze of lust. Belah's excited gaze met his but he could only blink dazedly at her. Iszak, he saw, had become just as aroused by simply watching Nikhil's domination by his brother.

"What in the everloving hell is happening?" Iszak muttered.

Nikhil could only shake his head in wonder. "I- I couldn't tell you. I don't swing that way, but if I must…"

Iszak chuckled. "I don't either, but this jury's still out on what to do with you yet. It seems we may not have a choice thanks to fucking Fate."

"Ah, speaking of Fate, I'd like to take Belah to her children soon. I'd prefer to keep that promise while the two of you are making a decision on what to do with me."

Belah's excitement was almost palpable, but she seemed to be waiting for her mates' permission. Was she always this way with them, or was it simply his presence that shifted the dynamic between the three?

"We do have to consider these developments," Lukas said, moving to face him and squatting so he was at eye level with Nikhil. Their gazes held for a long moment, Lukas's desire radiating off him like a furnace that warmed Nikhil from the inside out. "I can think of all sorts of ways to *torture* you. I imagine Belah has a few tricks up her sleeve she'd love to share, too. Maybe if Iszak and I are satisfied with your penance, if Belah still wants you when we're done, we'll let her have a turn. Until we decide, you had better not lay a hand on her. I want your word, *monster*."

"You have my word that no harm will come to her. I owe my life to her, and I owe my sanity to your sister, and so I am your humble servant. Anything you command, I will do."

Lukas's eyebrow twitched and his lips curled in a wicked smile. "I will hold you to that when the time comes." Then he leaned in and captured Nikhil's lips with his again. This time the kiss was soul-deep and filled with tender passion. How a man who'd been filled with hate only moments ago could turn his emotions around so swiftly left Nikhil dizzy with confusion. Then he remembered that these were the lips responsible for coaxing pleasure from his lover's body now, and the image of Belah bound and at the mercy of these two powerful, dominant males made him hungry for more than just a kiss. It made no sense, but he went with it, kissing Lukas back with desperate hunger.

"By the Winds you taste like her," Lukas whispered huskily when he pulled away again. "Now I know why Evie still wants Marcus even after everything. You will keep her safe, monster. But Iszak and I are not done with you yet. There's no way in hell we're leaving you alone with her. Wherever she goes, we go, too."

He moved away to stand beside Belah and his brother. At their nods, Belah gracefully bent by his side and tore the ropes from his wrists.

"Thank you," she breathed, and kissed him on the cheek. He still felt flushed and hot from Lukas's attention and her lips were smooth and cool against his skin, the sensation giving him a rush of sweet pleasure he didn't expect.

He raised his eyebrows at her. "Please tell me you're ready to leave now. I don't think I'm ready to deal with whatever those two have in mind for me, even if it would mean getting to make love to you again."

Belah gave him a warm smile. "I would like that, but

what's most important now is seeing my children. We are ready to leave when you are."

Nikhil stood and rubbed his wrists. "I need Sterlyn…" He turned, searching for the path he thought he'd seen his Elite run off toward. Instead, he found Belah's huge white-haired brother who had somehow silently manifested only a few feet away. Nikhil wondered how long he'd been there and how much of the scene he'd just witnessed.

"Sterlyn will stay here," Aodh said in a deep, even voice. "I will go with you to my sister's children."

Nikhil nodded and pulled out his blade, preparing to cut his palm. Aodh grabbed his wrist, stopping him before he could break the skin.

"You don't need blood if you have me, brother. Just lead the way."

Knowing better than to question the word of an immortal, he linked hands with Belah and her brother, Belah's mates closing their circle, and he fixed his mind on the time and place where his daughter was. A moment later the *drift* carried them to her.

*A*ll the way back along the path, Marcus only had the strength to focus on a single thought.

*Evie. Our baby. Ours.*

When they reached the bungalow at the top of the hill, Ked helped him inside and guided him to the bed, but Marcus refused to lie down. Instead, he turned and just stood there, all the remaining strength draining out of him at the sight of her.

She couldn't have been more beautiful to him, even though what he saw was a pale, haggard woman. Beside her stood a contradiction to the power he'd witnessed earlier—a huge man with a look more tortured than Marcus's own soul. Evie's slight body was dwarfed in the man's arms when Ked swiftly scooped her up just as her strength appeared to give out. Evie clung to him like her life depended on it.

Evie's eyes met his and he ached to touch her. She only watched him from the arms of the man who held her.

"You look like shit," he said to Ked. As surprising as it was, the man really did look like he hadn't slept in days. His strong face was drawn with worry, dark circles under his eyes.

"Sorry," Ked said. "Looks don't matter when we're dealing with Ultiori torture."

Marcus himself had done this. He'd been reckless enough to wish for one night with her before she was saved.

"Her wings…" he whispered, venturing closer. "God, he was so brutal."

"Her wings are restored," Ked said, brushing a hand over her back.

Evie shivered under Ked's touch and pressed a kiss to his cheek. "You guys like talking about me like I'm not here? If that gets you off, I'm game… Unless we're talking about the baby."

Marcus's eyes shot to her midsection and then up again.

"You pregnant with my baby does a lot more than get me off."

Evie grew still, moving her pale forearms to lay across her abdomen. "The baby happened in there." She had a haunted look on her face which he studied. He knew the truth of all the pregnancies. All the losses and heartbreak that occurred afterward.

"And our child will be raised out here," he said, aching to tell her how much he wanted exactly that. To have their child raised in a good place. Maybe it was foolish of him to wish for, though.

"All the others died," she said, finally looking at him with tears in her eyes.

Ked shifted with her movements, moving to sit on the edge of the bed and holding her with her back to his chest, his arms protectively wrapped around her waist.

"This one won't die," Marcus said. "We won't let it, will we?" He looked at Ked and the man nodded.

Marcus bent to his knees before them and opened his

arms. "I'm not letting this baby go without a father. Trust me."

Evie sank into his arms with a harsh laugh and he let her fall into him, reveling in the familiar contact and summoning every last bit of strength he could find, just to hold her.

They'd done this so many times. This back and forth of planning for their offspring's future. Before, it had been a fictional child they planned for, but now it was so very real. But only if she let it keep being real.

"Love this baby with me?"

"You bet." He said it as his skin prickled with the presence of their savior.

Ked's dark eyes bored into his when he looked up. A wash of darkness and doubt overtook him, stripping away all his senses, all his emotions, but the one thing that mattered. He was of this man, so he knew exactly what he looked for—the truth about whether Marcus still wished to die.

He fought back, flinging a hand out and gripping Ked's arm. He threw his own power at the intrusion.

He gave himself over then, willingly submitting his every desire to the man who had invaded his mind. But he would take the same if he could.

Ked's mind was less willing, but when Marcus's secrets seeped in, he felt the barrier weakening. Soon enough, he saw everything and what he saw staggered him. In the blink of an eye the full scope of Ked's and his siblings' pasts were revealed, including the origin of the man who had created Marcus and his brothers, and who had been indirectly responsible for the child he and Evie had created mere days ago.

*"You've seen my darkest secrets,"* Ked said, speaking into the shadows of Marcus's minds rather than aloud. *"There are no more secrets between us. Let me mark you. It will keep you alive.*

*It's the only way, save giving you my blood, but to shed our blood again would be to give tacit acceptance to his ways."*

Marcus answered silently, *"If the mark will work, I'll do this, but you need to tell me what it means for the baby that I have the blood of three dragons running through my veins."*

Silence.

He stared into Ked's face, waiting for an answer, but the man simply stared back. Evie finally broke the silence.

"Guys, this is a little uncomfortable. If you can't actually *talk* to each other, I am going to go take a walk."

Marcus grabbed her arm in desperation as she walked past. "I just got you back, baby," he said, though missing her was only half the reason he panicked at the idea of her leaving the room. He cast a sidelong glance at the large, black-clad man still seated on the bed.

"I'm not going far," she whispered to him, and kissed him gently. "I'll be with Sterlyn right down the path. You two need to work this out," she said.

Left alone in a room with the man who'd saved him shouldn't have felt uncomfortable, but it did.

Ked didn't smile. He didn't do any of the things Marcus expected a man might do to encourage him to mate a dragon. That was part and parcel of receiving a dragon's mark, he knew at least that much, and he would do it if it meant allowing his and Evie's child to live, but that didn't mean he'd enjoy it.

"I'm not going to mate you unless you ask me to," Ked said, standing and moving to the bureau at the side of the room. He poured a cup of water from the ewer and drank, then poured another and offered it to Marcus, who licked his lips and accepted the glass. "But you should be able to tell by now that the power Kris gave you is waning. If you want to live, you need *my* energy. Nikhil's attack the other night nearly bled you dry, and without enough of my magic running through your veins, you will remain too weak to provide enough energy for the child. Your powers will eventually fade, your humanity will return, and you will grow old and die within a matter of weeks. I can sense the power already fading from your body as it regenerates the blood you lost."

"I know. I can feel my body failing even with the magic Kris gave me. You just have to understand that as much as I may be a part of you now, I am not *like* you. Not that way." Marcus leveled a steady gaze at Ked, and the man only stared back without blinking.

"Evie's child is ours," Ked said. "Both of us created this baby. You, with mine and my brothers' blood in your veins, and your seed in her womb that night. You have a responsibility to follow through."

"I'm not a deadbeat," Marcus said.

"Neither am I," Ked said. "And fixing you means…"

"Fucking me," Marcus concluded.

"It won't be as distasteful as you seem to think," Ked said, his deep voice resonating with suggestive, velvety smoothness that mirrored the heat in his dark eyes.

Ked still kept his distance, but Marcus was acutely aware of the change in tension in the air between them. His skin tingled in a not unpleasant way and he forced his gaze away from the other man, staring fixedly out over the railing beyond the half-open sliding doors that served as one wall of the room.

"Your brothers are part of it," Marcus said, redirecting the conversation back to his earlier request. "Did I catch that right?" He swallowed thickly, throwing that detail back at Ked in an effort to delay the inevitable. "Does that mean what I think it means?"

Thankfully the observation shifted the focus of the tension, Marcus's comment distracting Ked from what felt like a single-minded need to seduce him. He hazarded a glance only to see the other man smiling sardonically.

"Yes, thanks to the little cocktail of blood that made you what you are, there's also a small part of their essence inside the child. And yes, it means exactly what you think, but to a far lesser degree of need than the child has for your essence or mine."

"Does Evie know this?" Marcus asked, his ire rising at the thought that this man who was supposedly Evie's soul mate would pawn her off to his own brothers so casually.

"She's not a stranger to our ways, Marcus. And my brothers are not monsters. If anything, they're more gentle than I am. Aodh is a regular teddy bear, compared to me. They will do it out of need as much as desire."

"Good. Don't be gentle with me. I'd rather you make it less palatable an experience."

"Far from it," Ked said, leveling Marcus with the full force of his dark gaze. Marcus struggled to suppress the tremor of anticipation that passed through him. "You'll enjoy every second as much as Evie does. I am a dragon, after all. It is in my best interest to ensure your absolute pleasure."

Ked took a step toward him, followed by another. Marcus's pulse raced and he involuntarily found himself retreating, but Ked just kept coming, as inevitable and ominous as a thunderhead. His eyes flashed with deep violet light that seemed to see straight into Marcus's soul the way he'd looked into Nikhil's only moments ago. What had he seen in the soul of his former master? Would Marcus's own soul be as much of an abomination as Nikhil's had to have been?

Marcus's back bumped against the sturdy wooden railing of the porch and he grabbed hold of it with both hands. He had nowhere to go now, and not even Evie as a buffer between himself and this man who had flowed through his veins for decades. Such an intimate connection as sex shouldn't have terrified Marcus so much after literally being filled with the man's very essence for so long. Hell, his life had been *defined* by Ked for the last fifty years. Perhaps longer if what he'd learned about himself and his brothers was true. He was destined to be the mate of a dragon, and the detour he'd taken into the Ultiori ranks hadn't changed that.

But to be mated to *this* dragon? Christ, he couldn't even imagine himself with a female of the race, much less the most imperious and dauntingly *male* member of the race he'd ever met. He hated himself a little for how much Ked's presence so close actually sent pleasant ripples of sensation over his skin, like that gaze sweeping up and down him had a tactile element to it—like he was, indeed, being physically caressed.

Yet he had little enough strength left to object. He was living on borrowed time and if he ever wanted to see his and Evie's child thrive, he had no choice.

Ked reached him and rested his hands on the railing on either side of Marcus, not touching but so close Marcus could feel intense heat radiating from his skin.

"You know I am capable of compelling you to do my bidding. In your weakened state, you wouldn't be able to resist me. But that would be a poor start to what I would like to be a mutually pleasurable beginning to a very, *very*, long and satisfying relationship for the three of us. I am fated to have a family with Evie, yet it seems Fate, as always, has thrown a knot into the tapestry. Evie loves you and she would be heartbroken if you died, not to mention we would likely lose the baby."

Marcus let out a stuttering breath. "Then do it already," he said, trying to goad the man into overpowering him. To hell if he was going to simply bend over and beg to be fucked.

Ked leaned in, his lips brushing against Marcus's ear. "Do what, Marcus? Hold you down, strip you naked, and have my way with your untried ass? That really isn't my style, or any dragon worth his horns. No…" Ked let out a soft laugh that tickled Marcus's cheek and set every nerve in his body alight. The man raised a large hand and clutched the back of Marcus's neck, pulling back just enough that their eyes met. "You *will* ask for it, but only because you can no longer stand the thought of not having it. I belong inside you, Marcus, one way or the other."

Closing his eyes against the confusing swirl of lust and expectation in Ked's fathomless black depths, Marcus said, "Did you already make love with her?"

"Not particularly relevant, but not yet. Not for lack of profound desire on both our parts. Her injuries and her worry for you held her back. Now that her wings are restored and you're coming around, she'll be ready. So far, we have kissed, and I've coaxed her Nirvana from her once. "

Marcus clenched his eyes more tightly shut, shaking a little at what he was about to do.

"Then we'll start where you started."

Steeling himself, he opened his eyes and stared into the twin voids of Ked's again. He hated how utterly helpless he felt in that moment. The man was only slightly bigger, and not more than an inch taller than Marcus, yet somehow Marcus had the strongest sense that, had Ked been the least bit inclined to, he could tear Marcus in half.

He was far less concerned for his physical well-being in that moment, however. More than anything, he had to admit to himself that he was scared—not of what would soon transpire between them—no, he was utterly, ball-shrinkingly terrified that he would *like* it.

That sense was only confirmed when Ked's eyelids lowered, his gaze falling to Marcus's parted lips. Then Ked's fingers slid up through Marcus's hair and he bent his head, tilted slightly, and pressed his lips against Marcus's mouth.

Marcus surrendered reluctantly, at first thinking he could simply imagine the mouth on his was Evie's, but there was no mistaking the utterly masculine, powerful pull of Ked's lips, or the thrust of the hot, sweet, velvet of his tongue into his mouth. Marcus could do nothing more than open up for the man, and once he did, something primal and instinctual seemed to take over.

A sudden blast of heat flooded his body as the need gripped him. He released his hands from the railing and clung to Ked's sides, fingers digging in hard as their lips and tongues tangled. With a push and a twist of his leg around Ked's, he spun them, pushing Ked back against the railing and grinding hard against him. Their hips pressed so tight, the friction of their erections rubbing together through their clothing was as overwhelming to him as the slide of Ked's tongue against his.

Marcus pulled back abruptly, gasping for breath.

"Jesus Christ," he panted, struggling to steady his vision. The world swam around him, as though all the blood had rushed from his head. And he supposed that's exactly what had happened.

He stared down between them where his own and Ked's thick erections bulged in heavy ridges side-by side beneath their lightweight trousers. In another life, he might have been repulsed by this type of intimacy with another man, but it was far from distasteful to him now. Everything about it felt *right*. Right down to the contours of their thighs pressed together, warm through the thin linen barrier between them.

"It's the Blessing," Ked said softly, his large hand still cupping the back of Marcus's head, fingers gently stroking his neck. "You were meant for me from before your birth. Or meant for a dragon, at any rate, but Fate and circumstance led you to me. You can't deny that this feels predestined."

"Evie…" Marcus began, finding it difficult to even form a full sentence.

Gathering his meaning, Ked smiled. "She's definitely a big part of it. We can wait for her to return before venturing further."

Marcus found himself fixated on the movement of Ked's lips, the hard lines and soft curves, flushed darker now after the pressure of the kiss and glistening slightly with wetness. Marcus's mouth watered, craving another taste.

"Take what you desire," Ked murmured in a low growl. "You can give in to that urge with me. You won't hurt me." The undertone in his voice hinted at an invitation for Marcus to not hold back.

Marcus raised both hands and tangled one set of fingers in the hair at the nape of Ked's neck, yanking his head back and testing his resolve. With his other hand shaking from need, he traced fingers over Ked's throat and hooked them into the collar of the woven, tunic-style shirt.

"What if I want you to beg me for it first?" Marcus asked, twisting the fabric of Ked's collar into his fist and pulling until the lightweight weave protested.

"Not much of a challenge," Ked said. "I want you, but I don't think you have the energy to follow through yet."

With a wrenching pull, Marcus yanked downward. The linen weave tore like paper and the shirt fell open, hanging haphazardly on Ked's wide shoulders.

Energized by the hunger for the body pressed against him, Marcus pushed the fabric aside and sank his teeth into Ked's shoulder, grazing lips, teeth, and tongue over the taut, salty skin. Under his tongue, the skin had an unusual texture, both sensual and foreign. When he slid his free hand down the center of Ked's chest, he felt the same thing. Opening his eyes, he accessed his waning power to see what he could only feel, and could make out the faintest outline of dark scales shimmering over every surface of Ked's body. The same dark scales he'd had in his dragon form.

His hand paused at the waist of Ked's draw-string pants. Did the texture of his skin extend to every extremity? Was he brave enough to find out?

As if belonging to another body, his hand rose up, finger-tips plucking at the ties and pulling. In slow motion, it seemed, the bow came undone, the gathered waist of Ked's pants loosened and slid down a few inches to reveal more of Ked's naked hips and dark thatch of curls—the culmination of the dark trail of hair that led south from his navel. But the pants snagged on the jutting thickness of Ked's erection.

"Go ahead," Ked said. "You clearly want to find out for yourself when you could have simply asked what you want to know. Or you can wait, and find out when I fuck you whether my cock is as smooth as yours or not."

From somewhere behind Marcus, a lilt of amusement in her tone, Evie said, "I've seen you naked. Definitely smooth."

Marcus snatched his hand away and stumbled backward in a panic, spinning on his heels. "Jesus, Evie, I… I was just…"

Just what? His mind somersaulted over all the ridiculous excuses until he caught the alarm on her face. The lovely image of her swam disconcertingly before it tipped sideways and she cried out his name. Something hard and cool hit his side and pain shot through his body. His vision went red, then darkness seeped in around the edges, finally taking over again.

*Dragon Monastery, Sunda Islands*
*Present Day*

Evie's pulse raced from the surge of adrenaline coming right on the wake of one of the most arousing scenes of her life. She bent to the side of her unconscious lover, a fresh wave of despair coming over her at seeing him unconscious again after finally learning he was alive.

"Marcus, baby, please wake up." She pulled his head into her lap, stroking his hair. "What happened?" she asked, looking up at Ked. She lowered her eyes abruptly at his state of his clothing, ripped and half falling off, his pants barely staying up, and his thick arousal as clear as day. "I mean, I can *guess* what happened, but why did he get so upset?"

Ked strode over to them, cinching his drawstring tight again before shrugging out of his ruined shirt and tossing it aside. He knelt down and examined Marcus's side.

"He was coming around, but not easily. I think it'll be easier, now that you're here. We can't take much longer, though. When he wakes up again, we need to go through with it. Before he deteriorates any more. Are you all right?"

His tone softened to tenderness and she glanced up again in time for him to reach out a large hand and cup her cheek. She smiled and pressed her lips to his palm.

"Yes, but I'll be infinitely better once the three of us have done what we can for the baby. Do you know that even from the very first day we met, he talked about having children with me? And even though I didn't believe it would ever happen for us, I gave into the fantasy. He was never really mine, but I wanted what he wanted so badly back then. And now... now I want it so much I can taste it."

Ked's expression darkened, but not in a magical way. Something troubled him and when Evie met his gaze with a question in her eyes, he looked away. "There's something I failed to mention before... about the child. Marcus and I aren't enough to ensure its survival. We can provide most of the energy it needs, I just want you to be prepared..."

"Ked..." she began in a quavering voice, fresh fear gripping her at her helplessness to provide for her own child and anxious what this new complication might be. "Please tell me it won't involve a lab and an exam table with stirrups."

Ked's head snapped back around. "Sweet Mother, no. It isn't anything like that. It's only that the way the Elites are made uses a mixture of my blood and my brothers' blood, in different ratios. Marcus's seed carries my energy primarily, but also small bits of Aodh's and Gavra's energy. To survive, the baby will need their energy, too."

Evie closed her eyes and let out a long sigh that ended with a soft laugh. "Oh, thank the Winds. As long as your brothers aren't repulsed by the idea, I believe I can overcome my reservations, too. They did restore my wings, after all." She opened her eyes and smiled slyly at him. "I don't know if the bed is big enough for all five of us, though."

"Ah… no," Ked said, smiling back at her. She could have been mistaken, but she was nearly dead certain that a slight pinkness tinged his cheeks.

"So, what did you have in mind? Is my entire sex life plotted out in your head now? I ran into Issa on my walk. The complications of her pregnancy sounded terrifying."

Ked waved a hand. "The timing of her pregnancy was unfortunate, and carrying a single Catalyst is hard on any dragon mother, much less twins. I don't know what our child will be like, but we will take care to ensure we all provide for it. But no…" He trailed off and looked down at Marcus. "He's having a tough enough time adjusting to the idea of being with me. I wouldn't want him to be traumatized by a tryst that involved my brothers, too."

With a smooth, graceful motion, Ked slipped his arms beneath Marcus's prone body and lifted him. His shoulders bunched with the considerable weight, but otherwise showed no hint of strain. Evie followed him to the bed and climbed on, positioning herself so that she could cradle Marcus across her lap. At least he seemed less unconscious and more asleep now, his breathing slow and regular.

The other side of the bed dipped as Ked walked around and climbed on, situating himself diagonally alongside Marcus and leaning down to press a kiss on Evie's lips. She tilted her head back, accepting his mouth, allowing him to command the slow tempo and depth of their kiss—their lips slowly moving against each other, with only the barest hint of tongue teasing between.

An involuntary shiver coursed through her when he raised a hand and tugged open the loose robe she still wore, baring one breast. Her nipple pricked and hardened in the cool evening air coming in from across the mountains outside. The warm pad of Ked's thumb brushed over it, and it hardened and tingled.

A deep groan rumbled up from Marcus and Evie pulled away to see if he woke.

Pale green eyes gazed back at her, confused at first, then a low heat built in their depths. "Don't you dare start without me," he croaked. "Assuming you're okay going through with this?"

"Oh, Marcus," Evie said, stroking the side of his face. "We both want this too much not to. I know that. And seeing you with him does exactly the opposite to me that you seemed to think. If any dragon could be a match to you, it's him."

Marcus pursed his lips and furrowed his brow, turning his gaze to Ked. Without a word, he simply nodded, as though some silent agreement had passed between them. After the quiet exchange, both men seemed to relax into the moment.

Marcus maneuvered above her lap, shifting enough to brace himself on one arm. He glanced around as though getting his bearings, and his gaze landed on Evie's bare breast. Ked's palm rested just beneath on her belly, his thumb casually stroking the underside of her breast. Seeing a worthy target within easy reach, he bent his head and captured the small peak between his lips and sucked.

Delicious warmth spread downward, pooling between her legs. Ked tugged her robe open and off her shoulders, then lowered his mouth to her other breast.

"Ohh," she sighed, tilting her head back and threading her fingers through their hair. After the harrowing experience of the last couple days and her recovery, she relished the plea-surable contact, all too eager for their mating to finally be under way.

Her eyes fluttered closed, but she opened them again when a hand gripped hers. Marcus tugged her hand away from Ked's black mane and pulled it down between them. Ked released her nipple and leaned back, kissing her neck while Marcus guided her hand lower. She thought he was urging her to touch him, but Marcus didn't place her hand on his own cock as she expected. Instead, he pressed her hand between Ked's legs onto his hardening cock and gripped her fingers tight around the thick length, now gloriously exposed, though she didn't remember Ked's drawstring coming undone.

"That's right, baby. I think together we can maybe make him beg, what do you think?" Marcus said, giving Ked a wicked grin.

Ked leaned back with a groan, but didn't make a move to stop them. Evie's eyes widened at the girth of him, too large for her small hand to surround, though Marcus's hand could easily grip him. Marcus sat up fully and leaned across in front of her, snagging the back of Ked's neck roughly and yanking him into a hungry kiss while his hand urged Evie's up and down Ked's steel-hard length.

Deciding to encourage them both, she found Ked's hand and followed Marcus's example. Ked took over, untying the closure of Marcus's pants and pulling out his cock.

The sounds of heavy breathing surrounded Evie, a rhythmic soundtrack harmonized with the sounds of their hands sliding over each man's stiff erections, stroking.

Marcus gave her a devious look that she remembered all too well from their first year together. The look usually signaled a wicked idea he'd come up with that would undoubtedly lead to pleasure for her. He pulled his hand away from Ked's cock and abruptly kicked his pants the rest of the way off. In a flash, he slid down the bed between her legs and opened the tie of her robe to finally expose her hips and the glistening mound of aching flesh between her thighs.

Rather than lie flat against the bed, however, he kept his knees bent, his ass in the air while he spread her open and ran his tongue between her folds. Her entire body tingled from the pleasure and she tilted her hips up, inviting more contact. Both men let out similar moans of pleasure—Ked's apparently in response to the sight of Marcus diligently teasing her cleft with his tongue.

Marcus kept her spread apart with one hand and reached with the other to reclaim Ked's cock, this time sliding his hand lower between Ked's thighs and cupping his balls.

"Sweet Mother, I can't bear more of your teasing," Ked said. He moved to kneel on the bed beside Evie's hips and hooked his hand beneath one of her knees, pushing it up to her chest. Marcus paused his slow, exquisite licking and glanced up at Ked with a curious smile. "Don't move," Ked said. "I've been craving a taste of her for days, but having you both together will be even more delicious."

With his dark, low-lidded gaze fixed on Evie's face, he slid his hand down her thigh and traced a circle around her juicy opening with two fingers before dipping in.

Evie let out a soft gasp when his thick digits pressed deep into her, massaging gently while his thumb grazed back and forth over her clit. His entire body seemed taut with restraint, and as he bent down to kiss her with his fingers still deep inside her, even his kiss held back, just a slow pull with no tongue.

"I need you wetter," he whispered.

Another sensation, warm and soft, encountered her wet core. She gasped and looked down to see Marcus licking her clit around Ked's fingers.

"Oh, God," she whispered, not quite clear why he was doing what he was doing, but surrendering herself to it nonetheless. Her pussy stretched more with the introduction of a third finger of Ked's hand.

The sensation drove her wild, her hands tangling in Marcus's hair and her hips writhing against them both.

"Oh, yes. That's what I need," Ked said, and drew his hand away from her.

Marcus, thankfully, kept his mouth latched onto her pussy and with her cry of protest slid his fingers into her bereft snatch.

She lost herself under his attention. He seemed distracted, but not so badly that he couldn't lick her the way he used to.

# CHAPTER 31

*Dragon Monastery, Sunda Islands*
*Present Day*

Jesus, the man was devious and talented.

And beautiful.

After kissing him the first time, Marcus had lost himself. It didn't matter how terrified he was of what would happen next—what he needed to do to ensure his and Evie's child survived—it did become difficult to remind himself that the baby was his entire reason for even going through with this.

*"Lie to yourself all you want,"* Ked said in his mind as his large hand brushed down Marcus's naked back.

Evie's body arched beneath him, near orgasm.

Ked's hand, which had just been almost entirely immersed into Evie, slid over Marcus's ass.

Marcus clenched his eyes shut, focusing on Evie's flavor under his tongue and the hot clench of her around his fingers.

"I need to fuck you. Not because I want you to be mine,

or because of the child. Those are valid needs. No, Marcus...
I need to fuck you because I can't bear another moment
without feeling your ass wrapped around my cock. Because
you are Blessed, and when you come with me inside you, I
need to know you're mine. I'm going to mark you while I
fuck you."

Ked's fingers, wet with Evie's juices slid between Marcus's
spread cheeks and teased.

Marcus took a deep breath to let go of the hesitation he
had and simply let this man touch him. He had Evie's clit to
worry about, after all. His own body was secondary.

The slick tease of Ked's fingers against his ass was too
nice to deny. When two pushed inside, Marcus cried out.
Evie's fingers tugged at his hair and urged him to look at her.

"Let him in, baby."

"I just want you."

"No... you want him, too. You just have to let him in."

"Let me in, too, Evie," he said. Fuck, he need a distraction,
and she was it. The man he'd spent the afternoon making out
with was just about to fuck him. He needed a little comfort
to temper the experience.

Evie, like the angel she was, spread her thighs and pulled
her knees to her ears. Marcus said a silent thank you to
whatever winds or mothers or gods or goddesses were out
there that he could bury himself in this woman while his ass
took a dragon.

But just as he pressed his lips to her cleft, the fingers deep
in his ass moved in a very distracting way and Ked's mouth
brushed his ear.

"I'm making you mine now. You can lick her pussy to
your heart's content, if you can maintain control while I fuck
you."

Marcus's cock twitched and he thought he might come.
He let out a sharp gasp at the sudden pleasure of the sensa-

tion. The fingers moved slowly in and out of his tight channel, the sensation filling, yet not painful. He kept his mouth on Evie's cunt, hungrily licking the way she liked but barely keeping it together. His ass was taking more than it could already with Ked's fingers.

And he'd seen the man's cock. Hell, he'd seen his own cock and wouldn't want to be fucked in the ass with it.

Those fingers, though… teasing into him, stroking. He'd never conceived what it felt like to *be* fucked rather than to simply fuck.

How many had Ked put into him? He tried to feel them all as he licked Evie's pussy. Her fingers were the only familiar fingers tangling with his body right now, wrapped up in his hair as her hips pushed up into his face. The fingers in his ass were foreign but so talented.

Two, he thought.

*"Two, and only two until you ask for more,"* Ked said, his voice resonating into Marcus's mind.

*"I hate that you can hear my thoughts. I hate more that I love how this feels. That I want you inside me in a way that doesn't feel like it's against nature."*

His desire was so alien to him, it *did* go against his nature, or what he'd once believed was his nature, but he hoped the words would throw Ked off even just a little bit. Marcus didn't like this feeling of powerlessness, even to his own desires. Yet he wanted more. He'd loved every second of those kisses he'd shared with Ked, as surprising as that was. His cock roused at the memory now. The only encounter more potent had been his first day with Evie, but they'd accelerated way past the make-out stage within minutes.

The fingers teased deeper.

"You're resisting," Ked said, giving one ass cheek a sharp smack.

"Quit teasing me," Marcus said, turning his head away from Evie to shoot a glare over his shoulder.

"You need preparation. And you really need to relax. Bear down so I don't hurt you."

Even though a part of him wanted the pain, Marcus obeyed, bearing down as Ked commanded. He closed his eyes when something that was distinctly *not* a finger swept wetly around his opening, causing a fresh bolt of lust to shoot through his cock and balls. Then the fingers pulled out and he moaned in protest.

*"Please, more."* He only managed the half-coherent thought while his tongue continued flicking over Evie's clit.

When Ked pushed in again, there were more fingers, as he'd requested. They fucked in deep, then out, then in again until they seemed to curve inward. Those expert fingertips met a part of Marcus's anatomy that he didn't even know existed. He let out a soft grunt and an "oh, God" before the fingers slid out again fully. When they disappeared, he felt even more bereft at their departure.

"I want more," he said, and fuck anyone who would judge him for it. Who would now, anyway? Naaz and Sterlyn? They were his closest friends. The only other people whose opinions he cared about were in this room. He glanced up at Evie, mesmerized by the hot stare she kept leveled on Ked. This was turning her on, watching him get fingered. And why shouldn't it? They'd talked about letting him watch her with another man, which he still fantasized about, so why shouldn't it go both ways?

God, those thoughts made his head spin even more as Ked's fingers left his ass and his tongue replaced them, just as thick, but softer and more delicate. It wasn't supposed to feel that good, but it did.

"Am I going to beg to fuck you or are you going to beg to take me?" Ked asked in a rough voice.

Christ, the man was serious, wasn't he?

"Fuck yes, I want that. Give it to me." What *"that"* was, Marcus couldn't really be sure. To take him? His fingers, his tongue, his dick?

"I will," a dark voice said. "If you ask for it explicitly."

Marcus groaned and pulled back from his distracted licking of Evie's delicious snatch. With his lips still brushing against her soft folds he took a deep breath.

"I want you to fuck me. Fuck me back to life. Shove that cock so deep inside me that my veins fill with your cum when it's over. So that from today onward, my life is yours in every single way. Blood, bones, flesh, magic. You are my sustenance."

"As you are mine," Ked said.

Ked pressed his hand against the back of Marcus's head. He pushed him back down between Evie's thighs and held him there. Marcus couldn't move an inch, so he did what he did best. He devoured her even as the thick head of Ked's cock pushed into him and the fingers on the back of his neck squeezed, holding him in place. Ked's other hand held tight to the side of his hip.

The man was huge, his slick shaft slowly spreading Marcus open and filling him inch by inch. Even if he could pull his mouth away from Evie's tangy, swollen flesh, he couldn't say no to any of it now. He'd already said yes so many times to letting this man into his body. He'd already had Ked inside him for years, and with only the prick of a needle and a bag of blood hanging nearby to flow into him. Gravity and a brutal tyrant of a master were all he needed to become powerful before. He'd been such a fucking cheat.

A harsh, searing groan scraped out of his throat, as rough as a serrated blade as Ked pushed deeper, his cock sinking in with a thrust almost as searing, but far more pleasurable.

It was for Evie and their baby, he thought, but when Ked's

breath fell into his ear and his cock thrust deep, he knew better.

No. The kind of lust and fucking Ked gave him was nothing like what Evie and he had together. He sank his tongue into her while pushing back hard as though begging for more. Humiliated and exhilarated at the same time.

*"Fuck me harder,"* he said in his mind, and Ked did.

God, Marcus needed more. He pulled a hand away from Evie's breast and reached between his thighs, his cock aching to be touched.

"No hands yet. Save your energy for her," Ked spoke into his ear, lips brushing so close Marcus's scalp tingled. But he obeyed, though he knew it would only take the lightest touch to make him come.

Ked seemed to have the endurance of an ox, however, and Marcus lost track of how long he pounded into him. He was only aware of every acute bolt of pleasure that shot through him with each inward thrust, and the nearly blinding ache of longing when Ked pulled almost entirely out. Each time he slammed back in hard, innately understanding that this was precisely how Marcus needed it to be.

He didn't need to be made love to, not the first time around. He needed to be ravaged. Ripped apart so hard he split into tiny pieces that could be made whole again with Evie's sweet touch. That was what needed to happen, and this man was the only person alive who could accomplish that task.

The fucking became more erratic, the fingers digging into his neck moved to grip his shoulder, pulling him back hard to meet each thrust. Marcus could feel his balls swinging with the same rhythm, smacking back against Ked's thigh over and over, simply intensifying his need to come.

Abruptly Ked let out a deafening cry that resonated through the room, his cock seemed to swell inside Marcus and he slammed hard into him three times in quick succession. The bruising invasion was followed up with an overwhelming flood of warmth that began in Marcus's lower extremities, then spread out and over him. The room went pitch black, yet somehow everything around him was illuminated, as though cast in vivid neon under a black light.

The most vivid was the sensation of something as sharp and stinging as a whip, searing into his back, from the top of his ass crack, up his spine, and in a wide, sweeping pattern that covered most of his back.

The pain of being a dragon's fucktoy was secondary to the lash of tongue over his back. As Ked's orgasmic wave of energy faded, he felt the cut of the inevitable mark burn into his skin. It was as swift as a whiplash but more accurate, and he could visualize in his mind the intricate pattern it made. It was dark and filled with magic, a perfect representation of the power given to him by the man who now owned him, body and soul.

His entire body thrummed from the energy flowing into him, his cock a heavy trunk of need pulsing between his legs. His weakness subsided and he ached to turn the tables, but Ked didn't release him. Instead, the man's chest pressed against Marcus's back and his lips hovered at his ear again.

"Time for round two. This time, it's for the both of you," Ked said.

Evie's frustrated moan reminded him that he'd neglected her, too wrapped up in the novelty of being fucked for the first time, and being filled with the potent energy of a dragon like Ked. But before he could remedy that, he was torn away from her when Ked wrapped both arms around his torso and rolled them both together. He let out a surprised protest that became another groan of pleasure when he found himself face up and wrapped in Ked's embrace, the dragon's thick cock still hard as a rock and buried in Marcus's ass.

They lay sprawled in a half-seated position, with Ked propped on the pillows of the bed and Marcus more or less in his lap. Fuck that—*impaled* by his lap, was more like it—but the new position had forced Ked even deeper to the point Marcus lost himself again in the void of pleasure, where everything that mattered appeared gilded and bright against a black velvet backdrop.

He braced one hand on the bed beside them and with the other reached for some kind of anchor. Groping wildly, his hand found Evie's and he tugged. Her beautiful face came into view and her hands combed through his hair.

Her mouth moved, but words were beyond him now. Language meant nothing. Her kiss meant everything when her sweet lips found his, her passion a delicate counterpoint to the stretching fullness of Ked's cock.

She released him and bent her head to the one beside his, kissing Ked with no less tenderness. Marcus let his head fall back on Ked's shoulder and gave Evie a pleading look when she met his gaze again.

Her lips formed the word *Yes*, though he still couldn't hear over the throbbing in his body. He needed to be fucked so badly nothing else mattered in that moment.

And like the angel she was, before his eyes, Evie's wings unfurled, dove gray, fading to darker variegations at the tips, and she stretched them out for balance as she raised up and straddled his cock.

Fuck yes, he needed to be inside her. Reflexively, Marcus's hips tilted up and the cock in his ass slid out creating a sweet friction that was only enhanced by the hot wetness the tip of his cock encountered at Evie's entrance.

"That's right. Fuck yourself on me," Ked said, his hands sliding to Marcus's hips and urging him to move. Evie's juicy slit spread wide and his tip sank in deeper, but she stayed poised, her chest heaving and her hand fluttering over her clit, barely touching as though she wanted to keep herself on the edge for him.

He loved her for that. She was as close as he was, but he wanted it to last just a little longer. Still, he couldn't resist the pull of desire that caused him to lift his hips high enough to sink his shaft into that hot channel. He kept his hips raised when she let out a little gasp and simply enjoyed the way her hot, slick channel clenched around him.

He relaxed his hips and sank back down, the ache in his cock and balls growing more insistent with the long stroke and rub of that delicious spot inside him that Ked's fingers had uncovered and his cock rubbed incessantly against.

"I'm not gonna last," he said by way of apology to Evie.

"Me neither," she panted, and bent over him.

He embraced her with his free arm, and Ked's arm slipped around her back, too, holding her close while Marcus pumped his hips between them.

Fuck, maybe he *had* died and actually gone to heaven. He couldn't imagine pleasure so filling he wanted to both explode and hold it all inside, just to enjoy it for as long as possible.

Evie's lips found his neck, kissing wetly as her hot, panting breaths gusted against his ear. "I love you so much. Thank you for coming back to me."

He couldn't stand it any longer. With a surge of energy he began pumping between them in earnest, needing to feel her come around his cock and to come himself.

With her head resting on his shoulder, her teeth biting into his neck, he twisted his head and caught Ked's mouth in a fierce kiss. The man seemed surprised, but gave in and thrust his hips up suddenly when their tongues tangled, causing Marcus to falter in his rhythm.

The hand Marcus had holding Evie against him was

engulfed in another large hand, and his fingers twined reflexively with Ked's.

This moment was both his resurrection and his destruction, all in one. He thought he'd never love anyone as much as he'd loved Evie, but now he knew better.

Her quivering collapse of an orgasm sent him flying, and his climax shot into her so abruptly he could've believed his essence was drawn to some gravitational field she possessed. At the same time, Ked let out a deep whimper followed by a sigh of pleasure and his hips jacked up against Marcus, his hot semen flooding in along with another beautiful wave of dark power infused with vivid color.

He lay that way, sandwiched between them, mindless and incapable of doing anything but languish in the energy the two of them had filled him with.

Evie let out a shuddering sigh atop his chest, but didn't seem the least bit inclined to move. She did murmur something nearly incoherent that sounded like "mark me," to which Ked replied with a low murmur, "I didn't forget, I'm just a little buried at the moment."

Evie laughed softly and Marcus took the hint. He wrapped his other arm around her and went to move off the man beneath his back, but both Ked's arms tightened around them.

"No, let me enjoy this for a moment. She's still having little tremors with you inside her. It's sending aftershocks of energy through you and into me. Can't you feel it?"

"I feel too many things right now," Marcus said. "My body's nothing *but* aftershocks."

But when he settled back and closed his eyes, he gave Evie a little thrust of his softening cock and she moaned and clenched around him.

Finally, she opened her eyes and gave him a look of mild

regret before sliding off and falling to her side on the pillow beside him.

Marcus winced a little as he extracted himself from Ked and lay beside her.

She gazed up at him with her her big storm-colored eyes, her long hair was a rat's nest and her cheeks were flushed, and she'd never looked more beautiful.

"I'm glad you're not dead," she said.

"Never again," he replied.

# CHAPTER 32

## KED

*Dragon Monastery, Sunda Islands*
*Present Day*

The pair gravitated toward each other in the aftermath so effortlessly, Ked took the opportunity to step out and clean up. The bathroom of the bungalow was carved out of the mountain to access the hot springs that bubbled up from beneath. Unlike the separate bathhouses higher up the mountain, this space resembled a grotto with its dark, steamy alcoves lit with the comforting magical lights he was accustomed to. It was one of the few buildings at the monastery that actually had hot running water.

Standing under the shower, a slight tremor passed over him that made his knees shake. He braced himself against the stone wall and let it pass. The sensation was not unpleasant, but made him dizzy, and his inner ears pulsed so loudly he couldn't even hear the beat of the water on his body. Was it some kind of feedback from Marcus? The man's orgasm hadn't felt the same as the energy Ked was used to from other partners. When Marcus and Evie had climaxed, Evie's orgasm had inundated him in a refreshing, airy cloak that sank through his skin.

Marcus's, on the other hand, had felt like a... *A tangle with a dragon more powerful than you,* Ked thought to himself. Another tremor passed through him and his dick hardened with a fresh flood of desire.

If this residue was any indication of how powerful the man had been as an Elite, it was good that Ked hadn't met any of them at full power during his mission.

But now that power burned in him, left him lightheaded and short of breath, both sensations utterly alien to him.

"Sweet Mother, what is he doing to me?" He pressed his hands against the rough-hewn rock and bent his head under the hot stream of water, letting it beat on the back of his neck. His mind kept replaying the moment he penetrated Marcus and the intensity of pleasure and emotion that accompanied that surrender by the other man.

No other emotion had existed for Ked, which in itself was unusual. That was the effect *he* had on others. At first he'd thought it was simply Marcus's impressions bleeding into his mind, but as he fucked deeper and deeper, it became painfully apparent that the elation highlighted like a shining beacon in his mind was his alone.

No one else had that power over him—the power to lay one feeling bare and raw like his chest had been sliced open and his beating heart lay there on display to the exclusion of every other feeling.

*No one but Marcus.* And of course, the Elite hunter who had been created from Ked's blood would have the same powers as he had himself. Once filled with the energy of Marcus's Nirvana, Ked's own frequency was enhanced to the point of distraction.

He wanted more—so much more—but feared what would happen if they exchanged power in that manner again. As the submissive party in the encounter, Marcus had accepted more of Ked's power than he believed he was capable of giving. The magic didn't simply flow through him in the normal fashion. A piece of his very soul had been given up to Marcus, too.

As he struggled to regain his bearings, soft, gentle hands began rubbing over his back, slick and fragrant with soap.

"You left us," Evie said just loud enough to be heard over the sound of the water. "We missed you." Her lips pressed against his back and her arms slipped around his waist, hugging him.

Ked sighed, but didn't let himself relax. The disconcerting pulse of his body kept him on alert. He turned his head to look over his shoulder at her and caught sight of Marcus leaning in the opening of the carved-stone shower's alcove.

Their gazes locked and Ked's cock pulsed harder. He needed to fuck something soon, but feared another exchange with Marcus would destroy him.

Marcus's green-eyed gaze swept over him as potently as a red dragon's might. The same level of interest blazed in those depths, too, albeit tinged with a sweet shyness that endeared him utterly to Ked.

With a sideways smile, Marcus stood up straight and spread his arms out in the archway, gripping the rock on either side until his arms and shoulders flexed.

"You fixed me. And who knew *that* would be so fucking amazing? Did you know?"

Ked laughed, but was unprepared for how disarmed and nervous he now felt in the other man's presence. Evie's light touches were a pleasant anchor for him. Fated for each other, she was his because he was undeniably hers, but he hadn't yet granted her the mark that would bind them.

Marcus, on the other hand, had the mark on his back to prove he belonged to Ked. Yet the dark aura spilling out of him like smoke said so much more as it filtered through the steam and coiled around Ked's lower legs. His own aura reached for it greedily, just as dark and thick.

"Sweet Mother, I need you," Ked said.

Marcus's smile disappeared, growing grave and determined. "You don't look so hot. But after a fuck that great? How can you not feel as invincible as I do?"

"Because I gave more than I intended. Your submission was so complete, I wasn't prepared for how much you would take of me. My willingness to give everything you required left me with a deficit. But not of my usual power—I have plenty of that. I gave up a piece of the essence that sustains my soul, because your body needed it."

"I don't understand," Marcus said.

Evie's pretty face slipped into view. "We'll give you whatever you need," she said. "Just say it."

Ked cupped her cheek and kissed her, grateful for her contact and her willingness to please him. He still needed to mark her, too, and the overwhelming urge to do so captured every bit of his attention for a moment. But would the same thing happen with her? Or was Marcus's nature the reason for that shift of magic?

*First things first, I need to be inside someone, and it can't be Marcus again until I figure out how this happened.*

He hooked his arm around Evie's waist and hauled her up in front of him. She let out a little yelp followed by a laugh as he pressed her against the wet stone beneath the streaming water. She hooked one leg around the back of his thigh.

"What I need is to fuck you," Ked said, kneeling down and spreading her fragrant folds with his forked tongue. He slid his tongue into her, tasting every inch of her tight channel, savoring the salty-sweet taste of Marcus lingering deep inside her. The flavor galvanized Ked, making him surer than ever of what he needed.

He pulled back and stared up at her, licking his lips. "And while I fuck you, he needs to fuck me."

"I need to what?" Marcus blurted. His eyes widened and he paled slightly.

Remaining on his knees, Ked did the one thing he never imagined he would do, in all the thousands of years he'd lived—he begged for the honor of submitting to another.

"Please. Fuck me. Fuck me so hard your soul meets mine when you find your Nirvana."

"How do you even know it will work?" Marcus asked. He'd regained his composure and stood with his arms crossed, eyeing Ked skeptically. His hardening cock betrayed his interest in the idea, however.

"Just look at our auras, Marcus. The way yours clings to me like iron filings to a magnet. Your energy wants inside, your soul commands your aura's behavior, but tell me you don't feel that need already."

Marcus's eyes closed and he dropped his hands to his sides again. He let out a rough, shaky sigh.

"God, yes. I need more. I don't think I'll ever stop needing more. Just tell me how you want me."

"Well, hard like that is a good start," Ked said, enjoying the other man's hesitance. "The blue jar on the shelf there will have the other thing you need."

As if preparing for what was to come, Evie pulled away and rested on the smooth stone bench that was carved into one wall of the shower. She simply sat with bright eyes watching, mouth parted and chest rising and falling. Her potent arousal met Ked's senses as thick and pungent as the fragrant soap she'd lathered his back with, and her aura glimmered around her, pulsing in time with the rapid beat of her heart.

Ked stood and moved to stand over her, then fell to his knees again, greedily burying his face between her thighs. He needed to bare himself to Marcus, but craved her essence as foreplay. Under his tongue, her delicious flesh fluttered and throbbed, her panting breaths growing to melodic cries that increased in volume until she spread her fingers through his wet hair and fell back onto the bench, her hips bucking into him and her song tingling in his ears.

"I'm going to mark you now," he said. Just as she got the syllable of affirmation out, his tongue darted out and swiftly traced a mark about the size of his palm into the creamy flesh over her womb. The pattern matched the one he'd given Marcus, and glowed with dark violet light.

With a swift, fluid movement, he hooked his arms beneath her knees and wrapped his hands around her behind, lifting her and standing just enough to lay her back down while he rested a knee on the edge of the bench.

"Not yet," Evie whispered, pressing a hand against his chest when he moved to mount her. He pulled back and looked down at her quizzically. "Take him first. I want to watch without the distraction of needing to come again."

Marcus hovered close behind, his anticipation thick between them. Evie rose to a sitting position and clutched at both sides of Ked's face, stroking gently as she urged his mouth onto hers. Sweet Mother, the woman was as much an antidote to his darkness as Marcus was a reflection of it. Acquiescing, he let her embrace him and bent low to rest his head on the tops of her thighs, spreading his legs so that there could be no mistake that he was ready.

"I submit to you," he said in the old language and that aching void in his soul seemed to throb with need.

To his surprise, Marcus replied in the same language. "You are mine."

Then, without any teasing or foreplay, not even a lick or a stroke, Marcus pressed his lubricated cock against Ked's ready opening and slid deep in with one long, glorious stroke. Pleasure exploded through Ked's body and he clung to Evie.

"Jesus Christ, I didn't believe you could take it, but I could feel your need so deep I didn't want to disappoint you." Marcus dug his fingers into Ked's ass cheeks and pushed a little harder, as if testing to determine whether he was all the way in.

Ked wrapped his arms around Evie's waist and groaned with pleasure at the slight movement. His need must be as transparent to Marcus as Marcus's own elation was to him.

"Bite me while you fuck me," Ked growled over his shoulder.

"My pleasure." Marcus twisted his hips in a slow circle as he pulled out, every increment of movement sending a continuous current of pleasure racing up Ked's spine and then back down to settle in his cock and balls. The thrust back in forced a soft grunt out of his chest and his cock twitched hard against his belly. Blood rushed to his head and his temples pounded in contrast to the gentle stroking of Evie's fingers.

Marcus bent over him, the wetness on his chest lending a slick warmth that mimicked the slippery feel of the cock buried inside him. Larger fingers threaded through Ked's hair, tightened, and tugged, pushing Ked's face down into Evie's lap. He chuckled to himself at the way the motion almost mirrored what he had done to Marcus, and snaked his tongue out to tease between Evie's thighs.

Hot breath gusted against his ear. "You want it here, right?" Marcus asked before nipping lightly at the back of Ked's neck in that sensitive spot that a dragon only gave up to the one they considered their superior in every way—to the master they chose to serve.

"Yes," he gasped against Evie's wet mound. His entire body screamed to have that part of him claimed by this man, to have his teeth sink into him and ignite that instinctive surrender. Marcus was more than just the host of Ked's essence, more than a simple Blessed human who needed to be marked by a dragon. He was the piece of Ked's soul that had been missing for much longer than the last hour since Ked had surrendered that magic up to the man. The void had existed for far longer.

And when Marcus's teeth sank into that tender flesh, the truth of his state crashed over him like a tidal wave as sweet and hot as Evie's juices flooding over his tongue. Her knees bent on either side of his face and her hands clung to his head, holding him against her core as he devoured her. Together, they claimed him, and between them he became whole again for the first time since the day he'd lost himself.

There was no denying when his life had shifted. It had been the day Ked executed *her*. Benedetta, the Elite Ultiori hunter who had first carried his essence. She had been so far under Nikhil's power, there was no saving her, in spite of the love Ked had for her. She'd been the first Blessed he'd encountered and his need to mate her had been so strong he nearly lost himself.

Ked had carried the regret of that death for centuries, along with the piece of himself that had died with her final breath.

Sharing his regret over her death with Nikhil had only been part of his penance. This was the rest. Letting these two possess him, use him. Falling at their feet was barely enough to assuage his shame. He needed to bury himself deeper beneath them. No others would ever see him this way, but Marcus and Evie were elevated in his mind to a status that rivaled his Mother. In their hands, he could be broken down to nothing and reborn.

One way or the other, he'd be released of his burden through them.

Marcus's teeth held on, his hot tongue probing the spot between. His cock slid out and back in again and again, each time a little groan escaped Marcus's mouth, his breath flowing over Ked's neck.

The sweet taste of Evie's snatch wasn't enough anymore, he needed to be inside her.

"Stay with me," he said, and rose up, supporting himself on one hand. He scooped Evie in his free arm and let her slide down his torso.

She let out a little laugh as her arms wrapped around his shoulders. "Fancy moves," Evie said smiling.

Marcus rose with him, his cock remaining a hot, welcome pressure inside Ked's ass. His arms wrapped around Ked's torso and his mouth laid kisses over Ked's shoulder.

"Jesus, you feel amazing. I'm enjoying fucking you too much to stop."

"Don't stop," Ked said. Meeting Evie's gaze, he said, "You ready for the fucking of your life?"

Her aura pulsed and she simply kissed him with a surprising hunger. Her lips pulled longingly at his and he returned her kiss, sliding his tongue into her mouth and savoring the sweet flavor and soft heat within.

He shifted his cock between them, let her slide down onto him, closing his eyes at the exquisite combination of sensations that overwhelmed him in that moment. Her tight channel engulfed his cock and squeezed, the feeling a counterpoint to the steady, almost violent thrust of Marcus into him from behind.

He held tight to Evie's hips, said, "I'm sorry for this," and did the thing he'd craved. He lifted her petite frame off his cock and pushed her back down. Lifted her up again, and slammed her down again, each time moving quicker and more urgently.

Evie clung to his shoulders and whispered in his ear over and over, "yes, yes, yes" each time he filled her up.

Pleasure more exquisite than he'd ever felt built at the base of his spine, flooding slowly through his lower extremities and upward. Each stroke of Evie's pussy on his cock matched the deep, hot friction of Marcus inside him until a balloon filled with every sensation seemed full to bursting. Ked emitted a resonant growl when he could no longer contain himself. Twisting his torso, he gripped Marcus by the back of the neck and hungrily captured his mouth, then did the same with Evie. Their faces stayed close to his, their mouths coming together in front of him, then parting. All three of their breaths mingled and their cries of ecstasy merged.

Ked could no longer contain his orgasm, and it erupted from him with a violent surge. His cock shot hotly into Evie and she clung hard to him, her entire body shuddering with her climax. Marcus grabbed both of Ked's ass cheeks and squeezed, spreading him open to take his final, urgent thrusts until Marcus, too, came hard into him.

"All I am is yours," Marcus murmured into his ear as the dark waves of energy flowed between them, converging in Ked's core along with the feather-light energy of Evie's Nirvana.

Ked closed his eyes and savored the way it fit, filling him still, even as Marcus slowly extracted himself. There, at the very core, was that bright, glowing piece. Not quite his own, but a piece that fit so perfectly it was far better than what he'd given up—a perfect hybrid of them both.

*North African Coast, near Alexandria, Egypt*

They arrived so swiftly, Nikhil wasn't sure the *drift* had even happened at first. Only a faint wave of dizziness had him spinning for a moment before the dim glow of the candles on the cave's ledges came into focus, illuminating the pair of stone effigies lying on the floor.

The smooth surfaces of their bodies shimmered with the subdermal lights and Belah fell to her knees between the pair, tears streaming down her face. Nikhil watched, barely able to contain his own emotions, and almost overwhelmed by the joy that emanated from the woman he loved and her two children.

He silently moved away toward the entrance to give them privacy, stopping at the shimmering edge of the temporal bubble that protected the two priceless treasures. If he reached out with his mind, he was sure he could eavesdrop on the conversation between mother and children, but he refrained, instead simply standing and looking out toward the small patch of light that came in through the cave's opening.

Footsteps came up from behind him and stopped at his side. Lukas stood with arms crossed, his stance relaxed, but guarded. Iszak moved to stand on Nikhil's other side.

Nikhil glanced over his shoulder once, and saw Aodh crouched near the heads of the two figures, one hand on Belah's shoulder and his other resting on the shoulder of his nephew.

"What happens with them now?" Iszak asked softly.

"Not sure. I'm hoping the dragons have a solution, though. This was the safest place I could bring them on short notice. I had to assume the chamber they were in before was known by the little fucking homunculus that lived in my head all this time. No piece of my life since Belah left me is a secret, I fear."

"I have this weird urge to thank you," Lukas said on his other side.

Nikhil turned to look at Lukas, eyebrows raised. "Not torture me with kisses?" he asked.

Lukas laughed. "Another time, I promise. You should know that before you showed up that night, we'd spent hours torturing Belah—only in the best way, I promise. We hated her until we knew her, and for good reason. Or so we thought. She was responsible for you, after all, and we *definitely* hated you." Lukas paused and Nikhil's power picked up on a glimmer of remaining animosity that the other man still warred with.

"What Lukas means is that, in a really fucked up way, we owe you for what you did. If she hadn't been taken from you, she may never have been ours. And the shit with Evie... I don't think she'd change things if she had a do-over, either, because she wanted Marcus so fucking bad at the start but knew he wasn't destined to be hers. What you did changed that."

Nikhil frowned. "What I did was the worst kind of torture. No one deserves what your sister had to go through, or Marcus. I would sooner kill a captive than put them through that. They weren't my enemies. Nor were they the enemies of the only goddess I have ever worshiped."

"And who would that be? Are you a follower of any of the old gods?" Lukas asked, seeming genuinely curious.

Nikhil glanced over his shoulder with affection before meeting Lukas's gaze. "She was Isis to her followers back then. My *Tilihatan.* My goddess. I never stopped worshiping her, but the darkness that had hold of me twisted my adoration to make me do unspeakable things in her name. Now I will do nothing without her explicit consent. Nor yours, for that matter. I will be her champion once more, willing to die in battle for her, until I can earn the right to be her lover again." He considered his position for a moment, then added, "Or even her pet, for that matter. A toy she keeps in a box and only takes out when she wishes to pleasure herself."

"By the Winds are you *whipped,*" Iszak said, chuckling and shaking his head.

"If that's her wish, I will happily provide the whip."

Both men grew oddly silent, their tension growing until it seemed to tap at the shell of their defenses—a desire seeking escape but not yet equipped to peck its way out. Rather than use his power to push his way in, Nikhil continued his earlier thought as if he'd only paused mid-sentence. "… though she prefers the lash herself. When she initiated me, she used other means besides pain. She's adept at domination, but prefers submission. I assume that's why she was drawn to you?"

"Fate's what put us together," Iszak said gruffly. "Ropes are what keep her happy."

"Or candle wax," Lukas interjected, darting a glance over his shoulder.

Nikhil smiled at a particularly vivid memory he had involving candles and Belah's sweet, round ass. "Aye, she does enjoy candle wax. The whip was always her favorite, though. Or the cilices."

"I think that's where we're falling short," Iszak said. He cleared his throat and looked at Nikhil, folded and unfolded his arms, then rubbed the back of his neck, clearly discomfited over whatever he needed to get out.

Nikhil said nothing, waiting for the other man to find a way to say what needed saying, though he had a good idea what the issue was.

Lukas said, "She needs more than we're capable of giving. She even tried to incite our rage at you to get us in the mood to … to beat her the way she wanted. I just can't… I mean, a little pain I'm cool with. It's fucking hot when she gets wet from having her nipples pinched or seeing her ass all red from being smacked. I can even do a belt. But a whip… she wants to bleed, I think. Or at least be abused in a way that would make a normal woman bleed."

Lukas paused and Iszak filled in. "And now that she's pregnant, the baby's making it even more difficult for us to please her. It gives her these cravings that are so deviant they make my head spin. I hate feeling this helpless to give her what she needs. It isn't enough just to whip her, but we need to be able to get off on it, too."

"Not as sadistic as you thought you were?" Nikhil asked, a surge of hopeful anticipation warming his chest.

"Not even fucking close," Lukas said. "So, man, you've gotta do whatever it is you need to do to get square with your conscience. We'll work on our side of it, but the sooner the better."

Get square with his conscience… There was the rub. How

long would that take? He'd only begun to start searching for the insidious creature that had taken over his mind and now seemed to be systematically taking control of his entire organization. Now that he was so close to having Belah back that he could almost taste it, he ached to stay and offer to give her mates the help they needed. But his honor dictated that he exact retribution on their enemy for what she'd done, and he couldn't be *square* with his fucking conscience until he knew where to find the slippery nymph who'd ruined his life and the lives of so many others.

Before he could formulate any kind of response, Aodh called to them.

"We're taking them to the sacred hibernation temple," Belah's brother said. "They'll be safe there until their fated mates can seek them out."

"And you just have one of these temples lying around?" Lukas asked.

"There are seven of them, in fact," Aodh said. "One for each generation of dragons who have ascended since the hibernations were instituted over three thousand years ago. The newest was completed several years ago, and was intended for this Ascension's children, but it won't be needed now that we've abolished the hibernation law. The temple would be unused otherwise. It's equipped with every safety precaution required to ensure no one but the intended mates of the hibernating dragons within are given access."

"The Ultiori can't get in?" Nikhil asked, this new knowledge filling in several gaps in his understanding of how dragons worked.

"The temple is heavily guarded with wards and locks. The keys hidden in separate secret locations, all of which require a trial for access. Within the temple we'll station guardians and shadows from the recently ascended brood. With the proper incentive they'll be willing."

Nikhil frowned. "The hibernations lasted five centuries. What kind of incentive are you giving these dragons to be imprisoned again for the rest of their lives?"

"They won't be," Belah said. "My children's mates are already born. They just need to pass the trial to prove they are the true mates of dragons. Any dragon who agrees to be a guardian or a shadow will only have to endure it for a short time. Their incentive will be their own mates arriving at the same time as Zorion and Asha's. The temple is designed to call to the mates of its six highest-ranking inhabitants once the dragons are asleep inside. The rest will take care of itself."

"I don't like it," Nikhil said, his gut clenching at the thought of his daughter being taken from him for an indeterminate amount of time. "Will I be able to drift in to see her?"

"No…" Belah said, her expression softening. She stepped toward him and rested a hand against his cheek. "I missed her, too, and the idea of being apart from her again so soon hurts, but this is the best way to keep them both safe until they can defend themselves. Hopefully it won't be more than a few months or a year, and then we can be with her for good. You'll be able to look into her eyes and tell her how you feel. Hold her in your arms, protect her. We can be a family." She glanced between Nikhil and her two mates. "All of us," she said, resting her hands against her belly.

Nikhil closed his eyes and took a deep breath, reaching out his mind to his daughter's.

*"Asha."*

*"I am here, Papa. This is the way it should be, you know. You must focus on getting Mama back while I am gone. Please find a way to make things right between you and my little brother's fathers. Make things right for all of them."*

*"I will,"* he said.

*"You will see me soon, I promise. I love you."*

Nikhil dropped to his knees beside the beautiful effigy

and cupped her face in his hands. *"I love you, too, Asha,"* he said, pressing a kiss to her smooth, cool forehead.

As an afterthought, he rested a hand on Zorion's obsidian shoulder. *"Be well, son of my goddess."* When he said the words, a sharp jolt hit the center of his palm, the pain surprising him. He snatched his hand away as if he'd been burned.

"What the fuck?"

Before he could ask Zorion if he'd offended him somehow, the familiar shadow darkened the edge of Nikhil's consciousness. *"You will need those blessings intact to do what needs doing, so I have repaired them for you,"* Zorion said. *"Seek out my uncle's secrets if you want to find the truth. Do not let his silence fool you—he has much to say, if you choose the right time to ask the questions."*

Nikhil carefully refrained from looking in the direction of Aodh, though his skin prickled at the bit of knowledge this strangely powerful creature gave him. He had no reason to doubt Zorion's word. In fact he was certain of the truth in a way he hadn't been about anyone's words in eons. Those blessings were the wedding blessings he'd received on the day of his marriage to Belah more than three thousand years ago. They'd been corrupted as a result of his atrocities not long after he'd lost control over his mind. But now they were whole and pure once more. To test it, he pinched himself, the little zing of pain inciting a giddy sense of elation that he had to bite his lip to suppress. He'd never enjoyed pain so much as he did in that moment.

Standing again, he forced his composure back to a solemn mask, said another silent farewell to Asha and turned toward the others. He regarded Aodh for a second before nodding at the huge man to indicate he was finished with his farewells.

He would have to tread carefully with Belah's brother, but he wondered if the power the dragon had to *drift* wasn't innate after all. According to Calder, none of the other races were able to do it without an infusion of nymphaea blood, and even then the ability faded over time.

"We must part ways now," Aodh said, stepping between Nikhil and the two effigies of Belah's children. "I will take them to the temple and arrange for their protection. Take Belah and her mates home."

As Aodh began to turn, Nikhil grabbed his arm. "You promise they'll be safe?"

"I swear on my own breath, and on your love for my sister," Aodh said.

Nikhil relaxed. Whatever the white dragon was hiding, he had no intention of letting any harm come to those who shared his blood.

They stayed long enough to see Aodh rest his hands on the two hibernating dragons. A moment later all three forms shimmered as though they were immersed in clear water and then disappeared.

Nikhil took a moment to allow the ache of Asha's departure to fade, grateful for the feel of Belah's hand as it slipped into his own and squeezed.

"We'll see her again soon," she said softly. "Will you take us home now?"

With Lukas gripping his other hand and Iszak holding Belah's, he let the *drift* carry them out, but found he could only travel as far as a deserted beach on the Indian Ocean.

"Without you up there, I can't get to the top," he said to Belah.

"I'll fly us," she said, her skin shimmering like sapphires in the sunlight as she began to shift.

"No, Belah," he said, putting out his hand to stop her. "I would love nothing more than for you to take me home with you, but there's too great a danger still out there for me to go. I have to find out who was responsible. I promise as soon as I have a lead, I will find you, but I have done too much harm to you and your family to accept any forgiveness yet. Let me prove my worth to you again. Let me be your greatest general, conquer your enemies for your glory, so you have a reason to love me once more."

"Nikhil..." she began, the glimmer of a tear clinging to the corner of her eye. At her side, Iszak and Lukas watched silently.

"No, little beast. Obey your mates and go with them until I return. I promise to come back to you as soon as I can."

"I have always loved you," she said, allowing her mates to pull her away.

Nikhil stood on the beach and watched while the three of them shifted, their wings kicking up sand as they rose into the air and flew off. He remained there until they were no more than specks high in the sky, indistinguishable from the seagulls.

When they disappeared into the band of fog at the top of the mountain, he turned and looked out across the water. The rhythmic sound of the ocean filled his mind and he closed his eyes. Once more he surrendered to the *drift*, bidding it to take him to the next location on his list: Alexandria, Egypt, where the Ultiori had first been born.

# CHAPTER 34

## EVIE

*Dragon Monastery, Sunda Islands*
*Present Day*

Waiting to find out whether or not her baby survived was the worst kind of torture for Evie. The not knowing haunted her even worse than the pain of having her wings ripped off.

She stood on the wide porch, naked in the morning light and flexed her wings again for the fourth day in a row after having them restored. She tested the muscles that had seared with pain when Ked found her a little more than a week ago. They still ached from disuse, but not from injury. The urge to shift and fly to truly test them was like a deep itch in her soul—to commune again with the wind for the first time in decades would do so much to improve her mood, but she didn't dare shift until after the baby was born.

Her mind wandered to the pair of dragons who had succeeded in making her whole again. Ked's brothers, Gavra and Aodh, had healed her completely during the long flight that brought her and Marcus to the safety of the monastery.

She had been resigned to being flightless after Nikhil had ruthlessly, brutally taken that from her. The two dragons deserved her thanks, and she had forgiven the man who had done the damage because she knew the moment he'd heard her song that he'd been a puppet for something far more vicious and evil.

Ked's conflicted emotions made her wonder if she'd made the right decision, but she had managed to avoid dwelling on that fact for the last few days, content to stay in bed and make love to her mates over and over until virtually every muscle in her body ached pleasantly. Yet her mind still returned to Ked's explanation that their baby needed the magic of all three brothers thanks to Marcus's physiology having been altered by the blood of all three dragons. She needed Ked's brothers more than she needed validation for forgiving Nikhil right now.

It hurt her to think of Gavra and Aodh, however, because when she saw the pair in their human forms, they reminded her acutely of Naaz and Sterlyn, who were still too wrapped up in the conflict that plagued the Ultiori to find their own peace and happiness yet.

"Good morning, angel," Marcus said, slipping up behind her and brushing his fingertips over the top of her naked hip.

Evie furled her wings and let them fade back into her body, then shrugged back into her lightweight robe, tying it at the waist. She leaned against Marcus and sighed when he wrapped his arms around her and tucked her head under his chin, placing a soft kiss at her temple.

"There has to be a way to help them," Evie said. "If he's so powerful, surely he can hunt down the thing that's responsible for all this suffering. Even Nikhil deserves to be happy, and you know Naaz and Sterlyn do."

Ked's deep voice carried from inside the room. "Easier said than done."

Evie and Marcus both turned to watch him stride out toward them, his eyes so filled with devotion for them both, Evie's chest grew warm.

"How so?" Evie asked.

"Nikhil allowed me to see inside his soul when he was here. When I did, the nature of the beast that held him in thrall was clear to me. The Lamia is the creature we seek, which means her true identity isn't clear at all. She was once Belah's physician, Meri, but has changed identities hundreds of times since. She's been able to slip into the shadows of the minds of humans for ages. The human woman you knew as Dr. St. George was the Lamia's last host, but that woman died several years ago. Nikhil's mind didn't have any fresh clues to her current identity, and there are thousands of humans in the Ultiori's ranks who she could have taken over."

Evie gazed up into his eyes when he came to the railing and bent to kiss her softly.

When he pulled back, Evie said, "There must be something we can do. Bring them all here, at least? Or take them to a turul enclave."

"Nikhil has control of the Canadian facility. They've set a trap there that they hope the true enemy will fall into, but she hasn't taken the bait yet. In the meantime, he says Naaz has already identified a faction of the Ultiori who are still loyal to Nikhil. It seems the organization is pretty evenly divided between the military and science divisions." He cast a meaningful glance at Marcus.

Marcus tightened his embrace around her and nodded. "Once the Canadian facility is secure, we're planning to use it as a base for a resistance. With any luck we'll have either captured the leader or at least someone who knows her identity."

Evie looked between the two men, hope rising up within

her like a strong wind holding her aloft. "So, what are you waiting for? Don't you need to go do some securing? Help them with their resistance?"

"We have more immediate priorities," Ked said. "Namely, you."

"We're still waiting for word from Naaz or Nikhil, but regardless, we aren't going anywhere until we know the baby is going to be all right," Marcus said. "And we're not about to leave you alone for more than a day or two until after the baby is born."

Evie's hands drifted down to her midsection. Having a dragon hybrid child growing inside her was going to be interesting. The cravings she knew about, after talking with Belah, whose own pregnancy was no more evident than Evie's. Ked's other two sisters shared their own wisdom of motherhood with her as well, and Evie had left the conversation dumbfounded to realize that the six ancient dragon siblings were, in fact, the progenitors of the entire race.

This was only her first real pregnancy—though her heart still ached for the two she'd lost. Except for Belah, Ked's sisters had all borne six children each, with human mates, thousands of years earlier. Ked and his brothers had also fathered eighteen children between them.

She gazed up at Ked with that awareness still fresh in her mind, simply taking in his strong features. This man—her *One*—was the oldest black dragon in the world, all other Shadows having descended from him. And the child growing inside her was as much his as Marcus's. What nature the child would take remained to be seen. The higher races had never interbred before.

Her pregnancy was barely more than a week old, but the cravings had begun. They came upon her in dreams at first, only the night before, and she'd awoken with a deep desire to taste both Ked's and Marcus's essence at once—to have their flavors flooding over her tongue. She didn't pause to articulate it, but woke them with her mouth, sucking hungrily on their cocks, back and forth until they roused and made her pause long enough to tell them what she needed. They'd happily acquiesced, stroking themselves to completion while Evie sucked the heads of their cocks together until that hot, salty flood slid down her throat.

She was slightly ashamed to admit the fresh craving that came upon her now that their conversation was over. It hit her so strongly when she hazarded a thought about Ked's brothers that her entire body trembled with it. She tried to brush it off, and pulled away from Marcus, heading inside, through the bedroom and out into the living area where their breakfast had been laid out for them already. She didn't have the presence of mind to marvel yet again at the efficiency of the monks who served the dragons. Even the sight and aroma of what she was sure was a delicious meal didn't appeal to her.

She lifted a carafe of juice and the liquid sloshed in her shaky attempt to pour herself a glass.

Ked's hand caught hers deftly and he took the carafe and glass away from her, pouring it for her.

"What do you need today, Evie. We are at your service—all you have to do is ask."

He ignored her reach for the glass of juice, instead putting the rim to her lips and tipping it up for her to drink.

She closed her eyes and swallowed, grateful for his help, but ashamed at the way the craving took over so completely. When he set the glass down, he took her hands and led her to a chair, sat down, and pulled her onto his lap. Marcus pulled another chair close and sat across from Ked, leaning his elbows on his knees and looking at her with a furrowed brow.

"Is it the baby?" he asked. "Do you need us to whip 'em out like last night?"

Evie chuckled. "No, but I can't promise that'll be the last time we do that. Sorry."

Marcus frowned, and Evie caught a glimpse of the distinct press of his erection inside his drawstring trousers.

"Well, you know where to find my dick. What's mine is yours, anytime you need. And his, of course." He eyed Ked with a wicked half-smile and a glint in his eyes.

"That I do," she said, almost wishing she had the same craving as the night before, but the need burning inside her now couldn't be denied. She turned to face Ked. "No, it isn't you two the baby needs today. I think it's time we had that talk with your brothers."

Ked's dark eyebrows rose. "Indeed? This is good news. I was worried you found the idea too distasteful to follow through with so soon."

"Distasteful isn't the word I would use," Evie said. "It's just that I was close to Naaz and Sterlyn. Being near your brothers seems strange to me after knowing them. But I can't deny this need now. Please take me to them."

Ked closed his eyes and his face became a placid mask, his eyes moving beneath his lids like he searched for something in the darkness behind those dark lashes.

"They'll meet us in the bath house," he said when he opened his eyes again.

"I'm starting to feel like the turul are the filthiest of the higher races. We don't spend nearly as much time in the water as the rest of you seem to."

Ked laughed. "I can guarantee you that dragons are far filthier. I'll let my brothers show you exactly how filthy we can be."

He urged her off his lap and she threaded her fingers through his with one hand and Marcus's with the other. The tingling burn of her mark sent little jolts of anticipatory pleasure between her thighs.

"Did you tell them why I need them?" she asked. They walked barefoot up the worn flagstone path that led through the lush vegetation of the mountain. The bathhouse rested up the hill from the luxurious bungalow she'd begun calling home for the last week since her rescue.

"They know everything," Ked said. "They're as eager as you are to help ensure the child thrives."

The scent of the aromatic steam from the bath house reached Evie before the building itself came into view. Inside, two of the oldest immortals would be waiting to make love to her. Turul custom might have made her hesitate if it weren't for the fact that going against turul custom to begin with had brought her to this place. She had not one, but two true mates as a result, and carried a child conceived of four fathers, though Ked and Marcus could claim greater credit.

The burn of her mark transformed into a solid, heavy ache between her thighs and wetness pooled and slid down, coating her skin around her core. She paused just inside the doorway, letting her eyes adjust to the shadows within the space.

On the far side of the pool they waited for her, one red, one white, tendrils of steam from the pool rising in a cloud around their feet. They were clad in the same style of loose clothing that Marcus and Ked wore, only in colors that matched their nature.

Gavra's red hair flowed in a loose, wavy mane over his shoulders, while Aodh's long, sleek hair was pulled back into a white ponytail at the back of his head. Their features betrayed their relationship. The same strong jaw and square chin graced their faces that she found mesmerizing whenever she looked at Ked, though their eyes were different enough to be disconcerting. It wasn't merely the color that stood apart, but the shape. Aodh's eyes slanted ever so slightly at the corners and regarded her serenely, while Gavra's were more deep-set and watchful.

"They're ready for you," Ked whispered in Evie's ear.

She released the tight hold she had on their hands and took a deep breath. Tugging at the tie to her robe, she opened it and let it fall to her feet, then took a step forward, keeping her eyes on the pair of men on the other side of the pool.

Without a word back to the men she left behind her, she strode forward. Gavra and Aodh's postures changed with her movement, becoming more alert and each taking a slow step closer to the edge of the pool. Now that they were in her sight, a steady, insistent pull began deep in her belly, urging her toward them. The need confused her when she tried to resist it, but soon discovered that giving in made her want it all the more.

She took slow steps down into the hot, fragrant water, never letting her gaze fall away from the pair of them. In unison, they also stepped into the water at their end, their clothing fading away in a second as though it had simply dissolved from the heat. Both glorious bodies sank slowly into the water and she drank them in from head to toe, lingering at their hips where their erections bobbed with each step they took.

The water came up to her breastbone at the deepest point, just covering the tops of her breasts. When she reached the center, she waited and they reached her a moment later.

"I never got a chance to thank you for restoring my wings," she said.

Aodh smiled and dipped his head. "Sharing this honor with us is more than thanks enough, sister. How may we please you?"

Evie let her urges dictate her actions, reaching out with both hands to each man's chest, leaving a trail of wetness over their shoulders and up the sides of their necks. They simply stood, patiently accepting her touch and seeming to await her command. She took a deep, shaky breath, trying to come to terms with the fact that two of the most powerful beings on the planet were offering themselves to her for her use.

She slid her hands back down their torsos, beneath the surface of the water, until she reached their hips. Watching their expressions raptly, she took each man's cock in a hand and stroked them. Aodh's eyes closed and he emitted a soft sigh. Gavra's expression heated, his gaze setting her on fire with the lust that blazed within.

"I want you both inside me," she said without thinking, but knowing without a doubt that was what she needed. As much as she needed the taste of both Ked and Marcus on her tongue the night before, she ached to be filled and stretched to the point of pain by the pair of long, thick cocks she held in her hands. "Right here, right now. Fill me up and let our child have the magic of both your essences at once."

In one smooth motion, Gavra took action, wrapping his arm around her and sweeping her up so quickly she let out a sharp gasp. With his other hand, he hooked her leg and wrapped it around his waist. She thought for a moment that he would simply shove right into her, but he merely pushed his cock between her thighs so that her slick lips rubbed along the shaft.

His mouth went to her ear, his hot breath making her shiver. "It would be our pleasure. But are you sure you want us both inside your hot little cunt? Aodh would be happy to fill you up elsewhere." In illustration, he let his fingers stray between the cleft of her ass. The teasing contact against her sensitive, puckered opening made her eyes flutter closed and her core pulsed even warmer. She pushed her hips against him, aching to have deeper contact anywhere.

"Am I allowed a second course of you two?" she asked, breathless. "If so, yes, but first I need this."

Aodh pressed his chest against her back and brushed his mouth against her other ear. "You're allowed whatever your heart desires. Our sole purpose today is to please you."

With her legs wrapped tightly around Gavra, Evie leaned back, letting Aodh support her. Between them, she felt nothing short of cocooned in their wet warmth, and gave herself up completely, trusting that they would do precisely what she needed.

"Don't go slow," she said.

Gavra held her higher up with one arm and beneath the water, between her spread legs, the pair of them pressed the tips of their thick cocks to her sopping wet slit. She leaned forward into Gavra and wrapped her arms around his neck, tilting her hips back a little to allow Aodh better access. They pressed together, pushing deeper a little at a time. They had no choice but to take it slow if they wanted to fit, she realized, and was grateful for the care they took.

Her muscles flexed and throbbed in anticipation of their entrance and soon enough, both smooth heads breached the barrier of her body.

"Hold on, doll," Gavra said into her ear a split second before they thrust deep into her in one swift, synchronous motion.

"By the Winds, yes!" she cried at the delicious press of them both inside her. Aodh's large hands slid up her sides and he cupped her breasts, teasing and plucking at her nipples until she was nothing more than a wet bundle of sensation.

"So tight," he practically groaned into her shoulder as he pressed his hips tighter against her.

"So perfect," Gavra said, raising a hand to her cheek and urging her to look at him.

His red eyes glowed like embers, their heat flickering and mirroring the pulse between her thighs. In those red depths, she saw his essence—the piece of him that had been transferred to Naaz through his blood. This time, with his cock already moving inside her, she wasn't disconcerted by the resemblance. Gavra's tenderness and lust were just as potent as Naaz's had been, and Evie knew she could accept it for what it was. Simply a favor for a brother and a friend to treasure her in a moment of need.

He kissed her then, his tongue teasing at her lips to gain entry. She simply hung there, suspended between them, floating in the water and on wave after wave of ecstasy as they plunged in and out of her. The rhythm lulled her even as the stretching friction of their cocks sent pulses of pleasure all the way through her body.

When she asked, they sped up, the water around them moving out in churning eddies as they moved together. Soon she was nothing more than a deep well for them to take their pleasure from, and to be filled with their desire. Together, the two men climaxed, their semen searing her insides with heat that sent her over the edge in its wake.

Evie sang through it all, and when their shared tremors subsided, she looked at Gavra only to see his eyes closed as though he'd been enjoying the sounds.

"You are a blessing, Evie North," he said, finally opening his lids, the red irises behind them flashing with pleasure. "My brother is a lucky, lucky dragon."

"Our baby will be the luckiest one, with uncles like the pair of you," Evie said.

Aodh released a reluctant sigh when he pulled out of her and they let her sink back into the water. Evie turned to face him and pulled him down to place a soft kiss against his mouth. Their energy had only scratched the surface of the craving.

"I've been promised that the pair of you will demonstrate exactly how *filthy* dragons can be, in spite of all this gratuitous bathing you seem to do." She dipped her hand into the water and playfully flicked wet droplets into the white-haired dragon's face.

Aodh grinned at her, then glanced at his brother. "I accept the challenge. And you, brother?"

Behind her, Gavra gripped her by the hips and pulled her back against him, pressing his fresh erection against her lower back. His hot breath gusted against her ear, sending a sharp thrill through her body.

"I am up for it until she sings for us to stop," he said.

His contact and the subtle threat incited a fresh ache of need inside her. She glanced around the bath house, seeking out her mates. When she spied them, she smiled.

Aodh turned his head to follow the direction of her gaze and laughed softly at the sight of Ked and Marcus entangled on a chaise at the side of the pool, all long limbs and rippling muscles. Ked was in the superior position again, and Evie wondered if his brothers had any inkling that their brother might let another man—a human no less—dominate him the way Marcus had.

"They'll keep themselves occupied just fine, I think," Aodh said. "Now, I believe we have some filth to demonstrate to our lovely turul angel."

*Dragon Monastery, Sunda Islands*
*Present Day*

Evie sat in a comfortable wooden chair on the porch, singing softly to her still-flat stomach. The latest craving was simply to hear her voice rising up to the sky, and she had learned not to deny the strange urges that would overtake her from hour to hour.

Marcus and Ked were somewhere nearby—they never strayed far. Lately, however, she had craved solitude. In bed at night, she would invariably fall victim to deep urges that required their presence, but during the day, she wanted her space, and they reluctantly granted it. They were certainly adept enough at entertaining each other when they needed. The thought made her smile, particularly because she knew all their little secrets, even the ones they chose not to tell her. Sound carried, after all. It wasn't as though she was eavesdropping—it was simply her nature to hear the words that weren't said when they spoke to each other around her.

When Ked said, "I love you" to Marcus, there was always

an underlying edge to it, and what Evie actually heard was more like, "I loved how well you fucked me last night."

Or when Marcus laughed and blurted out a playful, "Fuck you" after Ked said something smart-mouthed, Evie heard a promise that would likely involve one or the other of them on their knees later.

After a day of long-needed solitude, she'd wandered to the bathhouse looking for them, and found them with Ked's mouth wrapped around Marcus, eagerly sucking his cock. She'd been amused and surprised that Ked would debase himself in a place where others might wander in like she just had. More than that, she'd been turned on by the sight of Marcus's thick shaft disappearing into her other lover's mouth. She had stripped and swam to them, then simply straddled Ked's lap and sank down onto him while he continued sucking Marcus for all he was worth.

Being with them was so easy, and being apart was a comfort, too, but only as long as she was aware of where they were. At this particular moment, Ked was flying with his brothers, and Marcus was inside the house somewhere within earshot of her.

As if sensing her reaching out to mentally locate him, he popped his head through the wide opening between the porch and the interior.

"Hey, baby, you have a visitor."

Evie looked up to see Belah standing close behind him, smiling. She stood up and went to the woman, wrapping her in a tight embrace. Having grown up with two brothers, finally having a sister had been far more rewarding than she had ever expected it would be. Particularly since this woman knew her brothers as well as Evie did. And... well... Evie knew Belah's brothers just as well, after regular encounters with all three of them.

Sometimes she worried that the cravings were really her

own, and not the baby's, but the first time she tried to deny herself a day spent in the arms of Ked's brothers, she wound up violently ill to the point she became terrified that the baby was in jeopardy. She hadn't made the mistake again. And in spite of the presence of other enticing males on the mountain, it only seemed to be her own mates and Ked's brothers who she ever craved.

"Sister, you look well," Belah said, kissing her on the cheek.

"I feel amazing!" Evie said, shooting a look of thanks to Marcus, who simply smiled and shook his head before heading back to whatever it was he'd been doing.

"Your songs are such a welcome distraction during the day. I think the mood of this place is set to your tunes now. When you are sad, we all slow down to think, and when you are happy, the day seems more vibrant. My brother is nothing like the dark and broody mess he used to be. Thank you for that."

Evie thanked her and moved aside, inviting Belah out to sit with her.

"Not today," Belah said. "Actually, I have a bit of a surprise for you. If you'll indulge me, I'd rather not tell you what it is. Just come with me, all right?"

Evie nodded, perplexed by the invitation. She found Marcus and kissed his cheek and explained she would be with Belah for the afternoon. Before she could extract herself, he pulled her close and whispered in her ear, "Have fun. I'll miss you."

Thinking nothing of his ardor, she kissed him again and left, following Belah up the long path. Before long, she realized their destination must be Kris and Issa's temple-like home near the summit.

They reached the exotic, flower-flanked entry to Kris and Issa's residence, and Belah pushed the doors open. It was

Evie's first time here—usually she only interacted with the others around the grounds or when they would come to visit her. The monastery tended to inspire quiet, introspective solitude more than energetic activity, except for the sexual variety, anyway.

Inside was a large, jade-tiled room with high windows and several doorways leading off to other parts of the residence. It didn't strike Evie as a large place from the outside, but it was more opulent than any of the other buildings she'd been in at the monastery. Built from stone rather than wood, it was imposing in its beauty. The doors were massive constructions of luminescent jade, with windows that were made of the same stone, cut so thin that ethereal light filtered into the room.

Belah led her to one of the doors and out onto a landing that overlooked a huge garden area with a pool in the center.

When the door opened, a cheer erupted and several female figures stood, applauding.

Evie blinked, then laughed. They were all there, even women she didn't recognize, but who she knew must be connected to her somehow. Some were even visibly pregnant.

"It's too soon for a baby shower," she said, pressing her hands over her midsection. Even after a couple weeks, she could sense the life growing inside, but it was still so small.

"Not a shower," Belah said. "Just... a powwow, of sorts. It'll be good for all of us."

Evie's skin tingled, and she realized that she wanted this without even realizing it. Her gaze flitted over the figures gathered below. All of them were there. She recognized Ked's sisters, Numa and Aurum. Rowan and Issa stood nearby. Beyond them, she saw a collection of human females who she thought must be the mates of the other Court dragons. One of them broke away and made her way forward

The pretty, dark-haired woman was visibly pregnant, but not far along. When she reached Evie, she stretched out a graceful hand.

"I'm Hallie," she said. "Your mate is my mate's mentor."

"Mentor…Is that what you call it?"

Hallie shrugged. "Any other designation would take too many syllables. Kol reveres your man, and that's worth acknowledging somehow. Come sit with us."

She followed Hallie to a collection of benches in the garden, and found herself surrounded by human mates of dragons. The oddest sensation came over her then. That of not belonging but still wanting to fit in. They were human. They weren't turul or dragon or any other higher race. Yet they were mates to dragons just like she was.

She felt a little ashamed to by her awkwardness, as though she didn't quite belong with them simply because of her race.

Yet they all accepted her without question. One of them moved over and made room on the bench for her to sit.

"I'm Camille," the pretty blonde said. "Not pregnant yet. My mates are still arguing about it. That's… oh, you already met Hallie. She's fucking the hottest dragon and is knocked up, in case you couldn't tell. That's Erika…" Camille's grin widened. "She's our leader and always swore she'd never have kids but, check it out, she's pregnant, too. I guess it takes a hot red for her to let her sacred eggs get touched."

Camille paused and Evie's greetings fell silent. She looked at the two other females propped on the edge of a chaise. One dark-haired and petite, the other a leggy blonde.

"I'm Thea, not pregnant. And this is Jill… Not sure what you are anymore." She pointed at the blonde.

Evie raised an eyebrow.

Jill, the perfectly coiffed blonde, smiled just enough that on the surface she could appear put together, but Evie saw through every inch of her deflection. "I'm pregnant, too," she said. "But the circumstances are complicated."

The piercing cries of infants rang through the air, and every single woman's heads rose to attention. A moment later, the sounds stopped.

A soft touch pressed against Evie's back and she turned to see a beautiful, lavender-haired woman standing behind her.

"Issa!" Evie turned and hugged the woman, thrilled to see her.

"I'm so sorry about the noise. The boys are relentless. They want what they want, when they want it."

"By the Winds, don't worry. I love everything about today, babies and all."

Behind Issa, the other women came.

Rowan she knew, and hugged affectionately. Ked's other sisters she treated the same. Though she didn't know them as well. Beyond the one day of sharing, she hadn't seen them much. They intimidated her with their beauty.

Belah she was more comfortable with, even though her dark hair and pristine features were as surreal to Evie as her sisters'.

Belah's sisters were disconcerting to look at. Numa had dark-green tresses that looked black in most light, and green eyes that seemed to see more than Evie wanted to share. Aurum was easier to deal with, at least. Her golden hair was almost metallic in appearance, as was her skin, but it merely caught the light in an unusual way, making her glimmer magically.

They seemed oddly deferential to her, which was even more confusing. They'd been mothers before, she knew as much from the talk they'd had, but now...

"They didn't know the extent of your connection to us," Belah explained softly in her ear when her sisters wandered down to join the rest of the group. "Our brothers' energy is potent. If it were only Ked, they might not blink, but all three…"

"The baby needs all three," Evie said.

"Yes…" Belah said and gripped Evie's hand. "But we're a competitive family. They don't like the idea of being left out of what the boys do. I have my own distractions, thanks to your brothers, but Numa and Aurum are itching to have their moment. Our brothers have had you to occupy their time outside the glade. Until my sisters find their mates, they will be restless."

Evie watched the pair of women as they moved around the group, talking with the others. They were affectionate and familiar with all of them, carrying themselves with grace that Evie always hoped she pulled off but never quite believed it. She admired them deeply and it hurt a little to think they considered her any kind of rival.

"If it helps, it isn't because I don't find all of you amazing and enticing. The baby craves what it craves. Your brothers are part of that."

"It's no matter," Belah said. "They'll come around. Now, come down and relax with us. Food will be served shortly and I believe all the women brought gifts for you."

"I thought you said it wasn't a shower?"

Belah smiled. "I lied."

The next two hours were a whirlwind of activity. Their attention made her feel whole again in a way that the attention of her mates hadn't. Among these women, she was more than just a counterpart to her mates' male needs, even if those needs extended to making sure she was happy. She was a woman who hadn't realized how much she needed the company of other women until today.

When another pretty red-haired woman showed up, she instantly recognized Zamirah, who had only arrived at the monastery the day before and had barely shown her face after locating Sterlyn and holing up in a bungalow together. Evie looked for Neela, but didn't see the dark-skinned beauty anywhere, nor had she heard anything about Naaz in several days.

The other women showered her with attention, deep conversation, humor, and feminine wisdom. They gave her gifts, but the gifts were secondary in her mind to the camaraderie she felt being with all of them.

In the middle of the festivities, a shadow darkened the sky and a gold-winged leviathan bore down on them. Evie stared up in awe at the beautiful beast as it hovered above, wings flapping and claws extended as it lowered down into the courtyard. When it landed beside the pool, a petite figure slid off its back and the dragon quickly transformed into a pretty blonde who clad herself in a wisp of a conjured dress before following her passenger around to where Evie sat. Evie hadn't met the golden dragon, but knew her when Evie's new friend, Thea, walked to her and they shared a warm embrace followed by a tender kiss.

Evie stood swiftly when she recognized the dragon's passenger, who walked toward her with purpose. Her throat seemed to stop working and tears pricked at the corners of her eyes.

"Nanyo!" she called. She broke into a run and was in her grandmother's arms a second later. Her tears came unchecked and her grandmother held her, shushing her softly and stroking her back. She had so many questions after all the years apart. "Why?" was the least of them, but Evie already knew the answer to that one.

"It was because of them," she finally said, answering her own unspoken questions. She gazed into her grandmother's wizened features. The older woman nodded.

"Yes. They were your destiny. If I'd known the ordeals your path would lead you through, I would have done everything in my power to change the course, but that wasn't for any of us to know. Now I'm sure you have nothing but happiness ahead for a long time."

Abruptly her grandmother pushed her back and gripped her arms gently in her paper-soft hands. "Granddaughter, you aren't the only one I came to see today. Dreams have haunted me the last few nights, I need to see the green and golden females of your mate's blood. Will you take me to them?"

Evie blinked and wiped the stray tears from her eyes. "Follow me," she said, leading her grandmother around the pool to Ked's sisters, Aurum and Numa.

*Dragon Monastery, Sunda Islands*
*Present Day*

Evie's grandmother bowed to the pair of dragons when she reached them, then began to speak in a language Evie had never heard before. Numa and Aurum stood, graceful as ever, and listened silently. Evie could only catch nuances of the meaning of what her grandmother said to them, which was frustrating. She should have been able to understand any language, but this one was something different. The dragons understood it well enough, at least. During the course of her grandmother's story, their expressions shifted across a spectrum, from surprise, to cautious understanding, to excitement, then determination.

"We must call our brothers," Numa said, finally speaking in a language Evie understood. "If your visions are true, we need to take action now." She closed her eyes for a moment, and within the span of a breath, more winged shadows darkened the air above them.

Ked and his brothers landed, with Lukas and Iszak close

behind. Marcus slid off Ked's back and made his way toward her as the others shifted to their human forms.

Ked's mood didn't seem pleasant and grew less so when he started talking to his sister.

"Do you know what's going on?" Evie asked, moving away from the crowd to talk quietly with Marcus. "I'm still not quite sure, but it seems like a big deal."

"I don't know much either," Marcus said. "But whatever it is, it means we'll be heading back to the Ultiori facility sooner than we'd planned. I think maybe the trap they set has been sprung."

A sudden chill crept over Evie's entire body. "No fucking way." She stalked to Ked and stabbed a finger into his chest. "You are *not* going back there now! You said you would wait! What if that ... *thing* ... takes over your mind?"

"Evie," her grandmother said, laying a gentle hand on her back. "My visions don't lie. They were given to me by the Winds, and I told them in the Dragon Tongue to prove their truth. This is as it must be for them."

Ked pulled Evie into his chest and pressed his lips to the top of her head. "We'll be safe, angel. It's time for me and my siblings to stop hiding from our problems. It isn't just the enemy we're hoping to find. My sister's mate is out there, and we need to go find him."

"Then I'm going with you," Evie said. "You two said yourself that you can't leave me while I'm pregnant. Either you stay, or you take me."

Ked's grip on her tightened and she shivered again when the darkness started creeping into her mind. As swiftly as it began, it retreated. Marcus came to stand beside them and squeezed her hand.

"I'm going, too. Now that I'm healed, I can at least be an asset. If Sterlyn's along for the ride and Naaz meets us there, we should be able to overpower anyone who tries to fight us."

With a grumble, Ked said, "We are all going. I can't convince my sisters otherwise. But the second anything goes bad, you *all* have to leave. The Ultiori can't chase you through the air easily. We leave tomorrow."

It felt like the eve of the apocalypse that night, the wind carrying with it all the whispers of final words of love and regret. Secrets between lovers were so plentiful, Evie eventually let them wash past with the breeze.

All the Court were there, with their mates, invited for what was meant to be a celebration of the life in her belly, but had turned into something entirely different.

The humans would remain behind, but the dragons would be joining the excursion back to the cursed place she and Marcus had been prisoners for so long.

Evie's body was alive with the need for contact, as though the simple presence of the new life inside her had lit an unquenchable fire that either needed fuel to burn brighter or water to cool her from its incessant flames.

She needed to burn tonight and paced restlessly around the bungalow while Ked and Marcus plotted and planned with the others.

When she heard footsteps, she dropped her robe to the floor and went to meet them.

So perfect, they both were, simply greeting her naked presence with deliciously hungry expressions and not asking questions or even speaking. They just undressed right in the doorway, tossing their clothing to the side and accepting Evie's single comment as though they'd expected it.

"I need everything tonight."

What "everything" meant, she didn't know, but she was confident they would figure it out.

Marcus came to her first, his warm, soft skin brushing against her. Her skin came alive from his heat and her nipples pricked into hard peaks. He slid a hand up her arm and cupped her jaw, tilting her head so he could taste her lips. His tongue teased slowly between them and she opened with a sigh as Ked's anise-scented body enveloped her from behind.

Ked's hands rested at her hips, holding her tight against his erection like he just needed to feel her for a moment, then slid up to cup her breasts and tease her nipples.

Wet heat pooled between her thighs, accompanied by a painful ache. Just as she thought she couldn't bear the discomfort, they acted together. Ked pulled her back against his solid chest and lowered her to the floor, holding her against him.

In front of her, Marcus knelt and slid his palms up her inner thighs, spreading her knees as he bent between them. He kissed slowly along the sensitive flesh around her core and finally pressed his mouth to her swollen, throbbing clit and gave it a long, slow lick.

Evie moaned and spread her thighs wider, leaned back against Ked's shoulder and gratefully accepted his mouth when it found hers.

This place she found herself in, between the two of them, was nothing short of heaven. Ked's warm body supporting her, his hands on her skin, and Marcus giving her languid pleasure as though they had an eternity to make love, were all she needed in that moment.

The hard weight of Ked's erection against her back incited a fresh craving. Evie twisted in his arms, forcing Marcus to lean away and watch her. Evie came up on her knees between Ked's thighs, her mouth already watering with the thought of her intentions.

Ked's cock felt thick and so very present in her hand, like this was how and where he was meant to be. She stroked him slowly, loving the way his dark eyes closed and his head fell back. He could be so severe sometimes—so broody—but now he exuded nothing but pure need for what she could give.

She shifted lower and licked at his tip, tasting the salty moisture that had seeped from inside him. Ked twitched a little, then threaded his fingers into her hair, keeping his hand at the back of her head.

Evie bent again and wrapped her lips around the tip, then encompassed his length into her mouth, tasting every hot inch as she went. She loved the flavor and scent of him. Sweet and musky, and like no other man she'd ever known. He smelled like the darkness he exuded and she craved another taste of his essence.

Between her thighs, a hot, slick teasing began again. Marcus's tongue went to work, distracting her from her rhythm on Ked's cock, but in the best way. Her clit throbbed with his licks, his tongue delving deep into her and then pulling out to flick repeatedly over the sensitive bundle.

Ked's hand clutched her tighter, pushing her head down onto him while his hips rose up until his tip hit the back of her throat.

Evie's eyes watered with the need for relief. For a breath or for an orgasm, she couldn't decide. She needed something.

Ked's hand gripped her head and pulled her off his cock. She watched him, her swollen lips still wet from her saliva and his residue. The lustful look in his eyes told her what he needed and she moved. She spread her thighs to straddle him and sank down, closing her eyes as his massive girth stretched her.

Behind her, Marcus shifted close again, slipped his fingers between her thighs and encircled Ked's cock as it slid into her. He stroked her spread lips, teasing her clit in tiny circles while his tongue found her puckered opening between her cheeks and teased.

She moaned in encouragement. She wanted that. She wanted everything, just like she'd told them.

His fingers moved between her thighs, stroking over and over from where she and Ked were joined and up to circle around her ass again. After the third stroke, he pressed a wet fingertip at her opening and plunged it beyond.

Evie let out a soft gasp at the invasion, but wanted even more. Marcus gave it to her, adding another slick finger and pressing deeper.

Her entire body clenched with the addition of another finger that stretched her even wider. Ked's hands clutched the sides of her face and forced her gaze to his.

"Everything, you said," he whispered, then kissed her, his tongue filling her mouth and his lips pulling hotly at hers.

Then Marcus was behind her, his cock pressing against her ass and she pressed back, urging him inside her. His thick tip breached the barrier and they both emitted sharp cries of surprise. When he pushed deeper, all Evie could think was how much she loved them both. There was pain, but it swiftly turned to pleasure as Marcus sank into her. Then she felt suspended between the two of them as they fucked her, buoyed by the pleasure.

Ked's orgasm was the most beautiful thing she'd ever experienced. He always took a deep breath and seemed to pause, as though in suspended animation while his cock surged inside her, flooding her with his semen. In that second, she might believe he was simply a statue carved from pale marble. His lips and cheeks grew too flushed for her to believe he was anything less than alive, however. This time she didn't resist the urge to kiss him and he kissed her back, hungrily, while his cock still frantically thrust into her.

Her own orgasm hovered close, and the combination of Marcus's bruising slams into her ass and his finger slipping between her thighs threw her far beyond the realm of reason. She let out a harsh, surprised cry and bit down on Ked's lip, making him groan with pleasure.

Ked clutched at her and refused to surrender her mouth, his cock growing hard again and pushing deep.

Evie's body soared without even air or wings, her orgasm carrying her across the winds in the arms of the two men she loved. They filled her more than just physically in that moment. Every cell of her being held a piece of them inside that would never be relinquished.

*Dragon Monastery, Sunda Islands*
*Present Day*

A sense of dread filled Evie for the next day, but she clenched her teeth during their preparations to leave.

Maybe it was the baby in her womb making her feel this way, but it all seemed so surreal.

Her overwhelming happiness at having both her mates kept bumping up against the possibility of losing them. She'd spent so many years away from Marcus, finding happiness and pleasure in the cracks between… now that she'd had a solid span of time to enjoy peace and love, the prospect of losing it utterly terrified her.

She kept it tamped down, though. They needed to do this for the others—the prisoners still in the Ultiori's clutches, and those yet to be captured.

"Sister, thank you," Aurum said, startling Evie out of her concentrated packing to make sure her gear was dragon-worthy.

She looked up at the golden beauty, dazzled as always by Aurum's presence. The very proximity to the gold immortal made her happy and she said a silent thank you for the respite from her worries.

"Why thank me? It's your brothers who are the master-minds of this excursion."

"Thank you for going with us. I know you're only going to stay close to them, but your powers are something my siblings and I don't have."

"My brothers could have done as much as I can," Evie said, shrugging.

"Bullshit."

Evie's head shot up at the curse spilling from Aurum's perfect mouth. She stared, blinking at the woman like she'd grown another head. Had she just said that?

Aurum laughed softly. "I'm several thousand years old, Evie. You don't think I've learned how to curse?"

"I—don't know what I thought about you, to be honest. That you were in another league entirely. I mean… I know your brother… *brothers*, but somehow you, Numa, and Belah all seemed so… perfect."

Aurum walked to the bed and smoothed the cover out carefully, then turned and sat, as primly as someone immortal might.

"We can't die," Aurum said. She frowned, her face contorting in a way that seemed distinctly wrong for her features. Her blonde waves slipped over her shoulders when she slouched and rested her elbows on her knees. "I don't wish for death," she said, looking at Evie, "But I wish for a respite sometimes."

Evie didn't quite know how to respond. Their races were all long-lived, and had adapted. But thousands of years as opposed to a few hundred? Immortality didn't sound so fun, after all.

"Well, this trip is supposed to give you that, isn't it? I mean… you and your siblings are looking for your Ones now, right?"

Aurum looked at her, confused for a second. "Our Ones. Oh! Yes, something like that. Fate likes to fuck with us too much. If my dreams are any indication, mine apparently has four arms and four legs, but I haven't heard of any race who turns into spiders."

She shivered and grimaced.

Evie chuckled. "No. You're probably reading it wrong. Tell me what you saw. Let's see if I can find the truth in it."

She walked to Aurum and stood in front of the woman. Aurum looked up at her, golden eyes studious before she took Evie's outstretched hands and her eyelids closed.

She took a deep breath and her expression shifted inward, her eyes moving behind her closed lids. Evie held tight and waited for Aurum to speak.

"I'm swimming in a river, my eyes are open, blinking through the current. I test the flow, pushing against it and it pushes back. The stronger the current, the more I must test my strength. But then when I'm swimming upstream and reaching out, fingers thread into mine and pull. I swim against the current until I get to him. And he is beautiful. Blue-black hair flowing in the water, long and wavy, and he smiles and pulls me to him. His words sound like forest rain when he speaks in my ear, and it makes me want him."

Evie raised an eyebrow. If forest rain were words, she'd lose herself, too.

"But he isn't the only one. Another hand pulls from the other side and I wind up on the shore. Then it all gets very confused. Too many arms and legs."

"Story of my life," Evie said, laughing. "Can you handle more than one man? Because I think that's what your dream is telling you. There isn't just one. There are two."

Aurum's face transformed with a delighted smile. "Two? Oh, that makes more sense. How can you tell?"

"I'm good at hearing the wind between the words. The first man is a water nymph—a satyr—which is rare enough, isn't it? How many of them even exist anymore? The second is an ursa, tied to the earth. You may have to choose between them, or you could mediate to have them both. A female as powerful as you are might manage it."

Aurum closed her eyes and sighed. "It's true. He should not even exist, but your grandmother insisted my mate was still held captive and my brother confirmed that he spoke to a satyr in one of the cells when he went in to rescue you. The trick is finding the other one. I need your help with that, sister."

"That's what I'm here for."

Aurum gripped her hands suddenly, and Evie stared at her, surprised by the familiarity of Aurum's caress. The woman lifted a hand to Evie's cheek and leaned close.

"Let me give you a gift in return."

Evie snatched her hands away and stood, walking away a pace. "Not yet. I know what you were thinking, but we don't need it yet. Ked mentioned blessings might be needed to make sure the baby lives. Right now, I promise the baby is very vocal about what it wants, and that's the only sign I need about its health."

Aurum laughed. "Yes, the young ones are needy early on. If you need anything from me, you have it."

Evie smiled back and sat down again, gripping Aurum's hand. "If you need anything from me, you have it, too."

"What I need is both of these men to materialize in front of me now. I'm not used to being told who to mate or that it *shouldn't* be a human man. Is it crazy that it scares me what kind of baby might come of this union?"

Evie closed her eyes. Her baby had such dubious origins

she couldn't deny them, but it wouldn't be nice to let Aurum worry about that.

"You're not a new mother, Aurum. I know that much. Why does this bother you so much?"

The golden dragon stood and paced across the room. "My other child were all conceived from human men. They were each born nearly a century apart, and I loved them all dearly. They sated my maternal urges, and I've enjoyed not being a mother ever since. The role we play as Dragon Council is enough. But the higher races have never mixed their blood before. And even though I am ready to be a mother again, I'm frightened of not knowing what will come. You have the power of foresight that your grandmother has. When we get to the Ultiori compound, please don't hesitate to tell me everything you hear on the Wind."

"You have my word, sister."

# CHAPTER 38

EVIE

*Canadian Rockies*
*Present Day*

It took some convincing for Evie's mates to agree to let her join them. She had to promise that she would avoid shifting once they arrived, for fear that the change would harm their child. Since Belah had been transported a couple times via Aodh's drifting power and her child was still well, Ked and Marcus agreed that Evie could travel in the same fashion with them.

She dreaded returning to the compound where she had been held prisoner for so long. Not even Marcus's comforting arms the morning before they left could dispel the worry.

"I don't want to go back any more than you do," he said, "but this was the last place Aurum's satyr was seen. If there's a chance we can get him out, we need to take it for everyone's sake."

Evie squeezed his hand and turned to kiss him on the

cheek, trying to shed her fears through her intimacy with Marcus.

"I'm not worried about being captured again. I know Sterlyn and Naaz are on our side, and so is Nikhil. I just hate the idea of being that close to any of the Ultiori who might not be so friendly as long as the baby's doing well."

A few moments later they all stood in the same clearing Evie remembered from her rescue, but the place had changed even in the short time since they were there last. It was late Fall, so there shouldn't be many leaves on the trees anyway, but even the evergreens surrounding them were bare of needles, the entire area as silent as a grave. When the others shifted around her, she heard a collection of soft curses from the dragons.

"Evidence of Nikhil's curse is all it is. He was forced to absorb the life of the vegetation to heal himself before he came to surrender to us," Ked said, his darkness pulsing around him. He seemed far too eager to fly to the compound and confront whatever evil might lie in wait. Thankfully his brothers kept him reasonable.

"Let the Norths reconnoiter and tell us the situation first, brother," Gavra said, placing himself between Ked and the direction of the peak the Ultiori lair was nestled behind. "If this trap Nikhil says he set has captured the Lamia, we'll want to be prepared before we go inside."

Evie's brothers flew away again, disappearing into the gray November sky. While the rest of them waited, Evie closed her eyes and listened for any secrets that might be carried on the wind. Around her the bare, dead branches of the trees rustled eerily, causing her to shiver. The Wind itself spoke of sadness and pain, but that was nothing new compared to what Evie had experienced when she'd been there last.

Deep in the undercurrents, she could hear other notes.

Abandonment, deep regret, loneliness, hunger, despair. The notes came from the direction of the compound but sounded like long forgotten echoes from many instruments, their songs dissonant echoes carried on the wind. Except there were still two bright notes that called out to her, disguised by the sound of the rushing river on the other side of the compound. After hearing that river outside her cell for five decades, she'd learned to differentiate between its song and everything else.

Her brothers returned a few moments later, grave looks on both their faces.

"It's abandoned," Lukas said. "I could hear nothing inside. No life. Last time we were here, the place was full. Mostly with prisoners, but not even a rat is in residence now."

"There are two still," Evie said, surprising herself at the ringing strength of her voice. She was even more surprised when Lukas abruptly stopped talking and turned to stare at her, along with everyone else. "I may be out of practice, brother, but fifty years of trying like hell to hear *anything* has refined my senses. There are still two inside. I don't know more than that, but everything I can hear suggests that they were left behind—trapped and abandoned with the compound."

"Two?" Aurum asked, grabbing Evie by the arm. "Is it both of the males from my dream? Can you tell?"

Evie gripped the dragon's hand and squeezed. "I can't tell who it is. The place is deserted otherwise, though." She turned to tell Ked she believed it safe to go in, but he was already flying away, with her brothers close behind.

"Climb on my back, sister," Aurum said, her eyes wild with excitement and worry as she shifted and bent low for Evie to climb on.

They flew together, following the others up over the ridge line covered with dead pines and rocks. Aurum's massive wings pulled them through the air and in spite of Evie's elation at being aloft at all, she could sense the female's apprehension as though it were her own.

Aurum made a slow circle around the roof of the sprawling building that had been constructed into the mountainside over the rapidly churning river. Evie had only seen that view once in the dead of night when Ked had taken her away. Her only other memory of the river was from the view she'd seen the day she and Marcus had arrived. That day she'd thought it beautiful from within the glass trap she'd let herself walk into unknowing.

Now it seemed violent and unforgiving, the white caps of the water churning over the rocks.

When Aurum landed, Evie slid off and Aurum immediately shifted and walked toward the rest of the group. Evie followed close behind, hoping she would be able to hear any hint from the Wind that would give her insight into the situation. Ked was inside now, she could tell that much, and he'd taken Marcus in with him. She knew they'd gone together to more quickly navigate the place, but their absence now in the belly of this dead beast made her anxious.

The air currents shifted around them suddenly. Only Evie and her brothers seemed to notice, all three of them turning their heads at the whispers of approach.

At the other end of the rooftop, a dark cloud coalesced and Ked appeared holding a huge, limp body in his arms. Aurum and Evie both ran to him and helped him lay the body down.

The man's long arms and legs flopped to the rooftop and his head lolled to the side, but he was breathing.

"This isn't either of them," Aurum said with certainty. "The ones from my dream both had dark hair. This man has white hair. But he needs help, still." She turned and called over her shoulder. "Numa! Come help, please!"

Aurum's sister rushed over and knelt on the other side of the unconscious man.

Before Evie could reach him, Ked disappeared in a cloud again. Marcus had yet to make an appearance, and she guessed he was still inside.

Instead, she went to kneel beside the unconscious man.

He wasn't entirely unconscious. Numa touched his face gently, and he turned into her palm. His lips moved constantly, repeating words over and over. Sometimes they sounded like, "Mama, save me." Other times they were just gibberish. With a breath from Numa's lips, his ranting slowed and he slept.

Evie studied his white-haired features that seemed contradictory to his youthful appearance. Maybe youthful wasn't the word, though. He wasn't young, but he was by no means old, either. His huge body, in spite of appearing malnourished, was strong and fit. Yet he had long white hair and a white beard. He'd been inside for a very long time. And for fifty years she'd been in there with him, yet had never known him. She'd caught so many fleeting impressions of the residents on the days when her door had opened and she was led to the lab, but had no memory of his voice carried on the recycled air around the facility.

Before she could hear more from Numa's soft questions, an uproar came from behind her.

She turned in time to see Ked struggling with a black-haired man who kept yelling, "Let me go, I need to go after her!"

Beside her, Aurum let out an incoherent cry, and the air around Evie grew thick with her friend's power—a combination of utter joy and acute need for intimate emotional connection.

Every cell in her body gravitated to Ked and Marcus. She went to Ked and he met her, pulling her into a tight embrace.

Marcus materialized a second later, walked toward them, and embraced them both. She didn't understand this need to be with them until Ked grumbled, "She found him, I guess. Hard not to want to be with loved ones when Aurum's lit up like that."

They turned together and watched as Aurum approached the man who knelt a few yards away, raking his hands through his long, lank, black hair.

He wasn't just a man, though. Beneath his crouched form, Evie saw hooves rather than feet, though his upper half was entirely human in appearance. A very upset human.

Aurum knelt in front of him and he held completely still while the golden dragon spoke.

"Do you know me as I know you?" Aurum asked.

The man let his hands fall to his lap and bowed his head. Beneath him, his hooves transformed into human feet.

"You are she," he said. He let out a sigh through quivering lips. "I am not ready for you yet. I still have work to do."

"I still want you," Aurum said. She reached out to touch him, hesitating with her long, delicate fingers close to the edge of his face. She tucked a strand of his hair behind his ear and let her palm rest on his cheek.

His eyes clenched tighter and he turned away from her touch.

When he opened his eyes, he stared hauntingly down over the edge of the rooftop, watching the churn of the river beneath. He let out a sigh that reached Evie's ears a second too late. *Forgive me, my love, for I am yet unworthy of you*, was what Evie heard on the Wind.

Then he stood and in only a few swift strides, he vaulted off the rooftop.

They ran to the edge in time to see his body splash into the violently churning water of the rapids far below.

Before Evie's eyes, Aurum shifted and let out a roar. Her

massive gold-scaled shape swooped out over the ravine and down toward the river, following it until she was no longer visible.

They all stood there, still as statues. Evie took comfort in the touch of her mates, but they couldn't keep the tears from falling.

"How could he survive that?" Evie asked. The man hadn't even sprouted wings when he leaped off the roof. He'd just plummeted straight into the churning rapids of the river below.

"He's a satyr," Numa said in her melodic voice. "The last nymphaea male. The water won't let him die, if he's returning home."

A moment later, a dripping wet Aurum landed and shifted in front of them. "I lost him, but I'm going to find him. He's in the water now, so I'm going to the source. You'll help me, won't you, brother? I need you. I need all of you to help me find him."

"That looked like a suicide jump to me," Marcus said. "That was Calder. The mad goat, we always called him because he always spoke in weird riddles and indecipherable prophecies."

"He's a water elemental. A nymphaea," Ked said. "It explains his state of mind the first time I met him, but Numa's right—a leap into any body of water wouldn't have killed him. We have more immediate concerns, though." He pulled away and moved to crouch beside the other man who was still incoherent, but had calmed under Numa's touch.

"We have to leave now," Aurum said, frantic and pacing around them. "If we get to the source, we can find him, but we can't waste time."

"The source is protected."

They all stared at the man who had spoken. The white-haired stranger lying between them opened his eyes and looked around for the first time. He struggled to a sitting position and bowed his head, taking a deep breath, his bare, broad shoulders shuddering. Tangles of white hair fell over his bearded face. His voice and posture were weary, reinforcing Evie's sense that he was even older than the white hair suggested. But when his gaze landed on her, she saw no lines around his eyes and his skin was perfectly smooth and pale. It was then that she understood what he was.

The color of his features wasn't due to age, though he was no doubt much older than she was. He was so pale he seemed nearly translucent, the way a plant might when deprived of sunlight. The lack of sunlight had made her own skin paler, but her hair and wings had darkened over the past five decades in captivity. Not so for one of his kind, as bound to the Earth as the ursa were.

He glanced at all of them before his gaze fixed on Aurum when he spoke.

"Solstice. That's when we go. What day is it today?"

"November twentieth," Evie said.

"My mother will help us find him," he said. "You must take me home on Solstice."

"And who, pray tell, is your mother?" Numa asked.

Evie answered for him, the Wind already whispering the surprising name in her ears.

"His name is Stonetree. His mother is the Ursa Queen, Maia Stonetree."

His gaze shot to her again and he studied her, as though trying to understand how she knew. When a breeze blew past, whipping his hair around his head, he closed his eyes. The cock of his head and the imperceptible whisper Evie heard caused her eyes to widen in disbelief. He was most certainly an ursa male, and yet the wind was speaking to *him* just then. She glanced toward her brothers, who both stared back at her in shock.

Evie's fascination with the exchange was interrupted by Ked rising again and pushing her away.

"This is Aurum's ordeal, not yours. Be careful."

"You don't understand. He's different. How can he hear the Wind the way I can? He's an ursa, not a turul!"

"I am many things," the man called to her and Evie pulled away from Ked's tight grip.

"Please tell me," she said.

"My mother knew when I was born that I was more than just an ursa child. She gifted me with all my secrets when I was a baby, before they took me away from her." He stood to his full height then, towering broad shouldered and as tall as any of the dragons.

Turning his back toward Evie, he tugged the waist of his pants down low enough to display an intricate, bear-shaped scar near the base of his spine that glimmered faintly with power. When he turned around again, he focused intently on Evie. "I was conceived inside a place like this, hundreds of years ago. My father was an ursa male—a Windchaser—who was mutated with the blood of a turul before he was given to my mother to service her through her estrous. After she escaped, my father was destroyed for the sake of the Ultiori's cruel experiments. You carry a child like me inside you now, so you understand more than anyone what I am. Guard that child with your life when it is born, for the Ultiori will hunt you down to reclaim it if they learns that it exists. I know that if they could have killed my mother when they stole me back, they would have, but my mother was far too powerful, and the Ultiori dared not capture her as well, or she would have destroyed every last one of the hunters in her rage."

Evie had certainly heard stories about the fearsome power a female ursa could wield in order to protect her cubs. Turul mothers were protective, but their mates shouldered as much or more of the responsibility of ensuring their offsprings' well-being. Still, she reflexively placed her hands over her abdomen and was comforted by the solid presence of Marcus and Ked as they moved close to her sides.

"Was there no sign of the Lamia after Nikhil left you? Calder was supposed to be the lure to draw her in."

"She was here long enough to taunt us and cut off the power so we couldn't leave the cell. Then she did something to Calder so his powers wouldn't work—the words she said sounded like the ocean in my ears, but they made him go mad for a day and when he was himself again he couldn't let us out the way he used to be able to. We were trapped. We thought we would starve until you came."

Evie's skin prickled with goosebumps that had nothing to do with the chilly air. Words that sounded like the ocean, and mention of the Lamia made a sinking dread fill her belly. This creature they were after was more powerful than they had first believed.

"The Ultiori gave up on Calder a long time ago. I think they hoped for more from me, but when I refused again to share the secrets my mother bestowed on me, I was tortured." His eyes fell on Evie again. "Nicholas is the name Nikhil gave me because I was their first successful attempt toward breeding a hybrid. He treated me differently than the scientists did, at least when his mind was clear. I think he thought of me as a son. My mother did not have the chance to give me my ursa name before I was taken from her. I need to go home so I can learn my true name. And if you take me, I can help find Calder."

EVIE WATCHED with a pounding heart as the four dragons she'd come to love rose into the air. Nicholas rode on

Numa's back, his pale shape stark against her shining green scales.

The wind swept around them, carrying the dragons up the second they stretched their wings.

"Why are you crying?" Ked asked, sliding his thumb down her cheek.

Evie sank into him and let her tears flow. "To be taken from his mother so young and not even know his true name must have been horrible."

"She gave him what magic she could to protect him. It was the wisest thing she could do for a child born outside of the Sanctuary."

Evie nodded and accepted Marcus's large hand in hers, squeezing back. She hadn't considered names for her baby yet, but suddenly knew that she needed to go home before the baby was born. If the ursa were anything like the turul, they would have a naming ceremony, too, and Maia Stone-tree would not have wanted to give her son his ursa name until she could do it in their sacred place.

"I need to go home," she said.

"We can be back at the Monastery within the hour," Ked said.

"No," she said looking up at him. "I need to go to the Enclave where I was born. My family will be there for the winter. Plus, when our baby is born, she can be named on the mountain peak where I was named, with the North Wind to bless her. Belah and my brothers can join us."

"In that case, we'd better get moving if we want to reach the Enclave by dawn. Aodh needs to return with the others, so we'll be flying." Ked released her and in a cloud of swirling shadow shifted into his majestic black-scaled true form.

As Marcus helped Evie climb onto Ked's back, he asked, "Will your grandmother have breakfast ready for us? I've missed her cooking like you can't even believe."

Evie laughed. "I'm sure she can accommodate you if you ask nicely. Just don't make demands while she's in the kitchen. She's scary with a carving knife."

Beneath them, Ked let out a deep rumble of laughter. "I will never again argue with that woman while she's cooking."

Still vibrating with humor, Ked spread his wings and launched into the air, and with the rise in altitude Evie's spirits rose. She leaned back against Marcus and closed her eyes, happier than she'd been in as long as she could remember.

# EPILOGUE

## MARCUS

*Turul Enclave, the Appalachian Mountains*
*Present Day*

After a few weeks at the Monastery, followed by the even more rustic amenities of the turul Enclave, Marcus was a little ashamed to admit he missed some features from his life as an Ultiori Elite. Hot, running water and electricity were two of those things. Evie and Ked didn't seem fazed by the change, and adapted swiftly to the otherwise comfortable quarters the three of them had been given in one wing of the rambling stone lodge that was the focal point of the turuls' community.

The building seemed to have sprouted organically from the earth and trees of the mountain, part stone and part wood, added on bit by bit over the centuries, so he'd heard, until it was a warren of cozy nooks and crannies mixed with huge rooms for larger gatherings. Every room seemed to have a huge window looking out over the rolling hills of the Appalachian mountain range that was now covered in its first dusting of snow.

Their rooms were warmed by a huge fireplace that burned day and night. Unlike at the monastery, they weren't waited on. As Evie explained when they arrived, they were expected to be self-sufficient, and so he and Ked took it in turns to ensure they were well supplied with everything Evie would need to be comfortable and cared for.

Most days, she insisted on spending her waking hours among the other turul, usually helping her grandmother in the communal kitchen, playing music with her parents and her brothers and whichever other extended family chose to participate, and sharing meals in the huge, communal dining room with them in between the other activities.

He and Ked sat alone together at their regular dinner table, silent and immersed in their own thoughts. Evie would get her fill of socializing and join them, but until then, they both had taken to brooding over their own worries again.

They weren't the only strays in residence in the Enclave, though Marcus and Ked were given the widest berth of any of the outsiders, and he was sure it wasn't only because they were so new. Marcus was still an Elite, in spite of now being marked and mated by one of the most powerful dragons on Earth. Ked, being that dragon, was avoided as much out of fear as respect. So they often found themselves isolated from the bustling community with only Belah and Evie's brothers for occasional company once they arrived and announced their intention to stay until their own child was born.

Evie seemed to thrive in the attention of her fellow turul, so he and Ked subsisted with each other's company during the days, making sure to get their fill of the woman they loved in the evenings.

There was only one thing missing, something that had nagged at Marcus since the day Ked had marked them both. Those marks meant that he and Evie belonged to Ked, a fact that Marcus couldn't deny. Their shared blood was the connection to Evie through the bond as her fated mates. Yet Marcus had known her and loved her since long before he'd been turned into an Elite and become an extension of the dragon he was mated to.

He still couldn't shake the memory of the day he'd decided to run. The day that would have gone so differently, had he not received that letter.

It wasn't until Marcus sensed an amused presence in the corner of his thoughts that he glanced up to see Ked watching him with a half-smile over his dinner plate.

"You still want to propose marriage to her. Why didn't you share this detail before?"

Marcus's cheeks heated and he stared back down at his meal – yet another gourmet concoction from Evie's grandmother that left his mouth watering more with each bite. He chewed and swallowed, enjoying it enough to savor it the way Evie would, then took a breath.

"It's a little late for something so human and frivolous, don't you think?"

"Yet you kept the ring all this time. Was that what took you so long to come back out of the enemy's compound when we were there? You went back for it, didn't you?"

"It was the only thing of value I'd left behind. Even if I never gave it to her, I wanted a keepsake to remind me of when I first fell in love with her."

As Ked studied him, Marcus had the strongest sense of deep understanding. Sometimes the dragon surprised him with the well of wisdom he possessed, though he shouldn't have been surprised. He still wasn't quite sure how old Ked really was, but was occasionally privy to the most primal memories that must have predated civilization.

Today, Ked's ever-present connection to him somehow managed to discern the precise source of that hesitant tangle in Marcus's gut.

"She won't say no, and you know it," Ked said. "And she won't think it's a ridiculous question, either. She grew up among humans. She loves human traditions as much as any of us. Dragons rarely celebrate their matings publicly, but the other races do. She won't get a traditional turul mating ceremony because she shouldn't shift at this stage in the pregnancy. Not to mention, you can't fly. Sharing breath with you that night is enough for her, but I know she would love a more public ritual if you offered her an excuse."

Marcus only stared across the room to where Evie sat chatting with some new friends—two of the other dragons in residence and their human mate, a blonde woman who glowed as much from her own pregnancy as from the adoration of her mates. Melody was another Blessed, like him, but her mates had been less than hospitable to Marcus, just like almost everyone else at the enclave. He was less concerned about the others' opinions than he was about how Evie would respond if he actually managed to find the balls to propose to her for real.

"Turul love a good excuse for a celebration. Besides, the weight of that ring in your pocket is only going to get heavier the longer you wait. It's starting to weigh me down, too."

"Fuck, I feel like I'm back in high school, trying to get up the nerve to ask out my crush. Like it doesn't even matter that I woke up this morning with my dick halfway down her throat because she's decided I am breakfast for the foreseeable future."

Ked chuckled. "You aren't alone. In fact, I'm going to give you a little push."

Before Marcus could object, the world abruptly went pitch black, causing the entire dining hall to erupt in alarm. He cursed under his breath, but was acutely aware that the darkness covering them now was the cozy, cuddly version of

Ked's power, though he doubted the rest of the enclave, aside from Evie, and perhaps Belah, realized it.

"Don't be alarmed," Ked said through the thick, velvety blackness. "This is only a friendly nudge to my mate to take care of some long overdue business."

Around him the darkness lifted, light seeping in from a source Marcus couldn't discern. It was enough to illuminate him entirely, as though he sat in a spotlight. Around him, the others all stared from the darker shadows.

Across the room, Evie's startled face came into view in a similar circle of light. She turned and gave Marcus a bewildered smile.

"Marcus? What is this?"

Taking a deep breath, Marcus stood. He spent a moment trying to gather his thoughts, mostly sending a barrage of rude words to Ked, whose grin was almost bright enough to glow.

"Evie," he said, moving to walk toward her. "I think I have loved you since the first day I laid eyes on you, singing with your brothers in Central Park. It was spring in 1965, and it took me about a week to work up the nerve to even talk to you. The day you sang to me, I knew my life had changed. I had no idea what I was then, or what I would become. All I knew was that my life would only have meaning with you in it."

Evie's eyes widened and she turned in her seat to face him as he walked closer. God, could it have been any longer a journey to get to her? She was so beautiful, illuminated the way she was on that dark backdrop. A few faces were visible in the shadows around her, but Marcus only had eyes for her. In his mind, Ked was similarly enthralled, and Marcus sensed that the light that surrounded both him and Evie could only have been given to the two of them in that moment. He felt bathed in love so complete, it spurred him on to finish what he needed to do – what he had needed to do for five decades.

"I would have died without you, Evie. Now that we've made it through the darkest part of our lives together, I know we were always meant to travel that path, because it was the only path that led us here, to this place, to this day, to this moment.

"Fifty years ago, I knew I wanted to spend the rest of my life with you," he said, finally reaching her and falling to his knees before her. Their shared bubbles of light brightened around them enough to illuminate most of the room. Tears glistened on her cheeks and she bit her lower lip, watching him. "At the time I thought we'd spend fifty years happily married, have children, grow old together. Now I know we were given a much greater gift. We have forever now. I was going to ask you then, but I'm glad I had to wait. Angel, will you spend forever with me? Will you marry me?"

He held up the tiny circle of silver with the simple setting of three diamonds. It seemed such a trivial thing now, after everything they'd been through.

Evie's eyes brightened through her tears. "Yes, Marcus. Always."

She let him place the ring on her finger and then launched herself at him. Marcus laughed as he stood. He kissed her madly, barely aware of the return of the light and the rising sound of singing and music around them.

As the gathering erupted into an all-out celebration, Marcus found himself suddenly the center of attention. Praise and congratulations came at him from all sides, but none of it filled him with as much joy as Evie's kiss and the sparkling jewels on her finger.

"I've waited two hundred years for this," she said to him, curled on his lap where he sat, chatting now with a few turul who had barely even acknowledged his existence until moments ago.

Ked moved toward them finally, his smile fading and a look of longing in his eyes. In the back of his mind, Marcus received an impression of his mate, of eons of self-subjected loneliness. Now the loneliness was gone, but the memory of it had yet to fade.

"A drop in the bucket," Marcus said, his eyes meeting Ked's.

The Shadow's approach caused conversation to halt around them.

"Five thousand, give or take," he said. "Not that there's a competition, but you both are mine now, so I'd say I won, either way."

Thank you for reading "Dragon Void"! If you loved it, please visit the retailer and leave a review!

**But wait, there's more!**
The Immortal Dragons' quests for mates continues. Read about the Golden sister Aurum's quest for her mates by picking up "Dragon Splendor" today, or keep reading for a preview.

And don't forget, subscribing to the Dragon Beasties mailing list gets you **two free sexy dragon shifter stories** not available for sale anywhere.

## DRAGON SPLENDOR

NOBODY SAID FINDING your fated mates meant an instant happily ever after. But for Aurum, an immortal gold dragon gifted with the power of psychic empathy, love has never been simple.

Night after night, she has endured prophetic dreams about her pair of lovers, but finding them brings her no respite—the beautiful satyr, Calder, abandons her upon their first meeting, forsaking love for revenge, while royal ursa Nicholas...

Well, he looks nothing like the dark-haired man Fate promised her. So why does she find him so irresistible?

As war between ancient allies darkens the horizon, Aurum realizes the long-lost prince may hold the key to solving both her and Calder's problems, bringing together the fated mates for good—as long as he doesn't get them all killed first.

Their Fated connection doesn't make things easy. But for Aurum, Calder, and Nicholas, victory might just go hand in hand with surrender where matters of the heart are concerned.

*Read on for an excerpt, or* buy now.

∼

## Chapter One

FREEDOM WAS HIGHLY OVERRATED.

Nicholas had never felt so helpless, even during all the days and nights he'd spent locked up in that cell beneath the mountain. He was free now, carried out by the same dark dragon who had rescued the turul princess held prisoner for half a century just down the hall from him.

Except those four walls he'd grown up inside were *safe*. There was constancy in that little cell, even if he barely had room to move once he'd reached his full height. Now that he was free, he lay on his back beneath the sky, afraid to open his eyes to see it for the first time since he was a baby—afraid that he might fall into that vast emptiness if he didn't anchor himself to the earth somehow.

He was still weak from spending the last several days locked in a cell without food or even light. His entire body hurt from throwing himself at the door over and over, but he could never hit it hard enough to make it break. He'd only had Calder to keep him sane in the darkness and make him forget the pain.

His other senses told him that he was surrounded by the others—strangers to Nicholas, but he knew they were friends. Two of the female dragons knelt by his side, gently administering to his wounds. One lay a hand on his forehead, her skin smooth and warm, as comforting as he imagined the sunlight might feel, and it did comfort him.

"Shhh, be still," one of them said. Carried on her words

was the scent of citrus and sunflowers. It made his mouth water and his heart ache with longing.

The other female touched his sore shoulders gently. She smelled sweetly fertile, like summer rains that made him think of home. Even though he'd never been inside the Ursa Sanctuary, these two females reminded him of what he'd always imagined it might smell like. When he found his mother again, he would be embraced by such scents.

The dragon exhaled a sweet smoke reminiscent of mossy trees and forest floors that he gratefully inhaled. Her magic filled him, made him stronger, and healed his bruised body within seconds.

But the first dragon ... Nicholas took another deep breath, hungry for more of her luminous scent. It didn't just make him feel alive, but gave him the absolute certainty he would find joy in his life. He hazarded a crack of his eyelids, just enough to see a golden cascade of hair framing a beautiful face. Eyes the color of honey looked down at him for a split second before a noise distracted her and she was gone, leaving Nicholas aching for another touch—another scent of her.

When he tried to rise to go after her, the one that smelled of forests pushed him back down.

"You're still hurt. Tell me where you are injured."

Nicholas pushed back against her, frustrated at not being able to see what the commotion was behind him, or to follow the enticing scent of the other female, but this dragon was stronger than she looked.

"Let me go!" a familiar male voice yelled.

Nicholas twisted away from the grip of the dragon who had healed him and rose halfway up onto one elbow, ignoring the pain that shot through his side and the resulting dizziness that nearly made him collapse again. The others who had been gathered around him turned as well.

Nicholas's heart clenched when he saw Calder struggling against the hold of the male dragon who had carried him out of his prison moments earlier.

"Ked! Let him go!" the pretty, golden-haired female yelled.

Calder tore from the dragon's grip and stumbled to the ground, collapsing in anguish Nicholas felt deep in his own gut. They had failed. Their entire purpose for staying behind in this awful place had been in the hope of capturing their enemy, but she'd been too devious. She'd taken the bait, but they hadn't bargained on how powerful she would be, nor how angry when she learned she'd been tricked.

Calder bowed his head when the golden woman went to him and crouched, reaching out, almost too hesitant to touch, but clearly wanting it. The joy and love she radiated was infectious. Everyone around them stopped what they were doing to watch. A few of them gravitated toward each other and embraced tenderly.

She was the one, Nicholas realized with a start, and his heart broke a little bit in spite of the joy he felt for his friend. This female was the one Fate had set in Calder's path. The one Calder somehow dreaded meeting too soon, and the one Nicholas had always hoped would take her time arriving for his own selfish reasons.

He was no more prepared for Calder's reaction to the woman than she was. When Calder suddenly ran to the edge of the roof and vaulted over, Nicholas let out a yell and tried to rise to follow, but his body wouldn't cooperate. The golden dragon, however, did follow. She dove after Calder, shifting into her true form mid-arc and roaring her protest loudly enough to shake the entire mountainside. Her call echoed through the valley long after she disappeared into the distance, the pain of Calder's absence reverberating within Nicholas's heart just as loudly.

"Easy, child," the green dragon said, resting her hand on his arm and urging him back down. Nicholas's shoulders sagged in defeat and he stared at the edge of the rooftop where Calder had leapt over into the river beyond. The woman's shimmering green breath settled on his skin, sank in to heal him, but he could only feel the dull ache of loss.

He closed his eyes again, hoping to quell the heartache and jealousy. Nicholas had heard him speak to the female before he'd gone. His words had been filled with regret over leaving *her*. He hadn't even said so much as farewell to Nicholas. It didn't matter that they'd said their farewells the day before, in the dark confines of that prison cell, tangled together on Nicholas's tiny cot. He wanted Calder to acknowledge their parting in the light of day—it didn't matter that Nicholas knew Calder had no choice but to go.

He kept his eyes shut when the dark dragon who had rescued him came to crouch at his side, silently inspecting him. He continued to feign half-consciousness when the golden one returned moments later, wild with agitation.

"I lost him, but I'm going to find him. He's in the water now, so I'm going to the Source. You'll help me, won't you, brother? I need you. I need all of you to help me find him." Her footsteps were quick on the rooftop as she paced around them. "We have to leave now! If we get to the Source, we can find him, but we can't waste time."

Nicholas finally registered what "Source" she was referring to, and as much as it pained him to get involved, his conscience forced him to. Jealousy was a petty emotion, and there was far too much at stake for him to let it control him.

*This is for you, Calder, whether you like it or not.*

"The Source is protected," he said, then took a deep breath and opened his eyes.

Mentally bracing himself for all their questions, he struggled to sit up again. The green dragon's healing had helped, but he was still sore and weak, his muscles fatigued from his constant, futile efforts to escape his prison. His vision swam and he shut his eyes again briefly, taking in a deep breath and bowing his head while the world see-sawed around him.

When he opened his eyes to look around, the world had steadied. Nine pairs of eyes watched him. He looked at each one in turn, knowing them all from the dreams Calder had shared with him many times. He had known this day would come, but not even Calder's stories had prepared him for the pressure of this moment.

Finally, he took another deep breath and said, "Solstice. That's when we go. What day is it today?"

"November twentieth." The pretty, dark-haired female who spoke gave him a soft smile of recognition. He knew her voice well, and knew the man who held her even better. The turul princess and her Elite lover were finally together.

He gave her a nod of thanks. "My mother will help us find him. You must take me home on Solstice."

"And who, pray tell, is your mother?" the green dragon asked.

Before he could answer, the turul female said, "His name is Stonetree. His mother is the Ursa Queen, Maia Stonetree."

Nicholas stared at her, surprised until the breeze swirled around his head and he closed his eyes, anticipating one of the whispered secrets he often heard when the air currents moved around him just so. He cocked his head, listening, but the wind only encouraged him to continue the conversation.

The dark dragon beside him rose and swiftly moved to the turul's side, pushing her away from the group.

"This is Aurum's ordeal, not yours. Be careful," the dragon said to her.

"You don't understand," she said. "He's different. How can he hear the Wind the way I can? He's an ursa, not a turul!"

Calder had explained that very thing to him when he was much younger and trying to understand his own nature.

"I am many things," he called after them. The female pulled away from the dragon.

"Please tell me," she said.

Nicholas swallowed, realizing he would need to explain how he came to be. His dubious origins might make them hate him, but the only sure way to earn trust was by speaking the truth. Calder had given him his truth, at least, which was more than he could say for their captors. So he told them all he knew, even though much of it occurred before his birth.

Two hundred years ago, his mother had been captured by the Ultiori, held and experimented on in much the same way as the turul princess who had requested his tale. His mother had been locked in a cell with a captive male ursa during her estrous. The ursa—a Windchaser, Calder had told him—had been through dozens of experiments, his genetic makeup altered as a result. Nicholas was the product of those experiments, so was mostly ursa, except for the part of him that wasn't, which he understood now must be similar to what this turul female was, if the soft breezes spoke to her as they did to him.

Thankfully, his story seemed to be enough and they continued to question him about his captors. He told them everything, including the unfortunate outcome of Calder's plan to capture their enemy, but kept to himself the reason he managed to survive his captivity for so long without going mad like most of the ursa did. Instead, he confessed one of his deepest desires.

"My mother did not have the chance to give me my ursa name before I was taken from her. I need to go home so I can learn my true name. And if you take me, I can help find Calder."

The golden-haired female frowned at him. "What is he to

you?" she asked, spearing him with a gaze so intense he blinked and stammered.

"We … we were captives together for a very long time." He gritted his teeth, holding back a sudden surge of emotion. "I know what he wants and I know how to find him, that's all."

He closed his eyes, hating the lie and hoping he sounded convincing enough. When he opened his eyes again he caught the turul princess giving him a sad look, but was grateful she didn't call him out. The look on the gold dragon's face was enough to tell him she didn't entirely believe him, anyway.

"We'll take you back to the Monastery until Solstice," the dragon said, rising decisively. "When we get there you must promise to tell me everything there is to know about him. I have dreamed too long of the day we would finally be together. If that day isn't today, I at least want to hear what you know of my mate."

*Want to read the rest?* Buy now.

# ABOUT OPHELIA BELL

Ophelia Bell loves a good bad-boy and especially strong women in her stories. Women who aren't apologetic about enjoying sex and bad boys who don't mind being with a woman who's in charge, at least on the surface, because pretty much anything goes in the bedroom.

Ophelia grew up on a rural farm in North Carolina and now lives in Los Angeles with her own tattooed bad-boy husband and six attention-whoring cats.

Subscribe to Ophelia's newsletter to get updates directly in your inbox. If newsletters aren't your thing, you can find her on social media.

http://opheliabell.com/subscribe

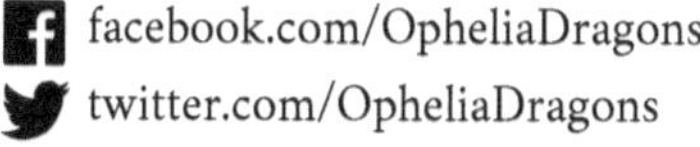

facebook.com/OpheliaDragons
twitter.com/OpheliaDragons

**Sleeping Dragons Series**

Animus

Tabula Rasa

Gemini

Shadows

Nexus

Ascend

Sleeping Dragons Omnibus

**Rising Dragons Series**

Night Fire

Breath of Destiny

Breath of Memory

Breath of Innocence

Breath of Desire

Breath of Love

Breath of Flame and Shadow

Breath of Fate

Sisters of Flame

Rising Dragons Omnibus

Dragon's Melody (a standalone dragon novel)

**Immortal Dragons Series**

Dragon Betrayed

Dragon Blues

Dragon Void

Dragon Splendor

Dragon Rebel

Dragon Guardian

Dragon Blessed

Dragon Equinox

Dragon Avenged

*Immortal Dragons Box Sets:*

Immortal Dragons: Books 1, 2, & 3 + Prequel

Immortal Dragons: Books 4-6 + Epilogue

**Black Mountain Bears**

Clawed

Bitten

Nailed

Stonetree Trilogy

**Fate's Fools Series**

Fate's Fools

Fool's Folly

Fool's Paradise

Fool's Errand

Nobody's Fool

Eye of the Hurricane

Fool's Bargain

April's Fools

Thieves of Fate

**Aurora Champions Series**

*(Set in Milly Taiden's "Paranormal Dating Agency" world)*

The Way to a Bear's Heart

Hot Wings

Triple Talons

Midnight Star

Once in a Dragon Moon

**Second Skin Series (Romantic Suspense)**

Mad Dog

Mile High

Valentine's Day

The Devil's Daughter

Marked Man

**Rebel Lust Taboo**

Casey's Secrets

Blackmailing Benjamin

Burying His Desires

Doubling Down

~

**Standalone Erotic Tales**

After You

Out of the Cold

www.ingramcontent.com/pod-product-compliance
Lightning Source LLC
Chambersburg PA
CBHW021223060726
47590CB00005B/1612